The Last Rogue

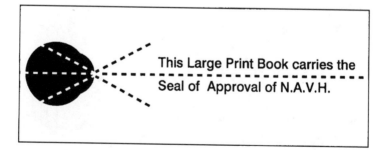

This Large Print Book carries the
Seal of Approval of N.A.V.H.

The Last Rogue

Connie Mason

Thorndike Press • **Waterville, Maine**

Published in 2004 by arrangement with Leisure Books,
a division of Dorchester Publishing Co., Inc.

Thorndike Press® Large Print Romance.

The tree indicium is a trademark of Thorndike Press.

The text of this Large Print edition is unabridged.
Other aspects of the book may vary from the original edition.

Set in 16 pt. Plantin.

Printed in the United States on permanent paper.

Library of Congress Cataloging-in-Publication Data

Mason, Connie.
    The last rogue / Connie Mason.
        p. cm.
    ISBN 0-7862-6786-0 (lg. print : hc : alk. paper)
    1. Cornwall (England : County) — Fiction.   2. Smugglers
— Fiction.   3. Nobility — Fiction.   4. Large type books.
I. Title.
PS3563.A78786L37 2004
813′.54—dc22
                                                    2004042263

The Last Rogue

As the Founder/CEO of NAVH, the only national health agency solely devoted to those who, although not totally blind, have an eye disease which could lead to serious visual impairment, I am pleased to recognize Thorndike Press* as one of the leading publishers in the large print field.

Founded in 1954 in San Francisco to prepare large print textbooks for partially seeing children, NAVH became the pioneer and standard setting agency in the preparation of large type.

Today, those publishers who meet our standards carry the prestigious "Seal of Approval" indicating high quality large print. We are delighted that Thorndike Press is one of the publishers whose titles meet these standards. We are also pleased to recognize the significant contribution Thorndike Press is making in this important and growing field.

Lorraine H. Marchi, L.H.D.
Founder/CEO
NAVH

* Thorndike Press encompasses the following imprints: Thorndike, Wheeler, Walker and Large Pr int Press.

Prologue

Lucas, Viscount Westmore, was doing what he did best, making love to a beautiful woman. He knew by the look on her face that he was pleasing her. Eyes closed, neck arched, she clasped her legs tightly around Luc's waist as he thrust between her plump white thighs. His cock was ready to burst, but ever mindful of the lady's pleasure, he gritted his teeth and held on until she screamed and shuddered in his arms.

Growling low in his throat, Luc unleashed his considerable lust upon the woman writhing beneath him. His naked loins pumped vigorously as he thrust deep into his lover's hot sheath, again and again, until he felt his juices rising, torrid and unstoppable.

No matter how carried away Luc became during his sexual encounters, he never forgot the code he and his fellow rogues lived by. The woman whose favors he was enjoying was a lady, and leaving her with a bastard was unthinkable. He wouldn't be rutting with her at all if she were an innocent. But there was nothing innocent about Lady Sybil Roxbury. She had set about seducing him with the expertise of a courtesan, and he hadn't resisted.

His climax was coming fast now. As was his custom with all his lovers, he started to withdraw so he could release his seed on the bedding.

But Lady Sybil Roxbury had other ideas. Locking her legs around Luc's pumping buttocks and her arms about his neck, she clung to him with desperate tenacity.

"Release me!" Luc cried. There was no stopping his climax. Even now his climax was speeding toward final culmination. "Sybil, for the love of God, let me pull out!"

Either Lady Sybil didn't hear or didn't care, for she wrapped herself around him like a clinging vine, her body arching up to receive his seed. Expelling a curse, Luc lost the battle. His self-control shattered and he spent himself in Sybil's grasping sheath.

When it was over, he reared up and stared into her guileless blue eyes. "Are you mad?"

Her arms and legs fell away; he rolled aside and leaped to his feet. "What were you thinking?"

Lady Sybil sat up, a look of satisfaction on her lovely face. "You'll post the banns tomorrow, of course."

"What in bloody hell are you talking about?"

Shoving long fingers through his dark auburn hair, Luc was livid. Turbulence flashed in his blue eyes, and his well-toned muscles tensed.

"You could have given me a child," Sybil said, refusing to meet his gaze.

"Whose fault would that be?" Luc charged. "I didn't get this far in life without knowing exactly what I was doing." His eyes narrowed. "You'll not trap me into marriage, my lady."

Sybil's expression grew frantic and she began to wring her hands. "What will I do if I caught a baby? My parents are elderly. This could kill them. My father will probably send me away. I'll be ruined. I'll never be able to show my face in society again."

"You should have thought of that before you lured me to your bed. Need I remind you, my lady, that you weren't a virgin? I knew that before I agreed to meet you. Virgins don't invite men to meet them at less than respectable inns." He sent her an assessing look. "Why didn't you let me pull out?"

Sybil flushed and looked away. "I got carried away."

Luc's brow arched upward. "Indeed."

"Why are you looking at me like that? Don't you believe me?"

Lucas Westmore was nobody's fool. He could add two and two quite well, thank you. Though he'd known Lady Sybil for some years, she had paid him little heed in the past, and he in turn hadn't been overly attracted to her, though her beauty was spectacular.

Then all of a sudden Sybil had taken notice of him, acting like a woman eager to have him in her bed. Not one to miss an opportunity, Luc had agreed to an assignation at an inn on the outskirts of London. The moment Luc slid inside her he realized she was even more experienced than he'd thought.

What had begun as an interesting interlude had turned into a wildly passionate coupling. He had taken Sybil twice, spending himself on the bedding the first time, but had been held captive inside her the second.

"Why me, Sybil?" Luc demanded. "There are men far richer than I whom you could trap into marriage. Why are you so desperate for a husband? You have a respectable dowry and good bloodlines. Either or both should get you a husband."

Sybil bit her lip and looked away.

"Damn it, Sybil! Neither of us knows if our coupling produced a child, so why the rush to the altar?"

Suddenly comprehension dawned. How could he have been so stupid? Sybil had a reason for haste, all right, but it wasn't going to wash with him.

"Whose child are you carrying, my lady?" he asked brusquely. "How far along are you?"

Sybil sent him a startled look, and Luc knew he had hit upon the truth.

"I . . . don't know what you're talking about."

Luc found his clothes and pulled them on with angry jerks. "Why don't I believe you? Come clean, Sybil — you want a father for your child. Why me? I'm not the best father material, or husband material, for that matter. Why don't you just marry the man who —" He paused, divining the answer to his question. "He's already married."

Sybil's brazen façade crumbled and she burst into tears. "I'm sorry, Westmore, but it had to be you."

"Would you mind explaining?"

"I knew a man of your reputation wouldn't remain faithful. Nor were you likely to care if your wife strayed."

"In other words," Luc said slowly, carefully, "once you passed your bastard off as mine, you would continue to carry on with your married lover."

Lady Sybil nodded. "Admit it, Westmore; you are an unrepentant rake. As long as your wife was discreet, you wouldn't care what she did. You were perfect for my needs."

Luc's handsome features hardened. "I am not a dupe, my lady. Nor am I willing to give your bastard my name. Who is the father?"

Sybil shook her head. "I can't say. I will never divulge his name." She burst into tears. "What am I to do? The shame will kill my mother."

Luc might be many things, but heartless wasn't one of them. Neither, however, was he going to wed Sybil. Only a fool was that honorable. A wife had no place in his life. He was having too good a time in his single state.

Sex was as necessary to Luc as breathing, and gambling and drinking was a way of life he had no intention of abandoning. Living on the edge of danger was exciting. Luc was a rake and a womanizer and was proudly upholding his reputation even though his fellow rogues Bathurst and Braxton were caught in the parson's trap.

He stared at Sybil's hunched shoulders, listening to her sobbing, determined to do anything he could to help her, short of marrying her. Even as he sought a solution, he cursed the man responsible for placing her in such an untenable situation. If he knew the man's name he would call him out. Then out of the blue came an answer to Sybil's dilemma.

"Dry your eyes, my dear. A solution is at hand. I will find you a husband."

She spared him a laugh. "Who would have me? You were my last hope."

"I'll find someone. Give me a fortnight to come up with a prospective groom. There are plenty of noblemen with empty pockets, or second or third sons looking for women with respectable fortunes. It shouldn't be too difficult to find you a husband."

With everything settled in his mind, Luc finished dressing. When he offered to help Sybil dress, she refused and waved him off.

"There's no need, Westmore, I can manage on my own. My coach will come for me soon. You needn't worry about seeing me home, as I have a small errand to attend to after I leave here."

"You'll hear from me soon," Luc promised, placing his top hat on his head and taking up his cane. He sent her a stern look.

"Meanwhile, promise you won't do anything rash."

She nodded bleakly. "Thank you, Westmore. You're very kind."

He laughed. "Kind is hardly the word I would use to describe myself." His expression hardened. "Are you sure you won't tell me the name of the man who put you in this situation?"

She shook her head. "What good would it do? He can't marry me. I . . . love him," she whispered.

Luc's hands fisted at his sides. It would do *him* good to beat the man to a bloody pulp. Lord knows he had loved and discarded countless women, but he had never left one with child. Nor was he married like Sybil's lover.

"Very well," Luc said, anxious to be off. "You'll hear from me soon."

"Westmore," Sybil said as he reached for the door latch. "Forgive me for trying to trap you. I . . . was desperate. I still am."

"Trust me," Luc said. "I'll bring a prospective groom up to scratch within a fortnight."

Luc strode down the steps, pausing at the bottom to search the crowded taproom. He recognized no one and was confident no one would recognize either him or a heavily veiled Lady Sybil when she appeared. He continued out the door, already considering possible husbands for Sybil.

Two days later, Luc, along with all of London, read the following article in a gossip column in *The London Times*:

"Last evening, Lady Sybil Roxbury's body was found floating in the Thames. Reliable sources reported seeing the disreputable rogue, Viscount Lucas Westmore, with the aforementioned lady at an inn the day before her body was discovered. However, Bow Street found no evidence to link the viscount's name to the unfortunate lady's death."

Chapter One

London, 1820

London was stunned by Lucas, Viscount Westmore's vow to give up sex. Word had it that guilt over Lady Sybil's death had led him to his startling decision.

What the *ton* did not know was that he was also leaving the temptations of decadent London behind for the wilds of the Cornish coast, where he intended to live in virtual isolation. Now all he had to do was convince his friends Bathurst and Braxton that his decision was final and irrevocable.

Luc was staring out the window sipping brandy and brooding when his two friends and reformed rogues were shown into his study.

"What in the hell is this all about, Westmore?" Bathurst asked, his vexation pronounced. "Your man said it was important."

"You said it was a matter of life or death," Braxton groused. "I had a business appointment this afternoon and had to cancel it after receiving your message."

Luc took a large swallow of brandy before making his plans known to his friends. "I'm leaving London."

"Is that all?" Bathurst snorted.

"For a year," Luc returned.

"A year!" Braxton gasped. "Does your leaving have anything to do with Lady Sybil's death?"

"It has everything to do with Sybil's death."

"Damnation, Westmore, you didn't shove her in the Thames, did you?" Bathurst blasted.

"Don't be ridiculous. Of course I didn't. But I still hold myself responsible for her death. As punishment, I'm giving up sex for a year and leaving London."

"You're mad!" Braxton vowed. "Have you thought this through? It isn't like you to let gossipmongers get to you."

Bathurst, ever practical, asked, "Obviously, something happened between you and Lady Sybil before her untimely death. Care to tell us about it?"

Luc began to pace before his two friends. "It's not a pleasant story," he said after a lengthy pause.

"It never is," Bathurst drawled. "Just

begin at the beginning. I always suspected you were holding something back when gossip linked you with Lady Sybil's death."

"You're right, as usual," Luc admitted. "Lady Sybil was most anxious to get me into her bed, and as a rule I never refuse a lady." Braxton started to speak, but Luc forestalled him. "I know what you're thinking, Braxton, and you're wrong. Lady Sybil wasn't a virgin. I wouldn't have agreed to meet her at the Thorn and Thistle if I thought otherwise."

"How did you know?" Bathurst queried.

"How many innocent, highborn ladies of your acquaintance would make an assignation with a man at a less than respectable inn?"

"You have a point," Bathurst admitted. "Go on."

"Sybil was already at the inn when I arrived, arrayed naked on the bed. I must say I enjoyed myself immensely, until . . . well, to make a long story short, I did not withdraw in time."

"And she demanded marriage," Braxton guessed.

"Damnation, Westmore, you're no green boy! Couldn't you contain yourself?" Bathurst said.

"Believe me, I tried. When I attempted to

18

withdraw, she wrapped her arms and legs around me and held me in place. Once started, I couldn't stop the flow."

"So you refused to wed her and she took a dive into the Thames," Bathurst said after considerable thought. "Strange. Why didn't she wait to see if your seed took?"

"I wondered that myself," Luc replied. After a long pause, he explained, "I soon realized what was driving Sybil. The lady was increasing and in desperate need of a husband. She chose me because of my reputation. She figured I would stray soon after marriage and wouldn't look closely if she continued her affair with her married lover."

"Blast and damn!" Braxton cried. "She was involved with a married man?"

"Indeed," Luc said dryly. "I refused to marry her but took pity on her and offered to find her a husband. Her bloodlines were good and she had a respectable dowry, so I figured I could find someone willing to accept her bastard. I told her as much and offered to bring someone up to scratch within a fortnight."

"That was generous of you," Bathurst said.

Luc gave a snort of derision. "Obviously not generous enough, since the lady took her own life."

"Why are you blaming yourself?" Braxton asked.

"If I had married Sybil, she would still be alive."

"She tried to trap you."

"I know, but that doesn't matter now, does it? She's dead."

"So you're punishing yourself for Sybil's death by giving up sex and abandoning your life in London," Bathurst stated. "The blame lies with the bastard who fathered Sybil's child. Do you know who he is?"

"Sybil refused to divulge his name."

"Can we talk you out of leaving?" Braxton asked.

"Not a chance. My agent has already rented a cottage for me near the village of St. Ives."

"You really *are* serious, aren't you?" Bathurst said. "Bloody hell, Westmore, we know you better than you know yourself." He stroked his chin. "I predict you'll have a woman beneath you within two months. I've never known you to go without sex two days, much less an entire year."

Luc squared his shoulders. "A woman is dead because of me. I'm leaving at the end of the week no matter what you two say. I plan to do a lot of hunting and reading to keep myself occupied."

"Don't forget cold baths," Braxton laughed. "I suspect you'll take plenty of those."

Luc ignored Braxton's good-natured ribbing. "I expect to emerge a better man at the end of my self-imposed exile."

"What do you plan to do with your randy cock during that time?" Bathurst jested.

"St. Ives is a tiny village, remote from the rest of England. I seriously doubt my resolve will be tested by a horse-faced milkmaid."

Bathurst chuckled. "My guess is any reasonably attractive country lass will tempt you."

Luc shook his head. "Nothing you say will dissuade me. Don't you understand? A woman is dead because of me. Wearing a hair shirt won't suffice. I have to punish myself in a way that will hurt."

"There's no reasoning with you," Braxton said, rising. "Will you keep in touch?"

Luc nodded and pushed himself to his feet.

"A word of warning," Braxton added. "I was talking with Sir Grafton, an official with the Home Office, the other day. He happened to mention the recent rise in smuggling activity in that area. Take care, my friend."

Luc grinned, his vivid blue eyes sparkling for the first time since the tragedy. "Smuggling — how interesting. Keeping an eye out for smugglers could be exactly what I need to take my mind off the lack of sex in my life."

"Steer clear of trouble, Westmore," Braxton advised. "Keep your eyes and ears open and send word if you learn anything vital, but let the king's excise men do their job."

"Heed Braxton," Bathurst said. "He's never steered you wrong. And now, my friend, we'll leave you to your packing. Keep in touch."

Alone with his thoughts, Luc tried to envision the isolation he'd have to endure during the next weeks and months. Could he remain celibate for an entire year? Then he envisioned Lady Sybil as she had been during their intimate encounter. Young, vital, beautiful. She shouldn't have died. Punishing himself for her death was the only way he could continue to live with himself.

A year of celibacy was a small price to pay for his self-respect.

Chapter Two

St. Ives, Cornwall

Luc awoke to the wind howling through the crevices of the crag upon which his cottage sat. It was said that Cornwall was the most savage coast in the world, and Luc believed it. It was as if he had come to the end of nowhere, where the arm of Cornwall thrust into the treacherous waters of the sea.

For an entire month Luc had listened to the wail of the wind in the night, fearing the cottage would be lifted from its foundation and tossed into the raging sea below. But the cottage was solid and sturdily built of stone, obviously constructed to withstand the famous Cornish gales.

Yet despite the furor of the nighttime storms, Luc usually awakened to sunlight pouring through the windows from skies as blue and cloudless as any he'd ever seen. The terrain was different from anything he'd known before. Below cliffs towering above the nearby coves, long stretches of beach were fringed with tall grasses.

There was a raw, stark beauty to the inhospitable land that Luc had learned to appreciate during the first month of his self-imposed isolation.

Loneliness was his worst enemy.

There were nights when Luc prowled the cottage, unable to sleep, his body aching with sexual tension. On those nights Luc made his way to the cove, scrambled down the steep path to the beach and plunged into the icy water.

Luc kept contact with the villagers at a minimum. He'd been to the village a time or two but had divulged almost nothing about himself. To the residents of St. Ives he was simply Mr. Westmore, a man in search of solitude.

At the Gull and Goose Tavern, Luc had inquired about someone to fill the position of part-time cook and housekeeper. Two days later Widow Pigeon had appeared at his door. Luc hired her on the spot. She came early each morning to clean, do laundry and cook enough food to last the day. At noon she returned to her own home.

Thus far the arrangement had worked well for both of them. The taciturn widow was exactly what Luc wanted. While Widow Pigeon was tidying up the cottage, Luc usually wandered along the cliffs or down to the beach, walking off his sexual frustration.

It was on one such walk along the cliffs that he saw her. She stood near the edge of a chalky crag, peering intently at the waves crashing onto the narrow stretch of beach below and the sea beyond.

She was tall for a woman. The wind coming off the sea molded her billowing skirts against long, long legs and pressed her bodice against rounded breasts he'd give his right arm to caress. Her long sable hair floated behind her like a banner, blown hither and yon by the wind. Her profile was startling in its perfection. Full lips, elegantly curved brows, high cheekbones and a small straight nose. He tried to guess her age and placed her in her early twenties.

Spellbound, Luc watched as the woman scanned the cove, one hand shielding her eyes from the sun. He felt himself grow hard beneath his tight trousers, and a small groan slipped past his lips. He hadn't realized that being deprived of sex would be so difficult . . . or painful.

Luc stood some distance away, partially hidden by a tree, quietly watching and waiting. Was she going to jump? If she moved one step closer to the edge, he would act, but until she gave some indication of her intention, he was satisfied just to look at her. She was certainly easy on the eyes.

The wind snatched at her billowing skirts and flung them up, exposing trim ankles and shapely calves. Luc swallowed hard. His cock was throbbing now, and the blood pumping through his veins ran hot.

He almost wished the woman would make a move toward the edge, for then he would know what it felt like to hold her in his arms as he dragged her to safety. But much to Luc's chagrin, she turned abruptly and strode away. It took all the willpower he possessed not to follow.

Collapsing against the tree, Luc took a moment to recover. Damnation, he hadn't expected to find an attractive woman in this remote village. And now that he knew one existed, how in bloody hell was he supposed to keep away from her?

As he strolled back to his cottage, he wondered what had brought the woman to the cliff's edge. Why was she staring so intently at nothing but vast expanses of blue sea? Who was she?

The rest of that day Luc's thoughts kept returning to the mystery woman. It took a great deal of fortitude to keep from visiting the Gull and Goose to inquire about her, or question Widow Pigeon when she arrived the following morning. But no matter how much he desired to learn the identity of the mystery woman, he did not take his vow of celibacy lightly; nor did he forget why he had taken the vow.

Luc did, however, return the next morning to the same spot where he had seen the woman, arriving about the same time as the day before. Disappointment lanced through him when she wasn't there. He was about to turn and continue his walk in another direction when she suddenly appeared. Fascinated, he drew closer, his gaze riveted on her.

She was as lovely as he remembered. The sun reflected off her hair, revealing golden highlights among the sable strands. Luc tensed when she approached the edge of the cliff, ready to intervene should she attempt to jump. He hoped it wouldn't be necessary, however, for his erection would make moving fast difficult.

His relief was enormous when the woman spun around and disappeared down the path to the village. Luc approached the edge of the cliff and looked down. There was nothing beyond the thin crescent of beach but water. What could she be looking for?

Luc returned to the same spot the following day and the day after that, never revealing his presence. On the fourth day, the woman approached too close to the edge of the cliff. Luc's heart jumped into his mouth. Only a reckless fool would attempt something so foolish, with certain death awaiting her if she lost her footing. She didn't seem to recognize the danger. The tilt of her head indicated that she was staring straight ahead. At what?

"Don't jump!" he shouted as he raced toward her.

Startled, the woman leaped backward, her hand at her throat. When Luc reached her, he pulled her against him and dragged her away from the ledge.

She went rigid against him. "Let go of me! What do you think you're doing?"

"Calm down, I'm not going to hurt you. I just want to help. Why do you want to end your life?"

"What are you talking about?"

"I've been watching you. I knew you intended to jump to your death the first day I came upon you."

"I do not!" she cried, pushing against him. "I was perfectly fine until you rushed at me like a madman. Release me."

"Not until you promise not to jump."

"You idiot! I never intended to jump."

"It certainly looked that way to me. Why

do you come here each day if not to work up enough courage to jump?"

Her pert chin went up. "That, sir, is my business. Who are you? Where did you come from?"

"I am Luc Westmore. I've rented the Beaton cottage on the outskirts of the village." He searched her face, finding her beauty even more entrancing close up. "Who are you?"

After a long moment of silence, she said, "Bliss."

Luc couldn't suppress his groan. Bliss. Her name was Bliss. How could Fate be so unkind as to introduce him to a woman named Bliss? Her name suggested all manner of sexual fantasies to his mind. And other places as well. Desire raged through him like wildfire.

Her eyes, which reminded him of the purest amber, narrowed suspiciously. "What are you doing in St. Ives?"

Luc shrugged. "Looking for solitude. I needed a rest from the hustle and bustle of London."

Bliss's expression registered disbelief. "I have to go."

"Wait, Bliss! Don't leave."

His plea was lost to the wind as Bliss turned and fled.

Who was she? What was she looking for? Would he see her again? Though his conscience warned him to mind his own business, his body marched to another drummer.

Bliss hurried along the path, fearful that the stranger would follow her. Who was he really? What was his purpose in coming to St. Ives? Why would a handsome man like Lucas Westmore leave London and the entertainment it had to offer for the dubious charms of St. Ives? He certainly didn't look the type to enjoy solitude. The handsome stranger was probably more at home in London's drawing rooms than in the peaceful village where Bliss had lived since her birth.

Perhaps Mr. Westmore's family had banished him for some indiscretion, Bliss thought. Strangers weren't welcome in St. Ives, and with good reason. The village had secrets; prying wasn't to be tolerated.

Bliss had to admit that Mr. Westmore was the handsomest man she'd ever seen . . . and more sophisticated than the rough fishermen of St. Ives. Lord, the way he filled his clothes fair took her breath away. He was tall and muscular, and his shoulders certainly didn't need padding, nor did any part of him. But he was a stranger and therefore not to be trusted.

The knowledge that Lucas Westmore had been watching her was disturbing. Was he something other than he pretended? She had to find out before he brought tragedy to the entire village.

Market day in St. Ives was a lively affair, and Bliss was greeted by people she had known all her life as she walked home. St. Ives was a fishing village; its citizens were sturdy, hardy and steadfast. They lived at the end of nowhere and survived the harsh elements and overwhelming poverty through sheer force of will. She loved these people and they loved her. Her father was the squire, a benevolent man respected by all.

But Bliss had too much on her mind right now to stop and chat. She was headed for Widow Pigeon's cottage. As Westmore's housekeeper, she might know what he was doing in the village.

Bliss found Widow Pigeon in the yard, hanging her laundry in the whipping wind. She hailed the widow as she walked to the white picket fence.

"How be you today, Bliss?" Widow Pigeon asked as she joined Bliss. "Any news? This will be my Billy's first time."

"Not yet," Bliss said, lowering her voice.

"Billy will know when the time arrives. I understand you work for the stranger who rented the old Beaton place at the end of the lane."

"Aye, I cook and clean and mind my own business."

Bliss sighed. "Can you tell me nothing about Lucas Westmore? Do you know why he chose our village to settle in? He doesn't look the type to rusticate in the country. Can we expect him to leave soon?"

"The man speaks no more than a word or two of greeting when I arrive at the cottage. He leaves soon afterward. I believe he takes long walks. I'm usually gone when he returns. He did say, however, that he had taken a year's lease on the cottage. Why do you ask?"

"I met him this morning. He's been watching me for some days. He thought I intended to jump over the cliff."

Widow Pigeon chuckled. "That's ridiculous." Her brow furrowed and her expression grew anxious. "He didn't see anything, did he?"

"No, there was nothing to see."

"Thank God for that. Have you spoken to Brady about him?"

"Not yet."

"Perhaps you should, and you might ask Vicar Brownlee to call on Mr. Westmore.

32

'Tis likely he'll learn more than you or I."

"Good idea," Bliss agreed. "Lucas Westmore could mean trouble for all of us. Meanwhile, keep your eyes and ears open."

Vicar Brownlee, a round man with jolly features, greeted Bliss effusively a short time later. "What can I do for you, Bliss? Has your father taken a turn for the worse? Perhaps a visit will cheer him up a bit."

"Papa is still weak and I'm sure he would welcome a visit, Vicar, but that's not why I've come. Are you aware that a stranger has moved into the old Beaton cottage at the end of the lane?"

The vicar nodded.

"I'm suspicious of him," Bliss confided.

"You think he's a . . ."

"I don't know. I was hoping you would call on him and sound him out. A man of Lucas Westmore's caliber doesn't settle in a remote area like this without a purpose. I don't like it, Vicar Brownlee. Why did he come to St. Ives?"

"I'll do what I can, Bliss. I had intended to call on him anyway."

"Thank you. I'd best be going. Papa will miss me if I'm gone too long."

"I'll let you know if I learn anything of importance," Vicar Brownlee said.

"Don't mention my fears when you call

on Papa," Bliss warned.

"He still doesn't suspect?"

"It's best that way. I don't want to worry him. He's been too sick to take an interest in what's going on around him, and I thank God for it. He'd put a stop to it, and then how would the villagers fare?"

"How indeed."

Bliss took her leave and returned home to the large stone house near the village square, where the Hartley family had resided for decades.

"Where have you been, daughter?" Owen Hartley asked when Bliss entered his bedroom.

"I went for a walk, Papa. Jenny was here to look after you, else I wouldn't have left."

"Forgive me, Bliss," Owen said. "I didn't mean to sound peevish or ungrateful, but I do so tire of this bed and this room."

"Soon I'll take you to London to see a specialist, Papa," Bliss informed him.

"That's wishful thinking and you know it, Bliss. A trip to London is too expensive as well as unnecessary."

"Don't worry about it, Papa," Bliss said, as she added figures in her head. It wouldn't be too much longer before she'd have enough money set aside to pay for the specialist her father needed.

The following day, Luc returned to the cove where he'd first seen Bliss, but instead of Bliss, a strapping lad of about eighteen stood watch on the cliff. Curious, Luc approached the young fellow.

"What are you looking for?" he asked.

"Nothing in particular," the lad replied. "You must be the man my mam works for."

"You're Widow Pigeon's son?"

"Aye, I'm Billy."

"Where's Bliss today?"

Billy started violently. "You know Bliss Hartley?"

"I met her a couple days ago."

Billy said nothing.

"The citizens of St. Ives appear to be a secretive lot," Luc probed.

"We don't like strangers poking into our business."

"I assure you I am here for rest and solitude and nothing more. I wouldn't dream of prying into people's lives. I have enough problems of my own."

"Then I bid you good day, sir," Billy said as he turned away from the cliff. The catchy tune he whistled lingered behind as he ambled along the path toward town.

Disappointed by Bliss's absence, Luc returned home. Curiosity was killing him.

Was Bliss married? She certainly looked old enough to be wed, and have a child or two besides. Did she come to the cliff to escape a brutal husband? Despite his resolve to abstain from sex for an entire year, Luc had to know more about the lovely and mysterious Bliss Hartley.

That night erotic dreams drove Luc from his bed in the wee hours before dawn. His body burned, his staff was at full mast, and hot blood pounded through his veins. As he had done on so many other nights since he'd left London, he donned his trousers, scrambled down the steep path to the beach and dove into the cold water. He swam until he was nearly exhausted, then returned to the beach. Panting and shivering, he sat down on a rock to catch his breath before returning to the cottage.

Damn his randy cock, he silently cursed as he envisioned Bliss with her gown plastered against her curves and her hair flying in the wind. Her simple beauty surpassed that of all the London ladies in their peacock finery. He wanted Bliss as he'd wanted no other woman. Bloody hell! Who would have thought he'd find a woman like Bliss at the end of nowhere?

The plunge into icy water had brought about the results Luc desired, and he prepared to retrace his steps home. As he turned to leave, he thought he saw a ship's lights bobbing in the cove. When the lights blinked out, he assumed his eyes had deceived him. Shrugging, he thought no more of it and returned to the cottage.

The next morning, Luc greeted Widow Pigeon with more cordiality than usual. "I met Billy yesterday morning. Handsome young chap. He seemed quite interested in the cove."

"Billy likes to watch the sea," the widow said without looking up.

"Does Bliss like to watch the sea also?"

The widow's head shot up. "You'll have to ask her." Then she scurried off before Luc could question her further.

Later that day, Luc's unquenchable curiosity led him down the path to the center of town. Things were not as they seemed in St. Ives. Strangers were looked upon with suspicion and greeted with reserve. Though he tipped his hat and smiled, his friendliness was not returned.

Luc walked into the Gull and Goose amidst a cacophony of sound. Men sat around tables laughing and quaffing ale, but the moment Luc entered the smoke-filled tavern, the lively conversation stopped abruptly.

"Gentlemen," Luc said, doffing his hat.

A man grunted a reply, and then Luc was ignored as conversation resumed. Luc walked up to the bar and ordered ale.

The bartender looked Luc up and down. "You don't look the type who'd enjoy the quiet life we lead in St. Ives."

"Looks can be deceiving," Luc answered.

The barkeep filled a mug and pushed it toward Luc. "How long be you staying with us?"

"I took a year's lease on the Beaton cottage. Since I intend to stick around for a while, I thought I should become acquainted with my neighbors. I'm Lucas Westmore. I've already met Billy Pigeon and Bliss Hartley."

"You met the squire's daughter?"

"Squire's daughter, is she," Luc said, pleased to have gleaned that small bit of knowledge. "Is she married?"

As he spoke with the barkeep, Luc was unaware that the room had quieted and others were listening to their conversation.

"No, she's not married, but Brady Bristol plans on changing that soon."

"You talk too much, Al," a rough-looking man said as he sidled up to Luc. "I'm sure our Bliss would have told the stranger her life story had she wanted him to know it."

Al nodded to Luc and walked away.

"Al's mouth runs faster than his feet. Pay him no heed."

Luc studied the man who had just spoken. He had a threatening air about him. "Who are you?" Luc asked.

"Fred Dandy."

"Do you live and work in St. Ives?"

"Aye, I'm a fisherman, like most men who live in the village."

"You sound as if you know Bliss quite well."

"Why are you interested in our Bliss?"

Luc went still. There it was again. *Our* Bliss. Was she the town whore?

"She's very beautiful," Luc allowed.

Several men half rose from their chairs. At a gesture from Fred Dandy, they resumed their seats.

"Don't go getting ideas about Bliss," Fred said. "She's not like your London women. We protect our own."

Luc recognized a warning when he heard one. Everyone in the tavern seemed excessively protective of Bliss. Instead of letting the matter rest, Luc became more curious than ever. What were these people hiding? What was Bliss hiding? Luc grinned. He had to admit that satisfying his curiosity would be more exciting than doing nothing all day.

St. Ives might yet prove to be quite interesting.

Luc returned home in a thoughtful mood. No sooner had he closed the door behind himself than an unexpected visitor arrived. Luc recognized his caller as a man of the cloth and invited him inside.

"Forgive me for not welcoming you to our village when you first arrived. I'm Vicar Brownlee."

"I'm Lucas Westmore," Luc said, extending his hand. "Please sit down, Vicar. May I offer you tea? Widow Pigeon left some delicious lemon cakes."

"Thank you," the vicar said. "I would love one of the widow's lemon cakes. No one makes them like she does."

Luc was knowledgeable enough about kitchen matters to brew tea and place a few lemon cakes on a plate. He waited patiently while the vicar devoured all but one of the cakes and sat back in his chair, patting his rounded stomach.

"As I said before, I am late in welcoming you," the vicar began, "but my welcome is no less sincere for that. Are you from London?"

"Yes, London is my home."

"You must miss the entertainments to be had in town."

"Indeed," Luc said, giving away nothing.

"What brings you to our fair village, sir?"

"I asked my agent to locate a cottage for rent in a remote village, and this is what he found. I wanted solitude, and St. Ives meets my needs."

The vicar fidgeted with the sleeve of his threadbare jacket. "Young men seldom seek peace and quiet. Something must have happened to send you fleeing into the countryside. You may confide in me, my son. Sometimes it helps to unburden your soul to a man of the cloth."

It sounded to Luc as if the vicar was pumping him for information. "I have nothing to confide, Vicar. I reached a point in my life where I needed to be alone to reassess my values."

Not exactly the truth, but close enough.

"Not all young men reach that point in their lives," the vicar said. "London is a wicked place." He leaned forward, his voice pitched low. "I hear that all kinds of perversions are indulged there. I commend you for walking away from temptation."

He took the last lemon cake and stuffed it into his mouth. "By now I suppose you've grown tired of country living."

"Not at all," Luc said. "I leased the cottage for a year and intend to remain until the

41

lease expires. I've just recently met a few of your parishioners. What can you tell me about Bliss Hartley?"

The vicar appeared flummoxed by Luc's interest in Bliss. He made no attempt to answer, but instead went back to the previous topic. "Yes, well, perhaps you'll change your mind about leaving once boredom sets in. This is a quiet place with no diversions to speak of."

With great difficulty, he pushed himself out of the chair. "I bid you good day, sir. Should you need my services, you'll find me at the rectory next to the church. I'm always willing to listen."

"Thank you, Vicar," Luc returned. "I'll remember that. Feel free to call again."

"I'll do that, young man, indeed I will," the vicar said in parting.

Vicar Brownlee went directly from Luc's cottage to Bliss's home. "Did you learn anything?" Bliss asked.

"He told me nothing," the vicar said, "except that he intends to remain here until the lease on his cottage expires. Quite frankly, I see little to fear in Lucas Westmore. I sensed no ulterior motive for his presence in St. Ives."

"I don't trust him," Bliss confided. "Fred

Dandy told me he was asking about me at the Gull and Goose."

The vicar grinned and patted her hand. "What's strange about that, Bliss? You're a beautiful woman. He'd be blind not to appreciate that. Now, if your father would like some company, I'd like to visit him."

"He'll be glad of your company, Vicar. But please don't say anything to upset him."

Bliss was on her way out the door to do the marketing when Jenny, the family cook and housekeeper, called to her.

"Billy is in the kitchen, Bliss. He brings news."

"It's about time," Bliss said, brushing past Jenny. "I was beginning to worry."

Billy sat at the kitchen table, devouring a slice of warm bread dripping with freshly churned butter. He stood when Bliss entered the room, but she motioned him back into his chair and joined him at the table.

"What news do you bring, Billy?"

Billy lowered his voice to a whisper. "It's time."

"Are you sure?"

"Aye, I saw the ship in the cove."

"Inform the others. Tonight's the night."

"Shall I tell Brady?"

"No, I'll tell him myself."

"What about the stranger?"

Instantly alert, Bliss asked, "What about him? Do you think he suspects?"

"Mam thinks he's no danger to us. He came to the cove while I was keeping watch. I think he was looking for you."

"We must do nothing to rouse his suspicion. Tell the others to have the wagons on the beach at midnight."

Billy finished his bread and hurried off. Jenny clucked her tongue in disapproval. "What would your poor father say?"

"He must never know, Jenny. The village was floundering before we began this enterprise. Now the citizens of St. Ives have enough food to eat, and money to buy fuel, clothing and other necessities."

"When will it end? I worry about you, lass. I'm sure the king's excise men are on to us."

"They've not bothered us yet, Jenny."

"Thank God for that, but it's not good to become complacent. Billy said the stranger was asking about you. Do you think he means trouble?"

"I don't think so. He came upon me by accident one day while I was watching for the ship. He thought I intended to jump. I don't believe he means us harm. Judging by his appearance, he's one of those dissolute gentlemen of the *ton* you read about in the gossip columns. I doubt that his reason for coming to St. Ives has anything to do with our operation."

Jenny searched her face. "Widow Pigeon says he's right handsome, and that he hasn't gone to fat for all his rich living in London."

Bliss shrugged. "Some might call him handsome."

She recalled the way his broad shoulders filled his jacket and his muscular thighs and legs stretched his trousers. The man might be a London dandy, but he knew how to keep his body in shape. She suspected that women fawned over him, and that he had bedded many of them. That thought brought a flush to her face.

"Will you keep an eye on Papa while I'm gone?" Bliss inquired.

"I always do, lass. Go about your business, but be careful."

Bliss left the house immediately and walked down to the small beach where the fishing boats were docked. Brady Bristol moved away from his fishing boat to greet her. Tall, blond and ruggedly handsome, Brady was a serious suitor for Bliss's hand. But though Bliss liked Brady, she had no plans to marry him.

"Billy already stopped by," Brady said. "So did Fred Dandy. I think you should stay home tonight. Let the men handle things. I don't like it that there's a stranger in town poking his nose into our business."

Bliss touched his hand. "You know I can't do that, Brady."

"I could order you to stay home."

Bliss laughed. "Order away and see what good it will do. I have to be there, Brady, and well you know it. This is as much my operation as yours."

"I don't like it," Brady said, reaching out to stroke her cheek. "I need to keep my woman safe."

Bliss bristled. "I've not yet promised myself to you, Brady."

"You will, Bliss; you will," he said confidently.

Neither Bliss nor Brady was aware that the very man they had been discussing was watching them. Luc had decided to explore more of the village and wandered down to the section of beach where the fishing boats were docked. When one was bored, even a fishing fleet could prove interesting.

What he saw was far more fascinating than fishing boats.

Bliss Hartley was talking earnestly to a handsome young blond man. The man seemed quite taken with the lovely Miss

46

Hartley. Did Bliss return his feelings? It certainly looked that way.

Suddenly feeling deflated and without purpose, Luc returned to his cottage.

His solitude was becoming more and more of a burden.

Chapter Three

Discomfort jolted Luc awake from a deep sleep. His erection throbbed painfully and his body was beaded with sweat. Fever raged through him. Another dousing in the icy water of the cove seemed in order. He rose and padded barefoot to the window. It was a moonless night; the wind howled through the trees, and shadows danced upon the water. He had started to turn away when he saw lights bobbing on the choppy water.

Would a fisherman be out this late at night? The answer was a resounding no. It suddenly occurred to Luc why the villagers were suspicious of strangers. It was as plain as the nose on his face.

Smugglers were out and about on this moonless night.

Apparently everyone in the village was involved, including the lovely Miss Bliss Hartley, her blond lover, and even young Billy Pigeon. Ignoring the danger he might encounter, Luc dressed quickly and left the cottage. Instantly he decided that spying on smugglers would relieve his boredom, and perhaps help England. Luckily, he had listened when Braxton told him about suspected smuggling in the area. Playing spy seemed a good way to take his mind off his randy cock.

Luc dressed and strode to the cove, stopping on the crag above the strip of beach where activity was taking place. He saw little except lanterns winking in the dark, but he had no difficulty recognizing the sound of wagon wheels and muffled voices. Since Luc had walked this way often in the past couple of months, he knew where the path leading down to the beach was located.

He scrambled down the steep track, cursing the loose stones that followed in his wake. Since there was so much activity on the beach, he reached the bottom undetected and hid behind a large rock, where he could watch the smugglers.

A dozen or more lanterns illuminated the stretch of beach, revealing much coming and going. He could barely see the ship anchored in the cove, but he knew it was there. Several longboats had already reached the shore and were being unloaded. Barrels, probably holding brandy, were stacked on the beach, waiting to be carted off by wagons. Luc could identify no one, for the men were all dressed alike in dark jackets and concealing caps.

One figure stood out, however. He directed the operation from a slight rise. Luc could tell little about the man except that he appeared to be the leader. And unlike the others, he wore a voluminous hooded cape that covered him from head to toe. Luc watched with interest as the leader directed his gang of smugglers with a precision that obviously came from experience.

Luc dropped to the ground and crawled closer to the activity. He could hear voices — strident, anxious. Someone called to the leader, and Luc strained to hear what was being said.

"The wagons are ready to leave, Shadow," Luc heard the man say.

Luc couldn't hear Shadow's reply as the man nodded and hurried off. Then the lead wagon rolled forward, followed by another and then another, until only Shadow and a man from the longboat remained. Luc crept through the tall sea grass, emboldened now that all but one lantern had been doused.

"Well, Shadow, another delivery completed successfully."

The man spoke French, a language Luc understood and spoke very well. Unfortunately, Shadow's voice was too low to be understood.

"Aye, look for us next month during the dark of the moon," the Frenchman replied to something Shadow said. "The same terms apply."

They shook hands and the meeting was concluded. The Frenchman returned to his longboat and soon disappeared into the thick fog rolling in from the sea.

Luc vacillated in indecision. Should he show himself and confront the leader or wait until he had more information to forward to Braxton? The decision was taken from him when Shadow was joined by a man who apparently had been waiting nearby for the Frenchman to leave. Shadow and his companion spoke not a word as they followed the same path as the wagons.

Luc had planned to follow until he noticed that the tide was turning, slowly gobbling the sandy beach. As the water rose, Luc scrambled toward the path. Of the wagons, he saw nothing, for blackness had swallowed everything around him.

Then the night seemed to explode as hoofbeats pounded along the cliff above him. The horses skidded to a halt, pawing the ground and snorting. Luc flattened himself against the ground.

"They're gone!" someone from above shouted. "We're too late. Spread out and search for the wagons. They can't have gotten far."

Luc remained concealed until the men and horses dispersed. It was nearly dawn before he found his way home and slid into bed. Sleep was not possible. He had too much to think about. Instinct told Luc that Shadow was someone from the village. Right off he could think of two likely suspects: Fred Dandy and the blond man Bliss had spoken to near the fishing boats. But Shadow could be anyone, including the squire himself. He suspected that every last citizen of St. Ives was aware of what was going on and condoned it.

How had the excise men learned that the smugglers would be receiving a shipment tonight? Was there a traitor in their midst? Belatedly Luc realized that Bliss must have been searching for the smugglers' ship when he had seen her poised at the edge of the cliff that first day. Obviously she was involved with the smugglers. Somehow that thought bothered him. If the smugglers were apprehended, Bliss would be, too.

Luc rose, performed his morning ablutions and went to the kitchen. Widow Pigeon had just arrived and was fixing breakfast. She had soon learned that Luc was an early riser. That hadn't always been the case, however. In London, Luc played all night and slept well past noon every day. Then he was off to practice swordplay with the best London had to offer or engage in boxing matches at a sporting hall.

"You look tired, sir," Widow Pigeon said as she poured tea. "Did you not sleep well last night?"

"I had a restless night," Luc muttered.

He picked up one of the week-old papers that had arrived by mail coach yesterday and began to read while he waited for his breakfast. But Luc had too much on his mind to concentrate on what had taken place in London a week ago. He folded the paper, replaced it on the pile and cleared his throat.

"Did you say something, sir?" Widow Pigeon asked as she placed a plate of eggs and ham before him. She reached for the teapot to refill his cup.

"I was wondering, Mrs. Pigeon, if you knew anyone in the village named Shadow."

The teapot slid from her fingers and shattered on the flagstone floor, spewing hot tea on Luc's ankles. He leaped to his feet.

"I'm sorry, sir, that was clumsy of me."

"No damage done except to the pot, Mrs. Pigeon."

Luc regained his seat, picked up his fork and dug into his food. Widow Pigeon was an excellent cook.

"You didn't answer my question, Mrs. Pigeon," Luc said around a mouthful of eggs.

"Sorry, sir, what did you want to know?"

"You've lived here a long time, have you not?"

"All my life, sir."

"Then you should know if Mr. Shadow resides in the village." He thought a moment, then said, "Perhaps it's a nickname."

Luc saw Widow Pigeon's lips quiver before she turned back to the hearth. "The name isn't familiar," she said without looking at Luc. "Perhaps you'll find the person you're looking for in Penzance or Land's End."

"Perhaps," Luc said, deciding to drop the subject since it clearly made the widow uncomfortable. But he was far from satisfied. One day the excise men would catch up to the smugglers, and Bliss could be caught in the middle. Though he barely knew her, he'd hate to see her hanging from the end of a rope along with her fellow lawbreakers. He needed to find Shadow and convince him to stop his illegal operations before he brought disaster to the entire village.

After breakfast, Luc went hunting and bagged a small buck. The widow offered her son's skills in skinning and preparing the meat, and Luc agreed to the arrangement. Though he could have done it himself, he had more important things to do.

Later that day, Luc walked to the village. His first stop was the Gull and Goose. Al had proved talkative before; maybe he would again, unless Fred Dandy was there to interfere.

The tavern was deserted when Luc entered. He slapped a coin on the bar, hoping the sound would bring Al out from the back room.

"Where is everyone today?" Luc called out. "Last time I was here the place was fairly bursting at the seams."

"The men are out fishing," a female voice answered. Luc swiveled around and smiled at the curvaceous blonde sauntering toward him. "I'm Millie. I work here."

"A mug of ale, please," Luc ordered. "Would you care to join me, Millie?"

Millie walked behind the bar, poured herself a mug of ale, took Luc's coin and raised her mug. "Here's to you, handsome." She drank deeply, wiped the foam from her lips and asked, "You must be the stranger who rented the old Beaton cottage. What brings you to St. Ives?"

Luc carried his drink to a table and sat down. Millie joined him.

"I'm here strictly for rest and solitude," Luc replied.

Millie preened for Luc's benefit. "You must be mighty lonesome by now." She slid her chair closer. "You don't look like a hermit. You're a handsome bloke. I'll bet women flock to you in droves."

Luc winced. Millie had come too close to the truth. "I gave up my life in London for the peace and quiet here."

Millie didn't look convinced. "When you get a hankering for a woman, I'm available." Her blue eyes sparkled as she licked her lips in a provocative manner. "I'll bet you know your way around a woman, unlike the rough fishermen who come into the Gull and Goose. Fred Dandy can't hold a candle to you."

"I'll keep your offer in mind."

"You won't be sorry," Millie purred.

"I'll bet you know everything that goes on in St. Ives," Luc probed.

Millie shrugged. Her bodice slid off one shoulder, the scooped neckline revealing more than it concealed. Luc stared. She had lovely breasts. He aimed his thoughts in another direction.

"I'm looking for information," Luc confided, "and I'm willing to pay well for it."

Millie sat back in her chair, immediately wary. "What kind of information?"

"I'm looking for Shadow. Can you direct me to him?"

Color seeped from Millie's face. "Why do you want Shadow?"

"I . . . have business with him."

Millie rose abruptly. "I'll find Al. You can ask him." She fled through a curtained exit behind the bar.

Luc cursed himself for blundering into this like a clumsy bull. He was a fighting man, not a spy. While he and Bathurst had fought together on the Peninsula, he had none of Braxton's savvy when it came to spying.

Al appeared from the back room.

"Millie said you were looking for Shadow. How well do you know him?"

"I don't know him at all," Luc admitted. "I . . . have business with him and thought one of the villagers could point me in the right direction."

"There's nobody around here named Shadow."

"If you don't know him, then I doubt anyone does. Sorry to have bothered you."

Luc finished his ale and left the tavern. It was apparent to him that Millie and Al knew more about Shadow than they were willing to admit. He wondered how the squire and his daughter would react to his questions about Shadow and decided to find out. Solving mysteries was far more exciting than brooding about past events. Once he had all the information he needed, he would send it along to Braxton.

The squire's house was the largest one in the village. Surrounded by a fence, it was a handsome, two-story edifice, built of stone. Obviously the squire was a prosperous man.

Luc passed through the gate and walked up to the door. Grasping the brass knocker, he made his presence known. A few moments later, the door was opened by a small woman of late middle age. The smile slipped from her face when she discerned the identity of the man standing on the doorstep.

"Can I help you, sir?"

"I hope so. I'm Lucas Westmore. I rent the cottage at the end of the lane. I thought it was high time I called on the squire. Is he in?"

"He's in, sir, but he can't see anyone. He's ill, you see, and receives no one but the vicar."

"Who is it, Jenny?"

Luc looked beyond Jenny and saw Bliss poised at the foot of the stairs. She was wearing a blue, sprigged muslin gown with a high waist and puff sleeves, looking even lovelier than he remembered.

"Someone to see the squire, Bliss," Jenny said. "I told him —"

"I'll take care of it, Jenny."

Jenny searched Bliss's face, then nodded and returned to the back reaches of the house.

"What do you want with my father?" Bliss asked.

"I merely seek to introduce myself," Luc replied. "May I come in?"

"Didn't Jenny tell you Papa was ill and not receiving visitors?"

"Indeed, but perhaps you'll grant me a few minutes of your time." He stepped inside and closed the door behind him.

The air between them seemed to have a life of its own. Bliss took a step backward. Why should this man produce such tumultuous feelings inside her?

"Since you're already inside, come into the parlor and tell me why you wish to speak to my father."

Bliss ushered him into a room furnished with comfort in mind. The room was light and airy, the floors were carpeted, and filmy curtains fluttered about the open windows.

"I fear this is far from what you're accustomed to in London," Bliss said when she saw him taking in his surroundings.

"I find it rather charming," Luc replied.

"Please be seated."

She chose a chair beside the hearth; Luc sat opposite her. "Now, Mr. Westmore, how can I help you?"

While Bliss waited for him to state his business, she studied his handsome features from beneath lowered lids. He was dressed casually today in buff trousers, a white shirt with an open neck, and a fitted coat. Fine-quality leather boots hugged his calves. She knew intuitively that were he in London he would be wearing gloves and a top hat and carrying a cane.

He must have said something, for he was looking at her as if expecting an answer.

"I beg your pardon — what did you say?"

"I inquired about the nature of your father's illness."

"We're not sure. The village doctor thinks he's just run down and wants to bleed him, but I won't allow it. I intend to take him to a specialist in London."

"Will you be leaving soon?"

Bliss studied her hands. "As soon as he's

able to travel." She stood. "I'll be sure to tell Papa you asked about him. Is there anything else, Mr. Westmore?"

Though Luc rose when Bliss did, he wasn't ready yet to leave. "I hoped to ask the squire about a man named Shadow."

The shock of Luc's words nearly staggered her. She swallowed hard and tried to conceal her shock. Her first instincts had been right. Lucas Westmore was a spy. Fred and Brady should be told immediately.

"I'm sure Papa knows no one by that name," Bliss said in a voice that trembled with nervousness.

Luc stared at her with such intensity, his blue eyes seemed to turn to smoke.

"Shall we dispense with formalities?" he asked. "This isn't London. Please call me Luc, and I shall call you Bliss. Now, where were we?"

Bliss moved to the window in an effort to escape the invisible cord that seemed to draw her to him. His eyes possessed the ability to look through to her very soul. She shuddered, completely unnerved by his charm, his handsome face and well-toned body. Comparing Luc and Brady was like placing a thoroughbred next to a nag. Before her thoughts got her in trouble, Bliss turned slowly and said, "I believe you were about to leave."

"In a moment. Are *you* acquainted with Shadow?"

Bliss's reaction stunned Luc. The color drained from her face, and her lips suddenly appeared bloodless. And lovely lips they were, lush and full, the bottom one slightly fuller than the top. Everything about Bliss Hartley was intriguing. Were he not celibate, he would have her naked and beneath him in a trice, her long legs wrapped around him and his name on her lips as he brought her to ecstasy.

Luc knew instinctively that Bliss would be passionate. He felt it in his bones. His every instinct was honed to keen perception where Bliss was concerned. His hands itched to touch her and his arms twitched, so eager to hold her he had to tighten his fists to restrain them.

"You are overly inquisitive for a man newly arrived in our humble village," Bliss charged. "What is your business with . . . Shadow?"

Luc's elegant brows rose. "That, my dear Bliss, is my business. Do you or don't you know him?"

Bliss's chin rose. "No, sir, I do not. Perhaps you should seek him elsewhere."

"Perhaps," Luc allowed.

He made no move to leave; he couldn't take his eyes off Bliss. Perhaps it was because he hadn't been with a woman in longer than he cared to admit, or maybe it was because Bliss was different from the women he usually bedded. Whatever it was, he seriously considered breaking his vow for one kiss from Bliss's lush lips.

Bliss felt lethargic, unable to move or think. Why was he staring at her like that? He made her feel all shivery inside. When Brady stared at her in the same way, she felt nothing. Brady wanted to marry her. What did Luc Westmore want?

Bliss learned the answer when Luc dragged her into his arms. Her voice rose on a note of panic. "What are you doing?"

"Something I shouldn't."

"Then don't."

"I can't help myself. I'm going to kiss you."

"My word! Why would you do that?"

He looked confused. "I truly don't know. It's just something I have to do, something I've wanted to do since I saw you standing on the cliff above the cove."

His mouth slanted over hers, stifling her protest. He kissed her hard, driven by deprivation and need. He swept his tongue between her parted lips, deepening the kiss, savoring her sweet essence. She clung to him, her fingers digging into his shoulders; only his arm around her waist kept her from falling. The kiss went on and on. He couldn't stop, even though he knew he was close to breaking his vow.

His hand slid around to her breast. He groaned against her mouth as the sweet weight of it filled his palm and her nipple hardened. He was guiding her toward the sofa when reason returned.

Bloody hell, what was he doing?

Abruptly he broke off the kiss and backed away. It was the most difficult thing he'd ever done. "Forgive me," he said, striving for control. "Despite the kiss, you have nothing to fear from me."

Bliss was panting, her breath coming fast and heavy. "How dare you!"

"I'm truly sorry, Bliss. But I spoke the truth. Your virtue is safe with me."

Bliss's curiosity was piqued. Luc Westmore was a man any woman who valued her innocence should fear. Just looking at him made her heart pound and her blood boil. "What do you mean? A moment ago you attacked me like a ravening wolf."

Luc shrugged. "I cannot be with a woman."

She let that sink in, then said, "You just kissed me."

"Ah, but that's all I did. I wanted much more than that from you."

"Thank God your conscience returned in time to stop you," Bliss ventured.

"Indeed, but that's not why I stopped. Before I left London I took a vow of celibacy. You are safe with me, even though it might kill me to keep my hands off you."

Bliss's mouth dropped open. She didn't know whether to laugh or express sympathy. She did neither. She accounted herself a good judge of character and she had marked Lucas Westmore as a rake and womanizer. She couldn't imagine him vowing to remain celibate.

"About Shadow," Luc prodded. "Perhaps one of your friends knows him. Who was that blond fellow I saw you with down by the fishing boats?"

Bliss bristled. "You were spying on me!"

"Not at all. I happened to be exploring the village when I saw you together. Nice-looking chap. Is he your lover?"

"Brady Bristol is most definitely not my lover," Bliss fumed. "Even if he were, it's none of your business. If you'll excuse me, I hear Papa calling me. Please show yourself out."

She turned to leave. Luc caught her elbow. "I'm not finished. My guess is that you know more about Shadow than you're admitting. I don't give a fig about him. I merely wish to warn you. Shadow will bring disaster to the village, and you could be caught in the middle."

"Who are you?" Bliss asked. "Why are you meddling where you don't belong?"

"I'm simply a man in search of solitude. But I'm also a man with two eyes in his head and a brain that works."

"I suggest you mind your own business, Mr. Westmore."

Luc stared at her lips. Lord, she was lovely. Her anger only enhanced her beauty. The one kiss he had stolen had whetted his appetite for more, but because of his vow he had deliberately denied himself. But it had been difficult to keep his hands off her when his randy cock was reminding him how long it had been since he'd had a woman. The need to touch Bliss, to kiss her, to bed her, was a fever in his blood.

Bliss stared at Luc's back as he let himself out the door. How did he know about Shadow if he hadn't been on the beach the night of the delivery? If he were a spy, why hadn't he notified the authorities? Had he done so, the whole lot of them could have been arrested in one fell swoop, Shadow included. Bliss had to know more about Luc Westmore.

Bliss touched her lips. They still tingled from his kiss. She had been kissed before, by Brady and some of the village lads, but their kisses were tame compared to Luc's sensual assault. His kiss had tasted of dark sin and mysterious secrets.

Bliss was astute enough to know that something in Luc's past had brought him to sleepy St. Ives. He might well be a spy, but she was willing to bet there was more to it than that. And what was his vow of celibacy all about? Luc's dark good looks and overt sensuality belied his vow. One had but to look at Lucas Westmore to know his sexuality was honed to a keen edge. As innocent as she was, Bliss recognized a rogue when she met one.

Jenny entered the parlor a few minutes after Luc left. "Does he know anything?" she asked.

"He was asking about Shadow. He knows something, but I don't know how much. I've got to tell Brady. The fishing fleet is probably in now. I'm leaving but should return before Papa awakens."

"I'll look after the squire while you're

gone. Do what you have to do, lass."

Bliss hurried down to the beach. The fishing boats had just arrived. She saw Brady washing down the deck of his small craft. She hailed him. He leaped to the ground and walked over to greet her, grinning broadly.

"To what do I owe the pleasure, love?" He pulled her into his arms and tried to kiss her. Bliss turned her face so his kiss landed on her cheek.

"Behave yourself, Brady Bristol," she said, swatting him playfully. "I have news."

Brady frowned. "Good or bad? The shipment got to where it was supposed to go, no trouble there."

"Lucas Westmore came by this morning. He was asking about Shadow."

Brady's hands tightened on her shoulders. "Damnation! I knew he was spying for the government. We have to get rid of him. Fred Dandy should be told. He'll slit the bastard's throat and toss his body into the sea if we ask him."

Color drained from Bliss's face as she pushed herself away from Brady. "We all agreed before we began this operation that there would be no killing. We need to be more careful, perhaps place a watch on the cliff above the cove. Luc must have been on

68

the beach during our last delivery. It's the only way he could know about Shadow. Besides, I'm not sure he is a spy, or even an excise man."

"What else could he be?"

"Perhaps he's a curious man with a penchant for intrigue. He heard a name, and is just bored enough with what the village has to offer to become involved."

"How do you know he won't betray our enterprise to the authorities?"

"I don't. I just don't want him dead. We don't do those things. Perhaps we should cease operations until Luc leaves St. Ives."

"Our next delivery has already been arranged. There's no way to call it off. Someone will have to keep Westmore occupied while we're working on the beach." He stroked his chin. "Mayhap Millie could help out. Westmore would probably appreciate a little romp in Millie's bed."

Bliss shook her head. "It won't work. You're not going to believe this, but Luc has taken a vow of celibacy."

Brady burst out laughing. "Never say it's true! The man is gulling you, Bliss." His brow furrowed, as if he were suddenly aware of the impropriety of what Bliss had told him. "He told you this?"

Bliss nodded.

"No gentleman would discuss such a delicate subject with a woman he hardly knows. What in hell were you thinking? You are not to speak to him again."

"You don't own me, Brady Bristol!"

"You're going to be my wife!"

"I do care for you, but I'm not going to marry you." She pulled away from him. "Just remember, no bloodshed. I'll handle Luc myself."

"Luc, is it?" Brady said with a hint of jealousy. "How did you get on a first-name basis so fast?"

"Now is not the time for jealousy, Brady. The man is celibate. He can do me no harm."

"Don't assume a simple vow will stop a man like that when he wants something. I think my idea is best. Fred Dandy will —"

"No! Leave Luc to me. I have to go."

Luc saw Bliss pull away from Brady and flounce off. Standing off to the side, he'd watched their heated exchange, taking great interest in their embrace. Unfortunately, he couldn't hear their conversation. Luc had known that Bliss would run to Bristol as soon as he left her house, so he had waited and followed. Their conversation had been quite intense, and Luc suspected they had been talking about him.

Luc was nearly convinced that Bristol was Shadow. Everything pointed to him. The man certainly bore watching, as did the lovely Bliss. Luc suspected that Bristol and Bliss were lovers, and for some reason that knowledge disturbed him.

Luc retraced his steps to the village and came face to face with Bliss, hands on hips, lips set angrily. "You followed me. How dare you?"

Luc shrugged. "I have to do something to ease my boredom."

"I strongly suggest that you return to London."

He looked past her, his mind wandering to the old haunts he'd frequented in London and the good times he'd had carousing, gambling and whoring. If he returned to London, he'd fall into the same routine without missing a beat. After his year of celibacy was up, he fully intended to take two women to bed at the same time and keep both of them very, very busy.

He returned his gaze to Bliss. How in bloody hell was he supposed to abstain from sex when Bliss tempted him beyond redemption?

"You seem lost in thought, Mr. West—"

"Luc."

"Luc, then. What were you thinking just now?"

"I was thinking how much I wanted to kiss you again. There's a lot we could do without breaking my vow."

Bliss had no idea what he was talking about, but she wouldn't give him the satisfaction of asking. "This conversation is inappropriate for casual acquaintances," she said. "I contrived this encounter to return the warning you afforded me this morning. Be careful — be very, very careful. I wouldn't want anything to happen to you."

Luc rocked back on his heels. Did the warning come from Shadow? "Thank you, Bliss, but you needn't worry about me. I can take care of myself." He tipped his hat and continued on his way.

Chapter Four

Bliss hadn't seen Luc for several days. The weather had turned ugly, not fit for man or beast. Rain had spilled from the sky nearly every day, keeping the fishing fleet beached and the villagers indoors.

Bliss knew that Luc was holed up in his cottage, for Mrs. Pigeon had told her. The widow said that Luc had kept himself busy by writing letters, and that worried Bliss.

Was he informing his superiors about what he knew of their smuggling operation? Or was he merely writing to friends? When she'd asked Mrs. Pigeon to act the spy and read his correspondence, the widow flatly refused. She had expressed loyalty to her employer, even though Bliss reminded her that he knew enough to present a danger to Billy.

The mail coach wasn't due to arrive for several days, and Bliss racked her brain for a way to get into Luc's cottage while he was out, so she could read his personal corre- spondence. It would help immensely if she were to learn Luc Westmore's secrets.

The opportunity she sought arrived sooner than she expected. Since there was a brief respite from the rain, Bliss decided to go marketing. She met Billy Pigeon in the marketplace; he told her his mother was ill with fever and chills and he was on his way to inform Mr. Westmore that the widow wouldn't return to her employment until she was feeling more like herself.

An idea occurred to Bliss immediately. She knew Brady wasn't going to like it, but her snooping would help everyone in the village.

"Don't bother going out to the cottage," Bliss said. "Tell your mother I'll take care of it."

"Mam will be relieved," Billy said. "She's grown fond of her employer. He pays well and seems to enjoy her cooking."

Bliss returned home, surprised to find her father sitting at the kitchen table. "Papa, should you be up?"

"Don't scold, daughter," Owen said. "I feel better today than I have in a long while. Maybe whatever ailment I had has finally run its course. Jenny is preparing me something besides that bland pap you've been feeding me."

"I'm happy to see you up and about,

Papa, but you shouldn't overdo. And that includes overloading your stomach with rich foods. We'll take your recovery a day at a time."

"Jenny told me I had a visitor a few days ago. I had no idea the Beaton cottage had been rented. What do you know about Mr. Westmore?"

"Not much, Papa."

"He's young and handsome," Jenny interjected.

"And a rogue if I ever saw one," Bliss added.

Owen finished only half the eggs Jenny had prepared for him and pushed the plate back. "You're right, daughter. My appetite isn't what it used to be. I think I'll go up to my room now and rest."

"Papa, I won't be here in the mornings for a while. Jenny will see to your needs."

Owen's brow furrowed. "Where will you be?"

"Widow Pigeon is ill, and I'm going to fill in as Mr. Westmore's housekeeper while she recovers."

"I knew we weren't flush, but are we that desperate for blunt?"

"It's not the money, Papa. No one else is available, so I'm just doing Widow Pigeon a good turn. It won't be for long."

"Do what you think best, Bliss. I trust you," Owen said.

"You should tell your father," Jenny advised once Owen left the room.

"I can't. He's the only law the village has. You know he'd break up the operation if he knew. He's not as well as he pretends. Did you notice how little of his breakfast he ate? And his complexion is far too ruddy. I need to take him to London as soon as our finances improve, and there's only one way to earn money in St. Ives."

"Be careful, lass. I worry about you and the others. Mayhap you should settle down, marry Brady and raise a passel of children."

"I don't want to marry Brady. Don't worry, Jenny, I'll be careful. I just need to know what Luc is about. I want to make sure he's no danger to us."

Bliss left the house before Jenny could voice further protest. It looked like rain again, so she hurried along, anxious to reach Luc's cottage before the skies opened.

Bliss let herself in the back door and quickly surveyed her surroundings. Then she walked into the larder, collecting the ingredients she needed to prepare Luc's breakfast. The rattle of pots and pans brought Luc into the kitchen.

"You're late this morning, Mrs. Pig—"

Luc stopped in his tracks just inside the door, stunned to see Bliss where the plump widow should be, her rounded backside raised temptingly as she bent over the hearth. He swallowed hard. "You're not Mrs. Pigeon. What in blazes are you doing here?"

Bliss rose and smiled at Luc. "Widow Pigeon is ill. I'm taking her place until she can resume her duties."

A tormented groan slipped past Luc's lips. Surely God was punishing him for his wicked ways. Why else would He place such temptation in Luc's path?

"There's no need. I'm perfectly capable of caring for myself."

"Are you capable of doing your own laundry and ironing your shirts?"

"Are you?" Luc shot back. "You're a squire's daughter, for God's sake."

"That doesn't mean I'm not capable. What would you like for breakfast?"

"I made myself tea and toasted bread when Mrs. Pigeon failed to show up at her appointed time. I require nothing more, thank you. Look, Bliss, this isn't a good idea. You're a temptation I can't afford."

"I'll try to make myself invisible."

Another groan slipped past Luc's lips. "Impossible," he muttered.

"I saw a freshly drawn rabbit in the larder, and some vegetables. I'll fix a nice stew for lunch, and there should be enough left over for your supper."

Luc watched her lips while she spoke. There were things a woman could do with her mouth that could drive men to madness. Just imagining her lush, red lips wrapped about his . . .

"Luc, are you listening? Does rabbit stew meet with your approval? I may not be as good a cook as Mrs. Pigeon, but my cooking won't poison you."

"Does Brady like your cooking?" Bliss nodded. "What else do you do that he likes?" What in bloody hell was wrong with him? His sexual innuendo was obviously lost on Bliss.

"Rabbit stew sounds fine," he said in a strangled voice. "Excuse me, I think I'll take a swim in the cove."

He left with indecent haste. He was so damn aroused, he couldn't think, much less carry on a conversation.

Bliss prepared the stew and placed it over the fire to cook while she finished her chores. She knew she must hurry if she wanted to search Luc's room before he returned. The cottage wasn't large. She found his bedroom with little trouble.

As Bliss made the bed, she became aware that his scent lingered on the bed linens . . . a combination of spice and fresh salt air. She inhaled deeply. Shaking her head to dispel the evocative aroma and the wicked thoughts it provoked, she moved away from the bed and ran a dustcloth over the furniture. Then she picked up a soiled shirt Luc had tossed aside and folded it neatly.

Aware that it had started to rain again and that Luc would return soon, Bliss walked to the writing desk and began rummaging through the drawers. She found an unsealed letter addressed to the Earl of Braxton's London address.

"Are you looking for something?" His voice stabbed into her with the potent heat of a searing flame.

Bliss spun around, her heart beating in time to the pounding rain. Luc was standing just inside the room, one shoulder propped against the wall, arms crossed over his chest. She dropped the letter into the drawer and forced a smile. "I'm cleaning your room. I believe that's one of Mrs. Pigeon's duties."

"Indeed." He pushed himself away from the wall and prowled toward her. Casually he closed the drawer. "If you're looking for something in particular, perhaps I can help you."

"I wasn't prying," Bliss argued. "I was merely —"

"— dusting." He stalked toward her, raised her chin with his index finger and asked, "Is Mrs. Pigeon really ill?"

"Of course — why would I lie?"

"I don't know, you tell me."

Bliss shivered. His blatant sexuality overwhelmed her. This man was more dangerous than she had suspected. Dark secrets lay beneath the facade of a London dandy. He radiated masculine power and sensuality. The strong column of his throat presented a dark contrast to the pristine whiteness of his shirt, and she was stunningly aware of the way his fitted trousers clung to his muscular thighs and legs. His penetrating gaze made her forget her name and purpose for being in his bedroom.

"Did Brady ask you to spy on me?" Luc asked after a lengthy pause.

"Leave Brady out of this."

"Do you love him?"

"Tell me about the mistresses you left behind in London and I'll tell you about Brady."

"Touché," he drawled.

Bliss felt a need to put distance between

them. She brushed past him and out the door. He caught up with her.

"Where are you going?"

"To check on the stew; then I'm going home."

"You can't."

"I most certainly can."

"Look outside."

Bliss walked to the nearest window and peered out. Early afternoon had suddenly turned into night. The sky was as black as pitch, and the wind howled like a hundred banshees. Sleet pelted the windows, and roiling waves pounded against the rocks below.

"I've walked in rain before," Bliss said, though in truth she didn't relish the thought of walking home in a violent storm.

Luc grasped her shoulders and urged her away from the window. "You're not going anywhere, Bliss. The storm will pass soon. You may as well share my stew while you wait."

Since Bliss could think of no polite way to reject his invitation, she headed to the kitchen. The stew was bubbling nicely but the vegetables weren't quite cooked, so she sliced thick hunks of bread Widow Pigeon had baked the day before and set out the butter. Luc surprised her by setting the kettle on the fire for their tea.

"You seem to know your way around a kitchen," Bliss remarked.

"I served on the Peninsula with my good friend the Marquis of Bathurst," Luc explained. "We had to fend for ourselves or starve on more occasions than I can count."

"Did you know Wellington?"

"We met on several occasions; he is a great man with a great mind. Those were difficult times, but Bathurst and I managed to survive."

Bliss found bowls in the cupboard and ladled stew into them while Luc measured tea into the pot. She felt so comfortable with him, she nearly forgot he might be a government spy.

"Very good," Luc said after tasting his first mouthful of stew. "You're as good a cook as Mrs. Pigeon."

Bliss accepted the compliment in stride. Jenny had taught her to cook after her mother died, but she didn't consider herself as accomplished as Mrs. Pigeon. Nevertheless, Luc's words pleased her.

When they had eaten their fill, Bliss said, "I'll clean up the kitchen."

Luc agreed with alacrity. Bliss smiled to herself. Though Luc might not mind lending a hand with the cooking, cleaning up was obviously not something he relished.

"I'll build up the fire in the parlor. It's getting chilly in here."

When Bliss reappeared in the parlor, she found Luc sitting on the sofa, legs stretched out in front of him.

"Would you care for a brandy?" he asked. "Or would wine be more to your liking?"

Since Bliss enjoyed a small brandy now and again, she voiced her preference for the amber liquid. She settled on the sofa while Luc poured their drinks. Then he sat down beside her and pressed her drink into her hand.

Her nearness hit Luc like a physical blow. Her flowery scent made his gut clench, causing his breath to catch. What would she look like with her hair tumbled across a pillow, her lips parted and her eyes half closed? He crossed his legs, grateful that Bliss seemed unaware of his growing arousal.

"Papa will be worried," Bliss mused.

"How is your father?" Luc asked in an effort to distract himself.

"About the same," Bliss answered.

"That's good," Luc said for lack of a better answer. If not for his vow of celibacy, he'd be seducing Bliss right now . . . and succeeding, for Luc never failed in that department. How far could he go without actual consummation? he wondered. A kiss or two shouldn't break his vow.

"You're very quiet," Bliss said. "What are you thinking about?"

"I want to kiss you," Luc admitted. "You're a fetching woman, Bliss. Your lover need never know that we shared a kiss or two."

"My lover? If you're referring to Brady, he is my friend."

"Of course," Luc said disbelievingly. His arm stole around her. Bliss resisted, but Luc held her firmly, bringing her against him. He removed the nearly empty brandy snifter from her hand and set it on the floor beside his.

"What about your vow?" Bliss reminded him as he lifted her chin.

"A kiss or two won't break my vow. I told you before that your virtue is safe with me."

"You're a rogue, Lucas Westmore."

Luc grinned. "I've been called worse." His voice lowered to a husky whisper. "Give me your lips, Bliss."

She held him at bay. "This isn't a good idea."

"It's the best idea I've had in weeks."

He slanted his mouth over hers, drinking from her lips like a man dying of thirst. His hunger was so enormous, he wanted to devour her. His tongue slid inside the heated velvet of her mouth, stabbing deep, taking complete possession as she made a soft, choked sound deep in her throat.

Luc felt her quiver and brought her hard against him, deliberately leaning into her, letting her feel the rigid pressure of his erection. Without quite realizing what he was doing, engrossed in the natural progression of seduction, Luc's hands found Bliss's breasts.

Pure animal hunger overwhelmed his conscience as he massaged her full breasts with his palms, then teased her nipples into hard points.

"Stop!" Bliss cried, struggling free.

Luc was a man possessed by unrelenting need. He wanted more than kisses but knew they were all he could allow himself. He eased her back until she was lying flat. If Bliss protested, he chose not to hear her. He tried to tell himself that this unaccountable hunger was caused by deprivation and not by any special need for Bliss. His body was starved for sexual gratification, and self-denial was killing him.

But a rational part of his brain argued that not just any woman would appease his appetite. It was Bliss he wanted . . . and

Bliss he couldn't have.

Without volition his hands slid down her ribcage, sliding around to her stomach. Bliss squirmed and tried to shove him away, but he was far too aroused to stop now. His right hand slid down, working its way between her thighs. She jerked reflexively as the heel of his hand pressed against her mound.

"Oh, God, what are you doing to me?" Bliss cried.

"Do you like that?" His voice was slow, rich, seductive.

"Yes . . . no . . . I don't know!"

He slid his hand beneath her skirt, raising it as his fingers skimmed past her knee and inner thigh. He nearly exploded when his fingers reached that moist, intimate place between her legs. She felt hot and swollen; just touching her there nearly undid Luc. When he found the tiny nub hidden amidst silken curls, he began to rub it.

Bliss nearly jumped out of her skin. What was Luc doing to her? The sensuous stroke of his fingers against that aching pulse sent jolts of white-hot reaction lancing through her. She arched upward, clinging to him as he continued kissing her. Something strange was happening to her. Her body was thrumming, hot blood was pounding through her veins, and her skin was afire. She knew she should stop him but she couldn't find the words.

"Ah, love, you're so responsive," Luc murmured. "I hope Brady appreciates you."

His finger slipped inside her, adding a new dimension to his torment. Bliss lacked the breath to speak. She was panting, her head thrown back, baring her throat for Luc's kisses as he continued tormenting her below. Suddenly she arched against his hand, moaning softly as his caresses created a growing tension that was exciting her beyond reason. Suddenly she stiffened; spasms ripped through her, sending indescribable pleasure exploding inside her. It was terrible. It was wonderful.

It was frightening.

The return of her senses brought a flood of anger.

"How dare you! You had no right." Disentangling herself from his arms, she rose and strode to the door.

"Where are you going?"

"Home." She was so confused, she hardly knew what she was doing or saying. All she knew was that she had to get away.

"You'll be blown away the moment you step outside the door."

"That's better than staying here with you."

She opened the door; a gust of wind nearly blew her off her feet. She struggled against the wind but got nowhere. Luc shut the door and latched it.

"Now will you believe me?"

"I don't believe anything you say. You said you were celibate, and look what happened."

"What happened didn't break my vow. I gave you pleasure while denying my own. No punishment could be more painful."

Bliss's curiosity was piqued. She edged toward a chair and perched on the edge. "Why are you punishing yourself?"

"It's a long story."

She glanced out the window at the raging storm. "I have time."

"You don't want to know. It isn't a pretty tale."

"It involves a woman, doesn't it?"

Agitated, Luc combed his fingers through his thick hair. "The best and worst moments of my life involve women."

Bliss believed him. She had never met a true rake, but everything about Luc screamed decadence and self-indulgence. Handsome and virile, he oozed charm. No woman had a chance against an experienced rogue like Luc. An innocent like her would be devoured by Luc's sexuality.

"Since we aren't going anywhere, why don't you tell me about it?"

Luc shook his head. "I can't. Suffice it to say, I'm punishing myself for something for which I hold myself responsible."

"So celibacy is your punishment." She searched his face. "Perhaps you're being too hard on yourself."

He gave her a smile that sent her pulses racing. "Are you inviting me to break my vow? Do you want me to make love to you?"

"No!" Bliss denied. "I have no desire to lead you astray."

"Too bad. Why don't you tell me about yourself?" Luc said, adroitly changing the subject. This kind of talk wasn't helping his aroused condition. Actually, just talking to Bliss was exciting.

"I assure you my life is quite dull. I was born and raised in St. Ives. As you know, my father is Squire Hartley. My mother died when I was fifteen, trying to give my father an heir."

"Why aren't you wed? Won't Brady make an honest woman of you?"

"Brady and I are friends, nothing more."

"Who besides Brady is vying for your hand? Perhaps you are aiming for someone of higher rank. Somehow I can't picture you as a fisherman's wife."

"Rank means nothing to me. Besides, marrying is out of the question while my father is ill."

"Why have you waited so long to take him to London to be evaluated by a specialist?"

"That's none of your business."

"It's lack of money," Luc guessed.

"I told you, it's none of . . . oh, look!" she cried, glancing out the window. "It's stopped raining." She jumped to her feet. "I should leave."

Luc rose. "Will you return tomorrow?"

"Yes, if Mrs. Pigeon is still ill."

She headed for the door.

"Wait! A word of warning. Don't get involved in anything dangerous or unlawful. I don't want to see you hurt."

Bliss went very still. "What does that mean?"

"I think you know. Think about it while I walk you home."

"I know the way."

"Nevertheless, a gentleman never lets a lady walk alone in the dark. And regardless of what you think, I am a gentleman."

She slanted him a look of total disbelief. But before she could voice her derision or question his warning, a loud pounding on the door interrupted her train of thought.

Luc strode to the door and flung it open. Brady stepped inside, his gaze settling on Bliss. "Jenny told me you were here, so I came to fetch you home. You should have let someone else fill in for Mrs. Pigeon."

"You needn't have bothered," Luc drawled. "I'm walking Bliss home."

"Stay away from my woman," Brady growled. "We don't want your kind in St. Ives."

Luc's eyebrows shot upward. "What kind is that?"

"That's enough, Brady," Bliss warned. "Let's go."

Brady shot a menacing glance at Luc as he ushered Bliss out the door.

"I wish you would stop referring to me as your woman," Bliss chided once they were out of Luc's hearing.

"Why? Everyone in the village expects us to marry."

"No, Brady, you're the only one who expects us to marry."

Brady grasped her arm. "What happened while you were alone with Westmore? Did he make advances?"

She twisted free, her flushed face betraying her racing pulse. Luc had given her pleasure, a fact she couldn't deny. But it was wrong and she knew it. She couldn't allow it to happen again and would guard against Luc's seduction in the future.

"The only reason I took Mrs. Pigeon's place was to pry into Luc's personal affairs. We all need to know what he's doing in St. Ives. If he's a government spy, our operation is in serious jeopardy."

"Did you learn anything?"

She deliberately refrained from mentioning Luc's thinly veiled warning. "I managed to rummage through his desk."

"What did you find?"

"Just a letter directed to the Earl of Braxton. I didn't have time to read it. It started to rain, and Luc returned home early. I'm going to try again tomorrow."

"Like hell! I don't want you anywhere near that spy."

"We don't know that Luc is either a spy or an excise man." *If Luc isn't a spy, why the warning?* Bliss silently wondered. Aloud, she said, "We need to know if Luc presents a danger to us. Besides," she said huffily, "you haven't the right to tell me what I can or cannot do."

"Don't I?"

Before Bliss realized what he intended, Brady grasped her shoulders, brought her against him and kissed her.

Luc had no idea why he was following Bliss and Brady. A misplaced sense of protectiveness, he supposed. Bliss neither wanted nor needed his protection, and that realization rankled. He knew Bliss must be involved with the smugglers, and despite her reluctance to trust him, he was determined to keep her safe. Experience had taught him to recognize people who kept secrets. And Bliss Hartley most definitely had secrets. He saw them behind those lovely golden eyes. He wouldn't be surprised if Bliss had been on the beach the night the illegal contraband had arrived, and that thought frightened him.

Luc continued to trail behind the couple. When they suddenly stopped, Luc did too. When he saw Brady drag Bliss into his arms and kiss her, his enraged mind told him to tear them apart, but rationality prevailed. His face set in harsh lines, Luc turned his back on them, intending to retrace his steps to the cottage.

A strangled cry from Bliss brought him spinning around. When he saw her struggling to escape Brady's attentions, Luc acted instinctively.

"Let her go!" he cried, racing to Bliss's defense.

A stunned look on his face, Brady shoved Bliss behind him and braced for a fight. "Keep out of this, Westmore. You don't want to mess with me. What does a London dandy like you know about fighting?"

"It's all right, Luc, I'm fine," Bliss said, stepping away from Brady.

Luc skidded to a halt, hands fisted, unafraid of Brady's tough stance. Luc had been trained to handle bullies like Brady, and had done so on many occasions.

"Did he hurt you, Bliss?" Luc asked through clenched teeth.

"No. Don't make trouble, Luc."

Though he didn't like it one damn bit, Luc followed Bliss's advice. But no matter how hard he tried, he couldn't forget the passionate interlude he and Bliss had shared. Though he hadn't been sexually satisfied in the traditional sense, he had received a great deal of pleasure just watching Bliss come apart in his arms. He'd do it again even if it did leave him aching and needy.

A resigned smile lifted the corners of Luc's mouth. It looked as if another dip in the frigid cove was in order.

Bliss slipped into the house and went immediately to her father's room. He was sleeping peacefully, so she closed the door and went down to the kitchen. Jenny was peeling vegetables for their supper.

"Can I help?" Bliss asked.

Jenny started violently. "My word, child, don't scare a body like that. That was some storm we had. I'm glad you didn't attempt to return home in that tempest. Did you learn anything?"

"Not a thing . . . except . . ."

Jenny put down the knife. "Except what?"

"Luc gave me a strange warning. He told me not to become involved in anything dangerous or unlawful."

Jenny shrugged. "You knew Mr. Westmore had observed the last delivery when he made inquiries about Shadow. How else could he know that? Listen to him, Bliss."

"You know I can't, Jenny. I'm as much a part of this as anyone. Besides, the villagers are much better off since our operation began. We can't stop now."

"Don't say I didn't warn you. Lucas Westmore is up to something, but it's not necessarily a bad thing. Had he wanted to, he could have informed the authorities already, closed down the operation and had you all arrested."

Bliss scarcely listened to Jenny as she

thought back to those intimate moments in Luc's parlor. How could she have allowed him to touch her like that? No man had ever known her as intimately as Luc. The very thought of anyone else touching her in such a manner was abhorrent.

The memory of pleasure lingered. Her breasts felt swollen, and that private place between her legs still tingled. What truly amazed Bliss was the fact that Luc had not sought his own pleasure. How many men would do that? How many men had that kind of control?

Before she died, Bliss's mother had explained how it was between men and women, and after that, Jenny had further elaborated, so Bliss was not unaware of what went on between men and women. She knew the danger of allowing intimacies and had deliberately ignored it today.

If she wasn't careful, she might lose more than she was willing to part with. Celibate or not, Luc Westmore was a master of seduction. Even an inexperienced woman like herself recognized Luc's blatant sexuality. Now that she knew, she had to avoid him. Unfortunately, that was easier said than done. The need to learn more about Lucas Westmore took precedence over her own safety.

Luc was shivering when he returned from his swim. This was becoming a nightly occurrence, thanks to Bliss Hartley. Had he any sense, he would stay far away from the entrancing beauty. But Bliss had made that impossible by showing up to take Mrs. Pigeon's place.

Luc removed his clothing and slid into bed, but his body was still too aroused to find sleep, even after a cold dip in the cove. His hand slid down to his member, and he found release in the only way he would allow himself during his year of abstinence.

Chapter Five

Luc left the cottage the next morning before Bliss arrived. He met her on the path, her arms filled with bundles. "What do you have here?" he asked, taking them from her.

"I noticed your larder was empty so I made some purchases at the butcher's and the miller's and the green grocer's and charged everything to your account. Where are you going so early? Come back to the cottage and I'll fix breakfast for you."

Being alone in the cottage with Bliss was the last thing Luc wanted. He didn't relish another cold dip in the cove.

"I have a letter to post. Then I'm going to get my horse from the livery and give him some exercise. He's probably as eager for a run as I am. But I'll carry the bundles up to the cottage first."

"There's no need," Bliss demurred. "I can manage on my own."

Ignoring her, Luc retraced his steps to the cottage. It was just a short distance and he really didn't mind. But he couldn't help noticing that Bliss appeared uncomfortable. He should have kept his hands off her yesterday, but Bliss Hartley was too damn tempting, and avoiding temptation had never been one of his strong points.

Bliss remained inordinately quiet as they walked side by side. She seemed almost relieved when they reached the cottage and Luc placed the bundles on the scarred kitchen table.

"Thank you," she said. "You can go about your business now."

Luc turned away, aware that he had to leave . . . immediately. If he didn't, he'd be pulling Bliss into his arms for a repetition of what had happened yesterday.

"By the way," Luc threw over his shoulder. "If you decide to search through my belongings again, I guarantee you'll find nothing of interest."

Luc smiled at Bliss's stunned expression and continued out the door. Aware that the mail coach was due this morning, he posted his letter to Braxton first. Though he hadn't mentioned the smugglers he had happened upon, he did say he was looking into a matter that might be of interest to the government.

After he posted the letter, Luc decided to call upon Squire Hartley again. There was a strong possibility that the squire was Shadow. Luc could discount no one. Not Billy, or Brady, or the squire.

Jenny answered his knock. "Is Squire Hartley feeling better today?" Luc asked. "I was hoping to introduce myself."

Jenny started to close the door in his face. "The squire isn't receiving visitors."

Luc placed his foot in the door. "Will you at least ask him if he'll receive me?"

"He's much too ill, sir. Some other time, perhaps."

"Jenny, is that the vicar?"

Luc pushed the door open with his shoulder. The man standing in the entryway wore a dressing gown and cap. His body was thin, his face unnaturally ruddy. It appeared as if he'd been ailing a long time.

"Who are you, sir?" Owen Hartley asked.

Luc sketched a bow. "Lucas Westmore, at your service. I'm renting the Beaton cottage."

"The Beatons left two years ago to join their daughter in Kent. Welcome to St. Ives. Please follow me to my chamber, sir, where we can have a nice chat. I seldom have visitors these days." He sent a censuring glance at Jenny. "My daughter and Jenny think I need seclusion. I am not, however, as ill as they believe."

100

"I've been hoping for a chat with you, Squire Hartley," Luc confessed.

He followed the squire to his room. Once they were seated in the comfortable study that had been transformed into a bedroom, the squire asked, "Are you from London, Mr. Westmore?"

"I am, sir."

"What brings you to St. Ives?"

"Peace and solitude. I asked my agent to look for a cottage away from London's hustle and bustle. St. Ives seemed to suit my purpose very well, so I leased the cottage for a year."

"My word. Whatever made you leave London?"

"It's a long story, one I'm not at liberty to tell."

"Ahhh," Owen said knowingly. "I understand completely. You aren't the first young man banished to the country to mend his wild ways."

Luc didn't correct him. The squire's supposition was as good an explanation as any for his self-imposed exile.

"How long have you been ill, sir?"

"Too long," Owen complained. "Some days are better than others."

"What does your doctor say?"

"Bah! All these country doctors know is

bleeding and cupping. They're butchers. My daughter wants to take me to London, but I'm against it."

As they conversed, Luc began to doubt that Owen Hartley knew anything about the smuggling taking place under his nose. But being a thorough man, Luc asked, "Do you happen to know a man named Shadow?"

"No, sir, I do not." The squire's expression convinced Luc that he was being truthful. "Is the man important to you?"

"Not really," Luc said, shrugging. "He could present a danger to the citizens of St. Ives, however."

"Our village has little crime," Owen said. "I should know, as I'm the local magistrate. As soon as I'm on my feet, I'll look into the matter for you."

"I would appreciate it if you didn't mention our conversation to anyone," Luc said, rising. "I could be mistaken about Shadow."

Luc left a few minutes later. His visit with the squire had convinced him that the man knew nothing about the crime taking place within his jurisdiction. Luc couldn't say the same about the squire's daughter, however.

There was one more piece of business Luc needed to conclude before fetching his horse from the livery. He walked to where the fishing fleet was anchored, looking for Brady Bristol. Luck was with him. Because of yesterday's storm, the fishermen were busy repairing damage done to their boats. Luc found Brady seated on the deck of his small craft, mending sails.

Luc hailed Brady and asked for a moment of his time. Brady motioned him aboard, and Luc complied.

Brady gave Luc a surly look. "What can I do for you, Westmore? Make it brief, I'm busy."

Luc perched on a coil of rope. "Are you Shadow?" he asked bluntly.

Brady half rose, his face turning red, the veins in his neck bulging. "What are you implying?"

"I think you know. I don't give a damn about you or your fellow smugglers. It's Bliss I'm worried about. She doesn't belong on the beach during a delivery. Your last delivery came close to being shut down by excise men. They arrived minutes after you and the others left. The raid could have had disastrous results."

Brady blinked, then blinked again. "I don't know what you're talking about."

"Don't you? I'm asking you point-blank if you are Shadow."

"And I'm asking *you* point-blank if you are an excise man."

"I am not," Luc said. "I merely happened to be in the wrong place at the right time."

"I'm not Shadow," Brady replied.

"I really don't care whether you are or not. I merely want your assurance that you'll keep Bliss away from the beach during your next delivery. You would do well to think about revealing Shadow's identity. He's a dangerous man. He could get you all killed."

"We'll take our chances with Shadow," Brady said. "Do you think I want to remain a fisherman all my life? Shadow is helping us escape the bleak existence we lead. We will follow him to our deaths, if need be."

"Does that include Bliss?"

"It's for Bliss that I want a better life."

"If you love her, you'll keep her safe. Don't let her become more involved in your illegal activities than she already is."

"Are you threatening me, Westmore?"

"Take it any way you want."

"Are you going to inform the authorities?"

"I will if you don't keep Bliss safe."

"You're the one who's dangerous," Brady said through clenched teeth. "Why did you come to St. Ives if not to spy on us? Go ahead, report us to the authorities; they'll find no proof of illegal activity in our village."

"I don't care about any of that. I just want to make sure Bliss is kept safe."

Brady waved his fist in front of Luc in a menacing manner. "Just how involved are you with Bliss? She's *my* woman, remember that."

Luc shoved Brady's fist aside. "You don't frighten me, Bristol. But I'm warning you — think carefully about what I just said."

During Luc's absence, Bliss searched his personal belongings for something to link him to the government. She found nothing but a letter from the Earl of Braxton. The contents told her little except that the ladies of the *ton* missed Luc, and that rumors abounded about his continued absence.

Bliss nearly laughed aloud when Lord Braxton wrote that most of the *ton* knew about his vow of celibacy, and that wagers had been placed in the betting books at White's as to how long Luc would remain chaste. The dates ranged from one week to several months, but the consensus was he would break his vow well before the end of his self-imposed exile.

So Luc had told her the truth about his

vow, Bliss mused. He really was set upon a course of celibacy. Another thought occurred to Bliss. If Luc was able to enter White's, a gentlemen's establishment, it was highly likely that he was titled. Why hadn't he mentioned his title?

Bliss placed the letter in the same spot she had found it and returned to the kitchen. The roasted venison she had prepared for Luc was cooked, and she moved it to the edge of the fire to keep warm.

Bliss heard a noise at the back door and turned, expecting to see Luc walk in. But it wasn't Luc; it was Brady.

"Brady, what are you doing here?"

"Your employer paid me a visit today."

Bliss swallowed hard. Had Luc told Brady what had passed between them yesterday? "What did he want?"

"He said that Shadow is placing everyone in the village in danger and warned me to keep you away from the beach during the next delivery."

"Perhaps he *is* an excise man," Bliss mused.

"He says not, and I'm inclined to believe him. He'd have the law down on us if he were a government agent. But he does want something, Bliss."

"Did he tell you what he wants?"

"Not in so many words, but it's plain to me that it's you he wants." He grasped her arm. "Why is he so possessive of you, Bliss? Have you given him what you refused me?"

"Let me go!" Bliss hissed. "You don't own me, Brady Bristol. You had best be careful how you treat me. Shadow might bar you from participating in our operation."

He gave her a strange look. "Shadow, bah! Don't threaten me, Bliss. Once we're wed, things will change. Shadow will be cast out as leader."

"Release me," Bliss repeated. "You're hurting me."

"You heard the lady, release her."

Luc! He must have come in the front door.

Brady thrust Bliss away from him. "I was merely having a private conversation with my woman."

Luc's eyebrows shot upward. Gently he raised Bliss's arm and examined the bruises on her wrist. "Since when does a private conversation include manhandling a lady?"

"Since when have you made Bliss your business?" Brady shot back.

"Since I learned about the danger she is in. You and your accomplices aren't doing Bliss any favors by letting her participate in your illegal operation. I don't want to see

Bliss hang along with the rest of you. And you can tell Shadow I said that."

Bliss turned deathly pale. Dear God! Luc knew everything. Everything except Shadow's identity.

"I can take care of myself," Bliss said once she found her voice. "How much do you know?"

"I know about the smuggling. I also believe your father has no knowledge of your involvement."

Brady pulled Bliss over to the door, where they could speak privately. "I say we get rid of him," he said in a low voice.

"Fool!" Bliss whispered. "You really are looking for trouble, aren't you? I don't think Luc presents a danger to us."

"I'm not so sure about that. I'll talk to the others and see what they think."

"Listen, Brady, Luc has some powerful friends, an earl and a marquis among them." Then she added in a louder voice, "I want you to leave so I can talk to Luc alone."

"A wonderful idea," Luc concurred. "But before you go, I suggest that you heed my warning. If I learn you've hurt Bliss in any way, I'll make you very, very sorry. Good day, sir."

Brady blustered all the way out the door.

Luc helped him along by slamming the door behind him. Then he turned to confront Bliss, his face as dark as a storm cloud. "Your lover is a bully. Why do you let him hurt you?"

"He didn't hurt me. He was just . . . trying to make a point."

"What point is that?"

"You know too much about the citizens of St. Ives and their activities, and Brady is worried."

"Worried enough to keep you off the beach during the next delivery?"

"How do you know I was there? Did you see me? Did you recognize anyone?"

Luc's brow furrowed. "Blast and damn! I didn't have to recognize anyone to know you were there. Don't try to deny that you're involved in the smuggling, for I won't believe you." He glared at her. "Unless you promise to remove yourself from danger, I'll be obliged to appoint myself your protector. Could your group use another pair of hands?"

Bliss's eyes widened. "You're mad! Shadow would never allow it."

"I'll speak to Shadow myself. Tell me where to find him."

Bliss backed away. "I have to go. Don't interfere, Luc . . . please."

He caught her before she reached the door. "I worry about you, Bliss."

"Why? You don't even know me."

"You don't recognize your own appeal. You'd be a sensation in London. If I'd met you there, I would have had no qualms about seducing you."

Bliss appeared visibly shaken. "You already have. You may have forgotten, but I haven't."

"I haven't forgotten a damn thing." He pulled her against him. "I've taken so many cold dips in the cove, my skin is beginning to shrivel. You make me so damn hot I can barely stand to be around you. If not for my blasted vow, you'd be in my bed right now."

"Don't," Bliss whispered.

Luc couldn't help himself. She looked so beautiful, so stunningly tempting, he couldn't resist testing his willpower again. He pressed her body hard against his, letting her feel the jutting ridge of his sex. Her gasp brought a smile to his lips. He knew Bliss Hartley was no innocent by the way she ground her hips against his erection.

When Bliss raised her head to stare at him, he took her mouth in a demanding kiss. If she hadn't regained her senses and struggled free, he knew exactly where they would have ended up — either on the floor or in his bed. Breathing hard, Luc made no move to follow as Bliss fled out the door.

Luc walked to his bedroom and picked up Braxton's latest letter, smiling when he read the part about the wagers placed in White's betting books concerning his state of celibacy. He gave a hoot of laughter. Only two months into his year of self-imposed celibacy and he was ready to renounce his vow, and all for a taste of Bliss Hartley's enticing charms.

God, he was pathetic.

Bliss marched straight down to Brady's boat. She hailed him, and he strode forth to meet her.

"You shouldn't have come to the cottage," Bliss scolded. "Now Luc wants to meet Shadow and join our operation."

"Does he suspect who Shadow is?"

"No, and he never will if I have anything to say about it."

"Surely you don't trust him, do you?"

"I . . . yes, I do. I found a letter in his desk from Lord Braxton. There was nothing in it to link Luc to the government." She paused. "He says he wants to join our operation."

"Why would he want to do that? Obviously he doesn't need the blunt."

"He believes I was on the beach during

the last delivery and wants to protect me."

"That does it!" Brady blasted. "I'm going to the Gull and Goose to talk to the men. I think they'll agree with me about getting rid of Westmore. Friends in high places or not, we can't afford to let him in on our venture."

Bliss sent him a quelling look. "You'll do nothing of the sort, Brady Bristol! We have no reason to suspect Luc of anything more than curiosity." So saying, she flounced off, feeling certain she was right about Luc.

But when she returned home and learned that Luc had visited her father, she became livid. His visit made her think that perhaps Brady was right, after all, that Lucas Westmore presented more of a danger to them than she realized. How dare he question her father!

The following morning, Bliss barged into Luc's cottage and slammed the door behind her. She had brooded all night about his visit to her father and couldn't wait to confront him. She didn't have long to wait. Luc strode into the kitchen, looking confident and virile. His welcoming smile displayed his dimple, and Bliss deliberately looked elsewhere in order to maintain her anger.

"Why did you call on my father after both

Jenny and I told you he wasn't receiving visitors?"

Luc had never seen Bliss so beautiful. Anger became her. Her golden eyes glittered and her face glowed. Her entire body was charged with energy.

"Your father invited me in for a chat. Didn't Jenny tell you?"

"What did you say to him?"

"Nothing to upset him. I introduced myself, and then we spoke of inconsequential things."

"Don't you dare call on him again!"

"Why not? Are you afraid he'll learn what his daughter has been up to?"

"He doesn't know."

"I suspected as much. Don't worry, I said nothing to upset him. Ask Jenny. My visit seemed to cheer the squire."

Bliss's fists balled at her sides. "If you say anything about . . . anything to Papa, you'll be sorry."

"Let's make a deal. You stay away from the cove during deliveries and I'll say nothing about your illegal activities to your father."

"I can't do that." Their gazes met and held. Bliss looked away first. "Brady thinks you're a danger to the operation."

"Is that what Shadow thinks?"

"I don't know. I didn't ask."

"Dammit, Bliss! Why are you being difficult? Are you the only woman involved with the smugglers?"

Bliss's chin angled upward. Luc surmised from the look on her face that she was the only woman brazen enough to place herself in danger. It was difficult to believe that smugglers would allow a woman to join their ranks.

"I'll have your breakfast ready soon," Bliss said, turning away.

Reaching out, Luc spun her around to face him. "Why are you being stubborn about this? Are you so starved for excitement that you would tempt fate?"

"Perhaps," Bliss admitted. "Then again, maybe I'm doing it for a share of the profits."

"You need the blunt to take your father to London. Is that it?"

"It's none of your business."

"I'm making it my business. I want your promise to stay away from the beach during future deliveries or . . ."

"Or what?"

"I'll tell your father what you've been up to."

"I can't guarantee your safety if you interfere," Bliss warned. "Don't you understand? You know too much."

Luc dragged her against him. "What I know will stay with me as long as you do as I say."

"Why do you care?"

"Damned if I know. Call it my protective instincts if you will. I love women . . . all women. I don't like to see them hurt."

The light left his face. Shadows gathered in the hollows beneath his eyes. Silence fell between them as Luc's thoughts returned to London, to that nondescript inn where Lady Sybil had begged him to marry her. After her tragic death, Luc had vowed that no woman would die as long as he had the ability to save her. Had Sybil waited, he would have found her a suitable husband, but he still blamed himself for her death. He wouldn't let the hangman claim Bliss Hartley.

"What's wrong?" Bliss asked. "You look so . . . so bleak all of a sudden."

The light returned to his eyes as quickly as it had departed. "Nothing is wrong." His expression hardened. "Do I have your promise, Bliss?"

Bliss wanted to lie, if only to satisfy Luc, but she couldn't do it. Besides, what she did or did not do was none of his business. Luc was as bad as Bristol, ordering her around as if she belonged to him.

"I can't promise you anything. Fortunately, this is my last day here. Widow Pigeon will resume her duties tomorrow. She has fully recovered from her minor ailment. You won't be able to badger me anymore."

"And you won't be able to snoop into my private correspondence," Luc shot back.

Bliss flushed, recalling the letter from Luc's friend she'd read. "It's no worse than you prying into village affairs."

His hands tightened on her shoulders. She twisted free. He caught her before she could flee, imprisoning her in his steely embrace. Panic swept through her. She knew intuitively that he was going to kiss her. Though Luc wasn't the first man to kiss her, he was the first to ignite a restless yearning and heated response that left her remembering the kiss long after it ended.

Her thoughts scattered when his mouth claimed hers with all the fervor she recalled from his previous kisses. There was no gentleness in him as he held her pinned against the length of his body. His kiss was savage and demanding and almost frightening. His tongue slid into her mouth, a heated spear that left her light-headed and reeling.

His body was unyielding, a hard pressure against her chest, belly and thighs. A shocked gasp left her mouth when his hand moved to her breast, shaping it in his palm, fingers stroking beneath the modest neckline of her bodice, sending shards of fire lancing through her.

He moaned.

A delicious throb ignited in her belly and between her thighs as Luc bared her breast, lowered his head and stroked her nipple with his tongue. Bliss felt . . . oh, God, this was insane. Had Luc abandoned his vow to remain celibate?

Luc seemed to know exactly what to do to arouse her as he rolled her nipple between his thumb and forefinger. She clung to him, feeling as if the floor were dipping away beneath her. The entire world was fading into nothing as delicious feelings swept through her. He continued kissing her, making her head spin and her heart pound. She clutched the front of his jacket to keep herself upright.

Bliss arched against him, blatantly aware of his long, hard-muscled legs pressing against her, of his hands and mouth doing things to her that felt wicked. She truly didn't know what would have happened or how far she'd have gone if Luc hadn't groaned and set her away from him.

She was breathing hard, feeling strangely

bereft. She wobbled drunkenly and caught the edge of the kitchen table. He reached out to steady her and then stepped back.

When she lifted her gaze to him, he appeared even more shaken than she was.

"Forgive me," Luc said in a tone deepened by desire. "You can't possibly know how badly I want you."

He turned away, needing time to compose himself before facing Bliss again. He was as hard as stone; his whole body burned with need. Why did he torture himself like this? There were worse things than breaking a vow. Then he pictured Sybil floating in the river and his erection softened. Only then did he turn to confront Bliss. She appeared to be struggling to control her body's reaction to his ill-timed seduction and was barely succeeding.

"Perhaps it's a good thing Widow Pigeon is returning," Luc muttered. He couldn't stand much more of the kind of temptation Bliss presented.

Bliss edged away from him. "I'll fix your dinner."

"I don't suppose I can convince you to sever your relationship with the smugglers," Luc said.

No answer was forthcoming as Bliss fled to the kitchen.

Widow Pigeon returned the next day. While Luc welcomed her, he missed Bliss. What in hell was wrong with him? Why should a country miss tempt him beyond reason when he had bedded sophisticated ladies of the *ton* who surpassed Bliss in beauty and experience?

The answer was simple and uncomplicated, or so he thought. He needed a woman, and Bliss was handy. He wasn't, however, going to succumb to Bliss's allure. Besides, she already had a lover.

Luc tried to entertain himself during the following weeks. Staying away from the village was no hardship, for Widow Pigeon kept him up on the gossip. She also did the marketing and paid his accounts with coin he gave her for that purpose.

Luc passed the endless days hunting, walking, riding and reading. His was a lonely life, but one he accepted as punishment for a woman's death. Maintaining a distance from Bliss was more punishment than he wanted, however. He missed her, missed their verbal sparring, the heated kisses they had shared and the feel of her curvaceous little body in his arms. She filled his dreams at night and occupied his thoughts during the day.

Bloody hell, if he didn't stop fantasizing he'd go mad!

Luc had been watching the phases of the moon carefully during the past weeks as he recalled the words the Frenchman had spoken to Shadow. The next delivery was to arrive during the dark of the moon.

For the past several nights, Luc had stayed up well past midnight, searching for twinkling lights in the cove. The smugglers might not want him on the beach during the delivery, but he was going to be there nevertheless, for he knew as surely as he lived and breathed that Bliss would be with them too.

A few nights later, Luc's patience was rewarded when he spied lights bobbing in the cove. Donning dark clothing, Luc loaded the pistol he had brought with him from London and left the cottage. The night was so dark and the path so treacherous that Luc had to pick his way carefully along the cliff. When he reached the cove, he wasn't surprised to see activity on the beach below.

He recognized Shadow by his hooded cloak. The leader of the smugglers was holding a lantern aloft, waving it back and forth in what Luc assumed was a prearranged signal. Luc flattened himself against the ground as Shadow turned his head and gazed upward, as if aware of his presence. Luc held his breath. A brief moment later, Shadow turned away and Luc let his breath out in a slow hiss. He had just started to scramble down the steep path when the earth beneath him began to shake.

Placing his ear to the ground, he identified the sound as hoofbeats pounding against the hard-packed earth.

Excise men!

Was Bliss on the beach? Instinct told him she was. Fear rode him as he stumbled down the steep path. When he reached the bottom, he filled his lungs with air and shouted, "Excise men! Run!"

Chapter Six

Work came to a standstill as the men on the beach searched for the source of the warning. Then one by one all lanterns but one blinked out as men began scattering. Some disappeared into the tall beach grass, while others climbed into the empty wagons being driven down the beach. The only person who remained was Shadow. He stood alone, frantically swinging his lantern in what must be prearranged signals to the ship anchored in the cove. Luc paid him little heed as he searched the beach for Bliss. Had Brady taken her to safety?

The ship's lights suddenly blinked out. Then Shadow's lantern went dark, too, and Luc was left in almost total darkness. But before Luc abandoned the beach, he needed to make sure Bliss had left with the others.

"Bliss," he hissed. "Answer me if you're still here."

Then he saw her, walking out of the mist rolling in from the sea. He called out to her. "Bliss, I'm over here."

"Luc!" Bliss cried, running into his open arms. "You shouldn't be here."

"Ungrateful wench," he muttered. Then he grasped her hand and pulled her toward the path. "We need to get out of here."

Bliss dragged her feet. "We could hide in one of the caves."

"The tide —"

"Not all the caves flood when the tide turns."

"The excise men will be searching most of the night. I prefer to have you tucked up in a warm bed. Hurry — we've almost reached the top."

Panting from the exertion, Luc pulled Bliss the last few feet up the steep path.

The pounding of hooves grew louder. "My God, they're nearly upon us!" Bliss cried. "What have you gotten me into?"

"Relax," Luc said as he brought her into the circle of his arms. "Kiss me."

"What? Are you mad? We're both going to end up in jail."

"Trust me. Let me kiss you, Bliss."

She lifted her chin. Luc pulled her hard against him, seizing her mouth and kissing her until he felt her relax. When he lifted his head, he saw that they were surrounded by red-coated excise men, some carrying lanterns.

One man separated himself from the troop, his horse prancing nervously beneath him. "Who are you?" he asked with a note of authority.

Luc sketched a bow. "Viscount Westmore at your service. Who are you?"

Luc felt Bliss stiffen when he revealed his title; he'd have some explaining to do later.

"Captain Skillington of His Majesty's revenue service. What are you doing out this time of night, my lord?"

Luc grinned down at Bliss. She hid her face against his chest. "Taking a midnight stroll with a lady. Is that a crime, Captain?"

"That depends," the captain said, eyeing them shrewdly. "Have you noticed any unusual activity on the beach tonight?"

Luc sent Skillington an amused look. "How could I when the beautiful woman in my arms had my full attention?"

Luc could tell the captain was becoming suspicious of his deliberately obtuse answers.

"Did you hear anything? Anything at all?"

"To tell the truth, we had just arrived at this spot. If there was activity on the beach, we neither saw nor heard it."

"What about lights? Did you see lights on the beach or in the cove?"

Luc looked down at Bliss, reaching out to

caress her cheek. "The only lights I saw were in my lady's eyes. Really, Captain, is this necessary?"

Obviously the captain thought so. "What are you doing so far from London, my lord? I know this region well and am aware of no large estate belonging to your family." He stroked his chin. "Westmore, you say?"

"Indeed. I maintain a home in London but came here for the hunting." He assumed a bored expression. "London can become tiresome. I've rented a cottage near St. Ives." He glanced at Bliss. "I think you'll agree that I have ample reason to remain."

The captain turned his probing gaze on Bliss. "And who might you be, mistress?"

"Her name is of no consequence," Luc answered in Bliss's stead. "I don't want to cause her undue embarrassment. If that's all, Captain, I'd like to take my . . . friend home. As you can see, the night has turned chilly, and my companion has forgotten her cloak."

"Are you sure, very, very sure you saw nothing suspicious in the cove?" Captain Skillington persisted.

"I'm sure, Captain. What is all this about?"

"We have it on good authority that smugglers are operating in the area. So far they've escaped us, but we'll catch them; our informant is trustworthy." He stared at Luc. "No one is above suspicion."

"Ah," Luc said, "an informant. How . . . interesting. Can you reveal his name?"

"I cannot, my lord." He tipped his hat. "I suggest you take your lady home, she's shivering. Good night, my lord."

Luc turned Bliss toward the path leading to his cottage. He didn't relax until he heard the captain give the order for his men to dismount and search the beach.

"My lord?" Bliss queried. "You're a nobleman! Why didn't you tell me?"

Luc shrugged. "It wasn't important. I wanted no special treatment."

"I understand nothing about you, *my lord*." She shivered and huddled against him.

"Where is your cloak? Whatever possessed you to go out without a wrap?"

"It was a warm night. I didn't think I needed one."

"That's your problem, Bliss, you don't think. Why didn't you leave the beach when I sounded the warning?"

"I was making my way to one of the caves when I heard you call my name."

"Where was Bristol? What kind of man is he? Does he care nothing for you? He should have secured your safety before looking to his own."

"I was in no danger," Bliss insisted. "I know every hiding place along this stretch of coast."

"What about the wagons? Surely no cave is big enough to contain three wagons."

"There's a break in the cliffs farther down the beach, and a road that has been widened to allow the wagons to pass. The wagons are driven to the Gull and Goose. Then they are unloaded and the kegs stowed in a secret place beneath the tavern. Once the danger has passed, the kegs are distributed to buyers by various methods. The profits are shared equally."

They had reached the cottage. Luc opened the door and ushered Bliss inside. He lit a lamp, built up the fire in the grate, then offered Bliss a snifter of brandy. She sipped it slowly as her thoughts returned to the captain and what he had said about an informer.

"What are you thinking?" Luc asked as he joined her on the sofa.

She sent him an assessing look. "There's an informer in our ranks. No one in St. Ives would betray us."

"Obviously someone has."

"No, that's impossible." A long pause

ensued. "You, on the other hand, are a stranger and a nobleman. How do I know you didn't alert the authorities? You snooped into our affairs until you ferreted out our secrets."

Luc reeled backward as if struck. "Surely you don't think I'm the informer."

"I don't know what to think, *my lord*. You're here for a purpose; what is it?"

"I've kept nothing from you, Bliss."

She snorted. Did he think her stupid? "You kept your title a secret."

"My title has no bearing on why I'm here. I had to leave London. My agent found this place, and it suited my needs. I happened upon your smuggling operation by chance. Bloody hell! Why would I work so hard to protect you if I meant you harm?"

Bliss rubbed her temples. She was too exhausted to think.

"Bliss, listen to me. I'm not the traitor. Could it be Shadow himself?"

Bliss started violently. "Impossible! Shadow is . . ." She swallowed hard. "Shadow is completely trustworthy."

"Tell me who he is. I'll investigate him for you."

Bliss shook her head. "I can't betray him. I *won't* betray him."

The curse that left Luc's mouth revealed

his disgust. "Damn it, Bliss, you're letting loyalty cloud your judgment. You and your friends could have been killed tonight had I not been there."

Bliss searched his face. "How did you know the excise men were coming?"

"I saw the ship's lights in the cove and headed down to the beach because I knew you'd be there. I intended to protect you with or without your approval. I was flattened against the ground, watching the operation from the top of the cliff, when I felt the earth tremble. It became apparent to me that trouble was on the way. I scrambled down the path and shouted a warning.

"I hoped you would be smart enough to leave when the others did, but I had to make sure. That's why I called your name. You can't imagine how shocked I was when I saw you running toward me."

"I've already explained my actions to you."

"What happened to Shadow? The last I saw him, he was signaling the ship in the cove. What did his signals mean?"

Bliss hesitated. How far could she trust Luc?

"Tell me, Bliss. You can trust me."

"Can I? I'm not so sure."

"I could have told the captain everything I

knew had I wanted to betray you."

Grudgingly Bliss accepted the truth of his words. "Shadow signaled the ship to return in a fortnight at a different location."

"Where?"

"I can't tell you. Shadow wouldn't like it." She stifled a yawn. "I have to go. Jenny will be worried sick about me."

Bliss rose, and Luc got up with her. There came a loud pounding on the door.

"Don't move," Luc said. "I'll see who it is."

Bliss followed him to the door despite his warning. His large frame shielded her as he yanked open the door.

"Captain Skillington — to what do I owe this pleasure? Were you afraid I wouldn't return home safely?"

"Not at all, my lord. I had no idea you occupied this cottage. We're searching every cottage in the village for the smugglers." Skillington glanced past Luc, stretching to see Bliss's face. "I see your . . . friend is still with you. Sorry to disturb you. Once again, I bid you good night, my lord." He tipped his hat and backed away. Luc closed the door and leaned against it.

"You can't leave now."

"Why not?"

"It's too dangerous. I don't think the

good captain is convinced of our innocence. He's probably left a man to watch the cottage. If you leave now you might be stopped and asked embarrassing questions. Since we were both careful to hide your identity, I don't think he got a good look at your face."

Luc's words made sense. If her identity was revealed, her father could become a suspect. They might even accuse him of being Shadow. What a coil.

"Very well, I'll stay until the excise men leave the village. They won't find anything, you know. By now the men are snug in their beds. Some of the caves have exits far from the beach. We know every one of them."

"What about Shadow?"

"What about him?"

"I need to talk to him, love. This can't go on. I need to convince him that he's endangering the entire village. Tell me his name."

She shook her head. No one would drag that information from her. "Ask me anything but that, Luc."

Luc's eyes narrowed. "What is Shadow to you? How well do you know him?"

"N-not very well," Bliss stuttered.

Luc searched her face. "You're lying."

Bliss bristled. "His identity must be protected."

"Bloody hell! It's Brady, isn't it?"

131

"No, and that's all I'm going to say on the subject."

This time she made no pretense of stifling her yawn.

"You're exhausted." Grasping her hand, Luc dragged her into the bedroom. "You can take the bed and I'll sleep on the sofa."

Bliss balked. "I can't do that. You take the bed and I'll sleep on the sofa."

"Don't argue. Let me play the gentleman. Get undressed and climb into bed while I build up the fire."

Bliss looked longingly at the bed, then at the small sofa. "We can share the bed," she blurted out. "I have nothing to fear from a man dedicated to celibacy."

Luc looked at Bliss as if she had just grown horns. Was she jesting? Didn't she know how close he was to breaking his vow and blaming it on his debauched nature? A man clearly on his way to perdition had few scruples, and he was beginning to learn just how few he had.

He wanted to bed Bliss Hartley. He wanted to seduce her into his arms and fill her with his rampant erection. He was out of control and knew it.

"That's not a good idea, Bliss. My control has limits. I'm a man accustomed to taking what I want when I want it. And I most definitely want you."

"Oh," Bliss said in a small voice. "I didn't intend to tempt you."

A heartbeat later she was in Luc's arms, his lips hovering above hers, his breath warm upon her. "Just looking at you tempts me, love." He kissed her, hard. "Kissing you arouses me beyond endurance." He caressed her breast, his touch light, teasing. "Just touching you drives me mad with wanting."

She pushed against his chest. "Then you shouldn't touch me or kiss me or . . . or anything. In fact, I should leave . . . now."

He backed away, his face revealing his frustration. "No, you can't leave. Go to bed. I'll sleep on the sofa in the parlor."

He left the bedroom and carefully closed the door behind him. He would have told her to latch it if the door had had a latch. He was shaking with need and would have taken a dip in the cove if the excise men weren't still prowling about. Damn, whatever had possessed him to take a vow of celibacy? A man of his vast and varied appetites should have realized how impossible it would be to honor such a vow. He might not be so needy, however, if he hadn't met Bliss.

Bliss was the cause of his misery and the

source of his elation.

During the next hour, Luc couldn't find a comfortable position on the sofa. It was far too short to accommodate his long legs. The floor would be far more comfortable, he decided. Recalling that the blankets were in a cabinet in the bedroom, he rose and tip-toed into the room where Bliss lay sleeping. His gaze went immediately to the bed.

Luc knew he'd made a fatal mistake the moment he saw Bliss. Her body made a tempting curve beneath the blanket; one hand rested atop the cover and the other beneath her cheek. Impulsively he approached the bed, and the devil inside him dared him to lie down beside her. He didn't intend to touch her; he just wanted to look at her.

Luc's good intentions flew out the window as Bliss sighed in her sleep and cuddled against him. Then she flung an arm around his middle, as if seeking his warmth. When he attempted to remove her arm, she opened her eyes. She smiled at him, as if it were the most natural thing in the world to wake up with Luc in her bed.

Luc settled more solidly against her.

"Am I dreaming?" she murmured.

"Yes," Luc whispered. "Kiss me, love."

She hesitated.

"It's all right. You can do anything you

wish in a dream. Let your inhibitions go. Let your dreams take you where they will."

"Truly?"

"Oh, yes. Tell me what you want."

"I want" — she placed her hand against his chest, wriggling her fingers beneath his loosened collar to feel his skin — "you naked."

Luc groaned. Why was he putting himself through this kind of torture? He knew the answer: because he couldn't resist Bliss's request, because he was a dissolute, unrepentant rogue controlled by his cock.

He rose and tore off his clothes.

Bliss loved this dream. She had wondered for a long time what Luc looked like naked. He stood before her now as God had made him, even more imposing than she had imagined. No woman could doubt his masculinity, for nothing about Luc was ordinary. Limned in the gentle glow of firelight, his sculpted muscles and toned flesh were as flawless as a marble statue created by an artist.

Her gaze traveled the length of his body, from the dark auburn swirls of hair on his chest, over his chiseled stomach and lower, to his proudly erect manhood. Excitement surged through her, around her, became part of her. Everything was unreal, but that was to be expected in a dream. A part of her she could not control yearned for the scent of his skin, the feel of his hands on her, the solid press of his body against hers.

Eyes half closed, she watched him place a knee on the bed. The mattress dipped beneath his weight as he slid beneath the blanket. She heard him groan as their bodies met and melded.

"I will pleasure you, love, if that's your wish. It may kill me, but you will have what you want from me."

His hand moved along the outside of her leg in a soothing stroke. He raised her shift and kissed her knee, her thigh, the indentation of her stomach. "I wanted to do this the first day I saw you."

She jerked violently as his head dropped between her thighs and he planted a kiss on the pouting lips of her womanhood. Her startled cry reverberated through the silent cottage. It was as if the air had been sucked from the room. Then she felt his fingers pressing her swollen folds open, felt his tongue touching the delicate nub between them. Oh, God, he was licking her in long, sinuous strokes that made her body arch up against him.

This was no dream!

Though she tried, she could not stop her hips from rising up to meet the wet strokes of his tongue. She had never thought anything like this was possible, much less enjoyable.

"Luc," she managed to gasp. "You must stop."

No answer was forthcoming as he plied his lips and tongue to her sensitive flesh with dexterity born of experience. Her breath hitched, her hips arched into his intimate caresses as flames consumed her. She felt his fingers pressing inside her while his tongue continued tormenting her, strumming, bathing, teasing. Then the sensations coalesced in a nearly unbearable peak, sending her spiraling to the stars.

Luc was more than pleased with Bliss's response. Had Brady never loved her in this way? Despite his vow of celibacy, Luc was too aroused to end it so soon. Nothing existed for him now except assuaging the terrible need to thrust himself into Bliss's hot sheath and finding the relief he had denied himself far too long.

He moved up her body, his cock hard as stone, his body tense enough to shatter.

"Open your legs, love," he whispered against her ear.

Apparently his softly spoken words returned Bliss to reality, for she tried to shove him away. "Remember your vow. You must not!"

"I must," Luc groaned. "Another dip in the cove will kill me. I'm so hot for you, I'll go mad if I don't have you."

Spreading her legs with his knees, Luc settled between them. He felt her stiffen and bent his head to kiss and suckle her breasts. He wanted her as eager for him as he was for her. His strategy must have worked, for she began moaning and arching upward, pressing her breast into the heat of his mouth and throwing her arms around his neck. Before long, her hips were grinding against his, as if begging him to enter her.

Luc flexed his hips, ready to thrust into her moist heat, when suddenly he paused. His damn vow was hampering his enjoyment of an act that had always come as naturally to him as breathing. As he pleasured Bliss, his vow intruded, diminishing his own pleasure. Damn the vow to perdition! Luc decided. It was no longer important. Two months of celibacy were punishment enough.

But Fate was a cruel mistress. Just as Luc had made up his mind to abandon his vow, he heard a loud pounding on the door. He tried to ignore it, but Bliss rose up on her elbows and shoved him away.

"Someone is here," she whispered, as if coming out of a trance.

Luc cursed loudly as he rose and pulled on his clothing. Who in blazes would be calling at this time of night? But it was no longer night. Fingers of dawn stretched across the eastern sky, turning darkness into daylight.

The pounding stopped, replaced by an irate voice. "Open the door, Westmore! I know Bliss is with you."

"It's Brady," Bliss hissed. "He can't find us like this. Where are my clothes?"

Luc gathered up Bliss's clothes and tossed them to her. Then he shut the bedroom door and strode through the tiny parlor to the front entrance. He opened the door, barring it with his body to keep Bristol from entering.

"What do you want?"

Brady tried to peer around Luc, with scant success. "Where is Bliss? Are you hiding her from me?"

Luc's temper flared. "I didn't see you trying to protect her last night. She could have been caught by the excise men and imprisoned. Where were you when she needed you?"

"Bliss doesn't need protecting," Brady

growled. "You don't know a damn thing about her, Westmore. You should keep your nose out of our business."

"I'm here, Brady," Bliss said from behind Luc. "Are the men all accounted for?"

"Aye. I'm here to walk you home."

"Are the excise men gone? It was too dangerous for me to be out and about while they were still in the village."

"They're gone. I don't expect any more trouble from them."

"Luc spoke with Captain Skillington, Brady," Bliss confided. "I learned something you should know. We have a traitor in our midst. Someone told the excise men about our delivery last night."

Brady glared at Luc. "We all know who the informant is, don't we? I tried to warn you about Westmore. The question now is, what are we going to do with him?"

He tried to push past Luc but failed.

"Luc isn't the traitor, Brady," Bliss argued. "Someone within our ranks is betraying us."

"So you say," Brady said, sounding unconvinced. "Are you ready to return home? Jenny is worried sick about you. She contacted me when you failed to return last night."

"I'm ready — let's go."

She tried to duck past Luc. He refused to budge. She glared at him.

"Not just yet, Bliss. We need to talk."

"You've had hours to talk," Brady said. His eyes narrowed. "Unless you and Westmore were doing something besides talking."

"Good-bye, Bristol," Luc said. "Tell Jenny she has nothing to worry about. Bliss is quite safe with me. I'll see her home after we've talked." He closed the door in Brady's face.

"Damn it, Bliss!" Brady shouted through the closed door. "Are you going to let a stranger dictate to you?"

"I'll be home directly, Brady," Bliss called back. Then she turned to Luc. "What do you wish to say to me? I really must go home."

Bliss was suddenly too embarrassed to look Luc in the eye. She had allowed him liberties that belonged only to a husband. He must think her wanton . . . or worse. Her breasts felt swollen and sensitive, her blood still pounded through her veins, and that place between her legs where he had loved her tingled and thrummed with sensation.

Bliss knew intuitively that Luc would have broken his vow if Brady hadn't appeared, and she would have let him. Lord, how could she face him?

"You can't leave yet, Bliss. Tell me where the next delivery is to be made."

"I . . . can't."

"Then tell me whom you suspect of betraying Shadow's operation."

"I wish I knew. I can't imagine why anyone would betray us. He would have nothing to gain."

"Very well, let's discuss another matter. You're to remove yourself from danger. You will most definitely not be present during the next delivery. Let the men handle it."

Bliss bristled. "I'm as good as any man. Besides, I need my share of the profits. Papa's sickness has almost depleted our resources. St. Ives is not now and has never been a rich community. Until Papa's illness, we managed quite well, but things have changed."

"I'll give you the money to take your father to London," Luc offered.

"You most certainly will not!" She glared at him. "Let me pass."

Luc leaned against the door. "Have you forgotten what happened between us?"

Her breath escaped in a loud hiss. "How could I? You almost broke your vow. I'm sorry. At first I thought you were part of a dream, a figment of my imagination. It didn't become real until you . . . joined me in bed. I should have stopped you."

"You wanted me as badly as I wanted you. I'm not sorry it happened. I wish we could have carried it to completion."

"Your vow . . ."

"For you, I would have broken it." He thrust his fingers through his hair. "How pathetic am I? I wanted to make you forget Brady and what you have with him. I wanted to be your lover, the man you turned to in your need."

"It's not like that between Brady and me. He's not my lover."

Luc's stunned expression showed his disbelief. "Don't lie to me, Bliss."

"But it's true. He has never touched me as you have. Your lovers are very lucky. But it can't happen again, Luc. I don't want to be responsible for a broken vow. I don't know what happened back in London, but it must have been serious to make a rogue like you mend his ways."

Luc chuckled. "I'm not sure I *have* mended my ways. I've come close to breaking my vow twice with you."

"Why did you make the vow in the first place?"

Luc shook his head. "It's a long and

painful story. Maybe someday I'll tell you."

"Perhaps I won't be around someday."

His expression hardened. "That's exactly what I've been trying to tell you. You're playing a dangerous game, love. The government is determined to stop the smuggling that's robbing the Crown of much needed revenue. Sooner or later, Shadow will be caught, and you and the others will be brought down with him.

"Think of the women and children left behind if their men are carted off to jail. What will they do? How will they support themselves? Shadow is a selfish bastard who thinks of no one but himself," Luc charged.

"I . . . never thought of it like that," Bliss mused.

"If you arrange a meeting between me and Shadow, I might be able to convince him of his folly."

"No — I'm sorry, but that's not possible. We don't contact Shadow, he contacts us."

"How?"

"I don't know. I'm not one of his confidants. Please let me pass. I really do have to leave."

Reluctantly Luc opened the door. Bliss brushed past him, and came face to face with Widow Pigeon.

"Bliss — my word," the widow said in a

startled voice. "I thought I told you I would be returning to work today. Did you forget?"

"Yes, that's it," Bliss readily agreed. "I'll be on my way."

Since it was now full light, Luc had no excuse to walk Bliss home, so he let her pass. He did, however, whisper a warning in her ear.

"I mean it, Bliss. If you refuse to heed me, I have no recourse but to protect you from your own folly, no matter what it takes."

Bliss rushed out the door, her face flushed and her mind spinning. In some ways Luc was right. She hadn't really thought of the consequences before. Their smuggling operation had been working flawlessly until now . . . until Luc had moved into the stone cottage.

Was Luc the informer?

She found that hard to believe. Luc had tried too hard to protect her. And Captain Skillington had seemed genuinely suspicious of Luc. But if Luc was not the one who'd tipped off the revenuers, who was?

Chapter Seven

Jenny was so happy to have Bliss home safely that she hugged her fiercely. "What happened, lass? Brady came here looking for you early this morning. I asked him to go out and find you, I was that worried. Did something go wrong last night?"

"Revenuers," Bliss said succinctly. "But we were warned in time."

"Come into the kitchen and I'll fix you some breakfast. You can tell me about it while you eat."

Bliss talked between bites of food, relating everything that had happened last night. Well, nearly everything.

"This has got to stop," Jenny warned. "Nothing good will come of it. It was a bad idea from the beginning."

"But everything was going so smoothly. Somehow the government learned of our smuggling venture and dispatched excise men to stop it."

"Brady stopped by after he left the stone cottage to tell me you'd return home soon,"

Jenny said. "He was upset about your spending the night with Westmore."

"I had no choice," Bliss said, avoiding Jenny's eyes. "With revenuers combing the area, I didn't dare leave."

"Are you sure that's all there was to it?" Jenny asked sharply.

"Of course. Why would I lie?"

"Mr. Westmore is a handsome man, and I believe a determined one. I've seen how he looks at you."

"He's *Viscount* Westmore," Bliss informed her. "The man's a bloody nobleman."

"Mind your language, Bliss. Why did he lie to us?"

Bliss shrugged. "Because it pleased him. How do I know? The man is a contradiction. If not for his warning, we all would have been caught. Yet . . . yet there's still a question in my mind about his reason for being in St. Ives. Tell me the truth. Do you think Luc's a spy, Jenny?"

"You know the man better than I do. He appears genuine to me, though why he concealed his identity is a mystery. However, I'm inclined to trust him."

Bliss finished her tea and rose. "I'm going to see Papa."

"Brady left a message," Jenny said.

"There's to be a meeting at the Gull and Goose this afternoon."

Bliss went still. "Shadow didn't call the meeting. I wonder why Brady assumed Shadow's authority."

"You'll have to ask Brady that question."

"I intend to, when I confront him at the Gull and Goose later today."

"You're going, then?"

"Oh, yes, I'll be there."

Luc was restless . . . his body, his spirit and his mind. He'd come so close to taking Bliss . . . her taste still lingered on his tongue, and the memory of her soft skin beneath his hands caused a clamoring inside him that begged for more. Brooding about Bliss and the danger she seemed to regard with little concern was driving him mad.

In the past, Luc had had no lack of women to assuage his sexual needs. Since that kind of relief was no longer possible, he decided to race his horse along the cliffs until the wind against his face blew the cobwebs from his brain.

With that goal in mind, Luc strode to the village to retrieve his horse from the livery. A soft rain had begun to fall but he wasn't going to let a little weather stop him from riding. He was just passing the Gull and

Goose tavern when he heard loud voices in heated discussion. Curiosity made him stop and push open the door. Fortunately, no one noticed him as he slipped into the shadows at the back of the room. He nearly gave his presence away, however, when he saw Bliss among the dozen or so men.

Stunned, Luc watched as Bliss motioned for silence. She didn't speak until the men gave her their full attention.

"Shadow didn't call this meeting," she began.

Brady Bristol's voice rose above hers. "Perhaps it's time to choose a new leader."

Murmurs of agreement followed Brady's words.

"I disagree," Bliss replied. "If not for Shadow you wouldn't have money in your pockets or food in your larder. This has been Shadow's venture from the beginning and should remain that way."

"Aw, Bliss," Fred Dandy whined, "we'll always be beholden to Shadow, but Brady's right. It's time for a change."

"What did Brady tell you before I arrived? Did he mention that there's an informer within our ranks?"

"It's that stranger!" Al the barkeep barked.

"You're wrong," Bliss argued. "Luc gave

the warning that saved our skins. Why would he bother if he were a spy?"

"I don't trust him," Brady maintained.

Luc tried to disappear into the woodwork. If he were seen, it would serve to reinforce Brady's view of him. But he couldn't leave yet — not until he discovered Shadow's identity.

"What does Shadow think?" a man Luc recognized as the miller shouted.

"Shadow . . . is inclined to trust Viscount Westmore," Bliss replied.

Brady appeared thunderstruck. "He's a nobleman? Blast and damn, why didn't he tell us? That's another strike against him."

Bliss shrugged. "Perhaps he had his reasons. Personally, I see no harm in his omission. If Shadow trusts him, so should you."

"What if excise men appear during our next delivery?" Brady asked. "Will Shadow still trust Westmore?"

"I think we should suspend operations after the next delivery," Bliss suggested.

"I disagree!" Brady said. "I like having money in my pocket. It wouldn't hurt, though, to keep changing delivery sites to confuse the excise men. Will Shadow agree, Bliss?"

Luc didn't stay to hear Bliss's answer. Afraid his presence would be discovered, he slipped out the door and continued on to the livery. Unfortunately, he had heard nothing to indicate that Shadow was present at the meeting.

Obviously Shadow was someone Bliss knew well. Just as obvious was the smugglers' trust in Bliss, and that puzzled Luc. Bliss's association with Shadow must be closer than he'd suspected.

Who was he? Where was he?

Luc wished he could have stayed in the alehouse long enough to learn Shadow's identity.

The meeting continued inside the Gull and Goose. Bliss was angry with Brady and she didn't try to hide it. Brady wanted to replace Shadow as leader of their operation and tried to convince the men to place their trust in him instead. Some men agreed, while others were satisfied with Shadow's leadership. The choice was put to a vote, and much to Bliss's relief, the group chose Shadow over Brady. Brady left in a huff immediately following the vote. Bliss chose to remain, hoping to discover who had betrayed their operation.

"The fact remains that someone betrayed us," Bliss said, searching each man's face for signs of guilt. She turned to the barkeep.

"Al, have you noticed anything unusual? Have any strangers turned up at the Gull and Goose recently?"

Al thought a moment, then shook his head. "Just Westmore. Why would a nobleman with no need of blunt be interested in our operation?"

"He isn't," Bliss assured them. "His presence here is merely a coincidence. We have to look elsewhere for our informer."

Absently Bliss glanced at Millie, who was distributing drinks to customers and seemed unconcerned with what was being discussed. Could she be the spy? Bliss discounted that thought immediately. Millie would have no reason to betray the smugglers. Though she didn't earn a share of the profits, she benefited from the generous tips she received after a successful delivery.

Since Luc was the only stranger in the village, all the evidence pointed to him. But Bliss knew in her heart that Luc was exactly who and what he said he was. In her opinion, Luc was not a liar and most definitely not the informer.

"Our next delivery arrives in a fortnight," the vicar piped up. "The odds are against us now. Too much is at stake. We all have wives and children to consider."

"If all goes well with this delivery, I say we

continue," Fred Dandy suggested.

"I'm not risking my life with a traitor in our midst," the miller replied. "I say we end it after our next delivery."

Several men echoed his sentiments. "I got a family to support," the blacksmith maintained. "I don't know how they would manage without me. I say we heed the vicar and end it after our next delivery."

"Caution is advised. We should station guards on the cliff above the cove," Al advised.

"Aye," the blacksmith agreed. "This is the last time, and then it's over and done with until we're sure the government has lost interest in us."

" 'Tis my opinion that Shadow will concur," Bliss said. "This operation was never meant to result in violence. We must avoid danger at all costs. We have our families to consider."

"That's it, then," the miller said, rising. "We all know where to meet the ship when it arrives in a fortnight. Vicar, will you pray for our success?"

"I will indeed," the vicar said. "I have as much a stake in the success of this venture as you do."

The meeting broke up shortly afterward. Bliss caught Vicar Brownlee before he left the alehouse. "Papa would enjoy a visit, Vicar Brownlee. He seems somewhat improved of late."

"Wonderful. I'll come around tomorrow, if that's all right with you."

"I'll tell Papa to expect you. It will give him something to look forward to."

Luc rode like a man possessed along the treacherous cliffs, then he urged Baron down the steep path to the beach and raced along the water's edge. It was exactly what he needed to clear his head, and the horse seemed to enjoy it as well. The sun was warm upon his back, and when he finally pulled up to rest Baron, he decided to take a swim.

Luc threw off his clothing and plunged into the surf, cooling his body as well as dousing his lurid thoughts. He hadn't been able to forget those exciting moments he'd spent with Bliss in his bed. Things had gotten out of hand quickly. He had consigned his vow to perdition and done everything but make love to Bliss.

Luc still did not believe that Bristol had never touched her. Bliss's passion seemed too powerful for an innocent. Her response to his seduction had thrilled and pleased him. Had they not been interrupted, he would have buried his cock deep inside her. His imagination took flight. He knew exactly how his name would sound on her lips when she reached her peak.

Luc plunged one more time into the surf, then began to swim back to shore. Water dripping down his long body, he rose from the surf and strode to where he'd left his clothes. He stopped abruptly, stunned to find them missing.

"What the hell . . ."

"Are you looking for these?"

Luc spun around, surprised to see Millie sashaying toward him, carrying his clothing and boots. "What are you doing here?"

Millie shrugged. "Does it matter?"

"Give me my clothes."

Millie hung back. "I rather enjoy looking at you. You look even better naked than you do with clothes on." She dropped his clothing onto the sand and stood sentinel over them. "Come get them if you want them."

Growling, Luc advanced toward her, making no effort to cover his nakedness. What good would it do? He had only two hands and they could shield only so much.

Luc tried to skirt around Millie, but she thwarted him no matter which way he turned.

"What do you want, Millie?" Luc asked.

"Isn't that obvious, *my lord?*"

"Who told you I was titled?"

"Everyone knows. News travels fast in a small village." Her hungry gaze slid down to his privates. "I've never done it with a nobleman. I'll bet you're good at it."

She sidled up to him, cupping his cock and balls. "I'm good too, my lord."

Luc felt himself harden in her hands. He'd never aspired to sainthood. His response was that of any healthy male. But it wasn't Millie he wanted. He removed her hands from his privates and held her at bay.

"What's wrong? I'm unattached and willing, and you look like a man in need of a woman."

"I've taken a vow of celibacy," Luc stated.

Millie laughed raucously. "You're daft if you expect me to believe that." She rubbed her breasts against his bare chest. "I know how to please a man."

"I'm not going to break my vow for the likes of you, Millie."

"I'll bet you'd break it for Bliss," Millie spat. "Forget her; she's Brady's woman."

Luc set her aside and swept up his clothes.

"Pity," Millie sighed as she stared at his manhood. "Women must be mad for you."

She sighed again. "Men in these parts aren't as generously endowed as you are. Do you intend to remain celibate for life?"

"God forbid," Luc muttered, raising his eyes heavenward.

"I'd like to be the first after you've had your fill of celibacy," Millie murmured, her voice a husky whisper.

Luc knew he had to turn the conversation before he was forced to take another dip in the ocean.

"You never told me what you were doing here. It's not someplace I'd expect to find you."

Millie shrugged. "I was taking a walk and saw you swimming in the cove. I thought you might like some company."

"It's not the best weather for walking. Why aren't you working?"

"The men went fishing, so there'll be little business until this evening."

"So you decided to take a walk," Luc probed. "Do you wander this far from the village often?"

She ignored his question. "Well, since you're not going to take me up on my offer, I'll be on my way."

"Can I give you a ride back to the village?"

"Er . . . no, thank you. I'll just amble off on my own."

Promptly forgetting Millie, Luc mounted Baron and urged him up the steep slope. When he reached the top, he let the horse have his head.

After his ride, Luc decided to call upon Squire Hartley. Though he would learn nothing about the smugglers from the squire, he had taken a liking to the old gentleman. Besides, he wanted to speak to Bliss. Judging from what he'd heard at the tavern, Luc knew the smugglers intended to be on hand for the next delivery of contraband despite the danger. He wished he could have stayed longer to hear the final outcome of the meeting, but he hadn't wanted to be discovered and labeled a spy.

Luc returned Baron to the livery, then continued on to the squire's house. Bliss answered the door.

"Luc — what are you doing here?"

"I've come to visit your father," he replied. "He did invite me to call again. Is he up to receiving visitors today?"

Luc could tell by Bliss's expression that she wanted to say no.

"I don't want you upsetting him," she warned.

"I have no intention of upsetting him. I merely thought he might enjoy some company."

"He's aware of your title, Luc. I already told him. He's pleased that a viscount has chosen to visit St. Ives."

"Bliss, about yesterday," Luc blurted, "we came very close to —"

"I don't want to talk about it. I'm too ashamed. I'm not a wanton, Luc."

"I know that. What happened is entirely my fault. When I set my mind to seduction, few women can resist. I'm considered quite the rake in London."

An understatement, Bliss decided. Still, she was as much to blame for what had happened as Luc. "It's my fault as well. At first I thought I was dreaming, but I didn't try very hard to stop you after I realized you were no dream." She turned away. "Can we forget it?"

"Not damn likely," he muttered. "Are you going to let that stop me from visiting your father?"

"No, he'd probably enjoy a visit from you. Follow me."

Luc followed Bliss to the converted study, admiring the way her skirts swayed around her shapely hips and ogling her delicate ankles and trim calves.

Squire Hartley greeted Luc effusively. Despite his high color, he appeared in good spirits as he invited Luc to sit down. "Will you ask Jenny to send tea, daughter?" the squire asked.

Bliss appeared reluctant to leave, but after slanting a warning look at Luc, she left the bedchamber.

"Bliss tells me you're a viscount," Owen said with a hint of censure. "Why didn't you tell me?"

"I abandoned London's amusements for a period of rest and privacy," Luc replied. "It served no purpose to reveal my title."

"But now that we know, you will be treated with the respect due you. What do you think of our village, my lord?"

"St. Ives is . . . not what I expected," Luc said frankly.

The squire searched Luc's face. "In what way? I know we are far removed from London society, but we differ little from other small villages. Do you know something I don't?"

Luc remained silent, deciding it was best not to air his concerns to an ailing man. But the squire surprised him by voicing his own anxiety.

"I may be confined to my bed, but that doesn't mean I'm unaware of what's going on around me. Even the vicar seems apprehensive on his visits. Something is going on in this village that I'm not supposed to know. Do you have any idea what it is?"

Luc sat on the horns of a dilemma. Should he tell the squire what was taking place under his nose? Would telling him be detrimental to his health? The decision was taken from him when Bliss entered the room.

"What have you two been talking about?" she asked brightly as she placed the tea tray on a bedside table.

"Nothing of consequence," Luc replied. "Your father seems much improved. Perhaps a walk around the village square would cheer him."

The squire brightened perceptibly at the suggestion, but Bliss voiced her opposition. "Absolutely not! Though Papa seems much improved, he is not strong enough to venture outside. Perhaps in a few weeks."

Bliss poured the tea and handed Luc and her father a cup. Then she poured a cup for herself and sat down to join them. Since the conversation the squire had instigated couldn't continue with Bliss in the room, Luc sipped his tea and listened to Bliss chat about the weather and inconsequential things.

Luc set his cup down on the tray and rose. "I really must be going. I don't want to tire you, sir."

"You'll come back, won't you, my lord?" Owen asked. "I'm most anxious to continue our conversation."

"I will indeed," Luc replied.

Bliss followed him out the door. "What did Papa mean? What conversation?"

At the bottom of the stairs, Luc pulled her aside. "Your father is no fool, Bliss. He suspects that something is going on, but doesn't know what. He asked me if I knew."

Bliss blanched. "What did you tell him?"

"There was no time to tell him anything. You made sure of that."

She grasped his lapels. "You must not tell him, Luc. He mustn't know. Promise you'll say nothing to him."

"It's not my place to tell him. He does appear to be on the road to recovery, however, and once he gets out and about, it's only a matter of time before he learns the truth. It's time to stop this nonsense, Bliss. Shadow has placed every man in the village in jeopardy."

"The villagers agree with you," Bliss confided. "They voted to make our next delivery the last until the excise men move on to new territory. We aren't the only smugglers in Cornwall. The entire coast is a haven for smugglers."

"At least someone has sense enough to

know when to stop. Was it Shadow's idea?" Luc ventured.

"Not exactly, but it was a majority vote."

"Was Shadow at your meeting today?"

"You know about the meeting?"

"Not much gets past me. Well, was Shadow there?"

No answer was forthcoming.

Luc searched his brain, trying to recall the men he had seen in the tavern. Nearly every man from the village seemed to have been present. Who among them had the leadership qualities to be Shadow? No one came to mind. Besides, judging from the conversation he'd heard, Shadow hadn't attended the meeting.

"I intend to be present during the next delivery," Luc contended. "Tell me where and when."

"I can't. No one betrays Shadow."

"Damn it, Bliss, stubbornness isn't a virtue. Besides, someone has already betrayed him. Tell me what I want to know."

"Very well. There's another cove north of the village. That's where we're supposed to meet the ship. It's one of our alternate delivery sites. The cove is smaller and harder to navigate, but more secluded. We keep changing delivery sites to throw the excise men off our trail."

"What about the informer? He could betray your operation again."

Bliss worried her bottom lip between small white teeth. "There's always that chance. But I prefer to believe that none of our men would betray our operation."

"Somebody already has."

"The men are more wary now. They've been warned and will be watching one another. I believe Shadow has taken the necessary precautions to protect us."

"Let me take your place on the beach, Bliss. I want you to remain home where you'll be safe."

"Are you mad? No one trusts you. They'll never let you join the operation."

"They allow you there, and you're a woman."

Bliss saw no way to thwart him, so she agreed. "All right, I'll stay home if that's what you want, although I don't know why you care."

Luc grinned. "My protective instincts, remember? I can't bear to see a woman in jeopardy. Leave the dangerous part to the men. We're agreed, then?"

"Yes! You can leave now."

"If that's what you want, love." He headed toward the door but was halted by a booming voice.

"Ask Lord Westmore to stay for dinner, Bliss," the squire said as he emerged from his makeshift bedroom in the study. "I feel invigorated enough to eat in the dining room tonight."

"I accept," Luc said before Bliss could offer a protest.

Bliss groaned. Why had Luc intruded in her life? He acted as if he owned her. Yet once he returned to London, she'd never see him again. She could only imagine the scores of women waiting to welcome him back into their beds. No matter what he said, she seriously doubted he'd spend the entire year of his self-imposed exile in St. Ives. To a man like Luc, sex was as necessary as breathing. He was already strung as taut as a bowstring, and she expected him to pack up and return to the life he'd left in London very soon.

"Are we going to stand here until dinner?" Luc drawled in an amused tone.

Bliss huffed out an invitation to join her in the parlor. Once he was seated, she excused herself to tell Jenny they had a guest for dinner.

"Help yourself to brandy. You'll find it in the cabinet beneath the window."

"French brandy, I presume?"

Bliss sent him a blistering look and

flounced from the room. Luc's chuckle followed her out the door.

"What's wrong, lass?" Jenny asked when Bliss stormed into the kitchen. "Did something get your dander up?"

"That *something* is Viscount Westmore. He's in the parlor. Papa invited him for dinner. Do we have enough?"

"We'll make do," Jenny returned. "Will the squire join us?"

"He said he would. He appears to be growing stronger." She paused, and then added, "And he's becoming curious. Papa was asking Luc questions."

"What kind of questions?"

"I'm not sure, but I don't like it. In the future, we shouldn't leave Papa alone with Luc. I'd best return to the parlor before Luc comes looking for me."

Bliss found Luc thumbing through some old copies of the *London Times*. "Anything interesting happening in London?"

"There's always something interesting going on in London. Whether it's newsworthy or not depends upon the reader. For instance," he pointed out, "did you read the gossip column in last week's paper?"

"I haven't had the time."

"Too bad. You'd find it interesting."

"London gossip doesn't interest me,"

Bliss said, though she was suddenly itching to get her hands on the paper.

Luc folded the paper and set it aside. "Then I won't bore you with the details. Tell me, does your father seem improved, or is it my imagination?"

"He does seem improved," Bliss agreed. "Frankly, I don't know what to make of it. He's been ill a long time. The local doctor hasn't a clue as to the nature of his illness, but little by little he's improving."

"Do you still intend to take him to London?"

"I believe it's a good idea."

"Do you have sufficient funds to cover expenses?"

"After the next delivery, I will."

Luc's mouth thinned. "Bliss, you promised."

Jenny poked her head into the parlor. "Dinner is ready. I've already told the squire. He'll be in soon."

Luc escorted Bliss into the cozy dining room and seated her. Squire Hartley entered, taking his place at the head of the table. Once he was seated, Luc selected a chair beside Bliss.

"I'm pleased you could stay, my lord," the squire said, beaming his approval at Bliss and Luc. "Do you have a fiancée or wife in London, Lord Westmore?"

Bliss nearly choked on a piece of bread. "Papa!"

"It's all right, Bliss," Luc assured her. "No to both, sir. I have neither fiancée nor wife."

"Excellent," Squire Hartley said. "Ah, here's Jenny. I'm sure she's cooked up something special to tempt your palate. It may be simple country fare, but you'll find it plentiful and tasty."

After the first course of fish, Jenny served roasted capon with vegetables. For dessert she'd prepared a strawberry tart with clotted cream. It was a fine meal, and Luc's compliments were genuine.

"I'd invite you into the parlor for brandy and cigars," Hartley said, "but I'm a bit weary. Bliss will entertain you in my stead." He rose unsteadily. "Good night, my lord."

Bliss jumped to her feet. "I'll help you, Papa."

Hartley waved her off. "I'm fine, daughter. See to our guest. I'll look forward to your next visit, my lord."

Bliss had no choice but to invite Luc into the parlor for an after-dinner drink. Luc immediately made himself at home, pouring drinks for both himself and Bliss. Then he leaned against the mantel and watched her through shuttered lids.

"Is something wrong?" Bliss asked.

"You're a beautiful woman, Bliss."

Bliss flushed. "Please, Luc, I don't need compliments."

"Every woman needs compliments."

"Apparently, the women you've known are shallow creatures. I've more important things to think about than how I appear to others."

Luc stalked toward her. He reminded her of a prowling tiger, graceful yet radiating strength and virility. She couldn't take her eyes off him. No man had a right to be as handsome as Lucas Westmore. His sensual nature had never been more apparent than it was at that moment.

Luc seated himself on the sofa beside Bliss, stretching his long legs out in front of himself. "What are you thinking, love?"

Bliss bristled. "Don't call me that. I am most definitely not your love."

"I'm going to bed," Jenny announced from the doorway. "Good night, my lord."

"Good night, Jenny. Thank you again for the wonderful meal," Luc replied.

"Perhaps you should leave," Bliss suggested. "It's getting late, and I want to wish Papa good night before he goes to sleep."

"Are you afraid to be alone with me?" Luc taunted.

"Any woman in her right mind would be afraid to be alone with you," she shot back. "If you recall, I've been a victim of your seduction."

Luc laughed. "I don't know if I'd say you were a victim, Bliss."

Bliss didn't contradict him. The truth was that she'd wanted him as much as he wanted her.

She rose abruptly. "I'll see you to the door, my lord."

"Just plain Luc will do. Forget the title."

"As you wish, Luc," Bliss replied, scooting past him.

Luc followed her to the front door. "I enjoyed the evening."

His arms went around her, bringing her against him. Curling a hand around her nape, he held her captive for his kiss. He kissed her until she went limp in his arms; then he set her away from him, sketched a bow and left her dazed and speechless.

Chapter Eight

It took a long moment for Bliss to regain her equilibrium after Luc left. The man was impossible. He turned her life on end and left her wanting more from him than he could give her.

Turning away from the door, Bliss went directly to the newspaper Luc had been reading. Though she'd claimed no interest in London society, she couldn't wait to see what Luc had found so entertaining.

She picked up the news sheet, turned to the gossip column and quickly scanned the article. About halfway down the page she saw what Luc had found amusing.

When will Lord W return to London? That question is on the lips of every gentleman and lady of the *ton*. With Bathurst and Braxton married and no longer available, London's leading rake is sorely missed. Also noteworthy are the wagers being placed in betting books at various gentlemen's clubs as to when

Lord W's state of self-imposed celibacy will end. Our dearest rogue celibate? Never say it's true! Come back to us soon, Lord W.

So Luc was telling the truth, Bliss mused, tossing aside the newspaper and going up to bed. The more she learned about Luc, the stronger was her belief that he presented no danger to the smuggling operation. If there was indeed an informer in their ranks, it wasn't Luc.

The next day, Luc awoke with a plan. He intended to find the informer who jeopardized the smuggling operation. He had learned a few things from Braxton, who had spied for the government during the war, and he intended to put his knowledge to good use.

After Luc ate the breakfast Widow Pigeon had prepared, he lingered over his tea in order to ask a few pertinent questions.

"Aren't you worried about Billy, Mrs. Pigeon? Getting involved with smugglers isn't the best way to earn a living," Luc said bluntly.

The widow regarded him solemnly. "I know you are aware that nearly every man in the village is involved in smuggling, my lord. We were desperate for a way to bolster our economy, and smuggling was the best we could come up with."

"So Shadow took over as leader and led the villagers into a life of crime," Luc replied.

"Everything has worked just as Shadow said it would," Widow Pigeon said defensively.

"Until now. On two separate occasions, excise men were aware that a delivery was in progress."

The widow shrugged. "A bit of bad luck."

"Not bad luck, Mrs. Pigeon. There's an informer in the organization."

"Shadow is taking precautions."

"So I've been told. That still doesn't make the danger any less. If you tell me Shadow's identity, perhaps I can persuade him to forget about the next delivery. If no one is on the beach when the ship arrives, it will leave and no one will get hurt."

The widow shook her head and backed away. "I'd best get on with my work, my lord. There's lunch and dinner to prepare before I return home."

The widow made a hasty exit, leaving Luc frustrated but not without options. There had to be someone in the village less protective of Shadow's identity than Mrs. Pigeon. Brady came to mind.

Luc strolled through the village, heading to the beach where the fishing fleet was docked. Some of the boats had already left and others were making preparations. As luck would have it, Brady Bristol hadn't left yet.

"Might I have a word with you, Bristol?"

"I haven't time for a chat, Westmore," Brady said with a sneer.

"I want to speak to Shadow. I know how reluctant you are to divulge his identity, but perhaps a guinea will loosen your tongue."

"You're wasting your time, Westmore." His eyes narrowed. "Have you talked to Bliss?"

"Of course. She's as stubborn as you are."

"You may as well give it up. No one in the village would betray Shadow."

"Somebody already has," Luc reminded him.

"I know. It was you, Westmore."

Luc realized this conversation was going nowhere. "You know better than that." He turned to leave. "I'll let you go about your business. I hope you fill your nets."

So saying, he strode off. His next stop was the Gull and Goose. A few men sat around telling fish stories while Al cleaned the bar and Millie served up mugs of ale. Conversation ceased when Luc entered. When he took a seat at an empty table, the talk resumed. Millie sashayed up to him, her ample hips swaying enticingly.

"What will you have, Lord Westmore?"

"Ale," Luc said. "Draw a mug for yourself and join me."

Millie complied with alacrity. "What brings you to the Gull and Goose?" she asked. "Might I hope it's me?"

"You might say that," Luc replied. "I'm willing to part with a gold guinea for information."

Millie immediately grew wary. "What kind of information?"

"I want Shadow's name. I mean him no harm, you understand. I just want to speak with him. He's placing the entire village in jeopardy."

"Did you talk to Bliss?" Millie asked.

"Several times," Luc said dryly. "She's no more forthcoming than you or anyone else I've spoken to."

The men at the next table had stopped talking and were staring at them. Though Luc had spoken in a low voice, he knew they had heard him. Millie cast a wary glance at the men and rose. "I can tell you nothing, my lord."

The buzz of conversation resumed. Before she left, Millie leaned close to Luc and whispered, "Bliss."

"Bliss what?" Luc asked.

It was too late. Millie had tripped back to the bar and disappeared behind a curtain. Luc had no idea what to make of Millie's hint, if that was what it was supposed to be. Did Millie mean he should question Bliss again? Luc knew what that would gain him. Absolutely nothing.

Scraping back his chair, he rose to his impressive height and said to the men at the table, "I'm prepared to pay handsomely for Shadow's name. I mean him no harm. I merely want to speak with him. Pass the word around." So saying, he strode out the door.

Luc had come to a dead end. The tightly knit group of smugglers wasn't about to give him anything of value. He was beginning to believe that Shadow was no one he knew, no one from the village. But for some reason, each and every man, woman and child was willing to protect Shadow's identity. What kind of man was he to earn such undying loyalty?

Luc walked to the livery and led his horse out of his stall. Baron whickered softly as Luc saddled him and mounted. Once he was clear of the village, he gave Baron his head. Luc rode like the wind, until clouds began to gather overhead. It looked as if a storm was brewing, and he didn't relish getting drenched.

Luc returned Baron to the livery and hurried down the lane to his cottage. He was halfway home when the skies opened. He broke into a run but stopped abruptly when he saw Millie racing away from the village. What was Millie doing out in the rain? A vague suspicion formed in his brain, and he locked it away to be taken out and examined at another time. Since their paths did not converge, Millie did not see him.

Rain continued to fall that day and continued relentlessly over the next several days. During those dull days Luc wrote letters to Braxton and Bathurst, read several books, and searched his brain for a way to keep Bliss safe during the next and, he hoped, last delivery. Though Bliss had promised to remain at home, he didn't believe her. She seemed to thrive on the thrill of danger, and she was too stubborn for her own good. Luc knew Bliss would be on the beach as well as he knew himself.

According to Luc's calculations, it was about time for the next delivery. After a dreary week the rain stopped, the weather turned fair and mild, and a half-moon rode the night sky.

Luc had neither seen nor heard from Bliss over the past several days, and he missed her. It was hard to believe that an unrepentant womanizer of his varied appetites could miss a woman he barely knew. There was a mystery about Bliss he would like to solve.

But what he really, truly wanted was Bliss moaning and writhing beneath him. He wanted to take her with the kind of passion and expertise that had made women swoon with ecstasy. How much longer could he hold out against his body's sexual demands?

Luc walked to the village the day after the rains ceased. His keenly honed instincts told him something was about to happen. The atmosphere in the village was heavy with tension. Villagers were gathered in groups, speaking in low tones, and little business was conducted.

Luc knew intuitively that the French ship had been sighted and that this was the night the smugglers would converge on the cove. Would the excise men be waiting for them? If he were an experienced spy like Braxton, he would already know the informer's name.

His face hard with resolve, Luc turned his steps toward Bliss's house and rapped sharply on the door. Bliss opened the door to him.

"Tonight's the night, isn't it?" he asked without preamble.

Bliss's gaze didn't quite meet his. "What makes you say that?"

"I'm no fool, Bliss. The tension in the village is thick enough to slice. I just wanted to remind you of your promise. You do recall your promise, don't you?"

"Of course I do. Why do you think I wouldn't?"

Luc chuckled. "I know you, Bliss. May I come in?"

Silence.

"Bliss?"

"Oh, very well, but you can't stay long. I'm busy."

Luc followed Bliss into the parlor. He waited for her to sit, and when she didn't, he asked, "Will you sit down?"

Bliss perched on the edge of a chair. Luc seated himself across from her. "How is your father?"

"About the same as he was the last time you saw him. Really, Luc, what is this all about?"

"You, Bliss. Your safety is important to me. I intend to be at the cove tonight. I won't reveal myself unless there's trouble. I want you to spread the word. If I see you there, I swear I'll beat you to within an inch of your life. Despite my probing, I'm no closer to finding the informer than I was a week ago."

Bliss glared at him. "I swear that Bliss Hartley will be nowhere near the cove."

"Does Shadow know?"

"Shadow is aware of everything."

"Good, very good." He rose.

Bliss wanted to wipe the smug look off Luc's face but stifled the urge. Losing her temper would only rouse his suspicion.

"It will be a relief knowing you're not placing yourself in danger tonight," Luc said. "That's one less thing I have to worry about. I was going to say I'd let you know tomorrow how the delivery went, but I'm sure you'll know the outcome before I can get back to you."

He walked to the front door, paused, and turned so abruptly that Bliss bumped into him. "I forgot something."

She gazed up at him. Her awareness of him was acute, so much so that she knew what he was thinking when his gaze dropped to her lips. She shuddered. His heavy-lidded gaze made her tingle from head to toe. Deny it though she might, Luc was a man women dreamed about, a man women fought over.

"What did you forget?"

"This," Luc said, dragging her into his arms. Then he kissed her and her world spun out of control. Her hands closed on his sleeves, holding him, fearing she would fall if she let go. Her senses came alive as his mouth moved over hers and her body tingled with awareness. She struggled to absorb the sensations, but the kiss ended quickly, far too quickly for Bliss's liking.

"I'll see you tomorrow," Luc whispered against her lips. Then he was gone, his words reverberating through her head.

Tomorrow . . .

Luc might be seeing me sooner than he expects.

Luc prepared for the night ahead. He dressed in dark clothing topped with a concealing cloak and pulled on sturdy boots. Lastly, he yanked a cap he'd purchased in the village down over his ears.

According to Bliss, the contraband was to be delivered at a secluded cove north of the village, one more difficult for the ship to navigate. Luc searched his memory for a place that fit that description, for he had come across many such coves on his daily rides.

Luc left early to fetch Baron from the livery. Since the stableman was probably on the way to the delivery site with the smugglers, Luc's presence went unnoticed. He rode through the deserted village, continuing along the northern ridge of cliffs. He recognized the cove Bliss had described when he came upon a narrow, rutted track leading down to a tiny strip of beach alive with activity.

Luc secured Baron out of sight in a stand of trees, then crept close to the edge of the cliff to wait and watch. He saw lights bobbing in the distance and realized the ship was waiting offshore for a signal from Shadow. Though the half-moon was partially obscured by a cloud, there was enough light for him to see the beach below, and to note the watchman standing guard a short distance away from where Luc was concealed.

The wagons had already arrived and men were milling about, waiting for the longboats to be launched. One man stood out from the others. He stepped to the edge of the water, swinging a lantern aloft.

Shadow.

With his cloak billowing in the wind, he looked like a huge bird of prey. Luc made no move to interfere as he watched. Then he felt the hair rise on the back of his neck and was suddenly overcome by a sense of foreboding. Immediately wary, he glanced around, but saw nothing that spoke of danger. The first longboat had reached the beach and men were swarming over it, their haste apparent as they carried kegs from the boat to the wagons. When a second boat arrived, Luc began to relax.

But his complacency was short-lived as once more his body thrummed with awareness and a pain in his gut warned him of danger. Rising, he pushed the startled watchman aside and stumbled down the rutted track. His intention of warning the smugglers was thwarted when at least a dozen men exploded onto the beach from the concealment of rocks, firing their guns. The smugglers began fleeing, leaving the wagons behind in their haste to escape.

Luc saw two men from the longboats fall beneath the revenuers' bullets. Frantically he searched the beach for Bliss. Another man fell, and Luc's heart began to race. Then he saw Shadow. The caped figure appeared stunned as his comrades scattered to safety. Luc saw him drop to his knees beside a fallen man and try to pull him to safety, wherever that might be.

As much as Luc hated the disaster

Shadow had wrought, he couldn't withhold his help.

Keeping low to the ground, he made his way to Shadow. "How is he?" Luc asked about the fallen man.

Shadow started violently. "What are you doing here?" His voice sounded husky, forced.

"You were told I'd be here. I'll help you carry your comrade to safety."

Shadow shook his head. "It's too late. He's gone."

Luc grasped Shadow's shoulders. "Where's Bliss?"

Shadow's face was so well protected, Luc couldn't see past his hood as he wagged his head in a negative manner.

"Damn it, man! Where is she? If she's hurt as a result of your stupidity, I'll kill you with my bare hands."

"We have to leave," Shadow growled.

Abruptly Luc became aware of their precarious position. The excise men were spread out along the beach; only moments remained before he and Shadow would be discovered. But how could he leave without knowing if Bliss was safe? Or even alive?

"Bloody hell! I have to find Bliss."

"You can't find her if you're dead."

Shadow's words made sense, but it was

probably too late for both of them. Men swarmed toward them amid an explosion of bullets. Then fate intervened. The half-moon slid behind a cloud, plunging the beach into darkness.

"This way," Shadow urged in a low, tense voice.

When Luc balked, Shadow grasped his sleeve and pulled him toward a spot farther down the beach where the cliffs reached down to the water. There was no beach, only rocks.

"Where are you taking me?" Luc hissed. "There's no escape this way."

"Trust me," Shadow hissed.

Luc was convinced they would end up in the water, or against a solid wall of earth and rock with nowhere to go, until he saw a tiny opening.

"We'll have to crawl through," Shadow said. "You go first. I'll cover our tracks and follow."

"The tide —"

"The cave only partially fills with water. There's a ledge we can rest on until the tide turns again. With luck, the excise men will have moved on by then."

Trusting that Shadow knew what he was talking about, Luc crawled through the mouth of the cave into total blackness.

Inching forward, he tried to find the ledge Shadow spoke of, and wondered if the smuggler had led him here to die in a watery grave. It would serve him right for trusting the bastard.

Luc heard voices outside the cave and then a gunshot, but he couldn't tell how far away they were. When Shadow failed to appear, Luc considered leaving and taking his chances with the revenuers. Then he heard a scraping sound and sensed the presence of another person.

"Westmore, where are you?"

"Here," Luc said. "What took you so long?"

"The revenuers have lanterns. I met with a spot of trouble while trying to cover our tracks. Fortunately, it's nearly high tide and the revenuers will have to leave the beach soon. Did you find the ledge?"

"No. Lead the way, I'll follow."

"Grab my cloak," Shadow whispered. "I'll lead you to the ledge. We'll be safe there."

Reaching out, Luc grasped a handful of coarse woolen material.

"The cave is too low for you to walk upright," Shadow warned. "You'll have to hunch over."

Shadow's words brought a realization home to Luc. Shadow was short for a man.

Luc recalled standing next to him on the beach and registering the fact that Shadow was a small man. He hadn't looked that way from a distance, but Luc was aware of it now.

"The ledge is to your right," Shadow said.

Extending his hand, Luc felt the damp, rocky ledge and scrambled onto it. Shadow followed moments later. The ledge was wide enough for them to sit side by side without touching. When Luc heard water rushing into the cave, he brought his legs up against his chest and wrapped his arms around them.

"How long do you suppose we'll be trapped in here?" Luc asked. While he was afraid of neither closed-in places nor darkness, something about being alone with Shadow disturbed him.

"Are you all right?" Shadow asked in a strangled voice that sounded unnaturally forced.

"I'll survive," Luc drawled. "This will give us a chance to have that chat I've been wanting. Why have you been avoiding me? I'm sure you're aware of how eager I've been to meet you."

"I saw no need."

Aside from Shadow's voice being still husky, Luc thought it had risen a notch and had a definite catch to it. "You saw no need! Bloody hell, man, do you care nothing about your comrades? The first time the excise men arrived at the cove should have warned you off. Why do you persist with this folly?"

"This was to be our last delivery until they turned their attention elsewhere."

"You knew about the informer. Your stubbornness placed the entire village at risk. There's at least one villager and two men from the French ship lying dead on the beach. How many deaths will it take before you come to your senses?"

"Enough!" Shadow growled. "This shouldn't have happened. There weren't supposed to be deaths."

Luc's voice turned hard, almost menacing. "Was Bliss on the beach tonight?"

A long pause. "No, Bliss was not here."

Luc frowned. Shadow's voice was beginning to lose strength. "If you're lying, I'll have your head on a platter."

"What does Bliss mean to you?"

"I care about her. Despite her penchant for trouble, I've grown fond of her. I know she joined your venture because she needed money to take her sick father to London, but I'm curious as to why you allowed it."

Silence.

"I didn't expect an answer," Luc huffed.

"Bliss is a beautiful woman. I suspect she used her natural assets to convince you of her worth as a smuggler. She has more bravado than brains."

Luc's words gained him a grunt.

"Now that we've had our chat, I hope you'll cease operations for good."

Another grunt.

"Grunt all you want," Luc warned, "but I mean business. If I hear of smuggling activities in this area after I return to London, I'll not hesitate to name names. I have friends in high places."

"Go to sleep," Shadow hissed. "We're stuck here until dawn."

"Do I have your promise to suspend smuggling activities?"

"Aye."

Satisfied, Luc leaned his head on his knees and nodded off to sleep. He awoke much later, aware of thin beams of light streaming through the cave's narrow opening. He glanced to his right and then to his left, stunned when Shadow was nowhere to be found. He cursed long and loud as he lowered himself to the cave floor and felt his way to the opening.

Luc poked his head out, saw nothing but a deserted beach, and cautiously eased out of the cave into daylight. After stretching to take the kinks out of his arms and legs, he headed toward the rutted track that would take him to the top of the crag. He was scrambling over rocks when he saw a bundle of black rags lying on the path ahead of him.

The closer Luc got to the object, the more convinced he became that what he saw was a body in a black cloak.

Shadow?

Luc's assumption proved correct. It was indeed a body, and most likely Shadow. His concern escalated when he saw bloodstains dampening Shadow's cloak. Carefully he turned Shadow over. Every nerve ending jangled as Luc lowered Shadow's hood for his first look at the master smuggler's face.

His breath caught in his throat when he saw Bliss's pale face revealed in the weak light of dawn. Thunderstruck with rage and grief, he shouted, "You little fool!"

He should have known. Why hadn't he suspected? So many questions crowded his brain that his head began to ache, but now was not the time to demand answers.

A cursory inspection revealed a bullet wound in the fleshy part of Bliss's upper arm. He found both the entrance and exit wounds. That she had lost blood was apparent from the vivid red stains on the cloak and man's shirt she wore. Fortunately, the wound did not appear fatal. His next concern was getting Bliss home so he could treat her wound.

Luc tore off the tail of her shirt and bound it tightly around her arm. Then he scooped her into his arms and carried her limp form to where his horse was tethered. Baron whickered in welcome.

Slowly Bliss regained consciousness, aware of Luc's strong arms around her and the heat of his body warming hers. She was so cold, so utterly exhausted, she could do little more than whisper his name.

Luc glanced down at her; his anger burned so vividly, she had to look away. "I'm sorry," she whispered.

"What happened?" Luc spat. "Why didn't you tell me you were shot?"

"A bullet caught me while I was covering our tracks. I knew it wasn't serious, so I didn't say anything."

"The pain must have been fierce."

"I managed. But the walk up the track proved too much. I never meant for you to find out."

"Obviously."

The cynical tone of Luc's voice convinced Bliss that nothing would ever be the same between them. But perhaps that was for the best. Nothing could ever come of her relationship with Lord Westmore. They lived in different worlds.

"Lean against my horse," Luc instructed. "I'll mount first, then take you up in front of me. Can you manage that?"

"Of course. Where are you taking me?"

"To my cottage; it's safer. Your wound needs immediate attention."

Bliss gritted her teeth against the sudden jolt of pain as Luc lifted her into the saddle before him. She reeled dizzily as Luc held her firmly against him with one arm and grasped the reins with the other.

"I hope you're able to hold up if we're intercepted by revenuers," Luc muttered. "It could prove disastrous if you fainted under questioning."

"Do you think they're still in the area?"

"Yes. They'll probably take their search to the village. That's another reason why you shouldn't go home right now."

His voice was so taut, so controlled and emotionless that Bliss could feel the rage emanating from him.

"You're angry."

His arm tightened around her. "How in bloody hell do you expect me to feel? You could have been killed. You and your friends ignored my repeated warnings, and look where your stubbornness has led you.

At least one of your friends is dead, and there could be others."

Silent tears streamed down Bliss's cheeks. Luc was right. The miller was dead. She didn't know how to tell his wife. Dear God, what had she done? Success had made her and the others incautious. She choked back a sob. She had to find the informer.

Luc felt Bliss's tears fall on his arm and tried to ignore them. He was still seething, his temper ready to burst at the slightest provocation. He wasn't finished with Bliss, not by a long shot.

It was full daylight when they reached the cottage. Fortunately, they had seen no sign of the excise men. Luc dismounted and lifted Bliss from the saddle. Holding her against him, he carried her inside. Widow Pigeon had just arrived and was in the kitchen. Billy was with her. Both rushed into the parlor when they heard Luc slam the front door behind him.

"Oh, no, not Bliss!" the widow cried. "Is she . . . is she . . ."

"She caught a bullet, but it doesn't appear to be life-threatening," Luc said, striding into the bedroom. He placed Bliss in the center of the bed and stepped back so the widow could examine her.

"What happened?" Billy asked. "We were

worried when Shadow failed to return to the village."

"We hid in a cave until the tide turned this morning," Bliss said weakly. "How many men have we lost?"

"Just the miller. We took up a collection for his widow and children."

Luc spat out a curse. The miller shouldn't have died. It could have been avoided if Bliss had listened to reason. "Where are the excise men?"

"Still poking around in the village. I came to warn Mam," Billy said.

"They'll come here eventually," Luc said. "Take my horse to the village and see to his care," he ordered crisply.

"I'm going to take Mam home with me," Billy said.

"Fine," Luc replied.

"What about Bliss?" Mrs. Pigeon asked. "Her wound needs stitching."

"Can you do it before you leave?"

"Yes, but —"

"I suggest you be quick about it," Luc said brusquely.

"Perhaps we should take Bliss with us," Billy suggested after his mother left the room.

"No, she stays with me. Since no one else seems able to handle her, I'll take care of her myself. Tell Jenny Bliss is safe with me, and that I'll bring her home when the time is right."

Mrs. Pigeon reappeared with a basin of hot water, soap, several clean cloths and a needle and thread. Luc and Billy left the room while the widow tended Bliss. Luc couldn't bear to watch the needle stab into Bliss's soft flesh. He'd rather he had taken the bullet instead of her. Nothing, however, could mitigate the rage he felt at being duped by a female with more courage than sense.

Luc stared out the front window. The lane was still empty; how long would it be before the excise men came knocking? His thoughts ran in all directions, but his main concern was keeping Bliss safe.

A few minutes later, Mrs. Pigeon came out of the bedroom, carrying the basin and bloody rags.

"How is she?" Luc asked anxiously.

"She'll be right as rain in a day or two."

"Get rid of that," Luc ordered, pointing to the basin. "Then you and Billy leave."

Ten minutes later, Billy and his mother left, taking Baron with them. His face molded into hard lines, Luc stalked toward the bedroom door, his anger escalating with each step he took.

Chapter Nine

Luc stormed into the bedroom, pinning Bliss with a furious glare. She glared back. She sensed the power of his anger and shrank from it. Elemental, potent, passionate. It swirled around her, then slammed into her like a physical blow. To Luc's credit, he kept it tightly reined, but Bliss felt seared by the heat of his rage.

She waited for him to speak.

"You realize what you've done, don't you?" His words blasted her with the force of a gale.

"I never intended for anyone to be hurt."

"Yet one man is dead and you were wounded. You barely escaped with your life."

She dashed away the tears welling in her golden eyes. "I know, I know! I was wrong. We were all wrong." She choked back a sob. "Why didn't you let me leave with Billy and his mother?"

"I'm the only one who can protect you. You're safer here than anywhere else. No one knows how long or how far the excise men will carry their investigation. How likely are they to find the smuggled brandy in the cellar of the Gull and Goose?"

"The last shipment was distributed long ago. They'll find nothing to link us to smuggling."

"I hope to hell you're right."

"How long are you going to keep me here?"

"As long as I deem necessary." He sat on the edge of the bed. His voice softened. "How do you feel?"

"Fine!" She'd not give him the satisfaction of admitting otherwise.

"Go to sleep," Luc growled.

"I can't."

"Are you hungry? I know my way around a kitchen well enough to fix tea and toasted bread."

Bliss started to refuse just as her growling stomach protested. "Tea and toasted bread sounds wonderful. Thank you."

Bliss watched Luc walk out the door. She had never seen him so angry. His body was tense, his steps stiff and measured. She truly believed that if she were not injured he'd give her a good thrashing.

God, how had things gone so wrong? Why hadn't she listened to Luc? Who was the informer? Apparently, the revenuers had lain in wait for the first longboat to arrive before launching their attack. That most of the men had escaped capture or death had been a miracle. Mr. Holly's death would be mourned for a long time, but it had taught them a lesson. Taught *her* a lesson, anyway.

Never again would she take anything for granted. She and her fellow smugglers had grown complacent after their successes. Now the entire village had come under scrutiny. Shadow was no more, and the prosperity of the village would decline with Shadow's demise.

Luc arrived with a tea tray. "Can you sit up?"

Using her uninjured right arm, Bliss scooted up, resting her back against the headboard. Luc placed the tray on the nightstand, poured tea into two cups and handed her one. Bliss grasped it firmly in her right hand and took a sip.

"It's good. Just what I needed."

He handed her a slice of toast smeared with butter and Widow Pigeon's famous elderberry jelly. She took a bite and licked her lips. "I was hungrier than I thought."

Luc picked up one of the four slices he had prepared and devoured it in three giant bites. "We'll have something more substantial later. Mrs. Pigeon picked up a nice piece of beef from the butcher this morning. I believe beef broth is good for restoring blood."

Bliss wanted to laugh at Luc's culinary skills, but his eyes suddenly fell to her breasts and her mouth went dry.

"Is that my shirt you're wearing?"

"I hope you don't mind. Mrs. Pigeon found it in your bureau drawer."

Luc's anger seemed to dissipate, replaced by a sexually charged gleam in his eyes. "I don't mind at all. It looks far better on you than it did on me. Are you finished eating?"

Bliss swallowed the last of her toast and nodded.

Luc removed the tray and perched on the edge of the bed. "Good. We need to talk."

Bliss grew immediately wary. "What is there to talk about? You already know everything."

"I still don't know why."

She met his gaze without flinching. "Yes, you do. The village has no industry, no way to earn money. My father was ill, and I needed funds to take him to London for treatment."

"You're a woman, Bliss. How did you get the men to follow you?"

"It wasn't difficult. It was my idea, after all. Brady was the only one who felt slighted. He thought he should be Shadow."

"Why wasn't he?"

"He's not smart enough," Bliss said without hesitation.

"I get cold chills when I think of the danger you faced every time you appeared as Shadow. You will never, ever do anything like that again."

Bliss bristled. "You can't tell me what to do, my lord. One day you'll return to London and forget all about me."

Luc seriously doubted he'd ever forget Bliss. She was unique in every way. But it wasn't just her physical attributes that made Bliss special. Her appeal defied explanation. No, he most definitely would never forget her. But more importantly, what in hell was he going to do with her?

A chuckle sounded deep in his throat. He knew what he'd like to do *to* her.

"Do I amuse you?"

"No, I'm laughing at myself. I have you exactly where I want you and yet I still can't do what I want."

"What do you want to do?"

"Kiss you, for starters."

Bliss lifted her face, her invitation blatant. "Why?" he asked softly.

"You saved my life."

"And you want to reward me with a kiss."

"Something like that."

Luc knew where one kiss could lead. To another and another . . . and then . . . Even knowing all that, however, he took Bliss's face in his hands and covered her lips with his. She kissed him back. Thrilled by her enthusiastic response and eager to enjoy the bounty of Bliss's mouth, Luc deepened the kiss, feeding his need, nourishing the lust within him.

He felt desire rise, felt his demons demanding more.

Felt the strength of his hunger as he devoured her mouth. Sheer arrogant masculinity demanded that he bring his body over hers, albeit carefully so as not to hurt her, pressing her down against the mattress, letting her feel the strength of his need. He was hard as a rock; he couldn't recall aching for a woman the way he did for Bliss. Spending so much time with her was fraying his resolve as well as his nerves.

She pushed against his chest. "You must stop. Your vow . . ."

Luc gazed into her eyes; the scent of her sank into his marrow as he shifted against her to ease the uncomfortable bulge stretching his tight riding breeches.

"What vow?"

His hands fell to the buttons marching down the front of her shirt . . . his shirt, and it had never looked more fetching. He worked one button free, then another and another.

"What are you doing?" Bliss asked on a gasp.

"Trying to get this bloody shirt off you. Hold still, I don't want to hurt you. That's it," he encouraged when Bliss stopped resisting.

He finally succeeded in getting the shirt off. Rising up, he let his gaze travel the length of her body and back. "You're beautiful." He studied the bandage covering her upper arm. "Does it hurt?"

She shrugged. "A little."

"Will it leave a scar?"

"It may, but it doesn't matter. I can't foresee any situation in which my arms would be bare."

Luc could. Indeed, he could picture her in a ballgown, the low bodice showing off the perfection of her breasts, shoulders and arms. Doubtless she'd set London on its ear should she appear as he imagined her.

Luc's hand shifted, tracing his finger over her lips, down the classic curve of her cheek and lower, to the pulse beating furiously in the hollow of her neck. Then he replaced his finger with his mouth, tracing warm patterns with his tongue. He heard her catch her breath. Emboldened by the sound, his mouth drifted lower. To the sweet curve of her breast. He touched her nipple with his tongue, swirled around it, bit down gently. She arched upward.

"Luc, your vow . . ."

"I know. I just want to kiss you and touch you. Don't deny me that small pleasure."

The words had barely left his mouth when he sealed any reply she might have given with a kiss. His mouth devoured hers with scalding enthusiasm. There was no evading him, no stopping him.

He released her lips; she waited breathlessly for his next move, for she knew there was more to come. How far could he take their lovemaking without breaking his vow?

Luc rose abruptly, removed his coat and boots and then returned to her, sprawling half atop her and taking her mouth again. His hands roamed over her body, his fingers playing upon her sensitive skin as his lips moved over hers. Her senses reeled as he traced her breasts, teased her nipples, then slid away to her ribs, her waist. Her breath caught as his hand glided to her belly, pausing just above that throbbing place that ached for his touch.

Dimly she wondered how it would feel to have him inside her. Not just his fingers but the aroused part of him that rose high and hard beneath his breeches.

His fingers drifted down her thigh, then up and down along the inside surface. Her hips tilted. His fingers drifted, settled, cupped, opened, pressed inward. She stirred restlessly, moving her thighs apart to give him better access. Another finger dove in beside the first. She tensed, waited, her body taut with anticipation.

Suddenly she felt something hot, hard and smooth prodding her stomach. The breath caught in her throat. He had opened his breeches! Surely he wasn't going to . . . Did he intend to break his vow? Then she felt his fingers withdraw, and something harder, hotter, more determined probed between her thighs. Too late she realized what was about to happen. Luc was seconds away from taking her virginity.

Then his mouth claimed hers and all thought fled. His mouth was warm, coaxing, utterly beguiling. He stripped away every last vestige of resistance as he kissed her deeply, commandingly.

After long pleasurable minutes, he slid down her body, spread her thighs with his shoulders and let his fingers glide over her wet, swollen flesh. Then he lowered his head and took her with his mouth.

Luc felt her buck beneath him. She was drenched with desire as he paid homage to her femininity with his mouth, his lips and his tongue. Clamping his hands around her hips to hold her in place, he feasted until he was but moments away from finding his release. He left her briefly to remove his clothing, heard her murmur of protest, and smiled. She was as eager as he was for consummation.

He quickly shed his shirt and trousers, then returned to her, covering her body with his. They were flesh to flesh, with nothing between them but his bloody vow.

"Open for me, love," he whispered. "I can wait no longer."

Her thighs fell open. He pressed; she shivered. He pushed harder; she stiffened. She was small, too damn small. Startled, he realized he was the first and felt something shift and crumble inside him. Then he cursed beneath his breath. Damn, she was a virgin!

"Relax, love. It will hurt less if you don't resist."

He slid out, then in again, going deeper each time. But he still hadn't reached the membrane protecting her virginity. He took her lips, trying to soothe her with kisses as he flexed his hips, thrust hard and broke through, sheathing his arousal to the hilt.

"Luc, stop! It hurts."

"Shhh. Kiss me. I won't move until you want me to. I'll just rest inside you until the pain eases." *Even if it kills me.*

It was nearly too much for Luc to bear. He'd been deprived so long, his usual control had been shattered. He feared he would expire if he had to wait another minute, and then Bliss made a tentative movement with her hips.

"Thank God," he groaned as he matched her movement with one of his own. "Are you all right?"

She clutched his shoulders, digging her fingers into his tense muscles. "Show me what to do."

"Move your hips with mine," Luc managed to gasp before his senses whirled out of control.

He thrust and withdrew several times, showing her the way. Bliss proved a quick learner as she met his strokes, tilting her hips and arching her back, taking him deep inside her. Her sheath clenched around him. Luc thrust faster, deeper, harder. He heard her cry out, felt her body tense; then she convulsed, and he groaned aloud, for he couldn't have waited another moment.

Grasping her hips, he thrust, held, then thrust again, and yet again. His climax began deep inside him. He felt it clear down to his toes as wave after wave of blistering heat seared him and incredible, earth-shattering pleasure speared through him. Convulsions racked his body, his eyes closed and he howled.

When he regained his senses, he became aware that Bliss was staring up at him with a bemused look on her face.

He rolled to his back, bringing her into his arms. "Did I frighten you?"

"Do all men go a little mad during sex?"

"They might, if they've been deprived of sex as long as I have. I'm sorry. Did I hurt you?"

"Only at first." Her face turned red. "Can we do it again?"

Luc laughed. "I've created a monster. Give me ten minutes to recover, love. Then I'll be happy to oblige. Very, very happy," he added.

True to his word, Luc loved her again, taking time to fully savor every nuance of her responsive body. He was an experienced lover, and knew precisely where and how to touch her to give her the most pleasure. No part of her remained unexplored by his mouth, lips and tongue as he kissed, touched, caressed and probed.

He brought her to climax once with his mouth and tongue, then again with him inside her. When it ended, neither Bliss nor Luc had the energy to move. They lay in blissful exhaustion, wet with perspiration, the scent of sex thick about them.

Luc didn't regret one moment of making love to Bliss, but he was swamped with guilt. Not only had he broken his vow, but he had taken a virgin, something he and his fellow rogues had always avoided. Yet he had never felt more invigorated or imbued with energy. He vaguely recalled why he had taken a vow of celibacy, but his passion for Bliss had clouded that memory.

"I should go home," she murmured.

"Your wound . . ."

"I hardly feel it."

"But —"

Luc was frozen in place when the door burst open and Captain Skillington barged into the bedroom. A knowing smile stretched his lips as his gaze flitted between Luc and Bliss.

"What the hell is the meaning of this?" Luc roared, throwing the sheet over Bliss to shield her from Skillington's prying eyes.

"I've come for Shadow," Skillington said.

"You've come to the wrong place," Luc

replied. "As you can see, there's no one here but . . . my fiancée." Disregarding Bliss's gasp, he continued. "We are celebrating our engagement. Now, if you gentlemen don't mind, my fiancée and I would like you to leave."

Skillington's gaze flicked over Bliss's sheet-covered form. "We have it on good authority that Mistress Hartley is the outlaw known as Shadow. I assume she's the woman beneath the sheet."

"Ridiculous!" Luc snapped. "Mistress Hartley has been with me the entire night, she couldn't be Shadow."

"The entire night and you're still in bed?" Skillington said. "It's mid-afternoon. You're a lucky man, my lord."

Ignoring his nudity, Luc surged from bed and pulled a blanket around his middle. "I'll show you to the door."

"I'm not leaving without Mistress Hartley. Our informer insists that she organized the smugglers and posed as Shadow. There's no escape. My men are waiting in the hallway should I need help."

"Name the informer," Luc demanded.

"That information isn't available to you."

"What evidence do you have against Mistress Hartley? I am not ignorant of the law. Do you have a witness? Word alone isn't enough to condemn an innocent woman."

"Nevertheless, my lord, I have the authority to arrest suspects and hold them until they are proven innocent." He proceeded further into the bedroom. "Move aside, my lord. Mistress Hartley is coming with us."

"I think not," Luc said in a tone that brought Skillington to a halt. "There's a law against breaking into a nobleman's home for no reason. As I told you before, I have friends in high places."

"I have sufficient reason," Skillington growled. "As for your friends, they are a long way off in London. I represent the law here."

"Very well, produce Mistress Hartley's accuser. Only then will I allow you to take my fiancée from my home."

Skillington appeared to consider Luc's request. Then he nodded, stepped to the partially opened door and spoke earnestly to one of his subordinates.

"I've instructed Private Billings to fetch the informant."

Luc refused to respond. He glanced down at Bliss. She poked her head out from the sheet. Her eyes were wide with fear, her face pale as death. He tried to reassure her with a look, but she was too distraught to interpret his silent message.

Luc sat beside her to wait, his hand curled around hers, offering what little comfort he could. After what seemed like hours but was in fact a quarter of one, Luc heard a commotion at the front entrance. Moments later, Private Billings appeared in the doorway and whispered something in Skillington's ear.

"What? Are you certain?"

Billings nodded. Skillington turned to Luc, his eyes blazing with fury. "It seems our informant left town suddenly."

Luc shrugged, striving to conceal his exultation. "Well, then, that's it." He swept his arm toward the door. "Good day, sir. My fiancée and I wish to be alone."

"I'll leave . . . for now," Skillington said, "but I'm not through here. The informer can't have gotten far. I intend to billet my men in the village until we find the proof we need. The Crown extends scant mercy to smugglers."

He strode from the room. Luc followed him to the door and slammed it behind them. Scarcely had the door closed than Brady Bristol pushed it open and charged inside.

"What happened?" Brady demanded. "We heard the revenuers had come for

Bliss. I saw them leaving just as I arrived. Where is Bliss? Billy Pigeon said she'd been wounded. Did they take her?"

"She's here."

"Where?" He pushed past Luc and charged into the bedroom.

Brady's eyes narrowed, as if he'd become aware of several things at once. Luc was nude but for a blanket wrapped around his lower body, Bliss was in bed, apparently naked beneath the sheet, and the scent of sex was overwhelming.

"Damn you!" Brady shouted. "How many women have you lured into your bed with your lies? Celibate, my arse!"

"Wait in the parlor while I dress," Luc ordered. "I'll explain everything after I'm decent."

He shoved Brady through the door and slammed it, bemoaning the fact that the door had no bolt. Had the door been bolted earlier, the excise men wouldn't have been able to barge in. But wasting time thinking about past mistakes was useless. An angry Brady Bristol was waiting for explanations, and a company of revenuers was clamoring for Bliss's arrest.

Bliss rose and picked up her clothing from the floor. The movement caught Luc's attention. "Where are you going?" he demanded.

"To calm down Brady."

"That's my job. Rest; you've been through a lot."

She ignored him. "You shouldn't have told the captain we're engaged. Whatever possessed you to lie?"

"It was the only thing I could think of in the circumstances. It probably bought us some time. Skillington isn't anxious to arrest the fiancée of a nobleman without sufficient proof."

"As it turned out, your noble gesture wasn't necessary since the informer has fled. Skillington has no case against me, no proof. But how am I going to explain this" — she gestured to the rumpled bed — "to Brady?"

"Stay here; I'll do the explaining." Bliss started to protest, but he cut her off. "I mean it, Bliss. You've had your way too long. It's time someone put a stop to your nonsense."

Bliss bristled. "Nonsense!"

Luc reined in his anger. "Do as I say, Bliss, I mean it. I'll return after I've sent Bristol on his way."

Luc opened the door and stepped through, closing it softly behind him. Brady confronted him the moment he entered the parlor.

"Bastard! Did it amuse you to seduce Bliss?"

"You're jumping to conclusions."

Brady laughed harshly. "I may be a lowly fisherman but I'm not stupid. The room reeked of sex." He paced away, then whirled back. "It doesn't matter. I'm going to marry Bliss tomorrow. You're not to see or speak to her after today. In fact, I suggest you return to London immediately. We don't want your kind here. Things didn't start going wrong until you arrived."

His fists clenched, Luc struggled to contain his anger. "Are you through, Bristol?"

"I've said all I needed to say."

"Very well, now be so kind as to leave."

"I'm not leaving without Bliss."

The reins of Luc's temper snapped. "You don't care about Bliss. If you did, you would have been more careful of her. She could have been killed or worse during your smuggling. All you and your friends cared about was filling your pockets."

"Bliss set up the operation. She's the one who dealt with the Frenchmen. She invented Shadow to protect herself. I couldn't have stopped her if I'd wanted to."

"Perhaps," Luc grudgingly replied, "but you could have done more to protect her."

Brady refused to meet Luc's furious gaze.

"You can show yourself to the door," Luc said. "If I were you, I'd be looking for the informer."

Brady hesitated, his expression stiff with resentment. "I'm not going anywhere without Bliss."

"I'm taking Bliss to London," Luc said, surprising himself with his spur-of-the-moment decision. "She's not safe here. The excise men will probably billet in the village and continue their investigation until they find enough evidence to hang you and your fellow smugglers."

"They won't find anything."

"Don't count on it."

Brady made an impatient gesture with his hand. "None of that matters. Bliss is my woman. I can protect her."

"You've failed thus far. The revenuers already suspect her. She's been fingered by the informant. They'll scrutinize her every movement. Is that what you want?"

"It's better than becoming the mistress of a dissolute rogue," Brady spat. "What will become of Bliss when you tire of her?"

"In case you haven't heard, Bliss has consented to marry me."

"I have not!" Bliss exclaimed. Both men turned toward her as she marched from the bedroom, fully dressed now in Luc's shirt and her own breeches and boots.

Luc sent her a fulminating look. "I thought I told you to rest."

"I had to know what was going on out here."

"You're coming home with me," Brady said.

"My *fiancée* is remaining with me," Luc returned hotly.

"Am I not allowed to speak for myself?" Bliss huffed.

"Not anymore," Luc replied. "You lost that right when you embarked upon a life of crime. You're coming to London with me. You need to get out from under the revenuers' scrutiny. What if the informant suddenly reappears? Think of your father. How will the knowledge of your illegal activities affect his health?"

Bliss considered Luc's words. She had been meaning to take her father to London anyway, so perhaps this was the time to do so. If they lived frugally, the money she'd saved, supplemented by Papa's income, would be enough to support them for several months, with enough left over to pay for a specialist. By the time they returned home, the revenuers would have moved on.

"Very well, I'll go to London, but not as your fiancée or your mistress. Papa and I will rent a small house in a decent neighborhood and remain in London long enough for Papa's illness to be evaluated and treated."

"You'll stay with me," Luc insisted. "There's enough room in my townhouse for several families."

Though Bliss didn't contradict him, she had no intention of marching to his orders.

"Don't let the rogue gull you, Bliss," Brady warned. "He'll toss you out when he tires of you."

Bliss rounded on Brady. "I'm not stupid, Brady. I told you before that I have no intention of becoming Luc's mistress. I'm going to London because I want to, because it's best for me and Papa. But even if I weren't leaving, I wouldn't marry you. You're a good friend, Brady, and I prefer to leave it that way."

Brady opened his mouth to blast out a reply but was interrupted by a loud pounding on the door. Bliss saw Luc tense and exchanged a glance with him. *What now?*

"Open the door in the king's name!"

Luc spied his cloak on a chair and tossed it around Bliss's shoulders, completely enveloping her in its dark folds. "I have no idea what Skillington wants now but it can't be good. Keep my cloak around you."

Luc flung open the door and stepped aside as Skillington strutted through. "I don't recall inviting you to return."

"I have the proof you demanded. I've returned to arrest Mistress Hartley."

Luc sighed. "I thought we settled that issue. Your informant has disappeared, so you have no case against my fiancée."

"We found the informer," Skillington said importantly. His lip curled as his gaze settled on Bliss. "Come along, Mistress Hartley. I'm taking you into custody." As if on cue, several men surged through the door and surrounded Bliss. One man curled his hand around Bliss's injured upper arm, wringing a cry from her.

Luc flung the man's hand away. "Don't touch her!"

"She's my prisoner," Skillington sneered. "Keep out of this, my lord. This is a matter for the courts."

Bliss glanced at Luc. His stricken expression spoke volumes. He was powerless to help her. Never had she felt such fear. When the soldiers escorted her out the door, she began to struggle. "Where are you taking me?"

"To Plymouth, and then to London, where you'll be tried before a high court of justice," Skillington replied. "Smuggling is a serious offense; I doubt the courts will be lenient."

"Luc . . ."

But Luc was as helpless as she to prevent her arrest. Why oh why hadn't she listened to his warning? What was to become of her?

Luc attempted to intervene. "I know the law, Captain. You're not taking Bliss until you produce the informant. He could have lied for the reward. I wish to question him myself."

Skillington spoke in hushed tones to one of his men. The man made a hasty exit, reappearing a few moments later dragging in the violently resisting informer.

"Tell Lord Westmore what you told me," Skillington prodded.

"Yes, Millie," Luc drawled in a voice taut with menace. "Exactly what did you tell the good captain?"

Chapter Ten

Millie cringed before Luc. "You don't understand, my lord. I've spent my entire life in St. Ives. I'd do anything to get away from here."

Luc pinned her with his hard gaze. "Even lie about a woman you've known all your life?"

Millie stiffened. "Who said I lied? Captain Skillington offered me money to finger Shadow, and I did. I always wanted to go to London, and now I have the means. I wanted to see more of the world than St. Ives."

"How could you do it, Millie?" Brady demanded. "You're one of us. When did you make Bliss your enemy?"

"Enough!" Skillington hissed. "Millie Partin is a credible witness, and I won't have her badgered. She'll come with us to Plymouth and then on to London, where she will tell her story before a high court of law."

Luc's eyes narrowed. "Without Millie you have no case."

"True, but we have Mistress Partin and intend to keep her."

"Will you start out immediately for Plymouth?" Luc asked.

Skillington glanced out the window. "No. It will be dark soon. Both women will be held under guard at the inn until daybreak."

"I'd like a private word with my fiancée before you take her away."

"From what I've observed, you've had sufficient private time together. Take her away, Sergeant."

The sergeant hustled Bliss from the house so quickly Luc could do little more than offer a brief word of comfort.

"Don't worry, love, I'll find a way to get you out of this." Then she was gone, and Millie with her.

Luc stood on the front steps, feeling bereft and helpless. It was the same empty feeling he'd had when Lady Sybil was found floating in the river. Only this time the victim was Bliss, a woman he truly cared about. He couldn't let her go to prison. He knew that smugglers were hanged. No judge would be lenient simply because Bliss was a woman.

Was he to blame for Bliss's desperate straits? Luc wondered. Was losing Bliss his punishment for breaking his vow of celibacy? His fists clenched at his sides. No! He wouldn't let anything happen to Bliss. He *would* find a way to help her. He had to think. But how could he concentrate when his brain was frozen?

Luc began to pace, formulating then discarding idea after idea. One thing he couldn't put off was speaking with Squire Hartley. He must be worried sick about his daughter.

"Lord Westmore."

Luc whirled, surprised to see that Brady hadn't left with the others. "I thought you'd left."

"No. Whatever you're planning, I want to help. I realize now that I don't have a chance with Bliss, but we've been friends since childhood and I don't want anything bad to happen to her."

"A fine time for those sentiments," Luc growled. "You and your fellow smugglers should have forbidden her access to the beach during deliveries."

"I know that, but Bliss is a stubborn woman."

"How well I know," Luc muttered.

"What are you going to do, and how can I help you? There isn't a man, woman or child in the village who wouldn't help if given the chance. Just tell me what to do."

"I don't know yet, Bristol. I'll contact you when I have a plan. Where can I find you?"

"Most likely at my cottage. I live three houses down from the vicarage."

Luc nodded curtly. "Very well, expect to hear from me soon. Meanwhile, I'm going to call on Squire Hartley."

They left together and parted ways at the squire's house. Luc strode up the steps and rapped on the door. It was opened immediately by the squire himself. He grasped Luc's arm and pulled him inside with surprising strength for a man who was ill.

"What has happened to my daughter?"

The squire's face had turned a mottled red. Luc feared he might suffer a seizure and attempted to calm him. "Let's go into the parlor where we can talk." He spied Jenny hovering nearby. "Jenny, please get the squire something to soothe him. Tea or whatever has a calming effect upon him."

"Don't try to cozen me, Westmore. I want to know about Bliss and I want to know now."

Luc steered Owen into the parlor and toward a chair. "Please sit down. Bliss is fine, for the moment. Captain Skillington has taken her to the inn for the night."

"What's this nonsense about smuggling? They're saying Bliss is Shadow, the brains behind the organization. How could that be?"

Luc sighed. Concealing the truth from the squire was no longer possible. The man was entitled to know everything that had gone on while he'd been ill.

"It's true, sir. Bliss organized the villagers and called herself Shadow to disguise her identity."

Owen shook his head. "How could this happen under my very nose?"

"You were ill, sir. The villagers wanted to improve their lives and fell in with Bliss's plan, and Bliss saw it as an opportunity to earn money to take you to a specialist in London."

"Humph! I told Bliss I would recover on my own, and so I have. Not entirely, grant you, but I'm well on my way to full vigor. I improve daily."

Jenny returned with a tea tray. She poured tea into two cups, sprinkled a powder into one and handed it to Owen. "It's nothing but valerian," she told Luc. "It soothes the squire's nerves."

Owen deliberately set the cup down. "My nerves don't need soothing, Jenny. What I need is assurance that my daughter will not be harmed." His unwavering gaze regarded Luc. "Tell me, my lord, what exactly happened between you and Bliss at your cottage. I've heard . . . unsettling things. Are they true?"

Luc had known the question was bound to come up, but he still wasn't prepared for it. What could he say to the father of the woman whose innocence he had stolen? That he'd merely been amusing himself with Bliss? Not true. That he was simply living up to his reputation? Perhaps. Luc was aware of his tendency to take what he wanted. He also knew that his friends and enemies alike regarded him as a womanizer and dissolute rake, and they were right.

To Luc, marriage was something other men did, not something he aspired to. He enjoyed his single state immensely, wasn't concerned about an heir and had managed thus far to escape the parson's trap.

"Westmore," Owen said, interrupting Luc's reverie. "Have you nothing to say for yourself? I know you and Bliss were found in a . . . compromising position. The vicar broke the news to me. He thought it would be better coming from him than from others."

Luc sighed. This was more difficult than he'd imagined. How in hell had the news of his indiscretion gotten around so quickly? "I accept full responsibility for my actions.

Bliss is not to blame in any way. I have considerably more experience than she does."

"What are you going to do about it?"

"Were you not told that I publicly announced my engagement to Bliss?"

"How will that help if she's tried and convicted of smuggling?"

"I intend to make sure that doesn't happen."

The squire's disbelief was palpable. "Just how do you propose to do that?"

Luc said words he'd never uttered in his life. "Do I have your permission to marry Bliss?"

"I see no other course open to you, or her, given the circumstances," Owen huffed. "However, that's easier said than done. My daughter is in custody, or have you forgotten?"

"I've forgotten nothing, but I promise that your daughter won't be put on trial." He turned to address Jenny. "Jenny, please pack a bag for Bliss. Just the essentials, a change of clothing or two, and whatever personal items you deem necessary. I'll take it with me." He paused. "There's something else you can do to help Bliss. It will require the aid of the innkeeper and his wife."

"Just name it," Jenny said. "I'd do anything to help Bliss, and so would every man, woman and child of her acquaintance."

Luc leaned close and explained the details of the plan he had contrived and Jenny's part in it.

"You can depend on me," Jenny said, grinning. She turned to leave.

"Pack a bag for yourself and the squire while you're at it," Luc called after her. "I'm taking you all to London. It's what Bliss wants."

"Absolutely not!" the squire protested. "Look what happened while I was ill. I'll not leave my people to their own devices again. I shall remain in St. Ives to provide leadership." He shook his head. "Smuggling. Who would have thought it? Had I been aware of what was going on around me, this would have never happened. In my own household, no less."

"Are you sure you're up to the task?" Luc asked. "Bliss always intended for you to go to London to consult with a specialist."

"It would have been a waste of money," Owen replied. "Bliss worries unnecessarily. I'll admit I was quite ill for a while, but I am well enough now to take charge. Had she trusted in my normally robust constitution, none of this would have happened. Though we aren't rich, we're not destitute and never will be. We live quite comfortably and have everything we need.

"I do wish, however, that the citizens of St. Ives had more gainful employment. But we will survive. Therefore, I entrust my daughter to you. Save her from harm and wed her promptly. I know you are above her in consequence, but she will make you an exceptional viscountess."

"Indeed," Luc said, already feeling the pressure of being leg-shackled, something he'd sworn to avoid. But the thought of Bliss crushed beneath the heavy hand of English justice was even more repugnant. It was too late to save Lady Sybil, and he still suffered guilt over her death; he wasn't about to stand idly by while another woman's life was destroyed.

"I'll go pack Bliss's bag," Jenny said, hurrying off.

"You'll hear from me soon," Luc said. "Not directly, but by messenger. I know you'll want to hear that Bliss is safe. I'll not fail Bliss, sir. I care about her."

"I should hope so," Owen muttered. "Bliss was an innocent until she met you. I expect you to do right by her. Wed her as quickly as possible, for there may be consequences from your lack of discretion."

An idea began to form in Luc's mind. Whether it worked or not depended upon the vicar, Brady Bristol and luck. When Jenny returned with Bliss's bag, Luc took his leave, strode briskly to the livery and ordered two horses, his and another, to be saddled and ready when he returned.

Then he called on the vicar. After a rather difficult conversation, the vicar agreed to Luc's request, albeit with some misgivings. Luc left immediately, found Brady Bristol's house with little trouble and knocked on the door.

"Westmore!" Brady cried. "Do you have a plan? Come inside and tell me."

Luc stepped through the door. "Yes. I'm going home first to pack a bag. Meet me outside the inn as soon as it's dark and I'll explain further."

"I'll be there. I can enlist others — the entire village, if you wish."

Luc grinned. "A half dozen should suffice."

Luc hurried home and packed a bag with a change of clothing and his personal items. The rest he could send for; he hadn't brought all that much anyway. Next he removed several gold guineas from his purse and placed them in his jacket pocket. He returned to the livery and attached his bag along with Bliss's to Baron's saddle. Then he led both horses through the descending darkness to the narrow alley behind the inn.

Luc studied the rear of the inn, his eyes lighting up when he saw stairs leading to the ground from the second floor. He found a rock, used it to tether the horses' reins to the ground, then sidled around to the front of the inn. He heard a hiss and saw Bristol and six brawny fishermen pressed into the shadows of the overhanging roof.

"We were beginning to fear you wouldn't show up," Bristol groused. "How are we going to work this? Are you going to take Bliss out from beneath the noses of the excise men?"

"I'm not taking Bliss anywhere."

"What? You said you would help her! What kind of man are you?"

"Be quiet and listen, all of you." Then Luc explained what was going to happen if they followed orders precisely. "Give me fifteen minutes before you act. Some of you could get hurt; if you wish, there's still time to back out."

"If it helps Bliss, it will be worth it," Fred Dandy said. The others agreed wholeheartedly.

Luc nodded and entered the inn. A discreet word with the innkeeper gained him the information he sought and a spare key, which he quickly pocketed. The innkeeper was no friend of the excise men. Then Luc boldly walked into the common room, sought out Skillington and loudly demanded that he be granted time with his fiancée.

Skillington looked up from the meat pie he was eating and frowned. "You are becoming a nuisance, my lord. You have no authority to make demands. I am but enforcing the king's law against smuggling."

Luc was protesting vigorously when Brady and his friends burst into the common room, wielding staffs and cudgels. Skillington dropped his fork and leaped to his feet. "What's the meaning of this?"

"We want you to release Bliss Hartley," Brady shouted.

Skillington's men, who had been taking their ease, rose to their captain's defense. A fierce fight ensued, just as Luc had planned. He kept to the sidelines until he saw the guard stationed upstairs rush to the common room to help his comrades. All but ignored, Luc crept toward the stairs, inching along the wall until he was sure he hadn't been noticed. Then he darted up the stairs, taking them two at a time.

He found the room he was looking for, fitted the key in the lock and turned it. The well-oiled hinges opened without a squeak, and Luc stepped inside. Millie was seated at a small table, eating her supper. She appeared unaware of Luc's presence until he softly spoke her name.

Fear etched Millie's face when she spied him leaning against the door. "How did you get in here? What do you want?"

"How much did Skillington pay you to betray Bliss?"

Millie swallowed hard. "Please, don't hurt me. I wasn't thinking straight. I'm sorry, truly sorry."

"I'm not going to hurt you; I'm going to help you get your wish."

Millie's breath caught. "What wish is that?"

"Answer my question, Millie. How much did Skillington offer you to betray Bliss?"

"Three gold guineas. That's more blunt than I've ever seen."

"I'm going to give you ten gold guineas and a horse. Once you're free of the village, you should be able to find your way to London." He handed her the guineas along with a folded sheet of paper. "Once you get there, you're to look up the Marquis of Bathurst and give him this note. He'll help you find a position to your liking."

Millie regarded the gold with round eyes. "You're going to do this for me despite . . .

everything? Why?"

"Without your testimony, it's my word against Skillington's that Bliss is Shadow. But we have to hurry. Brady and his friends are creating a diversion so you can escape."

"What about Bliss?"

"Let me worry about her. Will you do as I say?"

Millie looked at the gleam of gold in her hand and then at Luc. "Aye, my lord."

He urged her toward the door. "Let's get out of here. We'll leave by the back stairs. Do you know where they are?"

"I'm familiar with the inn."

Luc opened the door, saw that the hall was empty and motioned to Millie. She sidled past him and raced toward the rear exit. Luc carefully closed and locked the door behind him and followed. Sounds of the fight taking place in the common room spilled into the dark night.

"The horses are over there," Luc said, pointing. He lifted her into the saddle. "You're on your own now, Millie. Ride hard and ride fast. I suggest you sell the horse at the next posting station and take the stage-coach to London."

"Thank you, Lord Westmore. I hope Bliss will forgive me."

"Just stay ahead of the excise men and all

will be forgiven. Now go, and don't forget to look up Lord Bathurst. We are fast friends, and he will help you."

Luc waited to see if Millie made it safely from the alley before leading Baron around to the front of the inn. As unobtrusively as possible, he reentered the inn and sidled into the common room where pandemonium still reigned. While Bliss's friends looked somewhat battered, so did the revenuers.

Then the vicar showed up right on cue. "Stop!" he shouted. "Stop this nonsense now!"

Immediately the villagers stopped brawling and began backing toward the door.

"Thank you, Vicar," Skillington said. "In another minute I would have ordered my men to shoot. What in the deuce was that all about?"

"Mistress Hartley is one of our own," Vicar Brownlee explained. "I suspect the men were showing their displeasure over her arrest. Were I a brawler, I would have joined them."

"Rightly so," Luc said, making his presence known. "Thank you for your help, Vicar. The brawl could have had serious consequences had you not arrived when you did."

Skillington straightened his jacket along with his dignity. "Yes, well, it's over now."

Before Luc spoke, he made sure the brawlers, along with the vicar, had departed.

"Not yet, Captain. If I can't speak with my fiancée, I wish to question the witness. It's my right to do so."

"You may speak your piece before the magistrate in Plymouth," Skillington replied. "Once he hears the evidence, I'm sure he'll recommend that Mistress Hartley be taken to London to appear before a high court of law."

"How do I know Mistress Hartley won't be mistreated in your care?"

Skillington drew himself up to his full height. "I am a gentleman, my lord. Mistress Hartley will be quite safe in my care."

Though Luc desperately wanted to reassure Bliss, he thought it best not to press the issue. Her release depended upon Millie's escape. It was imperative that Millie's disappearance not be discovered until morning.

"Very well, Captain. I'll see you in Plymouth."

Luc left immediately. He planned to be in Plymouth well before Skillington arrived with Bliss.

★ ★ ★

When Bliss heard the ruckus in the common room, her hopes soared. What was happening? Had Luc come up with a plan to rescue her? She hoped not. It would be insane to challenge Skillington and his men. The noises grew louder. Pressing her ear to the door, she heard sounds of a fierce fight being waged but nothing more. Then she heard footsteps hurrying down the hall, and her heart nearly stopped. Was it Luc? The footsteps passed and she sagged against the door, abandoning all hope of escape.

Bliss moved to the window and stared out. Her life hung on Millie's testimony. She stared at the wall separating their rooms. Millie was as much a prisoner as she was right now. Skillington didn't dare let Millie out of his sight lest she disappear again.

Bliss walked to the separating wall and rested her head against it, wondering if Millie was suffering pangs of guilt. She wished she knew what she had done to earn Millie's enmity.

The murmur of voices inside Millie's room brought her head up. Who was Millie talking to? She pressed her ear against the wall but could hear nothing over the sounds of fighting below stairs.

If Skillington was busy quelling the tempest below, who was with Millie in her room?

The fighting stopped as abruptly as it had begun. Bliss waited for someone to tell her what was happening, but no one came. She returned to the separating wall and placed her ear against it. The voices had stopped. All was quiet. Too quiet.

Bliss remained wary, watchful, prepared for what would happen next. Nothing happened. After a long while, she lay down fully clothed on the bed and eventually fell asleep.

Fingers of sunlight stabbed against Bliss's eyes. It wasn't the light but the ruckus in the hall that had awakened her. What was going on? She arose and splashed cold water on her face. Once fully awake, she faced the door with a sense of impending doom.

Moments later the door swung inward. Skillington stood in the opening, his face red with fury. "Where is she?"

Bliss was truly puzzled. "To whom are you referring?"

"Don't play coy with me, Mistress Hartley. Is she with you?"

"Again I ask, to whom are you referring?"

"My witness. She's not in her room. The door was locked, but she is gone. I seriously doubt she flew out the window."

"And you think I had something to do with it?"

He sent her a long, searching stare. "I don't know what to think. How did she get out of a locked room? This is the second floor, and there is no convenient tree for her to climb down. A drop to the ground would have caused her serious injury."

Bliss's first thought was that Luc had arranged for her escape. Her second thought was that if Luc had freed Millie, why hadn't he freed her too?

"She must have had an accomplice," Skillington contended. He stroked his chin. "What confuses me is why they freed Mistress Partin and not you. Unless . . ." He scowled. "Of course, why didn't I see it? Without the barmaid's testimony, our case against you is without substance."

Ah, now Bliss understood. Had she escaped, the law would have pursued her, but without Millie to testify against her, she had a good chance of avoiding prosecution. How clever of Luc, for she had no doubt that Luc had somehow done the impossible. He had set Millie free under the very noses of Skillington and his subordinates. And he

238

had probably provided Millie with money and a horse.

"Perhaps you should release me," Bliss pressed. "You have no proof of wrongdoing on my part. Why would a squire's daughter resort to smuggling?"

"Tell it to the magistrate when we reach Plymouth, Mistress Hartley. He'll decide whether you should be taken to London for trial. We'll leave directly after you break your fast."

Bliss glanced down at the shirt and trousers she wore. "I'd like to change my clothes before I leave."

"Your clothes will be used as evidence against you. You'll wear them to Plymouth. Come along; you can eat while our horses are being readied."

Bliss pulled on her black cloak and followed Skillington to the common room below. She was surprised to see only four men seated at a long table. Bliss sat at the opposite end of the room. "Where are the rest of your men?"

"I sent them after my witness," Skillington snapped. "Never doubt it, mistress, we'll have her back in no time."

Bliss sincerely hoped not.

Peg, the innkeeper's wife, brought Bliss a plate of food. Bliss began to eat. When Peg returned with a mug of ale, she bent low to Bliss's ear and whispered, "The outhouse."

Bliss wasn't sure what Peg meant, but she implicitly trusted this woman she'd known all her life.

After Bliss finished a healthy portion of the food Peg had prepared for her, she asked permission to visit the outhouse.

Since Skillington could hardly deny her request, he sent her off with a guard trailing behind her. The moment Bliss entered the small, square enclosure, she understood Peg's words. Hanging from a hook were a dress and cloak, both of them hers. And what better place to dispose of the damning clothing she wore than down an odious dark hole?

Aware that her time was limited, Bliss changed quickly, dropped the clothing and black cloak she was wearing into the hole and watched them disappear. When she opened the door and stepped outside into the fresh, sweet-smelling air, the guard's mouth dropped open.

"Skillington isn't going to like this," he muttered as he escorted Bliss inside the inn.

When Bliss entered the common room, Skillington choked out a curse. "Where in God's name did you get that dress and cloak?"

Her lips clamped tightly together, Bliss remained stubbornly mute.

Skillington looked angry enough to explode. "The whole village is conspiring against me. What did you do with the clothing you were wearing?"

Bliss stared at him blankly.

"Hobart!" Skillington barked. "Check the outhouse. I want Mistress Hartley's discarded clothing."

Hobart hurried off. He returned a few minutes later empty-handed. Bliss wanted to laugh at the expression of disgust on Hobart's face but stifled the urge.

"The clothing has . . . been disposed of, Captain. Believe me when I say you wouldn't want it even if we could recover it."

Skillington slanted Bliss a murderous glance. "You, mistress, are defying me at every turn. The magistrate will be informed of your insolence. I specifically told you I wanted the clothes you were wearing as evidence."

"Did you? I don't recall."

Slapping his gloves repeatedly against his palm, Skillington looked as if he wanted to strangle her. To his credit, he turned and strode off. "Bring the woman," he ordered. "It's time we left."

Luc stopped during the darkest part of the night to rest and water his horse at a stream. Two hours later he resumed his journey, anxious to reach Plymouth before Skillington. It was afternoon before Luc saw the church spire rising above the city of Plymouth. He'd visited Plymouth several times in the past and rode to an inn he knew to be clean and respectable.

Luc dismounted before the King's Crown. A lad ran up to take his horse. Luc tossed him a coin. "Baron has had a hard ride," Luc said. "Give him a measure of oats and rub him down."

The lad pulled his forelock and led Baron off. Luc entered the inn and was immediately recognized by the jovial innkeeper.

"Lord Westmore, welcome! What brings you to our part of the kingdom?"

"Business, Peter," Luc replied. "I'd like your best room, if it's available. And a bath. I've been traveling most of the night."

"And something to eat, I'll wager," Peter said. "I'll ask Joan to prepare something special for you. It should be ready by the time you've finished your bath. Let me take your bags."

Luc followed Peter to a large room with a fireplace and wide bed. The bed looked so comfortable, Luc wanted to fall into it and sleep, but he had more important things to do first.

His bath arrived in short order. Though he would have liked to, he didn't linger in the tub. He washed quickly, shaved and dressed in clean clothing. By the time his food arrived, he was more than ready to eat the tasty meal of roasted beef and stuffed capon.

Luc left the King's Crown refreshed and eager to confront the magistrate. He didn't expect Skillington to arrive until sometime tomorrow, which left him plenty of time to plead with the magistrate on Bliss's behalf.

Since the magistrate had finished his hearings for the day, Luc was granted an audience. He introduced himself; Sir Halliday invited him to sit down and state his purpose.

"Since we are both busy men," Luc began, "I'll get right to the point. Captain Skillington has arrested my fiancée and is bringing her to your court. She is accused of organizing a band of smugglers."

"Your *fiancée?*" Halliday gasped. "A woman?"

"Just so," Luc allowed. "It's ludicrous. My fiancée is Squire Hartley's daughter and innocent of the charges. Skillington has no proof of her guilt. Why, I ask you, would a woman turn to smuggling?"

"Indeed," Halliday said, stroking his chin. "I know Captain Skillington. He's conscientious and devoted to his work. Perhaps he has proof you know nothing about." He paused, shaking his head. "A woman. It's highly improbable but not impossible."

"It's unlikely that my fiancée could be in two places at once. Mistress Hartley was with me the night she was supposed to be engaged in smuggling."

"The entire night?"

Luc looked him in the eye and said, "Yes. I know the information could ruin Mistress Hartley's reputation, but it could also save her life. We were . . . celebrating our engagement, if you catch my drift."

Halliday searched Luc's face. "Skillington must have valid proof, else he wouldn't have arrested your fiancée."

"He obtained false information from a jealous woman," Luc said earnestly. "A barmaid I rejected when I arrived in St. Ives told Skillington that Mistress Hartley had organized the smugglers. When the woman realized I preferred Mistress Hartley, she turned vindictive. I believe Skillington is using false information to convict an innocent woman."

"Surely he has more proof than that."

"Not to my knowledge. Mistress Hartley wasn't found in the vicinity of the smuggling or anywhere near the beach."

"I will listen most carefully to Captain Skillington's witness, and review what other proof he has, and weigh it against what you have told me. I find it difficult to believe that the fiancée of a nobleman would resort to smuggling. However, I am obligated by law to hear the captain's testimony."

"That's all I ask of you," Luc said. He rose. "Good day, sir. I will return when Skillington arrives with my fiancée."

Chapter Eleven

The journey to Plymouth took longer than Bliss expected. She had never ventured this far from St. Ives before. Skillington called a halt at a country inn just before dark. He arranged for Bliss's room while she took supper in the common room. While she ate, Skillington paced restlessly back and forth, as if waiting for something or someone. Bliss learned what had agitated him when one of the men he had sent to search for Millie returned to report that they hadn't found her, and that his companions wanted to know whether they should abandon the search.

Skillington became livid with anger. Bliss couldn't hear what he told his subordinate, but the man left immediately.

Early the next morning, the small party continued on to Plymouth. They reached the city before noon. Skillington wasted no time in hauling Bliss before the magistrate. A clerk went immediately to fetch Sir Halliday. While they waited, Skillington ushered Bliss to a bench. She hadn't been there five minutes before Luc entered the courtroom and sat beside her.

Bliss's hopes soared. Luc's timing was perfect. Skillington, however, looked far from pleased.

"What are you doing here, Westmore?" Skillington hissed.

"I'm here to support my fiancée," Luc drawled. He clasped Bliss's hand; she clung to him with tenacious fervor. With Luc there to support her, she felt she could get through anything.

The magistrate entered the room, sat down at his desk and bade Skillington to come forward with his prisoner. Skillington placed a hand beneath Bliss's elbow and brought her to her feet.

"State your case, Captain," Halliday ordered as he regarded Bliss's form and features with something akin to shock.

Skillington pushed Bliss forward. "Mistress Hartley is the leader of a group of smugglers operating out of the village of St. Ives, sir. She is known as Shadow and dealt directly with French smugglers, depriving the government of much needed revenue."

Disbelief colored Halliday's voice as he replied, "Those are serious charges, Captain. You have proof, of course."

"We had an informer with firsthand

knowledge of the operation," Skillington offered, "but somehow she slipped through our fingers. My men are searching for her as we speak."

"Aside from the elusive informer, what else do you have? It seems odd to me that a rough lot of smugglers would allow a woman to become their leader."

"W-we had the clothing Mistress Hartley wore when she was arrested," Skillington said. "She was dressed in men's trousers and shirt, much like the smugglers wear."

Luc jumped to his feet. "My fiancée would never dress in such outlandish clothing, Sir Halliday. No proof exists that she did."

"He's lying," Skillington argued. "Mistress Hartley is the elusive Shadow, I tell you."

"You have no proof to support your theory," Halliday charged. "A high court of law will require tangible evidence, which you lack. Did you see evidence of smuggling in the village? Has anyone besides your missing informer come forth with information? Where is the clothing Mistress Hartley supposedly wore? I find it difficult to believe that the woman standing before me is a menace to society."

"I'll admit it sounds far-fetched, but I

wouldn't have arrested Mistress Hartley had I not believed her guilty. The condemning clothing disappeared, as did our witness. I admit our evidence is flimsy, but I am convinced of Mistress Hartley's guilt. I suggest she be examined for wounds. One of my men insisted that he had wounded Shadow."

"May I speak in Mistress Hartley's defense?" Luc asked, approaching the bench.

"Very well, my lord, have your say," the magistrate replied.

"I am outraged. Examining Mistress Hartley's person is beyond despicable. I will not allow it. I intend to wed Mistress Hartley in a civil service immediately and take her to London. I took the liberty of purchasing a special license yesterday. Once we are wed, Mistress Hartley will pose no danger to the government — not that she ever did. Why Captain Skillington is bent on punishing an innocent woman is beyond my understanding."

"I'm inclined to agree with you, my lord. I see no reason to intrude upon Mistress Hartley's person." Halliday turned to Bliss. "What say you in your own defense, Mistress Hartley?"

"Sir, I present no threat to king or country. Captain Skillington has no proof of my guilt, or that the citizens of St. Ives are involved in smuggling. Shadow is but a figment of his imagination."

"Not true," Skillington retorted. "My men interrupted a delivery of contraband not far from St. Ives."

"There are any number of small villages up and down the coast involved in smuggling," Bliss said. "The captain should look elsewhere for the people responsible."

Luc stifled a grin. Bliss had clearly won the magistrate's sympathy. The odds were stacked against Skillington, and Luc couldn't wait to whisk Bliss away.

"Sir Halliday —" Skillington began.

"I've heard enough, Captain. I see no reason to hold Mistress Hartley or to remand her to a higher court of law. Mistress Hartley has suffered a grave injustice. She is free to go."

Though Skillington sputtered and fumed, he couldn't change Halliday's mind. He cast a venomous glance at Luc and stomped from the courtroom.

Bliss turned into Luc's arms. "Am I truly free?"

"Indeed you are, young woman," Halliday said. "Now, about that wedding — I'd be happy to do the honors."

Bliss sucked in a startled breath. She

wasn't ready to wed Luc. The only reason he had announced their engagement and purchased a special license was to keep her from going to prison. She knew he didn't really want to be saddled with a wife. Rogues didn't marry; they used their charm and sexual prowess to lure women to their beds. Then the hapless victims were discarded when another pretty face appeared. She didn't want to marry a man with a roving eye.

"Perhaps we should wait, Luc," she whispered in a voice meant for his ears alone. "We don't want to rush into anything. When I wed, I'd like Papa to give me away and all my friends to share in my special day."

"Sir Halliday, may I have a private word with my fiancée?" Luc asked.

"Of course. You may use the anteroom. It's the first door on the left. I urge you not to dally if you wish to wed today. My time is limited."

"This won't take long," Luc replied. Grasping Bliss's elbow, he escorted her to the anteroom and closed the door.

"I just saved your bloody neck, Bliss. The least you can do is show some sense. Marrying me will protect you. Do you really think Skillington is ready to let this matter drop?"

"I want to go home, Luc. I don't want to marry you and live in London. I know nothing about the *ton,* or what I'm supposed to do as a viscount's wife. All I know is . . ."

". . . smuggling," Luc finished. "That phase of your life is over. St. Ives is no longer a safe haven for you. You can't return."

Bliss regarded him with horror. "Ever?"

"I didn't say that. I merely said you can't return home now."

"What about Papa? He deserves an explanation from me. I can't go to London without him."

"I've already spoken with your father, Bliss. I offered to bring him and Jenny to London, but he refused. He said he won't abandon the villagers when they need him most. He knows everything," Luc added meaningfully. "I kept nothing from him. His only request was that I wed you immediately. He fears there might be an unexpected consequence of our . . . loving."

Bliss felt heat spread up her neck. "But it was always my intention to take Papa to London."

"Your father seems to be recovering on his own. He appeared quite robust when I saw him. He dismissed the idea that he was seriously ill. Do you have any other fears that need addressing before the magistrate marries us?"

"I hoped for love when I married, and fidelity. The thought of my husband seeking another woman's bed is unbearable. Can you give me that guarantee?"

"I can't promise love," Luc said bluntly. "I have little experience with fidelity. I can promise to keep you safe and act discreetly should I decide to stray. At this moment, I can truthfully say that you are the only woman I want. I won't lie to you, Bliss. I haven't led an exemplary life. My liaisons have been many and varied. I've been known to gamble away hundreds of pounds at a sitting, and have sampled every debauchery known to man."

"Oh, my God, it's worse than I thought."

"There's more, but I prefer not to divulge all at this time," Luc said, thinking of Lady Sybil's death. "But this I swear to you, Bliss. You'll never want for anything. I'll give you children, if you want them, and try to be a tolerable father. I'll never neglect you in any way or form."

"What if you fall in love with another woman?"

"That's highly unlikely," Luc scoffed. "I care for you, Bliss, and I always will."

"But you don't love me."

"I don't know. Do you love me?"

"I . . . don't know." She studied him intently. "But I could."

"Then we shall deal well with one another. I know little of love, but I'm willing to learn if you are. Shall we tell the magistrate we're ready?"

"Kiss me, Luc."

"What?"

"I need assurance that I'm not making the biggest mistake of my life."

His eyes glittered as he stroked the curve of her cheek with a single fingertip. Her breath quickened as he touched her chin and tilted her head. His mouth descended on hers, molding, coaxing. Boldly he parted her lips with his tongue, sliding it inside, stroking the soft inner surface of her cheek in a burning, demanding exploration.

The kiss was all that she expected, everything she needed. Light-headed and reeling, she wrapped her arms around his neck in a desperate bid for balance. Then she felt the rigid length of his sex through the barrier of their clothing and knew he wanted her. But was lust enough to make a successful marriage?

His mouth possessed hers with wicked skill as his hands roamed freely over her lush curves. Excitement built, but before it could explode, Luc pulled away. He looked as flummoxed as she did.

"Are you convinced?" he asked in a strangled voice. "I want you, love. This obsessive need I have for you could last forever. That's more than I've offered any woman."

Much as Bliss might wish for more, she decided to settle for what they had together and build on it. Love didn't develop overnight. It had to be carefully nurtured. Was she up to the task? Did she even care about nurturing a relationship that Luc had no intention of honoring?

He said he cared for her. Did he mean it?

"Bliss, the magistrate won't wait forever." He extended his hand, surprised to see it was shaking. He must be mad. It was the only explanation he could come up with for breaking his own rules and marrying Bliss.

At least he hadn't lied to her. She knew where he stood on the subject of matrimony. It held little appeal for him, but she certainly did. That was more than most marriages in this day and age had. He held his breath, waiting for Bliss to place her hand in his. For some reason he'd yet to discern, it was very important that she come to him, that she accept him as he was.

His breath left him in a loud sigh as their hands touched. His fingers curled around hers, bringing them to his mouth, brushing his lips against them.

"Let's go then, my lovely bride. We'll ask the magistrate to do the honors."

Halliday smiled when they returned arm in arm. "Is it settled then, my lord? Shall we get on with it?"

Though Bliss might have wished for a fancy dress and her family and friends in attendance, the brief ceremony was as binding as any fancy affair. She knew Luc had some fast friends and wondered what they would think when told of his marriage to a country miss with no dowry and nothing to recommend her. How could she possibly compete with the society women of Luc's acquaintance?

"Bliss."

Bliss looked up at Luc. "Yes?"

"You're supposed to say 'I do' now."

"Oh, I didn't know it was time. I do."

The rest of the ceremony passed in a blur. Only when Luc lifted her face and kissed her did she recall where she was and why. They were husband and wife. She was still in a daze when they took their leave of the magistrate and walked outside into the sunshine. Bliss blinked, as if coming out of a dream.

"We're married."

"Indeed."

"Where do we go from here?"

"I took a room at an inn when I arrived. You can have a bath and whatever else you'd like. We'll stay the night and then push on to London tomorrow. I've hired a coach to make the trip more comfortable for you."

"I wish I had some clean clothes to change into," Bliss said wistfully.

Luc grinned. "Your wish is my command. I had Jenny pack a bag for you before I left St. Ives. It's awaiting you at the inn."

"You're truly amazing, Lord Westmore."

"So I've been told," he said, tongue in cheek.

"How did you manage it?"

"Manage what?"

"All of it. Millie, the clothes waiting for me in the outhouse, the magistrate's compliance . . . everything."

Luc shrugged. "It wasn't difficult. A little prior planning helped, then things fell into place. I couldn't have freed Millie without the help of your friends, and the innkeeper was most accommodating. He gave me the spare key to Millie's room. Even the vicar played his part."

"Thank you," Bliss said sincerely. "I regret you had to go to such lengths to save me from my own folly. I should have listened to you. My stubbornness got the miller killed and placed my friends in danger. That's not the way I planned it."

"At least we agree on one thing. Ah, here's the inn. I'm sure you'll find it comfortable."

Luc made arrangements for a bath and asked that a meal be brought up in two hours. Then he escorted Bliss to their room.

"This isn't much of a honeymoon," Luc said, "but perhaps we can manage something more extravagant at a later date." He opened the door and handed her inside.

"It's very nice," Bliss said.

A smile stretched the corners of Luc's mouth when he noted the direction of Bliss's gaze. "I can attest to the fact that the bed is extremely comfortable. I'm sure you'll find that out for yourself very soon."

Bliss opened her mouth to speak, but a knock on the door prevented her reply. Luc opened the door, admitting servants carrying a large brass tub and buckets of water.

"Shall I help my lady bathe?" a maid asked shyly.

"There's no need," Luc said. "I will play maid for my bride."

The maid curtsied, giggled and made a hasty exit.

"Your bath awaits, my lady," Luc said.

"That sounds strange," Bliss mused. "I never thought to hear anyone call me that."

"Get used to it. It's your title now. Come here, let me help you undress."

"Really, Luc, it's not necessary."

"It's very necessary," Luc murmured.

With tantalizing slowness, he placed a finger beneath the first button on her bodice and released it. One by one, the rest followed. Excitement rushed through her when Luc's fingers brushed across her sensitive skin. Her bodice slid down her arms. He stroked her cheek, his touch as soft as butterfly wings. She shivered and gazed up at him. His fingers drifted to her throat, caressed the vulnerable curve, slid beneath her chemise to cup her breast.

"God, I want you." His hands fell away. Bliss was surprised to see them shaking. "First a bath, then . . ." He left the sentence dangling, and Bliss with it.

He undressed her with the speed and efficiency one would expect in a talented rogue. When he had stripped her naked, his hungry gaze feasted on her. She felt as if her skin were melting. She had nothing to hide behind, so she simply stood there and let him look his fill. Then he swept her up and lowered her into the tub.

When he started to undress, Bliss's eyes

widened. "What are you doing?"

He stepped into the tub. "Joining you."

She scooted backward as he lowered his big body into the cramped tub. Water splashed over the sides but it didn't seem to bother Luc as he took up a cloth and soap and proceeded to bathe her upper body. He washed and rinsed her hair next, then concentrated on the intimate parts of her body. A slow flush spread over her skin when his hand delved below the water to bathe her private places.

She gasped when Luc's talented finger delved into her sheath. A second finger followed. She felt her muscles clench around them, felt him thrust deep, then retreat, again and again, until his penetration brought her to the brink of climax. When she was ready to come, he removed his fingers, placed one arm around her hips and the other behind her back. She cried out in surprise and clung to him when he slid her onto his lap, positioned her so that she straddled him, and pushed his rigid staff into her body.

Grasping her hips, he thrust deep. Her flesh closed tightly around him, swallowing every solid inch of him.

She made a gurgling sound in her throat — not of protest but of pleasure. Panting, she rested her head against his, urging him on with soft little moans and frantic kisses.

With warm water splashing around them and Bliss's pliant body impaled on his cock, every logical thought fled from Luc's mind. He filled her sweet sheath in strong, upward surges, again and again, until her moans came one upon another, ending in a stifled scream as she clamped around him and convulsed.

Luc remained still, holding her against him, feeling her quivering around him, the depths of her body holding him snugly. Her spasms seemed to pull him deeper inside her; it was killing him not to release, but he wanted to draw out her pleasure, wanted to show her ways to love beyond her imagination.

Bliss drew back, gazing up at him through glazed eyes. "Aren't you going to . . . ?"

"Not yet. Don't worry, I'll have my turn."

He surged from the tub, bringing Bliss with him. He wrapped her in a soft cloth, drying her and then himself. He was still hard as a rock as he carried her to the bed and followed her down. He pressed kisses across her face, then lapped up a drop of water from the tip of her breast with his tongue. He raised his head. The sweetness of her lips tempted him, drew him like a bee

261

to honey. His mouth opened over hers, captured it fully, his tongue stabbing and withdrawing in an imitation of the sex act. He wanted to arouse Bliss slowly, savor every nuance of her response.

Reluctantly his lips left hers, traveling along the delicious curve of her chin, the lush swell of her breasts. Cupping a breast in his hand, he lavished attention on her rosy nipple, licking and nipping until the taut bud unfurled against his tongue. The other breast and nipple received the same undivided attention before Luc moved on to explore the tiny indentation of her navel, ringing it with his tongue and dipping inside.

"Do you like that?" Luc asked when a strangled sound escaped her throat.

"You're driving me crazy."

"Good. Now you know how I've felt since the first day I saw you."

His head moved lower, his hot breath fanning her skin, his hand sifting through the tangled curls between her legs. Then he spread her thighs and stared at her. Ignoring her gasp of protest, he opened the silken petals of her sex and kissed her there.

Bliss arched up, her hands tangling in his hair. "Luc, please . . ."

He raised his head. "Oh, yes, wife, I will

most definitely please you. Never doubt it."

His tongue swept over her tiny feminine bud; he drew it into his mouth and gently suckled. Her body began to tremble.

"Be still, love. Let me pleasure you."

"Luc . . ."

Completely absorbed in the tangy scent of her arousal, Luc ignored her plea as he blew a heated breath into her moist cleft. He heard her moan and cry out, but he needed more, much more, from her. His tongue parted the damp curls, finding the rose-tinted lips hidden beneath. His mouth ravished her, his tongue delving into her melting heat. With the tip of his tongue he teased her sex, and then stabbed relentlessly into the entrance of her body.

"Luc! Now! You're torturing me."

Frustrated beyond bearing, she reached down and tried to pull him up. She felt his laughter in a puff of air against her burning flesh. He brushed his lips against her swollen peak one last time before sliding upward and settling between her legs. His glittering eyes held hers captive as he thrust deep. He rotated his hips against her as his sex pounded into her, teasing and rubbing against her sensitive peak.

Stunning pleasure built inside her, gaining momentum, driving her higher and higher. She hovered on the brink, waiting breathlessly for release, aching for it, and then she tumbled. Violent spasms spread from her core; her senses overflowed as unspeakable pleasure exploded. She couldn't stop shaking. Nor could she have put two words together if she tried.

"That's it, love," Luc whispered against her ear as he continued thrusting, drawing long shudders from her.

"Is it your turn yet?" she asked between deep gulps of air.

"God, yes."

He tightened his hands on her hips, raised them and slammed into her, riding her hard and deep.

"You're so warm and tight," he murmured against her lips. "So sweet . . ."

Bliss watched his face as he stroked himself to completion. He became breathless. His eyes were closed, his head thrown back, his expression so intense it was almost feral. Overcome by a strange feeling of tenderness, she slid her hands over his back, caressing the curve of his spine, the deep slash of his buttocks, listening to the sound of his heaving breath.

Suddenly he buried his entire length inside her and jerked violently, releasing his passion with a guttural cry. She took his weight and held him close as he collapsed against her. Finally he sighed and rolled to his side. When he opened his eyes, she saw a flash of something she'd never seen before.

He smiled. "Did I hurt you? I didn't mean to be so rough."

She returned his smile. "You didn't hurt me. I should be embarrassed but I'm not. Does that make me a wanton? I was led to believe that a woman was supposed to lie still and let the man have his way."

"Most men dream about having a wife as responsive as you. I like you just the way you are."

"Did you dream about finding a responsive wife?"

Silence.

"Luc?"

Luc sighed. "I won't lie to you. I didn't dream about a wife at all, responsive or otherwise. I was quite happy with my unmarried state."

"What about an heir? All men want an heir."

"I have a younger half-brother who has already produced an heir for the earldom."

"You do? You've never spoken of your family."

"My father and stepmother live in Scotland, my stepmother's home. My stepbrother married a Scotswoman, and they reside near Edinburgh. I have a sister whom I adore. Mary Ann and her husband, the Earl of Belcher, are presently out of the country, but I expect them home soon.

"Father doesn't agree with the life I've chosen for myself and he disowned me, though not publicly. He has, however, cut me off financially."

"How do you live, then? You seem to have means."

"I inherited money from my mother and invested it wisely. I'm not as rich as Bathurst or Braxton, but I manage extremely well without Father's blunt."

"When was the last time you saw your family?"

Luc shrugged. "Shortly after I returned from the Peninsula and embarked upon a way of life Father couldn't tolerate."

"So you're in line for an earldom," Bliss mused. "You shouldn't have married me. I'm ill prepared to become the wife of an earl. It's bad enough being a viscountess."

"You'll manage," Luc said. "You organized a band of smugglers well enough. Besides, Father may still disinherit me in favor of Travis."

"It won't matter one whit to me." She snuggled against him. "I hope you don't intend to sleep separate from me once we reach London. I rather like company in bed."

Growling, Luc reached for her, but whatever he had in mind wasn't to be. There came a soft knock on the door.

"Our food," Luc said on a sigh of disappointment. "Come in," he called, causing Bliss to dive beneath the covers.

"How could you?" she hissed, pinching him in a vulnerable spot.

A chuckle rumbled from his chest. "Place the food on the table, please," Luc commanded.

Bliss heard servants bustling about and the rattle of dishes. Then she heard the door close.

"You can come out now, coward. We are married, you know."

Bliss peeked from beneath the sheet. Luc grabbed it from her fingers and flung it aside. "Shall we eat? I'm famished."

So was Bliss, but the thought of sitting at the table without a stitch of clothing was unsettling. "Allow me to dress first."

"No," Luc said, his eyes sparkling wickedly. "Nakedness is a natural state. I want to look at you while I eat . . . all of you, just as God made you."

Bliss gasped. "You're a wicked man, Lord Westmore."

"So I've been told." He surged from bed and extended his hand. "Will you join me? The food smells delicious."

Self-consciously Bliss placed her hand in his and let him seat her at the small table groaning with a variety of tempting food.

They started with oyster soup, then ate their way through turbot in lobster sauce, partridge and truffle pie, veal with walnut stuffing, candied carrots and apple pudding. Instead of ale, Luc had ordered a fine red wine.

At first Bliss wanted to cover herself with her hands, but then she decided it was too late for modesty and concentrated instead on the delicious food. Luc, however, seemed unable to take his eyes off her. Several times during their meal she felt his considering gaze on her. He looked as if he'd rather partake of her than the food. She tried to focus on her meal, but with his naked body displayed in all its magnificent glory, it became increasingly difficult to keep her eyes from straying.

"How did the cook prepare all this in such short order?" Bliss asked as the tension between them intensified.

"I ordered a bridal feast early this morning, before you arrived."

"How did you know I'd be released?"

Luc gave her a smug smile. "If you hadn't, I would have been very surprised. I spoke to Halliday before your arrival. I told him you couldn't possibly be guilty of everything Skillington claimed and proceeded to explain why."

Bliss swallowed hard. "What did you tell him?"

"That you were in my bed the entire night."

Her face reddened. "What must he think of me?"

"Who cares? We're married. I made an honest woman of you and saved you from the hangman."

"How clever of you," Bliss mocked.

Luc's brows lifted. "Indeed. It wasn't just luck that Millie disappeared when she did. Or that you were able to dispose of the evidence in such a way that it couldn't be retrieved. Thank God the magistrate didn't follow Skillington's suggestion and have you inspected for wounds."

Reaching out, he ran a gentle finger over her healing wound. "The stitches need to come out. I'll see to it myself. Are you finished eating?"

"I can never recall eating so much. All I want to do now is sleep."

"Sit still while I get the scissors from my

kit. I'll have those stitches out in no time."

"Are you sure you know what you're doing?"

"I should. On the Peninsula we didn't always have a doctor around during the worst of the fighting and had to make do."

Rummaging in his kit, Luc retrieved a flask of whiskey, removed the top and poured a small amount over his scissors.

"What did you do that for?"

"One learns many things on a battlefield. We found that disinfecting instruments before each use helps prevent infections." He grasped her arm above her elbow. "Hold still, this won't hurt nearly as much as placing the stitches did."

With great skill and more gentleness than Bliss would have credited of him, he removed the tiny stitches and dabbed the wound with whiskey.

"You're healing nicely," Luc observed. "Does it pain you?"

"A little." She looked longingly toward the bed. Sitting naked for so long was becoming increasingly uncomfortable. She wanted to cover up.

Her gaze drifted downward, her eyes widening when she saw that Luc's sex was no longer quiescent. It was hardening and lengthening before her eyes.

"I agree with you," Luc whispered, as if reading her mind. "The bed does look inviting. The way you're looking at me is making me hard. I want to love you again."

He raised her up and brought her against him. The moment their flesh touched, her exhaustion evaporated. He scooped her into his arms and carried her to bed, and made love to her in all the ways that made him the most sought-after lover in England.

Chapter Twelve

The coach Luc had hired was waiting for them the following morning. With Baron tied behind the vehicle, they started out on a glorious late summer day. Since they were in no hurry to reach London, the coachman was instructed to travel at a relaxed pace. They stopped at country inns when it became too dark to travel, ate a leisurely meal and retired to their room early, making love each night until their bodies were sated.

The passing scenery enthralled Bliss. She never tired of looking out the window at the changing terrain as the miles sped by, for she had not traveled so far inland before.

On the two days that it rained, the coach rolled through mud and rutted roads that made the vehicle lurch awkwardly. But the occupants didn't seem to mind. On those days Luc showed Bliss how pleasurable making love inside a pitching coach could be.

They reached the outskirts of London seven days after leaving Plymouth. As the coach rambled across London Bridge, Bliss was agog with excitement. She tried to take everything in at once — houses crowded together, their balconies overhanging the narrow street, vendors hawking their wares, beggars with their hands out, women dumping night soil into the gutters and upon passersby, and an occasional streetwalker propositioning a potential customer.

"Some sections of London are not safe," Luc warned, "especially for a woman. It's always wise to take a footman or maid with you when you venture abroad, even in the better neighborhoods."

Aghast, Bliss asked, "You mean I can't go out alone . . . ever?"

"That's correct. London isn't St. Ives. Besides, you're a viscountess now and must follow the dictates of society."

Bliss sent him a disgruntled glare. "Do you follow the dictates of society?"

Luc laughed. "Me? No, I follow my own dictates."

"Then so shall I," Bliss declared.

Luc's frown signaled his displeasure. "It doesn't work that way. Society women are more restricted in their movements than the women of your acquaintance. That's the way of the world."

"Not my world," Bliss argued. "I've

always come and gone as I pleased. I'm not sure I'm going to like London. Does your family have an estate in the country?"

"I have my own estate, but I rarely go there. Westwind Manor in Kent belonged to my mother. As you know, I don't fancy country living. I keep a skeleton staff there and have an excellent estate manager."

Bliss perked up. She could always retire to the country when London began to pall. But that might not be anytime soon. She was completely fascinated by London and couldn't wait to sample everything the city had to offer.

When the coach entered an area of broader streets with well-dressed people strolling about, she knew she was seeing a different side of London.

"That's Hyde Park," Luc said, pointing to a huge green area with serpentine walkways, horse trails, benches, tall trees and trimmed shrubbery. "It's *the* place to be seen. I'll take you for a carriage ride in the park one day soon. There are many things about London you'll enjoy — Covent Garden, Vauxhall Pleasure Gardens with its pavilions, bandstand and nightly fireworks, and the opera."

Bliss clapped her hands. "Fireworks? I've heard about them. When may we go?"

"Soon. There will be plenty of time for you to enjoy all the entertainment London has to offer. This is Mayfair —" He gestured as they passed by imposing mansions. "Some of the most influential and wealthiest people reside here. The Marquis of Bathurst and his family live in that house," Luc pointed out.

Bliss gawked at the palatial manor partially hidden by a high wall.

"He must be immensely wealthy," Bliss mused.

"Indeed," Luc agreed.

They passed row after row of mansions before entering an area of elegant townhouses rising two and three stories above the street. Luc rapped on the roof and the coach ground to a halt.

"I live at number twenty-nine. It's not a mansion by any means, but it suits me well enough."

The coachman opened the door and put the step in place. Luc stepped down and handed Bliss out. "Welcome home, Bliss," Luc said as he offered his arm. "Shall we go inside?"

Bliss placed her hand on Luc's arm. When they reached the front entrance, Luc rang the bell. It was opened immediately by a footman. Though his expression remained bland, one look into his eyes was all it took for Bliss to know that the man was shocked to see Luc back in London.

"Welcome home, Lord Westmore."

Another man, older and more distinguished than the footman, strode from one of the back rooms into the front hall. "Lord Westmore — we weren't expecting you." His gaze settled on Bliss, then darted away. "I'll have your rooms prepared immediately."

"Would you summon the staff, Partridge? I'd like to introduce them to my wife."

Partridge's shock was so apparent that Bliss had to stifle the giggle that rose from her throat.

"Immediately, my lord."

"You've shocked your butler," Bliss said after Partridge departed.

"I imagine he won't be the only one," Luc muttered. "I'll never hear the end of it from Bathurst and Braxton."

The staff began to assemble, from the housekeeper to the potboy. "My staff isn't extensive," Luc said. "Those I do have serve my needs well. This is Mrs. Dunbar, my housekeeper."

Bliss greeted the tiny woman with gray hair and spectacles and offered her hand. Mrs. Dunbar looked confused for a moment, then extended her own hand and curtsied. And so it went down the line: Mrs. Starkey, the cook; the two maids, Suzy and Tillie, who kept the house in order; William, the footman; Plumb, Luc's valet; and Partridge, the butler. Lastly, Luc introduced her to Mick, the potboy.

"I'm sure we will get along famously," Bliss said with more bravado than she felt.

"My wife will need a ladies' maid," Luc announced.

"Luc, I don't —"

He silenced her with a look. "I'll leave the hiring to you, Mrs. Dunbar."

"My lord," Suzy said timidly, "my sister is looking for work. She has little experience but is a quick learner. Her salary would help support my younger brothers and sisters."

"I'm sorry, but she won't do," Luc replied. "I prefer someone more experienced for my wife."

Bliss saw the hope die in Suzy's eyes and knew the family must be in desperate straits.

"Please, Luc, let's give her a try. I don't require much in the way of attention." She leaned close and whispered in his ear. "I believe the family needs the money."

Luc stared at Bliss a long time before agreeing. "Very well, we'll give the girl a chance to prove herself. What's her name?"

"Birdie, my lord," Suzy said. "Thank you ever so much. You won't be sorry. Birdie can be here tomorrow."

The staff dispersed. "Shall I show you the house while our rooms are being prepared?"

Bliss nodded eagerly. "I'd like that."

What Bliss saw was small but elegant. The front hall with its marble floor, sparkling chandelier and wide staircase leading to the upper floors was a showcase for Luc's excellent taste. The ballroom on the ground floor had mirrored walls to make it appear larger. Through a set of French doors was a wide terrace with stairs leading to a beautiful garden.

Luc's combination study and library was an extension of himself. Books lined the walls, and the room was filled with comfortable pieces of furniture that seemed to fit his character. The centerpiece was the highly polished walnut desk.

"This is where I take care of business and relax when I want to be alone."

"Do you do that often? Want to be alone, I mean."

He gave her a sizzling look that made her skin burn. "I have a distinct feeling that I won't want to be alone as long as I have a wife like you."

Speechless, Bliss followed him from the

library to the drawing room. Though not large, it was elegant and would be perfect for entertaining. The dining room was equally sophisticated with its papered silk walls, frescoes and burgundy drapes at the tall windows.

Bliss followed Luc down a long hall to the kitchen and housekeeper's room. The kitchen was spotless and well equipped; the cook and her day helper, whom she introduced as Mollie, were working diligently to prepare their dinner. From there they returned to the front hall and ascended the open staircase to the second-floor gallery.

"Our suites are on this floor, along with several guest bedrooms. The third floor is given over entirely to the staff."

"We each have suites?" Bliss asked. "That means we'll have separate bedrooms."

"Connecting bedrooms," Luc corrected. "That's the way things are done in London."

Bliss wrinkled her nose. "Who made that rule, a man who couldn't stand his wife?"

Luc opened the door and ushered her inside a large chamber that looked as if it had seen little use. The rose-colored draperies at the windows and bed hangings needed a good shaking, and the furniture, though beautifully fashioned, was covered with dust.

"As you can see, this room has never been used," Luc said. "I fear it's been sadly neglected. My servants are aware of my aversion to marriage and left this room virtually untouched. I'll have the staff see to it immediately."

The words had no sooner left his mouth than Mrs. Dunbar and both maids bustled into the room, armed with brooms, mops and various cleaning supplies. William followed, bearing a bucket of water.

"We'll put things to rights in no time, my lord," Mrs. Dunbar said as the maids, with William's help, began removing the bed hangings.

Luc guided Bliss through a second door. "This is the dressing room, which separates our bedchambers. The small room beyond the door to the left contains a water closet. It was just recently installed. There is no separate bathing room, but I hope to remedy that soon."

Luc opened the door to his chamber and ushered Bliss inside. The room appeared just as Bliss had imagined Luc's private quarters would look: heavy dark furniture, forest-green draperies at both windows and bed, and a carpet in varying shades of green and brown. It looked comfortable as well as inviting. Dimly she wondered how many women had shared this bed with him. She didn't ask though the question burned her tongue.

"What do you think?" Luc asked. "Is there anything you'd care to change?"

Only the sleeping arrangements. "I . . . can't think of anything. Give me time to settle in. Do you think I might have a bath?"

"Certainly. I'll make the arrangements on my way out. You can use my room while yours is being prepared."

"You're leaving?"

Luc gave her a strange look. "Surely you don't expect me to stay home and wait upon you, do you? You have a great deal to learn about society marriages, my love. Perhaps I shall see you at dinner. We don't keep country hours, so I expect dinner will be around nine. Enjoy yourself."

He turned to leave. "Luc! Where are you going?"

He spun around. "We're in London now. Don't expect answers from me. As soon as word gets out about our marriage, we'll have plenty of routs, balls and such to attend as a couple. We'll have to do something about your wardrobe, however. To-morrow I'll take you to one of the best seamstresses in town."

He gave her a jaunty salute and left. Fuming, Bliss followed him to the door and slammed it behind him. Whatever she had expected of their marriage, it wasn't this. She'd never thought Luc would abandon her so soon. Now that he was in London, she supposed he'd return to his hedonistic ways. Would that include womanizing? Did he have a mistress? How many of Luc's former lovers could she expect to encounter?

Luc left the house with unusual haste. Taking a wife hadn't seemed so confining in the country, but the moment he'd reached London and escorted Bliss into his townhouse, he'd felt the walls closing in on him, as if he were being suffocated. He had never imagined himself leg-shackled, or being responsible for another human being. He had lived his life selfishly, sampling every vice known to man. It was going to be difficult if not impossible to end that part of his life and begin another.

Bathurst and Braxton had given up debauchery for the women they loved, but Luc couldn't imagine loving anyone like that. That was why he had left Bliss to her own devices. He hoped his obsession for her would abate once he returned to his old haunts, enjoying the wilder side of London.

Luc created a sensation when he entered White's.

"I thought you were still in the country?" Lord Hoffington said in greeting.

"I decided to return," Luc drawled.

"The ladies have been bereft since you abandoned them," Viscount Cowerly offered.

"Well, man, tell us!" Lord Wellingham cried, his voice rising with excitement. "Who wins the bet? How long did you last?"

Luc knew what he was about to say would come as a shock, but he couldn't keep his marriage a secret for long in a town filled with gossips. "I was married one week ago and brought my bride back with me to London."

A stunned silence followed. "Never say it's true!" Wellingham gasped. "Not you! Not the last rogue! Bloody hell, your lovers will be devastated."

There was a rush to the betting books to see who had won the wager. Cowerly came away with a disgruntled look on his face. "It's Braxton, damn his hide!"

"What did I do?" Ramsey, the Earl of Braxton, asked as he strolled into the room.

"You won the bet," Cowerly said.

"What bet?" He saw Luc and stopped in his tracks. "Westmore, when did you return?"

"Today."

"Wait until Bathurst hears this. We shared a private bet. He gave you even less time than I did." He slapped Luc on the back. "Welcome home, old man. You've been missed."

"Tell him, Westmore," Cowerly prodded.

"Tell me what?"

Luc cleared his throat. "I've returned to London with a wife."

Clearly Ram was taken aback. "The devil you say!"

The subject was left dangling when the Earl of Mayhew joined the group, his penetrating gray eyes boring into Luc with unsettling intensity. Luc recognized Lord Mayhew as an acquaintance, but the man was not someone he would trust or call a friend.

"So you're back," Mayhew said without inflection. "You're not going to leave us in the dark as to why you fled to the country, are you?"

"Mayhew," Luc said, acknowledging the earl's greeting. "I believe my reasons are mine to reveal or conceal, and I prefer to keep them to myself."

"Come now," Mayhew persisted. "You must have had some reason to leave so precipitously. The gossip mill grinds on, you know. I heard your departure had something to do with Lady Sybil's death, hmmm? Do you know something that we don't, Westmore?"

His temper flaring, Luc's hands fisted at his sides. Why did Mayhew bring up Sybil now? What did he hope to gain? Suddenly Luc recalled why he didn't like Mayhew; the man fancied himself a ladies' man. Luc had thought him a sly fox with little to recommend him. Some had hoped Mayhew's recent marriage would change him. It appeared not. The man was as obnoxious as ever. One more word from him and Luc would issue a challenge.

Braxton must have recognized the state of Luc's tautly stretched temper, for he placed a hand on his shoulder and said, "Steady, old man. I need a drink, how about you?"

"I wanted to kill him," Luc hissed as they walked away.

"I know. Never did like him myself."

They ordered drinks from a passing footman and found an unoccupied corner with two comfortable chairs. Luc sprawled into a chair and stretched his legs out before him, his expression dark and forbidding.

"Forget Mayhew, he's a predator," Braxton said. "Tell me about your wife. You're the last person I expected to get caught in the parson's trap. She must be really something. Where is she from? How did you find her?"

"Damn it, Braxton, let me catch my breath," Luc said gruffly.

The footman arrived with their drinks. Luc swallowed his brandy in one gulp. "It's not what you think. It's not a love match. I married Bliss because . . ." His voice faltered.

Braxton's eyebrows shot up. "Bliss, is it? Catchy name. I hope you found bliss with her."

"I told you —"

"I know, I know, it's not a love match. Exactly what happened in St. Ives? Something must have convinced you to take a wife."

"It's a long story."

"I've got time."

Luc gave a long, strained sigh. "To make a long story short, I became involved with smugglers."

"You what? Bloody hell, man, you should have heeded my warning. How is your marriage connected with smugglers?"

Another long sigh. "Bliss organized the

smugglers; she was their leader. I married her to save her from the hangman."

"Go on," Ram urged. "This is unbelievable. It reminds me of Bathurst and his Olivia. She was a highwayman, if you recall."

"I recall very well," Luc said. "I also remember that you and everyone else thought your Phoebe stole a priceless Egyptian artifact."

"Things turned out well in both cases," Ram pointed out. "We fell in love with our wives."

"That's not going to happen to me," Luc vowed. "Once we reached London, I realized I didn't want to give up my former habits."

"Are you saying you're going to be an unfaithful husband? That you're going to continue your wicked ways?"

Luc winced. Braxton made it sound so sordid. Most marriages in the *ton* were arranged; he wouldn't be the first husband to stray. If he had learned one thing about himself since his marriage, it was that Bliss had too much control over his emotions. Wives shouldn't have that kind of power. Husbands were *supposed* to gamble, drink and take mistresses.

But if he was perfectly honest with himself, Luc would admit that the thought of Bliss in another man's arms brought a vile taste to his mouth and filled him with jealousy. But husbands and wives went their own ways, didn't they? He couldn't picture himself enjoying hearth and home night after night. The inactivity would drive him mad.

"What are you thinking?" Ram asked.

Luc flushed. "Nothing much."

"Continue your story, I can hardly wait. Tell me what made you abandon your vow to remain celibate."

"It's complicated," Luc said. "My intentions were good, but my body betrayed me. About a month after I left London, I encountered Bliss. I wanted her immediately but fought my desire for her.

"Neither of us trusted the other. She thought I was a government spy, and I believed she was involved in the smuggling operation I had happened upon one night during one of my midnight swims."

Ram's eyebrows shot upward. "Midnight swims? What was that all about?" He chuckled. "No, don't tell me, I already know. Did they help?"

"Not much," Luc admitted. "But that night I learned about Shadow, the leader of the group."

"Bliss," Ram guessed.

"Indeed. But I didn't know it until the excise men laid a trap for the smugglers. Bliss and I were hiding in a cave, but even then I wasn't aware of Shadow's identity. She left the cave while I was sleeping. I followed shortly afterward and found her lying on the ground. She'd been shot. I took her home and my housekeeper treated her wound. It wasn't serious. Then Captain Skillington came to arrest her."

"How did he know she was Shadow?"

"An informant."

"Bloody hell! I hope your Bliss is not a fugitive from the law."

"No, indeed." He grinned. "The informer mysteriously disappeared. So did the clothing Bliss wore as Shadow. With no evidence in hand, the magistrate dismissed the case."

"That still doesn't explain why you wed Bliss. Why didn't you send her back to her village?"

"I didn't trust her to stay out of trouble. I feared she would return to smuggling and that Skillington would be waiting for her to make a mistake and arrest her."

"Does Bliss have family?"

"Her father is Squire Hartley, but he had little control over his daughter. He's been ill but appears to be recovering. He made me promise to marry Bliss once I freed her."

Ram's eyes narrowed. "Why would he ask that of you?"

Luc cleared his throat. "It seems we were caught in a . . . er . . . compromising situation."

"How compromising?"

"We were found in bed together."

Ram threw back his head and laughed. "How typical. How long did you remain celibate? Two months, three months? I knew you couldn't keep your cock in your trousers for an entire year. I wish Bathurst were in town to hear this."

"Where is he?"

"He was called to his country estate on business and took Olivia and the twins with him."

"Who would have thought Bathurst could become domesticated? That's not me, not me at all," Luc vowed.

"Don't look now," Ram hissed, "but Mayhew is heading this way. What do you suppose he wants?"

"I say, Westmore," Mayhew began. "I believe an apology is in order. Please forgive my impertinence."

Luc nodded curtly. "As you say, Mayhew."

When Mayhew didn't leave, Ram asked, "Is there something else you wish to say?"

"Actually, there is, but I hope you won't think ill of me for bringing it up."

"Spit it out, Mayhew," Luc snapped.

"It's about Lady Sybil."

Luc's eyes narrowed. "What about her?"

"I understand you were the last person to see her alive. Did she say anything that might suggest she intended to take her life?"

"Even if she had, I wouldn't tell you," Luc gritted out.

"Why does Lady Sybil's death interest you?" Ram asked. "It happened months ago."

"I'm a friend of her father. The poor man continues to grieve, and I thought to offer him words of comfort. Can you tell me anything? Anything that would make Lord Horsely feel better?"

"Did you know Lady Sybil well?" Luc asked curiously. "Your personal interest is . . ." Luc's words fell off as a thought occurred to him.

Mayhew went pale. "I didn't know her at all, only her father. What makes you ask? Did she mention my name?"

"No," Luc said bluntly.

"I say, Mayhew," Ram interjected, "how is married life treating you? I hear you married an heiress, and that her money saved you from debtor's prison."

"Well . . . er . . ." Mayhew stammered, backing away from them. "I bid you good day. My wife is expecting me home." He executed a curt bow and hurried off.

"What in hell was that all about?" Ram asked.

"I'm not sure," Luc replied. His curiosity was engaged, however. "Does he actually know Lord Horsely?"

"I don't know, but I'll find out if you think it's important."

Luc shrugged. "If you wish; it really doesn't matter one way or another to me. The guilt for Sybil's death is solely mine."

"Not true," Ram disagreed. "You told her you'd find her a husband. What more could you have done?"

"I could have been more convincing. I actually *did* intend to find her a husband. I didn't lie."

"Of course you didn't." Ram finished his drink and rose. "I'm going home. I'm sure Phoebe will want to give a ball to introduce you and Bliss to society. Tell Bliss that Phoebe will call upon her once she's settled in."

"I suppose something must be done to bring Bliss into society," Luc acknowledged. "Give Phoebe my best."

"Are you going home?" Ram asked.

Luc shook his head. "I think I'll try the tables at Brooks's. I'm in line for some luck."

"Perhaps your luck is better than you think," Ram said in parting.

Luc mulled over Ram's words as he left White's. Was he lucky to have Bliss? He wasn't sure. What he *was* sure about was his need to sink inside her vibrant heat and ride her to completion. He wanted to bury his face in the fragrant valley between her breasts and suckle her tender nipples. He imagined her crying out his name as she climaxed, her skin flushed with passion.

Cursing his erection, Luc mounted Baron and headed toward Brooks's. He was deep in thought when a carriage pulled up beside him and a woman stuck her head out the window.

"Westmore! You're back. How marvelous. You've been missed, you know."

With a smile Luc greeted Lady Blythe Carstairs, a wealthy young widow. Their short affair had lasted but two months. He had dropped her because he didn't like possessive women. The sex had been good, but not good enough to put up with her demands.

"How kind of you to say so, Lady Blythe,"

Luc said courteously.

"You can't know how much I've missed you, Westmore," Blythe said in a throaty purr. "I'm still available to you, my dear. We had some good times together, if you recall."

"Indeed," Luc said, wishing she would drive on. He wasn't about to take up again with Blythe. He'd analyze his reason more thoroughly later. "I'll keep that in mind. Good day, my lady."

"Westmore, wait!" Blythe said when he would have ridden off. "When can we get together again?"

"I'm afraid, dear lady, that's impossible. I'm newly married, you see, and must attend my wife."

"Married!" Blythe gasped. "Never say it's true. Who is she?"

"No one you know. Bliss comes from Cornwall."

Blythe gasped audibly. "My God! Whatever possessed you to marry a country mouse? It's so unexpected of you. Is it a love match, then?"

"I . . . didn't say that," Luc stammered.

"Excellent. Then I see no reason why you can't continue on as you have in the past. I'm sure we will meet again." She motioned to the coachman and the carriage rattled off.

If Luc wanted news of his marriage to spread, he had told the right person. Blythe was a notorious gossip. He continued on to Brooks's, but somehow his heart wasn't in it.

Bliss finished her bath and wrapped a sheet around herself while she waited for Mrs. Dunbar to return the dress she had carried off to freshen and press. She wanted to look her best when Luc arrived for dinner.

Suzy helped to tidy Bliss's hair and help her dress. Then Bliss paced while she waited for Luc. The dinner hour came and went. She rang for Partridge and asked if Lord Westmore had returned.

"Not yet, milady. Lord Westmore rarely takes dinner at home."

Bliss felt tears well up in her eyes. It had started already. Luc couldn't stay away from his old vices. Not even for her. But what did she expect? That he would change overnight? He probably didn't even remember he had a wife. A country nobody like herself couldn't compete with highborn society ladies. The sooner she learned that, the better off she'd be.

"I see," she choked out. "If it isn't too much trouble, would you ask Mrs. Dunbar to prepare a tray for me? I think I'll eat in my room tonight."

"No trouble at all, milady," Partridge said with a hint of sympathy.

Luc just couldn't concentrate on his cards. He had promised Bliss he'd return home for dinner and had deliberately let the dinner hour pass. He was trying to prove something to himself, but it wasn't working. Scooping up his winnings, he bade his companions good night.

"What ho, Westmore. Not leaving already, are you?" Lord Thomason asked. "You can't quit without allowing me to recoup my losses."

Luc had no sympathy for young Thomason, who was rapidly losing the bulk of his new bride's dowry. Luc already held several of Thomason's markers.

"Sorry, Thomason," Luc said, "but I must get home to my bride."

A collective gasp echoed through the card room.

"Surely you jest, Westmore," Lord Thomason said. "Men like you don't marry. How will London manage without its last rogue?"

"Very well, I would imagine," Luc said in parting.

Luc could feel dozens of pairs of eyes following him as he took his leave. His announcement had shocked his acquaintances into silence, but if he were perfectly truthful, his own shock was just as great. This need to return to Bliss was both unexpected and inexplicable.

As Luc rode past some of his old haunts he looked neither right nor left, feeling no compulsion to gamble or drink or whore.

Damn Bliss! How could she do this to him? He had been thoroughly satisfied with the life he had carved out for himself before he met her. His obsessive need for his wife stunned him.

What the hell was happening to him?

Luc entered his townhouse and stormed past William, who stood sentinel at the door. Taking the stairs two at a time, he burst into Bliss's room to confront his demons. But the moment he saw her, his mind went blank. He could think of nothing except taking her to bed and thrusting his randy cock inside her.

Chapter Thirteen

Startled by the sudden intrusion into her bedroom, Bliss dropped the book she was reading. When she saw Luc, she retrieved the book from her lap, too angry to acknowledge him, much less speak to him.

He strode into the room with the panache of a conquering hero. "I'm home," he announced grandly.

"So you are," Bliss replied without enthusiasm.

"Have you had dinner?"

"Hours ago."

"I'm hungry."

"Dinner is at nine o'clock," Bliss replied, repeating his own words.

Luc walked to the hearth and held his hands out to the heat. "Aren't you glad to see me?"

Carefully Bliss laid the book down in her lap, finally giving him her full attention. "Not especially. Should I be? What happened to bring you home early? Did one of your lovers rebuff you?"

"*You* brought me home, Bliss," Luc admitted sheepishly. "I wanted to make love to my wife."

Bliss yawned. "I'm not interested." Being at Luc's beck and call whenever he got the urge to make love to his own wife wasn't her idea of a happy marriage.

The implacable look on Luc's face made Bliss's heart race. Despite her sour disposition, anticipating Luc's lovemaking sent excitement rushing through her. However, she would not succumb to Luc without receiving at least a token apology for his inexcusable behavior.

"Not interested?" Luc repeated, clearly amused. "You're my wife!"

Bliss's eyebrows lifted. "How very clever of you to remember. I waited for you; the dinner hour came and went. You said you'd join me."

"I didn't say *positively* that I would join you. I'm not accustomed to being tied to a woman's apron strings. I like to come and go as I please."

"It pleases me to be alone tonight," Bliss retorted.

"Would it help if I apologized for leaving you alone this evening?"

Bliss's gaze lifted to his, softened. "Do you mean that?"

Luc found he meant it with all his heart. He touched her gently, his fingertips tracing the silken curve of her cheek. "Yes, every word."

Bliss made no protest as he drew her to her feet. His head lowered and he captured her mouth. The sweetness of her taste inspired him to part her lips with his tongue and deepen the kiss. Luc never tired of kissing Bliss. Her response was freely given, her passion stunning despite her lack of experience, unlike some of his previous lovers who pretended what they did not feel.

There was no pretense to Bliss. Her emotions were honest and uncomplicated. He kissed her and kissed her until he felt her melt against him, felt her legs buckle.

"Undress for me," he whispered as he broke off the kiss and stepped away from her. He reached out to steady her when she wobbled and then retreated.

She hesitated a long, breathless moment before she began undressing . . . very slowly, her provocative movements teasing him, tempting him. He was utterly transfixed. She unbuttoned her dress and shrugged out of the bodice. He groaned. Then, more slowly, she removed her stockings and shoes. She paused, her fingers clutching the hem of her chemise, her gaze meeting Luc's.

"Everything, Bliss."

He sensed her uncertainty as she lifted her chemise and stripped it off. He reached for her, but she skillfully evaded him.

"Not yet," Bliss said archly.

Luc's hands dropped to his sides, disappointment making his voice harsh. "What are you doing? I don't enjoy being teased."

"Don't you? Take off your clothes."

Luc's eyebrows shot up. "Are you giving me orders, love?"

She gave him a seductive smile that nearly melted the skin from his bones. "Turnabout is fair play."

He returned her grin. "It is, as long as we both get what we want in the end."

Her golden eyes sparkled mischievously. "I guarantee it."

His fingers tore at the buttons on his shirt, ripping the garment apart in a frantic effort to free himself of his clothes. He had grown so hard, he feared his erection would rip his trousers open.

"Wait!"

"Bloody hell, what is it now?"

She approached him with languid grace. Standing on tiptoe, she rubbed her breasts against his naked chest. His breath hitched; he grew harder, thicker. He ached.

"What are you up to, Bliss?"

She pointedly looked down at his erection. "What are *you* up to, my lord?"

"Far more than you are, my lady. What are you doing?"

"Giving us what we both want. But first . . ."

Luc knew immediately he wasn't going to like what "but first" meant. "What is it you want . . . clothes, jewels? Name it and it's yours — within reason, of course."

"It's not as simple as that, Luc. What I want is more of your attention. You changed the moment we reached London. I know I'm an unwanted wife, but can't you at least pretend there's something about me you like?"

Her lips began to tremble, as if she feared her next words would push Luc away instead of drawing him closer. But her anxiety didn't seem to affect her determination. "I want your promise to remain faithful for six months. Are you capable of giving that much of yourself to me for that short length of time?"

Luc scowled. "Only six months? What happens after that?" Why was he debating her time schedule? *Perhaps because Bliss only wants you for six months,* a voice inside him warned.

"That's for you to decide." Her arms

crept around his neck, her mouth so close to his, her breath warmed his lips.

His arms tightened around her. His need for her was so desperate, he would have agreed to anything. Remaining faithful for six months shouldn't be a hardship, for Bliss was the only woman he wanted . . . right now. How long would his obsession for her last? At least six months. He saw no problem with granting her request.

Scooping her into his arms, he carried her to the bed. Bliss scrambled into a sitting position. "Does this mean you won't bed anyone but me for six months?"

"I'm here, aren't I? If I didn't agree, I'd be headed out the door. You have me solely to yourself for six months. Does that please you?"

"Enormously. Oh, Luc, you won't regret it."

"How can I regret something we both want?"

He removed his boots and rolled his trousers down his legs, tossing them aside. His staff sprang free, jutting upward with a life of its own.

Bliss couldn't look away. Her mouth went bone dry as her appreciative gaze raked over him. A golden brown mat of hair covered his chest and groin. His arms were knotted with muscle, his loins and stomach lean and taut. His turgid flesh grew even more enormous as her gaze roved over him. The mattress dipped as he came down beside her.

A shudder rippled through her as a strong male hand cupped her breast, taking the tip in his fingers, stroking it softly. A shiver of pleasure trekked over her skin as he nuzzled her breasts, then licked the valley between them. His mouth captured her nipple; she felt the sensitive bud tauten against his tongue.

His mouth began inching downward, the roughness of his tongue leaving a trail of fire as he kissed and licked his way toward more intimate flesh. He gave a hoarse grunt when Bliss pushed him away and flung herself atop him.

"What the devil are you doing?"

"This," Bliss said, then covered his flat male nipple with her mouth.

He arched upward, seeking the warmth of her mouth. "Bloody hell!"

Ignoring his outburst, Bliss moved to the other nipple, teasing it with the tip of her tongue. Luc cursed again and tried to dislodge her.

Bliss raised her head. "I never want you to regret the six months of sexual favors you're withholding from your lovers."

Her lips fluttered against his stomach. He lurched against the butterfly pressure of her mouth. She didn't stop — she was too close to her goal. Her tongue found his sex, and she was surprised to discover a drop of moisture on the distended head. She lapped it up and closed her mouth over the hot blunt tip.

He gave a low groan. "Bliss, have mercy!"

His staff felt like velvet-covered iron beneath her tongue. Her teeth grazed its length; then she drew as much of him as she could into her mouth, savoring the musky scent of his arousal.

She moaned her approval when his hips began flexing restlessly beneath the soft sucking of her mouth. For several long moments she pleasured and aroused him, while he writhed and twisted beneath her loving.

"If you don't stop, this will be over all too soon," he warned in a rough growl.

"Not yet . . ."

She continued her gentle torture, her mouth playing upon him until he cursed and reared upward. Bliss bounced once and landed on her back. Luc pounced on her, rose up on his elbows to keep the bulk of his weight off her and gave her a deliciously wicked grin.

"Where did you learn that?" he asked.

"From you."

Bliss caught her breath as his hand slid down between their bodies and parted the tender folds between her thighs. She felt his finger slide inside her, then another, his thumb teasing her sensitive bud. A hum of pleasure burst from her chest.

The touching, the closeness, the intimacy seemed remarkably natural, as though they'd known each other a lifetime instead of merely weeks. She traced the indentations of his chest, every familiar muscle, every dip, every marvelous plane. Then her thoughts shattered when he positioned himself at her entrance and filled her.

With his hands gripping her hips, he rocked her against him, slowly at first, then with increasing vigor. Shuddering under the force of his thrusts, she writhed against him with desperate yearning. A roaring sounded in her ears as intense pressure built. Tossing her head wildly, she pumped her hips against him in frantic need.

When he lowered his head and latched onto her nipple, she arched and cried out his name. Exquisite pleasure spiraled upward, outward, inward, ebbing, flowing . . . until . . . Then it happened. She clung to him as she scaled the peak of rapture. Convulsions racked her as he continued to pump into her. Then he exploded, flooding her with his warm seed.

Bliss cradled his head where it rested against her breasts. She felt as if she could remain this way forever. If only Luc felt the same way, life would be perfect. But at least she'd have him to herself for six months. She sighed. If every aspect of their marriage could be as satisfying as the physical part, they would be blissfully happy till the end of their days.

Bliss knew she was being fanciful, that Luc had no inclination to settle down to one woman, but dreams were cheap and hurt no one. Dimly she wondered if she loved Luc. Could she enjoy the intimacies of sex with a man she didn't love? She didn't think so. She needed to believe that love existed between them.

Luc took a deep breath as a hard shudder vibrated through him. She felt it travel through him to her. He raised his head and kissed her mouth before rolling off her. Then he hugged her against him and held her close. That was the last thing Bliss recalled before drifting off to sleep.

When she woke the following morning, Luc was still sleeping beside her. She was so happy that he hadn't left her bed to go to his, she wanted to clap and laugh out loud.

Luc awakened slowly. When he stretched his legs and arms to work out the kinks, he felt the warmth of another body snuggled against him. His eyes flew open. Bliss was looking at him, her eyes crinkling with suppressed glee. It came to him like a bolt of lightning. He had spent the night in Bliss's bed! Bloody hell, that was not what he had intended.

He had wanted to make love to Bliss last night, that much was true. Thoughts of loving her had ruined his outing the previous evening. While trying to enjoy himself at his old haunts, he had pictured Bliss exactly as she was now, her hair tumbling around her shoulders, her skin flushed and her lips swollen from his kisses. The vision had ruined his enjoyment of the evening. Like a doting husband he had returned home, and like a doting husband he had fallen under Bliss's spell.

He rose abruptly and gathered up his discarded clothing.

Bliss rose up on her elbow. "Are you leaving?"

"Plumb is probably waiting to shave me and help me dress. We have a big day ahead of us, Bliss. We must spend at least five or six hours with Madame Bileau, so I'd like to get an early start."

"Who is Madame Bileau?"

"One of the best mantua makers in London. I suggest you ring for your maid. I'll meet you in the morning room in an hour."

Luc knew he was being deliberately abrupt, but he'd been startled to wake up in Bliss's bed. He had expected his need for Bliss to abate after he made love to her. Instead, he'd held her in his arms after making love and hadn't wanted to let her go. Devil take him! Something strange was happening to him, and he wasn't sure he liked it. It had begun the day he wed Bliss.

Or maybe not.

Perhaps it had started the day he saw her standing on the edge of the cliff.

Luc summoned his valet and began preparations for the day. He appeared in the dining room precisely one hour after he left Bliss's room. She hadn't arrived yet, so he filled his plate, picked up the newspaper and perused it while he ate.

Bliss arrived a few minutes later.

"Are you satisfied with your new maid?" Luc asked as he folded the paper and laid it beside his plate.

Bliss walked to the sideboard, studied the array of food and placed her preferences on her plate.

"Birdie seems capable enough." William seated her, poured her tea and promptly withdrew. "She's young, but surprisingly good at arranging hair."

Luc's gaze wandered over her, from her neatly coiffed sable hair to her breasts. Her travel-worn gown had seen better days, but he was about to remedy that. He wanted to dress his wife in the latest fashions and parade her before the *ton*. He froze with his fork halfway to his mouth. Where did that thought come from?

They ate in relative silence. Bliss's appetite was nearly as good as his, Luc noted, and he wondered how her body stayed so slim. A smile twitched his lips. Last night's vigorous bed sport must have left her as famished as it did him. Luc finished his breakfast and laid down his napkin.

"I'm ready whenever you are."

Bliss rose. "Just give me a moment to fetch my cloak."

Luc followed Bliss from the dining room. William handed him his hat and cane and held the door open when Bliss arrived a few minutes later. Luc had ordered his high-perch phaeton to be brought around earlier and he handed Bliss inside, taking up the reins himself.

"How far is it to Madame Bileau's?"

"Not far. She's the best London has to offer."

"Probably expensive, too," Bliss muttered.

"Indeed. However, you must be decked out in fashion if you expect to pass muster with the *ton*."

Bliss snorted. "Just how well dressed do you suppose a smuggler should be?"

He gave her a disapproving stare. "Never, ever mention that again. You are my wife; the past no longer matters."

Luc concentrated on the road, trying to ignore the jolt of fear Bliss's words gave him. What if Skillington found new evidence and came after Bliss? If Bathurst was in the country and unable to help Millie, what had happened to her? Had Skillington traced her to London?

"You're angry," Bliss said, shattering his introspection. "Since arriving in London, the only time we speak to one another is in bed. What have I done now?"

Luc regarded her sternly. "When you make mention of your illegal activities, it frightens me. I married you to save you from the hangman, and I'd hate to see my efforts wasted."

Bliss bristled. "I know exactly why you married me, Luc. You don't have to remind me."

Luc sighed. He certainly was making a mess of things. He didn't want to hurt Bliss. He truly cared for her or he wouldn't have taken such extreme measures to save her from her own folly. The difficulties they were having just proved how unsuited he was for married life.

Luc hauled on the reins before an elegant shop on Bond Street, and the carriage rolled to a stop. The wide street was lined with shops of every nature, and the people Bliss saw were dressed in the height of fashion. Luc hopped out, lifted Bliss to the sidewalk and escorted her to the door.

A small woman with bright eyes and fluttering hands met them. "Ah, Lord Westmore," she said in a heavily accented voice. "It's been a long time since you've brought me your custom." She cast a dismissive glance at Bliss. "What can I do for you today?"

"Madame Bileau, I present my wife, Viscountess Westmore, to you."

Madame's mouth worked soundlessly as she stared at Bliss. A moment later, she found her voice and her manners and dropped a curtsy. "My most humble felicitations on your marriage, my lady, my lord. How may I help you?"

"Lady Westmore needs a complete wardrobe, Madame. She'll require two frocks with appropriate accessories and undergarments immediately, as well as a gown for evening wear. At a later, not too distant date, she'll require morning dresses, walking dresses and two ball gowns. Oh, yes, and night wear. Something sheer."

"Luc!" Bliss hissed, mortified. But Madame seemed to understand, for she smiled and nodded. Then she clapped her hands and a helper appeared from behind a curtain.

"Bring materials and fashion dolls for Lord Westmore's perusal," she said crisply.

"You're ordering far too much," Bliss complained. "I only need a frock or two."

"London is not St. Ives," Luc replied. "Once you're introduced to society, you'll be on display."

Bliss blanched. "Can't I live quietly in the background?"

"I'm afraid that's impossible. Lady Braxton will call on you soon. She's planning a ball in our honor. I want you decked out in fashion for the affair, for you'll be thoroughly scrutinized."

Bliss groaned. Her life in St. Ives hadn't

been half as stressful as it promised to be in London. A smuggler's life was simple compared to that of a society matron. She didn't have the manners or knowledge to be the wife of a peer. She hadn't a clue how to dress or act.

Madame Bileau whisked Bliss away to a small dressing room where an assistant took measurements while Madame exclaimed over her hair and figure, seeming pleased with what she had to work with.

"I'm not sure about colors or styles," Bliss said hesitantly.

Madame made a dismissive motion with her hand. "Your husband has excellent taste, my lady. He will know exactly the styles and colors that suit you."

"I want nothing immodest," Bliss insisted.

Madame rolled her eyes. "Piffle. Today's styles will suit your slim figure perfectly. Let your husband decide."

Bliss wasn't pleased. Apparently, Luc was well known to Madame, which meant Madame dressed his mistresses. The thought of Luc paying for his lovers' finery was intolerable.

After she was measured, poked and prodded, Bliss was allowed to return to Luc. She found him surrounded by an array of fabrics the likes of which she had never seen. Silks, satins, muslins, brocades, velvets and filmy linens were spread out on a table for Luc's inspection.

"I prefer jewel tones for Bliss, but I think this champagne silk trimmed in lace will make a splendid ball gown," Luc said. Madame nodded her approval. "The ruby satin should do nicely for the second ball gown."

Luc pulled out length after length of fabrics and held each beneath Bliss's chin. Some he approved for day gowns, others for walking gowns, and some he discarded. When it came to night wear, he chose the sheerest material Madame had on hand. Bliss had little say in the selections. Luc seemed to know what he was doing, so she merely observed, though she wasn't certain she approved of all his choices.

Minutes stretched into hours. Tea and light refreshments were served while Luc selected fabrics and styles. Finally he rose and clapped on his hat.

"I think we are finished here, Madame. We'll require two day dresses by the day after tomorrow, and a gown suitable for the opera no later than a week from today. Can you have the remaining order ready in a fortnight?"

"Indeed, my lord, it will be as you say," Madame replied.

The door opened and a fashionably dressed woman, accompanied by her maid, breezed through. She stopped in her tracks when she saw Luc and tapped his chest playfully with her folded fan. "Westmore, you naughty boy, wherever have you been? I have missed you dreadfully."

"Hello, Lillian."

She extended her hand. Luc bowed over it, his lips not quite touching her fingers. Bliss had been standing some distance behind Luc, speaking to Madame, when she heard the door open. The sound of a woman's voice and the low rumble of Luc's acknowledgment had caught her attention.

"I heard you'd returned to London with a wife," Lillian said. "I can hardly credit it, my dear." She flicked her fan against the placket of his trousers. "Couldn't keep your trousers buttoned, hmmm? Such a pity. You're definitely not father material. I heard your wife is from the country."

Bliss saw Luc stiffen and wondered if he would defend her. He did.

"It would please me, madam, if you did not disparage my wife. I don't know if I'll be a good father, but when that time comes, I'm sure I will rise to the occasion."

Lillian snickered behind her fan. "Westmore, you're absolutely wicked. You *always* rise to the occasion. I've never known you to fail."

Bliss decided it was time to make her presence known. "I'm ready, Luc. Shall we go?"

"Lady Broadmore, may I present my lovely wife, Lady Westmore?"

Bliss extended her hand. Lillian stared at it as if she expected it to bite her. Sniffing disdainfully, she briefly touched Bliss's fingers.

"Is this your wife, Westmore? Why, she's —"

"Beautiful," Luc finished, his message clear. He smiled at Bliss. "Shall we go, love?"

Even though Bliss knew Luc's endearment was for Lady Broadmore's benefit, she still savored it. "It was a pleasure, my lady," Bliss tossed over her shoulder as she swept past Lillian.

Luc handed her into the carriage. "Was that one of your lovers?"

Luc shrugged. "You knew I was no angel. Admittedly, I've led a life of sin and excess. I never thought I'd have to account for my actions to a wife."

Bliss had nothing to say to that.

"We have a few more stops before we return home," Luc said. "You'll need slippers to match your dresses, and gloves and hats."

Bliss sighed and followed where Luc led. Once their shopping spree ended, however, she was able to relax and take in the scenery as the phaeton rattled through the streets of London. The sights were as varied as they were mind-boggling. People in St. Ives wouldn't believe the things she'd seen on the streets of this vast city.

Luc turned down a narrow side street to avoid congestion caused by an overturned cart in the middle of the thoroughfare. "I hope you know where you're going," Bliss said.

"I know London like the back of my hand. This street will eventually exit near Mayfair. It is rough and somewhat narrow, but negotiable if one is careful."

Bliss heard the sound of another vehicle approaching and glanced behind her. "That coach is coming up fast," she warned.

"I see it. Where the devil does he think he's going in such a hurry? Can't he see the street is too narrow for that kind of speed?"

Apparently not, for the driver increased his speed instead of reducing it.

"Bloody hell, he's coming right at us! Hold on."

Luc flicked the whip across the pair of matched grays' backs. Bliss held tight as the phaeton bumped along the cobblestones, clenching her teeth to keep them from rattling.

Luc spat out a curse. "What does the bastard think he's doing?" He guided the horses as close to the curb as he dared.

A frisson of fear shot up Bliss's spine. "Is there enough room from the coach to pass?"

"If there isn't, we're in big trouble."

The coach drew abreast of them. Luc held his horses under tight rein. The coach was plain black with thick curtains covering the windows, giving no hint as to the identity of the occupants. The coachman's face was disguised by a scarf. Then, to Luc's utter horror, he saw a pistol poke through the curtains.

"Duck!" he cried at the same time the pistol exploded. He felt a burning sensation near his ear and pulled back on the reins, allowing the other coach to race past. Were he alone he would have given chase. Instead, he brought the phaeton to a halt, his concern for Bliss obliterating every other emotion.

He pulled Bliss into his arms. "Are you all right?"

She shuddered. "I . . . think so. Did someone shoot at us?"

"I fear so."

"Why?"

"Damned if I know. Are you sure you're not hurt?"

"I'm sure. What about you?"

"I'm fine. Let's go home."

"Luc, you're bleeding!" She touched his neck, and her hand came away wet with blood.

Bliss fished out her handkerchief and dabbed at the blood. "The bullet grazed your neck below your ear, but it doesn't look life-threatening. You were lucky."

His expression grim, Luc flapped the reins and the horses stepped smartly forward.

"Who do you think did this?" Bliss asked.

"I don't know. I haven't slept with anyone's wife lately, nor have I insulted anyone. I haven't the foggiest idea who might want me dead."

"Luc, maybe the bullet was meant for me," she said quietly.

"That's preposterous. Who would want to harm you?"

"Maybe one of your former lovers. Or

perhaps Skillington."

"Skillington is an unlikely suspect. He's a lawman, not an assassin. As for my former lovers, they will shrug and move on. It's the way of things."

"Why would anyone want *you* dead?"

A vague suspicion began to form in Luc's mind, but he couldn't quite make himself believe it. "I don't know. Perhaps I have a powerful enemy I'm not aware of."

They reached Luc's townhouse. Bliss descended without his assistance and hurried around to help him down.

"Don't fuss, Bliss. The injury is just a scratch." He removed the bloody handkerchief he'd been holding against his neck as if to prove the insignificance of his wound. "See, the bleeding has already stopped."

"I hope Mrs. Dunbar has some antiseptic on hand. Infection can lead to serious consequences."

Luc opened the door and ushered Bliss inside. William glanced at the blood oozing from Luc's neck and rushed forth to offer his aid. "Milord, you're hurt!"

"It's nothing, William. Ask Mrs. Dunbar to bring a basin of hot water and antiseptic to my bedchamber."

"Immediately, milord."

Luc started up the staircase. Bliss followed close behind.

"Milord, let me assist you!"

Luc glanced over his shoulder, surprised to see Partridge looking most undignified as he took the stairs two at a time.

"Really, Partridge, it's only a scratch."

"But the blood . . ."

"Help His Lordship to his bedchamber," Bliss ordered. "The wound doesn't appear to be serious, but he has lost some blood."

Luc sighed. Bliss was making far too much of this, although the thought of someone using him for target practice certainly was unsettling.

Luc had just settled in a chair when Mrs. Dunbar bustled into the room. "This is beyond ridiculous, Mrs. Dunbar," he maintained. "A dab of antiseptic and I'll be right as rain."

The housekeeper pulled away the bloody cloth, cleansed the wound of blood and swabbed on antiseptic. "Shall I wrap a bandage around your neck?"

"There's no need."

"What happened, milord?"

"A bullet gone astray," Luc drawled.

"I suggest you stay out of the path of bullets in the future, milord."

Still trembling from Luc's close encounter with death, Bliss wholeheartedly agreed. Not once in her smuggling career had she been this frightened.

Who would want Luc dead?

Chapter Fourteen

Luc didn't go out that night. After dinner he escorted Bliss to her door and retired to his own room. It wasn't that he didn't want to make love to her; he just needed a clear mind to think through the events of the day.

Luc was no stranger to danger. He was a seasoned warrior, one who'd used cunning and skill to survive the Peninsular War. He and Bathurst had protected each other's backs and both had come home safely. But being used for target practice by an unknown assailant was a sneaky kind of warfare. Obviously, his enemy feared a face-to-face confrontation.

It was common knowledge that Luc was an expert swordsman and a crack shot. It was also known that he practiced fisticuffs at least once a week. Apparently, his enemy was too cowardly to meet him face to face, which deepened the mystery.

Who hated him enough to kill him? What had he done to earn an enemy?

Luc paced his room far into the night,

searching for answers. None came to mind, though somewhere from his deepest psyche the name Lady Sybil emerged. He shook his head to clear it. What the devil would Sybil have to do with the attack upon his person? The association made no sense.

Luc glanced at the door separating his room from Bliss's. His stomach clenched with need. Was it too late to go to her? Would she welcome him? The thought of making love to Bliss became a powerful need, and his cock reacted accordingly.

Bliss wasn't asleep. She could hear Luc prowling his room and was debating whether she should go to him when she heard the connecting door open. She sat up, waiting for Luc to cross the room to her.

"Why aren't you asleep?" His husky whisper was filled with need.

"I wasn't sleepy. Are you all right? I heard you pacing."

He dropped his robe and crawled into bed beside her. "I was trying to find answers."

Bliss scooted over to make room for him. "Did you find them?"

He caressed her cheek. "No, and I'm tired of looking. I'd rather make love to you."

She placed both hands on his hard-mus-cled chest. His skin felt hot and firm beneath her fingers. She ran her hands down his body, exploring his hair-roughened torso, his lean waist, his flat belly . . . his rigid erection.

Luc groaned. "Does that mean you're agreeable?"

Her hand closed around him. He tensed. Deliberately she fondled his hard length. "Did you doubt it?"

She loved the feel of him, the way he pulsed and jumped at her touch, the way he enjoyed and encouraged her explorations. She loved just about everything about him.

A growl of impatience rumbled from between Luc's clenched teeth as he flipped her atop him. Straddling his waist with her thighs, she leaned forward and kissed him. She held his gaze for several breathless moments, then scooted downward and impaled herself on his straining staff.

Luc took over from there, driving them both to a fever pitch of desire, fanning the flames devouring her with forceful thrusts that spun her into oblivion.

Bliss slowly came to her senses, aware that Luc was no longer lying beside her. She rose up on her elbows. "Are you leaving me?"

"You'll be more comfortable without me disturbing your sleep. My mind is so unsettled, I'll probably toss and turn the rest of the night."

So saying, he disappeared through the connecting door. Bliss was disappointed but understood. If someone were shooting at her, she'd certainly be upset. It bothered her, however, that she wasn't able to offer the comfort Luc needed. Though she satisfied him sexually, obviously her presence wasn't enough to ease his troubled spirit.

Though Luc had reached a decision of sorts during his long hours of contemplation, he had found no answers. His decision was to enlist Braxton's help. Two heads were better than one, and perhaps together they could come up with the name of the man who hated him enough to shoot him. Luc knew that Braxton's family hadn't arrived from the country yet, and that Ram would offer his help out of boredom if not in the name of friendship.

Luc had finished breakfast and was reading the paper when Bliss entered the breakfast room. She looked as tired as he felt. "Didn't you sleep after I left your bed?"

"A little," Bliss replied. "I hope you don't intend to go out today. Every time you leave the house, you're vulnerable to another attack."

"I can't hide in the house, Bliss. I'm not a coward."

"I never said you were." She inhaled sharply. "But what if you're attacked again?"

"I'll be prepared the next time. I don't intend to leave home unarmed. Are you satisfied?"

"I want to go with you. The first of my dresses should be finished today; you can take me out without being ashamed of me."

Luc's mouth tautened. "I've never been ashamed of you. You'd look lovely in rags. I didn't want you to feel you were lacking. That's the reason I wanted you to be decked out in style before we ventured out."

Luc's words clearly surprised Bliss. "Will you take me riding in the park?" she asked hopefully.

Luc's eyes shuttered. "Yes, as soon as I learn who wishes me dead and see him behind bars. I refuse to endanger your life."

Bliss laughed. "I've done that plenty of times without your help."

"Indeed. I wonder," he mused, "if it wouldn't be better to send you home. Your father said he would put a period to the smuggling. You could be in more danger here than in St. Ives."

"You want to send me away?"

"Only for your own safety."

Bliss's mulish expression persuaded Luc that she didn't think much of his idea.

"Absolutely not," Bliss said through clenched teeth. "You can't send me away; I won't go."

"Bliss —"

"No, Luc, don't even think it. You're not getting rid of me that easily. We're just a few days into the six months you promised me."

Luc cursed. "The situation has changed. I want you out of harm's way until matters are settled here."

"Forget it, Luc."

Luc threw down his napkin. He had wed the most contrary woman on earth. She didn't take orders, constantly spoke her mind and disregarded his advice. What was he going to do with her?

Accept her as she is, a small voice inside him whispered.

Luc uncoiled his long frame from the chair. "I have to work at my desk for a while. I won't be going out until later."

Bliss rose. "I'm going with you. You need protection."

"Like hell you will! How do you expect to protect me when I couldn't protect myself?"

Bliss drew herself up to her full, unimpressive height. "I was a smuggler. I defied

beggared anyone at the tables. But someone sure as hell wants me dead. I hoped you'd help me solve the mystery. Your instinct for this kind of thing is sharper than mine. Spying is your line of business, not mine."

"It *was* my line of business," Ram corrected. "Thank God Phoebe hasn't arrived from the country yet. She'd have my balls if she knew I was involving myself in danger again."

"You can always refuse," Luc reminded him. "Our friendship won't suffer for it. I understand that your family has to come first now."

"Oh, no, you don't. Do you think I'd let one of my two best friends face something like this alone?"

The footman arrived with their drinks. Ram sipped thoughtfully, and then said, "Let's put our heads together and see what we can come up with. Shall we begin with your past dealings? Who are your enemies?"

Luc chuckled. "I probably have lots of enemies, but none that would wish me dead." He fell silent. When he resumed speaking, his voice held a note of sadness. "I have this nagging feeling the attack has something to do with Sybil's death."

Ram pondered Luc's words. At length, he

said, "I see no connection."

"Neither can I, but the feeling persists. Have you any other ideas?"

"Well . . . I —"

"Good afternoon, gentlemen."

"Mayhew," Luc acknowledged. "I'd ask you to join us, but we're discussing a matter that wouldn't interest you."

"Sounds serious," Mayhew said. "Perhaps I can help."

"I doubt that," Braxton replied in Luc's stead. When Mayhew made no effort to leave, Ram said, "Shall we continue our conversation elsewhere, Westmore?"

"Indeed," Luc agreed. "Good day to you, Mayhew."

Mayhew finally got the hint. He bowed stiffly and strode off.

"There's Wellingham and Thomason. They look as if they're coming our way," Ram observed. "Let's get out of here."

They made a hasty exit and paused in the street. "What now?" Luc asked.

"Shouldn't you go home?"

"No. The farther away I keep from Bliss, the safer she'll be. Shall we try the tables at Brooks's?"

"What does your wife think about the attack upon your life?"

Luc laughed. "She wants to protect me.

333

She threw a fit when I suggested that she return to St. Ives."

Ram shook his head. "Women! Whatever would we do without them?"

"Precisely," Luc said dryly.

"You really do care for her, don't you, Westmore?"

"Of course, else I wouldn't have married her."

"Do you love her?"

"If that means am I willing to abandon the life I'm accustomed to, then no. Bliss asked for six months of my undivided attention, and I agreed. That's more than I've given any other woman."

Ram snorted. "How generous of you. Shall we take your carriage or mine?"

"Let's walk. It's not all that far."

"It's starting to rain."

"I don't mind if you don't." Ram gave him a hard look, then nodded. "Very well, we'll walk."

They strode off down the street. Daylight was beginning to fade when they entered Brooks's. They made straight for the tables, joining in a game of whist. When Luc began to lose, he dropped out. His mind wasn't on the cards. He watched the play for a while, then wandered off.

Friends hailed him. He stopped to chat,

evaluating each man he spoke to, watching his face for signs of animosity. He saw nothing, heard nothing but friendliness. Thomason and Wellingham came in later with a group of friends. Luc wasn't surprised to see Mayhew among them.

"Fancy meeting you here, Westmore," Wellingham said in greeting. "We were going to ask you to join us when we saw you and Braxton at White's earlier, but you took off before we could extend our invitation." He glanced about. "Where is Braxton?"

"He's playing whist, and winning as usual. My mind isn't on cards tonight, so I thought I'd watch the play."

"Something bothering you?" Mayhew asked. "Is married life beginning to lose its attraction?" He laughed. "Join the crowd. I doubt there's a happily married man here tonight."

"Don't include me in your assessment, Mayhew," Ram said as he joined the group. "I am more than happy with my marriage. I wouldn't trade it for anything."

"Have you quit the tables already?" Luc asked. "I thought you were winning."

"I was . . . I am, but I became bored with the play. I could use something to eat, Westmore. How about you?"

Luc had to admit he was hungry. He'd

had nothing but a light lunch at noon. "Let's adjourn to the dining room. They serve a decent roast beef here."

They made their farewells and strode off. "What do you think of that lot?" Luc asked once they were alone. "Did you detect any animosity there?"

"I saw nothing alarming," Ram said. "Thomason and Wellingham are decent sorts. Mayhew hasn't seemed happy since his marriage. He wouldn't have wed Barbara if he hadn't been empty in the pockets. If you're asking if any of those men could shoot an unarmed man, I doubt it."

"I don't know," Luc mused. "I have no proof, but there's something about Mayhew that bothers me."

"I don't know the man all that well; does he have a reason to hate you?"

"None that I know of. Perhaps it's my imagination."

A waiter seated them and took their order. The conversation turned to less troubling matters as they ate. Afterward, they tried the tables again. This time Luc won. He continued to win until Ram placed a hand on his shoulder and suggested that they leave.

Luc was more than willing. He wanted to go home to Bliss. It was late when they walked out into the dark, moonless night. The rain had slowed to a drizzle, but a thick fog had rolled in from the river. Luc pulled up his collar to shut out the dampness.

They walked along in companionable silence until they reached the street where they had left their carriages. Then they separated, each going to his own vehicle after bidding each other good night.

Luc's carriage was parked some distance behind Ram's. He strode off, unperturbed by the impenetrable darkness closing in on him as he left the circle of light provided by a streetlamp. He was but steps away from his carriage when four men rushed out from a dark alley between two buildings. By the time Luc realized he was in danger, he was surrounded by thugs wielding daggers and thick cudgels. Luc whipped out his pistol, which was primed and ready.

"What do you want?" Luc asked. "If it's my purse, you may have it."

A burly man whose face was muffled by a scarf waved his dagger in Luc's face in mute reply.

Luc's eyes narrowed as he slowly raised his pistol. "I'll take one of you with me. Who shall it be?"

"Ye haven't a chance, Lord Westmore. There are four of us to one of you."

They know my name. Someone had definitely put them up to this. "Who paid you?"

"Enough talk."

Suddenly Luc was attacked from all sides. He fired his pistol, heard a yelp and felt a moment of satisfaction. But it didn't last long. Someone lashed out with his dagger, slashing through Luc's sleeve and leaving a gash on his upper arm. But Luc wasn't entirely helpless. He drew out the hidden sword from his cane and fought his assailants with the skill of an accomplished swordsman.

Luc knew the odds were against him as he fought for survival, knew he was fighting a losing battle. Blood flowed freely from both him and his assailants. Little by little he was being forced toward the gaping hole of the alley. He lashed out with his sword again and again as daggers and cudgels came at him from every direction. He took a blow to his thigh that nearly sent him to his knees, and a cut on his arm below the elbow. Just when he thought the fight was lost, along with his life, Braxton appeared at his side.

"What took you so bloody long?" Luc growled.

"I wanted to see how many you could take down on your own," Ram drawled.

Ram's sword turned the tide. After a brief

scuffle the attackers slunk off, proving no match for the combined forces of Luc and Ram. Panting from exertion, Luc surveyed the dark, deserted street, finally allowing himself to relax his grip on his sword.

"How badly are you hurt?" Ram asked.

"A few bruises and cuts here and there. Nothing serious. I owe you my thanks."

"No thanks necessary. I was in my carriage, ready to drive away when I heard a shot. I realized you were in trouble, but it took a few minutes to set the brake and reach you. Did you learn anything from them?"

"They were after my life, not my purse."

"Come on, I'll drive you home."

"That's not necessary, I can . . . Damn!" When Luc took a step toward his conveyance, his leg gave out beneath him. Ram reached out to steady him.

Extending an arm for Luc to lean upon, Ram guided him toward his carriage and helped him into the seat. Then he climbed up beside him and took up the reins. The horses jerked forward into the deserted street. It wasn't a long drive, and they soon reached Luc's townhouse. Ram jumped to the ground and helped Luc down.

"I feel like a bloody fool," Luc said, leaning against Ram and limping up the steps. He stopped at the front door and searched his pocket for his key. Ram took it from him and inserted it in the lock. Luc pushed the door open and both men stepped into the hall.

"Ring for Partridge," Luc said. "He can take over from here."

Ram found the bell pull and gave it a yank. "I'll help you up the stairs. It might take a while for Partridge to get here."

Luc didn't object. He was beginning to feel a little woozy.

Ram picked up a candle from the hall table to light their way up the stairs. They had reached the halfway mark when Partridge arrived, his dressing robe flapping around his skinny ankles.

"Milord, you're hurt!" He set the candlestick he was carrying down on the hall table. "Let me assist you."

The commotion must have aroused Bliss, for she appeared at the top of the stairs, wearing a sheer nightgown and dressing robe. Luc groaned when he saw her shapely legs exposed beneath her filmy garments.

"Good God," Ram muttered, "is that Bliss? No wonder she has you in a dither. Very nice, Westmore; very nice indeed."

"Bliss, return to your room," Luc ordered.

Bliss ignored him as she bounded down the stairs. "What happened? Didn't I warn you about going out alone? Why must you court danger?"

"Leave off, Bliss," Luc growled.

"I'm Braxton," Ram said. "I was with Westmore when he was attacked by four armed thugs. Please move out of the way, madam. Westmore has suffered an injury and needs attention."

Bliss flattened herself against the wall as the trio inched past her. "How could you let this happen, Lord Braxton?" Bliss scolded. "Luc told me you were one of his best friends. Why didn't you protect him?"

"For God's sake, Bliss, enough," Luc growled. "I need Mrs. Dunbar's skill. Please summon her."

Bliss knew she was on the edge of hysteria but couldn't help herself. Twice someone had tried to kill Luc, and the next time he might succeed. She had a right to be worried. It took a few minutes for her to rouse the housekeeper from a deep sleep, but once Mrs. Dunbar understood she was needed, she rallied quickly. While she gathered what she needed to treat Luc's wounds, Bliss returned to his bedchamber.

Luc was sitting in a chair before the hearth. Partridge and Braxton had undressed him down to his trousers. Bliss saw the numerous cuts and bruises on his arms and torso and staggered backward. Then she pulled herself together and knelt beside him.

"Tell me what happened."

"It happened pretty much the way Braxton described. We had said our farewells and parted. I was very near my carriage when four men rushed me from a dark alleyway. They were armed with daggers and cudgels."

"If Luc hadn't shot off his pistol, I might not have known he was in trouble," Ram said, continuing where Luc had left off. "After a brief scuffle, the thugs scattered." He paused. "I don't believe we were properly introduced."

Luc did the honors. "Bliss, this is Ramsey Dunsmore, Earl of Braxton. You can thank him for saving my life."

Ram bowed. "My pleasure, Lady Westmore. My wife is due to return from the country soon; you can expect a call from her."

"The pleasure is all mine, Lord Braxton," Bliss said. "Thank you for saving Luc's life."

Mrs. Dunbar chose that moment to shuffle into the room. She wore a practical woolen robe belted at the waist and carried a basket over her arm. William entered behind her bearing a basin of steaming water. Plumb trailed behind.

"What have you done now, milord?" Mrs. Dunbar asked in a no-nonsense tone.

"Someone attacked him," Bliss answered.

"So it appears. Well, let me have a look."

Her gaze slid over each wound as her fingers probed and prodded Luc's naked torso. "Not too bad," she said after a lengthy assessment. "That nasty slash on your upper arm is the only one that will need stitching. Salve and a bandage will do for the rest."

Mrs. Dunbar set to work immediately. She took care of the stitching first, then treated Luc's bruises and numerous cuts.

"Is there anything else that needs attention?" she asked.

"No, thank you, Mrs. Dunbar. You can return to your bed."

"Wait," Ram said as the housekeeper prepared to leave. "I believe Lord Westmore suffered a leg injury. Perhaps you should check it for broken bones."

A cry of distress left Bliss's lips.

Mrs. Dunbar turned back to Luc. "Where were you injured, milord?"

"My right thigh got in the way of a

cudgel," Luc drawled. "I'm sure it isn't broken."

"Let me be the judge of that." She knelt at his feet and touched his right thigh. Luc jerked.

"Hmmm," Mrs. Dunbar murmured. She probed deeper and moved the leg this way and that. "I believe there are no broken bones. If you'd like, I can send William for the doctor."

"I'll take your word for it," Luc said. "Good night."

When William started to follow Mrs. Dunbar out the door, Luc stopped him.

"William, please awaken Appleby and ask him to take Lord Braxton to fetch his carriage." To Ram, he said, "Thank you, my good friend. We'll speak soon. These attacks must stop."

Bliss silently agreed. Whoever wanted Luc dead wasn't going to give up until he saw Luc in his coffin. "I'll see Lord Braxton out while Plumb helps you into bed."

Ram followed Bliss out the door. "I can see myself out, Lady Westmore. I know you'd rather be with your husband."

"I wanted to talk to you out of Luc's hearing," Bliss confided. "Is there anything helpful you can tell me? These attempts on Luc's life are frightening me."

"Unfortunately, I have no idea who is behind the attacks, nor does Luc. We made the rounds tonight to see what we could turn up, and came away without a clue."

"Is there nothing you can do? Am I just supposed to sit back and wait for another attempt on my husband's life?"

"I'll do whatever I can," Ram replied. "First thing in the morning, I intend to hire Bow Street Runners. One way or another, we'll solve this mystery." He searched her face. "You love him very much, don't you?"

Bliss flushed but didn't deny it. "Is it that obvious?"

"To me it is."

"What did Luc tell you about our marriage?"

"Everything."

"Everything?"

"I am aware of your . . . er . . . former profession."

"Then you know Luc married me to save me from the hangman. He doesn't love me, Lord Braxton. He promised me six months of faithfulness, but after that, I expect him to return to his former lovers and dissolute ways."

"You're not giving Luc enough credit. I doubt he would have married you if he didn't want to, and I know him better than you do."

Bliss's heart leaped, but she didn't dare hope.

"Luc needs someone like you, just as I needed Phoebe and Bathurst needed Olivia. Even unrepentant rogues can be reformed. Take it from someone who's been there and fell hard."

"You don't have to make me feel better, my lord," Bliss said, "but thank you anyway."

"Good night, my lady. Take care of your husband."

Bliss closed the door behind Ram and hurried back to the bedroom. She found Luc in bed, with Plumb fussing over him like a mother hen. Partridge had departed.

"Thank you, Plumb, you may go," Bliss said.

"Are you sure, milady? I don't mind staying up in the event His Lordship has need of me."

"I can manage from here, Plumb. Go to bed."

Plumb left, albeit reluctantly. Bliss firmly closed the door behind him. Then she turned to confront Luc, hands on hips, angry tears spilling from her amber eyes.

She stamped her foot. "How dare you! I

warned you not to go out tonight."

Luc sighed. "Come to bed, Bliss. I'm too weary to argue with you."

She picked up the candlestick from the nightstand and held it over him. "I want to see the bruise on your thigh."

"You heard Mrs. Dunbar. The leg isn't broken."

Bliss grasped the cover and pulled it aside. The livid bruise on Luc's thigh gleamed darkly in the dancing candlelight. She sucked in her breath and let it out slowly. "No wonder you couldn't walk on your own."

He pulled the cover up to his waist. "Quit fussing and come to bed."

Bliss shed her robe. She started to climb into bed when Luc's growl stopped her. "What?" she said.

"If I could see through your gown and robe, so could Braxton and the others."

Bliss puffed out an angry breath. "Excuse me for not dressing properly, but I was more concerned about you than my appearance."

Luc grabbed her and pulled her into bed. "No more arguments, love. I need you."

Bliss slipped from his grasp. "What you need is rest. I shudder to think what would have happened if your friend Braxton had not intervened. Must you be so reckless, Luc?"

Luc pulled her against him. "Don't scold, Bliss. Let me love you."

"No, you'll hurt yourself."

He turned her on her side and snuggled behind her. His hand slid between her thighs, touching her intimately. His fingers came away wet with her dew. "You're ready for me."

"I'm not."

He held his damp fingers up for her inspection. "I think you are."

Allowing her no further argument, he lifted her leg, opened the petals of her sex with his fingers and entered her in one forceful thrust.

Bliss choked out a moan. She'd had no idea there were so many different ways to make love. But Luc, mindful of his injuries, had found a way to satisfy both her and himself without aggravating his injury.

They climaxed simultaneously, exploding in jolt after jolt of endless passion, clinging together in the blissful aftermath.

Chapter Fifteen

Bliss tried to convince Luc to stay in bed the next morning but he stubbornly refused. He wanted to be up and about his business.

"Will you stay in bed until noon?" Bliss wheedled. "Your bruised leg needs a period of healing."

"Bliss —"

"Please, Luc, for me."

"Very well, if you insist. Instruct Plumb to attend me. He can shave me while I'm cooling my heels in bed."

"I'll bring up tea and toasted bread. That should hold you until Cook can prepare something more substantial."

Stifling a grin, Bliss hurried to the kitchen, where she found Mrs. Dunbar and Cook discussing the day's menu.

"What can I do for you, milady?" Mrs. Dunbar asked. "Does His Lordship require my assistance?"

"No, but I do. His Lordship insists on getting out of bed today."

The housekeeper shook her head and

sighed. "I expected he would."

"You know how stubborn he is," Bliss said, and Mrs. Dunbar nodded in agreement. "I hoped you might help me. Does your knowledge of herbs include sleeping potions? Can you prepare something to put in Luc's tea to make him sleep several hours? He really shouldn't be roaming about the city, making a target of himself. I'm sure you're aware that his life has been threatened twice in as many days."

"The entire household is aware of His Lordship's difficulty."

"Will you do as I ask? It's for His Lordship's own good."

"Of course; how can I refuse? We'll dose Lord Westmore's tea with valerian; he'll never suspect."

"You took long enough," Luc groused when Bliss returned with a tray holding a pot of tea and a plate of toasted bread. He was sitting up in bed, a sour expression on his face.

"I'm sorry. I had to find Plumb and give him your instructions." She poured the tea and handed the cup to him. "I told him to wait until after you've finished your tea."

"I don't know why you're fussing, love," Luc said in a conciliatory tone. "I'm fine."

"Drink your tea."

Luc sipped his tea until his cup was empty. Then he nibbled on the toast while Bliss poured him a second cup. He drank that in one gulp and pushed the tray away. "I feel like a bloody invalid. Where's Plumb?"

Bliss removed the tray from his lap and fluffed his pillow. "How do you feel?"

"Like I've been run over by a carriage. What's that got to do with anything? I'm not sick. A few aches and pains never stopped me before; why should they now?"

Bliss sighed. "Lie back and relax while I summon Plumb."

Luc grumbled beneath his breath. Ignoring him, Bliss left. If the herb-laced tea didn't work, she'd never be able to keep Luc in bed.

While silently berating himself for giving in to Bliss, Luc had to admit he probably wouldn't have been able to walk down the stairs on his own. Why did Bliss have to be right? Perhaps that was why he'd never considered marriage before. He didn't like the constrictions. He smiled. On the other hand, marriage did have its benefits.

As Luc contemplated those benefits, he began to feel drowsy, and then he lost the ability to connect his thoughts coherently.

What the devil was wrong with him? He was suddenly too tired to hold his eyes open. What had Bliss done? He wasn't feeling at all like himself. It was as if he were floating and looking down upon himself. Then he knew no more.

"He's sleeping," Bliss said, motioning for Mrs. Dunbar to follow her into Luc's bedchamber. "It's safe to change his bandage and inspect the stitches now."

Mrs. Dunbar bustled past Bliss and leaned over her patient. Luc didn't move a muscle as she removed the bandage, spread the wound with salve and applied a fresh wrapping.

"Will you take a look at His Lordship's thigh? I know Luc wouldn't allow it if he were awake, but since he's sleeping . . ."

Bliss eased the blanket away from Luc's injured thigh, taking care to shield his privates. She stifled a cry when she saw the huge purple bruise and swollen flesh surrounding it.

"My word, that *is* a nasty-looking bruise," Mrs. Dunbar observed. "I recommend cold compresses to ease the swelling. I'll send William up with a basin of cold water and cloths. There's little else that can be done."

When William arrived with the cold

water, Bliss began applying cold compresses to Luc's bruised thigh while he remained blissfully asleep. Two hours later, after she noted a definite improvement, she left Luc to his sleep.

Daylight was fading when Bliss heard a loud bellow echoing down the staircase. Lifting her skirts so she wouldn't trip, she took the stairs two at a time and rushed into Luc's bedchamber. She came to a skidding halt when she saw him standing at the open window, as naked as the day he was born.

"Luc, what is it? You shouldn't be out of bed."

"Blast you and everyone else in this household! What did you do to me?" He gestured at the dark shadows outside the window. "It was the tea, wasn't it?"

"Don't take it out on the staff, it was my idea. You refused to remain in bed, so I asked Mrs. Dunbar for a sleeping potion to put in your tea."

He strode to the bell pull and gave it a yank. Plumb appeared almost immediately. "Are you ready to be shaved, milord?"

"I was ready hours ago," he snapped. "I'm going out. Lay out my clothes."

"Luc," Bliss pleaded, "listen to reason. What could possibly be more important than protecting your health?"

Luc waited until Plumb left to fetch hot water and his shaving gear before answering. "Making my own decisions. Now you know why I never wanted a wife. Don't interfere in my life, Bliss."

"I was only trying to keep you safe."

"I've lived this long without your help. Ah, here's Plumb. We'll discuss this later, wife."

Bliss shot him an angry look and stormed out, slamming the door behind her.

Dinner had just been announced when Luc appeared, newly shaven and dressed in black trousers, a yellow brocade waistcoat over a pristine white shirt embellished with lace, and a fitted black coat.

"May I join you? I haven't eaten all day."

Still upset over his boorish behavior, Bliss gave a curt nod.

"I'm sorry," Luc began. "I didn't mean to snap at you, but you must admit I had good reason."

"How do you feel?"

"Not bad, considering. The bruise on my thigh isn't nearly as painful, and I could swear the swelling has gone down. The stitches on my arm pull a bit, but it's nothing I can't handle."

He escorted Bliss into the dining room

and seated her. William came in bearing the first course. "Just put everything on the table, William; we'll serve ourselves," Luc instructed.

"This is nice," Bliss allowed. "We always dined informally at home. Sometimes Jenny even joined us."

Conversation lagged for lack of a safe subject, so they ate in silence. After dessert, Luc asked, "Would you like to attend the opera tonight? Braxton's private box is always available to me. I'll send a note around informing him of my intention to use it."

"Do you mean it?"

"I wouldn't ask if I didn't. It's still early. You'll have plenty of time to dress. While you're at it, I'll arrange for a couple of Bow Street Runners to provide guard duty."

"Lord Braxton has already taken care of that."

"What?"

Luc strode into the hall and peered out the side window. Sure enough, two men patrolled outside the house. Luc opened the door and beckoned to them.

"Do you intend to go out, milord?" one of the men asked.

"Yes. Did Braxton employ you?"

"He did. I'm Temple and this is Burns.

We've seen nothing out of the ordinary to-night."

"I'm taking my wife to the opera and I don't want anything or anyone to harm her." He glanced at his pocket watch. "We'll leave in an hour. You both may ride in the coach with us."

"No need, milord. We'll follow on horse-back and keep an eye on things from the outside. Lord Braxton informed us that attempts have been made on your life."

"Indeed. But your main duty is to protect my wife. She is to be guarded at all times."

"Your pardon, milord, but Lord Braxton hired us to protect you. He didn't seem to think your wife was in danger, but rest assured we'll keep an eye on her."

Luc nodded; the men retreated into the shadows. He closed the door and returned to the dining room.

"Milady has gone to her chamber, milord," William informed him. "She said to tell you she'd be ready in an hour. Birdie is with her now."

Luc wished he had thought to buy her some jewelry, but his mind had been on other matters. Precisely one hour later, Bliss appeared at the top of the stairs. Unprepared for her stunning beauty, Luc felt his mouth drop open. Then he recalled himself and waited for her to descend.

Bliss was exquisite in ruby satin trimmed with rosettes and pearls. Cut in the current Empire style, the gown was caught just below her breasts with a ribbon. The skirt was narrow, falling close to her body, the bodice square and low. Her elbow-length gloves hugged her arms like a second skin, and a shawl the same color as her gown rested in the crook of her arm. Luc made a note to compliment Madame Bileau when next he saw her.

Bliss should have rubies around her throat and hanging from her ears, Luc mused. Her sable hair had been done up in a French knot, emphasizing the slim line of her neck. As she descended the stairs, he could see her red slippers peeking out from beneath her skirt. He'd never seen a more fetching sight.

Then she stood before him, her amber eyes shining with excitement. "I'm ready."

Luc smiled down at her, and then his smile faded. He hadn't realized the gown was cut *that* low or so close to her body.

"What are you wearing under that?"

"Not much. Madame Bileau said the gown was to be worn with but a single garment underneath." She twirled for his inspection. "Does it meet with your approval?

Madame said it's the latest style."

"You look fabulous, as you well know, but I'm not entirely happy with the way the gown turned out. It's . . . rather revealing."

Laughing, Bliss handed him her shawl. "It's too late now. What opera are we going to see? I've never been to the opera, or to a play, for that matter." She sobered. "Are you sure you'll be safe?"

"Perfectly safe. We're going to the King's Theater in Haymarket to see *The Magic Flute*. I think you'll enjoy it." He laid the shawl across her shoulders and placed her hand in the crook of his arm.

William opened the door. The coach was waiting at the curb. Appleby set the step in place and Luc handed Bliss inside. After giving Appleby directions, he settled across from her.

"I hope those are the Runners following us," Bliss said after a nervous glance out the window. "What if they're —"

"They're Bow Street Runners," Luc assured her. "I spoke to them earlier. They're the reason I'm taking you to the opera tonight. They will protect you."

"I'm not the one in danger," she reminded him.

Luc let that remark slide by. He didn't want to get into it now. Instead, he talked about the opera and what Bliss could expect.

Soon they approached the horseshoe-shaped auditorium and lined up with the other conveyances awaiting their turn to discharge passengers. "Performances are always crowded," Luc explained, "and tonight is no exception. You're in for a treat, love. I believe the prince is here. That's his carriage — the one with the royal crest."

"The prince?" Bliss whispered. "Oh, my, I hadn't expected that. Do you know him?"

"Yes — quite well, actually."

A footman opened the door to their coach and handed them down. Her eyes bright and shiny in the sparkle of the carriage lamps, Bliss took Luc's proffered arm and tried to look everywhere at once as he escorted her inside. The auditorium was lined in five tiers of boxes, rising one above the other, and the huge gallery appeared large enough to hold several thousand people. Luc led her up two flights of stairs, then stopped before a box and drew the curtain aside so she could enter.

The breath caught in Bliss's throat. The box was elegantly appointed, sporting purple velvet curtains and chair seats. She moved to the front of the box and chose a seat next to the rail. Luc sat down beside her.

"What do you think?" he asked.

"It's . . . I can't find the words. I can hardly wait for the performance to begin." She searched the rows of boxes. "Which box belongs to the prince?"

"Look to your right. He's just entering his box. He's surrounded by so many people, you can hardly see him. You're not missing much," he chuckled.

Bliss was still gawking at the prince's box when the curtain behind them parted, admitting Lord Braxton and a woman Bliss supposed was his wife.

Luc rose. "Braxton, did you get my note? I hope I'm not imposing."

"Not a bit. I received your note and decided it was a perfect time to introduce your wife to Phoebe. She arrived from the country yesterday."

Introductions were made. Phoebe took the seat beside Bliss while Luc and Ram sat behind them. Shyly Bliss glanced at the other woman; Luc hadn't told her how beautiful Braxton's wife was. Her shiny black hair was piled atop her head in an elegant style, and her intelligent blue eyes literally sparkled with curiosity.

Bliss was startled when Phoebe leaned close and confided, "I'm so glad Westmore found someone. I was beginning to worry about him."

"I'm not sure you'll approve of me," Bliss returned.

A smile lurked behind Phoebe's eyes as she patted Bliss's hand. "Ram told me everything, and I don't think any the less of you. I just arrived in town and I'm already planning a ball to introduce you to society."

Bliss swallowed hard. "I'm not sure I'm ready to meet society. I'd never even met anyone with a title until Luc came to St. Ives."

"You'll do just fine," Phoebe assured her.

"Ram told me you have a child?"

Phoebe bristled with pride. "We have a son. He's but a few months old but is already displaying a personality and temper to match his father's."

Then the house lights were snuffed out and Bliss turned her attention to the opera. It was wonderful and magical. The singing was superb even if she couldn't understand the words. When intermission came, Bliss sat back in her chair and sighed.

"How did you enjoy the performance thus far?" Luc asked.

"Very much. Thank you for bringing me."

"Would you care to go downstairs for refreshments? Or shall I bring you something?"

"I'll go with you. I don't want to miss anything."

"We'll go down, too," Phoebe said.

Bliss soon found herself standing in a crush of people. Somehow they became separated from Lord and Lady Braxton, but she clung to Luc with desperate tenacity. Bliss was introduced to so many people, she was certain she'd never remember their names. They moved through the crowd until Luc was able to snag a glass of champagne for each of them. As she sipped the bubbly liquid, her gaze wandered over the crowded foyer. When she turned to remark on something to Luc, he was no longer beside her.

Panic seized her as she searched for him in the throng of people milling about. Crowded and jostled from every direction, she could hardly draw a breath. Her only hope to escape this crowd, she decided, was to return to the box.

"Lady Westmore."

A woman stepped into Bliss's path. Bliss recognized her immediately as Lady Broadmore, Luc's former paramour whom she had met at Madame Bileau's. "Good evening, Lady Broadmore. Are you enjoying the opera?"

Bliss thought the lady's smile was rather forced. "The opera is simply a place to be seen. I really can't say I enjoy all that caterwauling."

"I thought the singing superb," Bliss replied.

"How refreshing. Where is your husband?"

"We became separated."

"It's no wonder in this crush. Knowing Westmore as I do, he's probably making an assignation with one of his numerous lovers."

"Are you jealous?" Bliss shot back.

Lady Broadmore's eyes sparkled with malice. "Indeed not. I'm sure I'll see a great deal of him once he tires of you. I know Westmore well, my dear. He isn't attracted to women like you. He prefers bold, sophisticated women, not timid country misses. Furthermore, he discards his lovers as frequently as his shirts."

She stared at Bliss's middle. "He may have gotten you with child, but don't expect to domesticate him. He's not the type."

Bliss had nothing to say to that, for she suspected Lady Broadmore spoke the truth. She could very well be with child, but that was not the reason Luc had married her.

To Bliss's vast relief, Luc appeared at her

elbow. "There you are, love. Let's get out of this crush. You'll excuse us, won't you, Lillian?"

Lady Broadmore sent Luc a seductive smile. "Of course, my lord." Playfully she tapped his chin with her fan. "I expect to see you soon. My husband is returning to town next week."

"How fortunate for you, my lady," Luc said dryly.

When he said nothing more, Lady Broadmore flounced off. "What did Lillian say to you?" Luc asked as he guided Bliss through the throng of people.

"Not much. She just made it very clear that she expected to warm your bed in the near future. She believes quite seriously that you'll soon tire of your 'country miss,' as she so aptly referred to me."

They started up the staircase. "Pay her no heed. She's already found someone else."

"She's married," Bliss said. "Doesn't her husband care?"

"Lord Broadmore has mistresses to console him."

Aghast, Bliss said, "I was told London was a decadent place but I had no idea morals were so lax among married couples."

"You're naïve if you think marriages are

contracted for love. Most marriages are business transactions. After the wife provides an heir, both partners are free to seek lovers, as long as they're discreet. Discretion is not always the course followed, however, as Lillian has just demonstrated."

"I don't like London," Bliss said. "Why don't we retire to your country estate? Yes," she decided, warming to the subject, "it should be safe for you there, and I prefer country living."

When they reached Braxton's box, Luc felt a prickling sensation down the back of his neck. Whirling, he searched for the cause and saw nothing. The wall sconce had gone out; the corridor was not only dark but deserted. Before Luc could escort Bliss inside the box, a man stepped out from the shadows near the curtain. Luc shoved Bliss behind him when the man made a threatening move toward them.

Luc heard people approaching but didn't dare turn his gaze or his concentration away from the thug. Bliss had no such qualms and she screamed, "Help! Someone help!"

Moments later, Luc heard Braxton say, "What in blazes happened to the light? Hang on, I'm coming!"

A vile curse spewed from the thug's mouth as he took to his heels, disappearing down a rear exit that led to an alley. Braxton reached Luc and Bliss seconds later.

"What happened? Are you all right?"

"We're both fine," Luc answered.

"A man stepped out from the shadows," Bliss explained. "He would have attacked Luc if you had not arrived."

"He was only one man," Luc drawled. "I could have easily subdued him. Shall we take our seats? The opera is about to resume."

"I'll get Phoebe and join you. I left her behind when I heard Bliss's call for help. What happened to the light?"

"Deliberately snuffed out, I suppose."

"How can you be so unconcerned? You could have been killed," Bliss cried.

He seated her before he replied. "I doubt that. We're not even sure the man was armed. I think he just meant to frighten me. I wish I knew what this is all about. If I did, I'd take steps to stop it."

"Are you all right?" Phoebe asked as Ram ushered her into the box.

"A minor altercation," Luc explained.

Then the curtain rose, putting an end to the conversation. But Luc wasn't as entranced with the performance as Bliss seemed to be. The thought that someone would attack him at the opera, of all places, was disturbing. He had ordered the Runners to remain outside, assuming he and Bliss would be safe inside the theater. Who would go to such lengths to end his life? More importantly . . . why?

Once the opera ended, Luc hurried Bliss out the door and into their waiting carriage. Both Runners were nearby, keeping watch. Appleby closed the door, and moments later the coach rattled off into traffic.

"Have you thought any more about retiring to the country?" Bliss asked. "I really do think it would be a good idea."

"I'm not going anywhere, Bliss. But I think you should. Whoever is after me is determined. I don't want you hurt."

"I'm not going anywhere without you," Bliss informed him. "There are too many Lady Broadmores in London for my liking."

Luc sent her a wicked grin. "Jealous, my love?"

She shrugged. "I suppose. You promised me six months, and no one, not even Lady Broadmore, is going to rob me of them."

"What a fierce little cat you are." He stroked her cheek. "I promised you six months, and so you shall have them. Keeping you safe is what's worrying me, however."

His hand slid down the willowy column of

her neck, his fingers outlining the low neckline of her bodice. He heard her breath catch and decided the only way to change the subject was to occupy her thoughts with something else, something they both enjoyed.

His hand dipped into her bodice, finding an unfettered breast, covered by a single layer of material. A groan rumbled from his throat.

His hand cupped the warm mound of her breast, his fingertips caressing the nipple into a taut nub. Then he kissed her breathless. Bliss arched against him, making Luc wish he had instructed Appleby to take a turn or two around the park. A slow grin curved his lips as he wondered what the Runners would have made of that.

Reluctantly he removed his hand from Bliss's bodice and broke off the kiss. They scarcely had time to straighten their clothing before Appleby opened the door. Luc stepped down, swept Bliss into his arms and strode to the door.

"Luc, put me down. The Runners . . . Appleby . . ."

". . . will pay us no heed. You're dismissed for the night," Luc called over his shoulder to the Runners.

Appleby raced ahead of them and rapped

sharply on the door. William must have been waiting, for the door opened almost immediately. Luc strode for the staircase with Bliss still in his arms. He couldn't wait to make love to her. She had looked so delicious tonight, he wanted to taste her all over. He didn't set her on her feet until they were inside his bedchamber.

"I've never seen you so impatient," Bliss said as he began to undress her.

He stopped long enough to kiss her. "I beg to differ. I'm always eager to make love to you."

"Don't rip my dress," Bliss said when his hands became rough. "It cost a fortune."

Luc didn't care how many fortunes the blasted dress cost, he just wanted her out of it. Finally they were both naked. In a trice they were in bed, making glorious, abandoned love.

Afterward, while Bliss slept in his arms, he thought about the six months of fidelity he'd promised her. He'd never been faithful to one woman that long, but he really did think Bliss would last longer than the others. A year, perhaps? Six years? Sixty years? Good Lord, where had that thought come from?

The attacks on Luc stopped as inexplicably as they had begun. After a fortnight of nothing untoward happening, Luc dismissed the Runners and returned to his usual activities.

During that time, Bliss and Phoebe had become fast friends. Luc was pleased, for Bliss had not as yet been accepted into society. He had thumbed his nose at the *ton* once too often, and Bliss was paying for his slights. The ball the Braxtons were giving to introduce Bliss to society should help establish her social standing, especially since Bathurst had agreed to attend. It never hurt to have a marquis in attendance, and his lovely Olivia would accompany him.

"Are you excited about the ball?" Luc asked over breakfast one morning. "The champagne-colored gown will look lovely on you. You'll be the belle of the ball."

"I don't want to be the belle of the ball," Bliss groused. "I don't even want to attend the ball. Your friends don't like me."

"Most of my friends don't even know you, and those who do, like you very much."

"I'm not talking about your male friends." She sent him a dark look. "Speaking of your friends, they see more of you than I do."

"I've honored my pledge to you, Bliss. You're the only woman in my life, the only

370

woman in my bed. I can't just drop my friends. They'd think I was in love with my wife and couldn't bear to tear myself away."

Bliss threw down her napkin and leaped to her feet. "Damn you! I know you don't love me, but do you have to rub it in?" Spinning on her heel, she stormed off.

Luc spat out a curse. He couldn't believe those words had come out of his mouth. He really did care for Bliss or he wouldn't be ignoring the invitations for romantic trysts that came his way each night. The problem was that he was afraid to spend too much time alone with her. Once Bliss was introduced to society, Luc felt certain that invitations would start arriving and they'd spend more time together in the safer setting of social events.

As the days passed, Luc had the strange feeling that he was being stalked. The sensation wasn't something he could prove, yet it plagued him wherever he went.

Three days before the ball, a message arrived while Luc and Bliss were eating breakfast. Partridge brought it to Luc on a silver salver. The message was written on a single sheet of paper and folded over. Luc read it quickly, then stopped Partridge before he departed.

"Who brought this?"

"A street urchin, milord."

"Where is he now?"

"He handed me the note and ran off. Bad news, milord?"

"Er . . . no, thank you, Partridge."

The butler bowed and retreated.

"What is it, Luc?"

Luc crumpled the paper in his hand, his expression fierce. "Nothing you need worry about." He rose. "Excuse me — I'll be in the library if you need me."

"Luc, don't you dare leave! Tell me what the note said. Who is it from?"

"I told you, it's nothing. We'll talk later." So saying, he strode from the room.

Once in the study with the door shut, Luc carefully reread the note. It was a warning, cautioning him that if he told anyone what Lady Sybil had confided to him before she threw herself into the Thames, his days were numbered.

So that's what the attacks upon his person had been all about, Luc mused. But what in God's name had Sybil told him that was so significant? He thought back over their last conversation, and the answer suddenly dawned on him.

The father of Sybil's child feared that Luc would ruin him if Sybil had confided in Luc, and was trying to murder Luc in order to silence him. Little did the bastard know that Sybil hadn't seen fit to divulge her lover's name.

Suddenly the door opened and Bliss burst into the room. "You can't dismiss me like that, Luc. I have a right to know if you're in trouble. You're not leaving this room until you tell me what this is all about."

Aware of Bliss's tenacity, Luc handed her the note. It was time she knew the truth about him.

Chapter Sixteen

Bliss read the note twice but still didn't understand it. "Who is Sybil? What did she tell you?"

Luc sighed. "She didn't tell me anything."

"Apparently, someone thinks she did. Where is she now?"

"Dead. She threw herself into the Thames."

Bliss inhaled sharply. "Why?"

"Sit down, Bliss. This story is long and ugly. When I finish, you'll understand the kind of man I really am."

"You're frightening me, Luc. What did you do? You didn't push the lady in the river, did you?"

Luc looked away. "I might as well have. I was the last person to see Sybil alive. We were . . . we had . . . arranged a tryst at an inn on the outskirts of London."

"Oh."

"I told you it wasn't pretty."

"Go on."

"I was preparing to leave when she said I had to marry her. She wasn't a virgin, Bliss. I knew that before I agreed to meet her. I don't make a habit of despoiling virgins."

"You refused to marry her," Bliss guessed.

"I wish that were all there was to it. Sybil finally admitted she was carrying her lover's child. Her *married* lover. She begged me to marry her, and I refused. But I told her to be patient, that I would find her a husband within a fortnight. I knew several second and third sons who would gladly have married Sybil for her generous dowry, child or no child."

"Why did she choose you for a husband?"

"I suppose because of my scandalous reputation. She figured marriage wouldn't stop my decadent way of life, and that I wouldn't care if she continued seeing her married lover. She was wrong, however, to think I would accept another man's child."

A long silence ensued. Luc was the first to speak. "When Sybil was found floating in the river, I was overwhelmed with guilt. I felt as if I had pushed her into the water myself. Had I agreed to marry her, she'd still be alive."

"You promised to find her a husband."

"Nevertheless, if I'd realized how desperate she was, I would have done things differently."

"Would you have married her?"

"God, I don't know. I might have, to save her life. Her senseless death is not something I can dismiss." He closed his eyes and swallowed hard. "I should have married her."

"It was guilt that drove you to St. Ives," Bliss surmised. "Am I to assume that you gave up sex because your guilt demanded it?"

A smile kicked up one corner of Luc's mouth. "We both know how that ended."

Bliss glanced at the note. "This is ridiculous. Your life is being threatened because of information you don't even have. Is there nothing you can do to resolve this?"

"Even if I knew who fathered Sybil's child, there's little I could do about it. Sybil's parents were devastated by her death. They assumed it was an accident. Bringing this all up again would only torment them."

"Meanwhile, your life is still in danger." She stamped her foot emphatically. "That simply won't do, Luc! If you won't do something, I will."

Amusement colored his words. "What, pray tell, do you intend to do?"

"Go underground, if I have to. Follow you around to make sure no one attacks you. There are any number of things I can do. Don't forget, I operated outside the law for a long time."

"How can I forget when you keep reminding me?" Luc said dryly. "You're not to meddle, understand?"

"But, Luc —"

"No more, Bliss. I'm going to do this my way." He rose. "Concentrate on the ball. Phoebe went to a lot of trouble for us, and I want it to go off without a hitch. Everyone who's anyone will be there."

"What are you going to do?"

"I have something in mind, but I'll need Braxton and Bathurst for it to work. Fortunately, Bathurst just arrived in town. I'm going to send notes around, asking them to meet me here at two o'clock."

"Can I attend the meeting?"

"Absolutely not! Why don't you visit Phoebe this afternoon? In fact, I insist upon it. I'll tell Braxton to inform Phoebe of your visit. With the ball but three days away, I'm sure you two will have a great deal to discuss. William will accompany you."

Luc left before Bliss could offer an argument.

Luc prowled his study, waiting for Braxton and Bathurst to arrive. He had gone over his plan again and again, and though it had flaws, he was convinced it would work, unless Bliss interfered. Her meddling could ruin everything. In an effort to foil her curiosity, he'd sent her off with William five minutes before his fellow rogues were to arrive. The only thing that bothered him was Bliss's willing compliance. It wasn't like her to give in so easily.

Braxton and Bathurst arrived together promptly at two o'clock.

"What's this all about?" Ram asked. "Were you attacked again?"

"Braxton explained your problem on the way over here," Gabriel, Lord Bathurst, said. "How can we help you?"

Luc offered Gabriel his hand. "Good to see you, Bathurst. Will you remain in town for the season?"

"Yes. We arrived yesterday so we could attend the ball Phoebe is giving in your honor. Olivia is eager to meet your bride. Congratulations." A wicked grin turned up the corners of his mouth. "I take it celibacy didn't agree with you. I must admit, old boy, you're the last person I expected to see leg-shackled."

"Ours isn't a love match," Luc muttered.

Ram and Gabriel exchanged amused

looks. "For a rogue it never is . . . at first," Ram drawled.

"All levity aside, gentlemen, I have a matter of grave importance to discuss with you."

"So we assumed," Gabriel said.

Luc handed the threatening note to Ram. "This arrived this morning."

Ram perused it and offered it to Gabriel. Gabriel's eyebrows rose. "Now we know why you were attacked. The father of Lady Sybil's child would be ruined if it became known that he was responsible for her death. Do you have any idea who it is?"

"No. That's what makes this so bloody stupid. Sybil refused to divulge the man's name. All I know is that he's married."

Ram stroked his chin. "Apparently, you have a plan to draw the man out of hiding. Do you want to share it?"

"First things first. How big of a bash has Phoebe planned for Saturday night, Braxton?"

"She's invited everyone. It's going to be a terrible crush, but she wanted to do it up right for you and Bliss."

"Good," Luc said. "Then we can assume my nemesis will attend."

"I don't follow you," Gabriel said.

"It's simple," Luc explained. "You and

379

Braxton are going to spread rumors."

"What kind of rumors?"

"You're going to mention, quite accidentally, of course, that I know something about Lady Sybil's death that could ruin a member of the *ton*."

"Damn, you do enjoy living dangerously, don't you?" Ram said. "You're deliberately placing yourself in harm's way. If your man is at the ball, he can easily find you."

"That's what I'm hoping," Luc replied. "I'm going to make myself an easy target. The renewed gossip and speculation about Sybil's death will make him desperate to silence me . . . permanently."

Gabriel shook his head. "It's too dangerous. Both Braxton and I will try to protect you, but we can't guarantee that the culprit won't get past our scrutiny in the crush of people."

"That's what I'm hoping," Luc said. "I don't want either of you following me and scaring him away. I want a face-to-face confrontation. I want to look the bastard in the eye and let him know what I think of him. I intend to wander off alone, making myself an irresistible target. Don't worry, I'll be armed. Your job is to feed information into the gossip mill before the ball; I'll take care of the rest."

"I don't like it," Ram groused. "Do you enjoy putting yourself in danger?"

"Not especially, but I don't have any other choice. I want this settled once and for all, before Bliss is dragged into it."

"I can understand that," Gabriel said. "Are you sure, very sure you want to go through with this?"

"Positive. Will you do your part?"

"Aye, but I don't like it," Ram growled.

"Same here," Gabriel echoed. "Braxton and I will do our best to protect you and keep track of your wife. Both Olivia and I are quite anxious to meet her. Anyone who could bring the last rogue to his knees is tops in my book. It's about time you joined those of us who have already fallen."

"I told you, it's not a —"

"We know, we know," Bathurst laughed, "it's not a love match. Methinks you protest too much."

Bliss crouched outside the study, her ear pressed to the door. William had believed her when she'd said she had forgotten her reticule and had to return to the house, and he patiently waited in the coach for her to return while she eavesdropped on Luc and his friends. She hadn't heard everything, but had caught enough of their plan to re-

381

alize what Luc intended.

When they began to speak of other things, Bliss tiptoed away. After a brief apology to William, she stepped into the coach and it rattled off.

During the short drive, Bliss mulled over what she had heard. Luc's idea to lure his attacker into the open was dangerous and foolhardy. Though she knew she would not be able to dissuade him, there was something she *could* do. She wouldn't let Luc out of her sight the entire evening of the ball. She'd cling to him as if they were joined at the hip. And she'd be armed. On her next outing, she intended to purchase a pistol small enough to fit into her reticule.

Luc smiled as he roamed through White's that evening. Braxton and Bathurst had done an excellent job of bringing Lady Sybil's death back to the tip of everyone's tongue. Bits and pieces of gossip had already reached him. Lord Thomason and Lord Darlington were the first to inform him of the gossip currently making the rounds.

"Don't know who stirred up ancient news, old boy," Thomason said. "Sybil has been dead for months. Still," he mused, "there was some question about her death.

It was all rather mysterious, if you recall."

"I would take it as a compliment if you confided in us," Darlington said. "Exactly what *do* you know, Westmore?"

Since Thomason was newly wed, Luc had no reason to suspect him. Darlington, on the other hand, was an unknown. "I haven't heard the gossip, so I have no idea what you're talking about."

Wellingham joined them in time to hear Luc's comment. "Come now, Westmore, it's common knowledge that Lady Sybil's death hit you hard. She's the reason you gave up sex and left town. We'd all like to know the secrets you're hiding."

Since Wellingham was happily married, Luc doubted he would have taken up with Sybil, but no one was above suspicion. Luc declined to answer the questions posed to him and politely excused himself. He left White's, more than satisfied with the way his friends had revived the interest in Sybil's death.

At Boodles's, Luc was besieged by avid gossip seekers. He pretended innocence and dismissed the gossip, but purposely left everyone wanting more than the tidbits of information they had garnered. From Boodles's he went to Crocker's gambling hall, and so it went, until he decided to

might be true for Luc, it wasn't for her. She loved him. Unfortunately, he didn't share her sentiments.

Despite Luc's reluctance to confide in her, she was determined to save his life. Her thoughts scattered when Luc stripped off her nightgown and began to kiss her: her throat, the corner of her mouth, her lips. She couldn't find the will to maintain her anger. Instead, she melted into his arms, willingly sacrificing herself upon the altar of his passion. But it wasn't really a sacrifice. Luc might not love her, but she loved him enough for both of them.

He kissed her senseless, cupping her breasts and kneading them while his tongue plunged rhythmically into her mouth. His taste, his touch, his scent filled her with longing. She whimpered into his mouth and arched against him, filled with a pulsing urgency to meld their bodies. But Luc was in no hurry as he continued to stoke her passion to a fever pitch.

White-hot heat scalded her insides as Luc's mouth descended, leaving a trail of fire as he licked and kissed his way down her body. When his mouth found the tender folds of skin between her thighs, his tongue darted into her liquid heat.

The first time Luc made love to her he

had branded her with his desire, and she had been his ever since, body and soul. She moaned as he grasped her hips, holding her firmly in place despite her wild gyrations.

Luc felt her response, felt the convulsive thrust of her hips against his mouth as animal hunger escalated between them. He couldn't wait much longer. His control nearly at the breaking point, Luc reared up and thrust deep, the erotic pleasure of feeling her contract around him almost too intense to bear.

Shuddering under the force of his thrusts, Bliss rocked back and forth against him, pulling him deep, needing all of him. The excruciating pressure built; sensation upon sensation pulsed through her body. Tossing her head wildly, she pumped her hips against him, whispering his name as frenzied need made her nearly incoherent. Her climax came abruptly and violently.

She screamed his name and sank her nails into the smooth flesh of his shoulders as feral pleasure rippled through her.

His muscles clenched and his neck corded; every tendon in his body hardened. He drove into her one final time, then stiffened. A hoarse cry burst from him, and then his orgasm exploded in a potent stream.

She clung to him in the aftermath, her

love for this exasperating man causing her to say things she knew she'd regret later. "I love you, Luc."

Luc stiffened. "What did you say?"

Bliss wished she could call the words back. "Nothing. I said nothing."

He reared up on his elbows and looked down at her. "You said you loved me. Is it true? Do you truly love me?"

Bliss shook her head, refusing to answer.

"Don't."

"Don't?"

"Don't love me. I'm not worthy. A young woman is dead because of me. I vowed to remain celibate for one year and didn't last three months. My reputation is tarnished." He took several gulps of air. "I'm not even sure I can remain faithful the entire six months you asked for. My past record is deplorable, love."

"Is there someone else?"

"No! It's just . . . my sins are legendary. I'm not sure I can make you happy."

"I can't stop loving you, Luc, no matter what you say. Look at Bathurst and Braxton. Have either one of them strayed since marrying?"

"Not to my knowledge, but both are desperately in love with their wives."

"And therein lies the problem," Bliss said

bitterly. "You don't love me. I know that, Luc, but I won't give up on you. You cared enough to marry me, and that should count for something."

"It should indeed," Luc replied in a puzzled voice. "After this business about Sybil is finished, perhaps we can sort this out. Meanwhile, don't put too much faith in me. I'm not sure I can live up to your standards. Right now, however, I want no one but you, and I love making love to you."

"But you don't love me."

His voice shook with unexplained emotion. "How the hell do I know? I've never asked for nor sought love. I'm not even sure I'm capable of loving."

Bliss felt something break inside her. Her heart? Nevertheless, she wasn't going to give up on Luc. He wasn't unredeemable, he just thought he was. She had faith in him. He needed to search his heart for answers.

"Forgive me, Luc, I didn't mean to upset you. I know you have a lot on your mind right now. You're right, we'll discuss this later." She cuddled against him. "Go to sleep, but don't expect me to leave your bed. I rather like it here."

"I have never asked a lady to leave my bed." He kissed her and curled his body around hers. "Good night, love."

The following days passed quickly. Bliss was a nervous wreck on the day of the ball. Though she knew her debut into society was important to Luc, she still felt like an outsider looking in. But mostly she worried about Luc.

Just as she had planned, she had slipped out one day with only Birdie for company and purchased a small silver pistol. It could only fire once, but once was all she needed. Her aim was true. Brady had taught her to shoot before they ventured into smuggling.

Sitting before the mirror, Bliss watched Birdie arrange her hair in a becoming style atop her head. When Birdie finished, she stood back to inspect her work.

"You look lovely, milady. Milord will be proud of you. Shall we get you into your dress?"

Though Bliss was in no hurry to face the *ton*, she knew she couldn't delay the inevitable. Besides, Phoebe had worked hard to make the ball a success.

The champagne silk ball gown fit Bliss's figure to perfection. The bodice, encrusted with seed pearls, dipped low, baring the tops of her breasts, and the full skirt, embellished with yards and yards of cream lace, belled out from a fitted waist. Champagne satin slippers with jeweled buckles and silk stockings tied above her knees with ribbons completed the captivating outfit.

Bliss felt like a princess. Birdie confirmed her silent assessment. "You look like royalty, milady."

"Indeed," Luc said from the doorway. He strolled into the room. Birdie withdrew, closing the door behind her.

Bliss couldn't help gaping at Luc. He was resplendent in a dark blue cutaway jacket and trousers, a champagne brocade waistcoat, a white shirt dripping with lace and black shoes with jeweled buckles. No matter what he wore, he cut an imposing figure.

Luc circled her slowly, stopping in front of her and tilting his head. "You look magnificent, but the gown lacks something."

Bliss's face fell. "I think it's perfect."

"It lacks sparkle."

Bliss had no idea what Luc was talking about.

When Luc took a velvet pouch from his pocket, Bliss still didn't know what he intended. But when he spilled the contents into his gloved palm, Bliss lost the ability to breathe.

"Are those diamonds?" she choked out.

"They belonged to my mother. Since I never intended to marry, I had forgotten about them. When I mentioned going out to buy jewelry for you, Partridge reminded me that my mother's diamonds still reposed in the safe. Will you wear them?"

Bliss released the breath she had been holding. "I left at home a few pieces of semi-precious jewelry that were gifts from my father, but I've never owned diamonds. They're magnificent. Are you sure you want me to wear them?"

"My mother earmarked them for my wife, and since you are my viscountess, they're yours." He handed her the earbobs and removed his gloves. "Turn around. I'll fasten the necklace while you attach the earbobs."

Obediently Bliss turned. She felt the coolness of diamonds surround her neck and really did feel like a princess. Once the diamonds were secured around her neck and in her ears, Luc turned her toward the mirror.

"What do you think?"

The necklace consisted of several strands of small diamonds attached to a large diamond pendant. Two large diamonds dangled from her ears. The diamonds seemed to change the appearance of the ball gown, making it even more elegant.

"There's something else," Luc said.

He stood behind her as she perused herself in the mirror. She lifted her eyes to his.

"What else could there be?"

"This," he said, holding up a tiara that matched the diamonds. "Don't move."

She stood perfectly still while Luc carefully affixed the tiara atop her shining curls. Then he stood back to admire her. "The jewelry completes you. You were splendid before, but you're without equal now."

"I don't know what to say," Bliss said, speechless for the first time in her life.

His blue eyes sparkled as brilliantly as the diamonds he had presented her. "You can express your gratitude later, after we return home." He found her new velvet cloak and placed it over her shoulders. "Are you ready to leave?"

Bliss pulled on her elbow-length gloves and picked up her reticule. The comforting weight of the pistol hidden inside eased her mind about tonight. She wanted to be prepared should someone make an attempt on Luc's life. "I'm ready."

Luc ushered her down the stairs. William handed him his hat and cane as they headed out the door. Since Braxton lived but a short distance away, Luc suggested that they walk, avoiding the crush of carriages. Fortunately, the weather was cooperating, and Bliss readily agreed.

They reached the Braxton mansion

without incident. They were early, which gave them a few minutes to chat with the Braxtons before joining them in the receiving line.

"Are you nervous?" Phoebe asked Bliss when Luc moved off to speak privately to Ram.

"Very. What if the *ton* decides I don't measure up? I'm only a squire's daughter, and everyone knows it."

Phoebe gave her arm a squeeze. "My father wasn't a nobleman, and I was accepted. Just be yourself and everyone will love you."

Bliss sincerely hoped Phoebe was right. Then Lord and Lady Bathurst arrived and Bliss met the marquis and his wife, Olivia, for the first time. Now she knew why the three handsome rogues had been the darlings of London before they wed. Each man was exceedingly handsome; each presented a powerful presence, exuded sensuality and had a body men envied and women vied for. Despite the attractiveness of Luc's friends, Bliss thought her husband outshone the other two.

Olivia was extraordinarily beautiful, with flaming red hair and green eyes. Bliss found it difficult to believe she was once a highwayman. Olivia squeezed Bliss's hand and promised to visit soon, hinting that they had a great deal in common.

The guests began to arrive, and Bliss had to concentrate on greeting people in the reception line. She stood beside Luc as members of the *ton*, whose names she was unlikely to remember, were introduced to her. She smiled until she thought her face would crack and murmured politely to each person presented to her.

Then Luc introduced her to the Earl of Mayhew. "Where is your lovely wife tonight, Mayhew?" Luc asked.

Lord Mayhew was about Luc's age and quite handsome, if one liked mustaches and sharp features. Bliss didn't.

"Barbara is in the country, awaiting the birth of my heir," Mayhew replied.

"What are you doing here?" Bliss blurted out. "Shouldn't you be with your wife?"

Mayhew turned his curious gaze to Bliss. "So you're Westmore's wife. I must say you're not what I expected." His eyes dropped to her flat stomach.

Bliss didn't like Mayhew and felt sorry for his wife. Then he moved on and others took his place. Wellingham and his wife, Darlington and his lady, and Lord Thomason, who had come without his wife. Lady Patrice, Bathurst's grandmother, the dowager marchioness of Bathurst, was the last to arrive.

"So you're the gel who brought Westmore up to scratch," the old lady cackled. "Never thought it would happen. Westmore needed taming, and I warrant you know just how to handle him. Felicitations, my dear."

Bliss blushed and murmured an answer. Then Lady Patrice moved on. Everyone must have arrived, for no one remained in line. Bliss breathed a sigh of relief when Phoebe said, "Shall we sit down a moment, Bliss? Ram can see to our guests while we rest our feet."

Bliss readily agreed. Phoebe led her through the crush of people to a small alcove behind a huge fern. The sofa was unoccupied, and Bliss settled into it with a sigh of relief.

"This is just what I needed before facing all those people again," Bliss said.

"It's not as bad as you thought it would be, is it?"

"So far, so good," Bliss sighed. "Did you notice where Luc went?"

"He's with Ram. Why? Do you need him?"

"I . . . I'm afraid to let him out of my sight for fear that something will happen to him," she confided. "I overheard something I shouldn't have. Luc plans to lure his enemy out in the open tonight. He received a threatening note and wants to finish this business once and for all." She leaned close to Phoebe's ear. "I'm not supposed to know, so don't mention it to your husband or Lord Bathurst."

"My word," Phoebe said. "What can I do to help?"

"Help me keep an eye on Luc. If he disappears, even for a moment, let me know."

"I'm sure Ram and Bathurst are aware of Luc's plans. They'll protect him."

"Nevertheless, I'd feel better keeping him in sight."

Phoebe rose. "We should return to our guests, the orchestra is warming up."

Luc made sure he was seen by everyone, going from group to group while waiting for Bliss to join him. After he led her out for the first dance, he intended to leave Bliss in Phoebe's capable hands and seek secluded places, hoping to encourage his enemy to follow.

"There you are," Luc said when Bliss joined him. "Shall we promenade until the orchestra begins playing?"

"If you wish," Bliss said, placing her arm on his.

They didn't promenade far, for they were constantly stopped by Luc's friends and acquaintances, eager to speak to him and his bride. When they bumped into Lady Broadmore and her husband, Bliss forced a smile.

"Congratulations, Westmore," Lord Broadmore said in a booming voice. A suave, handsome man with thin features, Broadmore's smile seemed as insincere as his greeting. Bliss wondered if the man knew his wife had once been Luc's lover.

"Your diamonds are truly magnificent, Lady Westmore," Lillian purred. "They must have cost a fortune." She sent Luc a heated look before her husband pulled her away.

The music began, and Luc led Bliss out on the floor for the first dance. When the dance ended, Bliss was mobbed by men wanting to dance with her, and she saw no way to gracefully refuse.

When she turned her head to look for Luc, he had disappeared.

Chapter Seventeen

After making sure neither Braxton nor Bathurst was watching, Luc slipped out the veranda door into the relative coolness of a late summer night. He was alone. Apparently, everyone was on the dance floor. He lit a cigar and waited. He was about to give up when Wellingham appeared, wiping perspiration from his forehead.

He spied Luc and joined him. Luc stiffened, preparing for a confrontation. He tossed away his cigar, his hand hovering over his jacket pocket, where his pistol rested.

"What a crush," Wellingham said. "If not for the wife, I wouldn't be here." He laughed. "She had to meet the woman who had finally brought the last rogue up to scratch. Your wife is stunning, Westmore. I can see what attracted you."

"Thank you," Luc replied. He heard nothing threatening in Wellingham's words and relaxed.

"Well, I'd best return to the wife or she'll

come looking for me."

Suddenly Bliss burst through the French doors. The wild look in her eyes told Luc that she knew what he was up to. She skidded to a halt beside him.

"Are you all right?" she demanded in a low voice.

Wellingham greeted Bliss with a knowing smile. "Your wife is anxious for your company, Westmore. If she were my wife, I'd give her exactly what she wants." Then he strode off.

"Was that the man?" Bliss asked.

"I don't know what you're talking about."

"Don't play dumb with me, Luc. I know you and your friends are planning to expose Lady Sybil's secret lover tonight."

Luc's brows shot upward. "How do you know that?"

She shrugged. "I put two and two together and figured it out."

Luc didn't believe her, but he didn't press the issue. He still had Sybil's lover to trap. The only thing he'd learned thus far was that Wellingham wasn't his man.

Luc grasped her elbow and escorted her to the door. "Shall we return to the ballroom?"

"Are you going to disappear again?"

"Probably."

"Luc, this is insane."

"So are attacks upon my person and threatening letters. Don't interfere, Bliss; I know what I'm doing. Ah, here comes Braxton. I believe he wishes to dance with you."

"I don't want to dance."

"But you will."

Braxton bowed and asked Bliss to dance. Bliss shot Luc a quelling look before placing her hand on Ram's arm. Luc gave Ram a grateful smile and promptly sidled off into the throng of people.

Lord Thomason caught up with Luc. "Westmore, might I have a private word with you?"

Luc arched a brow. Thomason was his least likely suspect. "Of course; follow me to the library."

"This will take but a moment," Thomason said.

Thomason was sweating profusely, making Luc wonder if he had something to be nervous about.

They entered the library. After making sure no one was there to disturb them, Luc closed the door. "What can I do for you, Thomason?"

Thomason cleared his throat and ran a finger under his shirt collar as if it were choking him. "This is rather personal."

"So I surmised. Go on, I'm all ears."

"It's about a lady you know quite well, or did know, if you catch my drift," Thomason hinted.

Luc began to believe that Thomason was his man until he said, "I want to become Lady Lillian Broadmore's lover."

Luc's jaw nearly hit the floor. "Lillian? Are you serious? The woman is a man-eater. Are you sure you can handle her?"

Thomason bristled. "Of course I can. I wouldn't confide in you if I wasn't sure of myself. I want to know what it takes to please her. She invited me to her home for an assignation after her husband leaves on a business trip next week. She has given him an heir, so he doesn't interfere in her affairs. Can you offer any advice? If you're still not interested in her, that is."

"I thought you were happy with your new bride."

"Is any man ever happily married?" Thomason snorted. "Bernice was my parents' choice, not mine, though we rub along well enough together. I'm rather nervous about this. Lillian is one of the most sought-after women in London. I don't know why she chose me."

"If you're looking for advice, Thomason,

there's not much I can say, except I don't think you're prepared to handle a woman like Lillian."

"I beg to differ," Thomason said stiffly.

Luc sighed. "Suit yourself. Lillian isn't difficult to please as long as you are willing to spend money on her. She loves jewelry, the gaudier the better. She's an inventive lover and has no qualms about telling you what she likes."

"Thank you, Westmore, I appreciate your honesty. Are you sure I won't be stepping on your toes? If Lillian is your property —"

"Not at all, old man. I have no interest in Lillian, or any other woman."

"That's all I wanted to know." Thomason pumped Luc's hand and rushed off.

Luc's lack of interest in any woman other than Bliss gave him pause. What was wrong with him? The thought of bedding any of his former lovers was repugnant to him. Bloody hell! He felt the noose tightening around his neck.

Thus far Luc's plan to lure Sybil's lover had produced no likely suspects. Had the threatening letter and attacks come from someone he was not acquainted with? It was possible but improbable, for he knew everyone who was anyone. And he'd bet his last crown that Sybil's lover was a peer.

Disappointed but not yet ready to accept defeat, Luc decided to choose another place to lure his prey. His decision to leave the library was forestalled when the door opened and Lord Mayhew stepped inside. Luc's first thought was that his enemy had finally arrived.

"Thomason told me I'd find you here," Mayhew said. "Do you have a moment?"

Luc faced him squarely. "What is it, Mayhew? I'm sure my wife is searching most diligently for me."

"I know we haven't been the best of friends," Mayhew began, "and I want to apologize for my rude remarks."

"You? Apologize? Forgive me for being startled."

"Once I met your wife, I realized my remarks about her were uncalled for. She isn't at all what I expected. She's exquisite, and quite charming. Truthfully, I was jealous. I could see you were smitten, and wished for that in my own marriage. Will you accept my apology?"

Luc couldn't believe his ears. Smitten? Him? Good Lord, was he that obvious?

"We've never been what you would call fast friends," Mayhew continued, "but we've always been on speaking terms. I would like that to continue."

Luc nodded. "Very well, apology accepted. If you'll excuse me, I'd like to find my wife. I owe her another dance."

Luc's emotions were confused. He had been convinced Mayhew was his man. All the clues pointed to him. He had married for money, was secretive in his dealings and didn't seem overly fond of his wife. Now Luc was right back where he started.

Bliss must have spotted Luc the moment he entered the ballroom, for she marched up to him and demanded, "Where have you been?"

"Don't fuss, Bliss. As you can see, I'm fine. Shall we dance? They're playing another waltz."

"Have you learned anything?" Bliss asked as they whirled around the dance floor.

"Three things," Luc said dryly. "Sybil's secret lover is neither Wellingham, nor Thomason, nor Mayhew."

"That really narrows the field. It's probably someone you least expect." She frowned. "Of the three, I would have guessed Lord Mayhew. He's a rather nasty sort."

Luc decided to keep Mayhew's apology to himself until he and Bliss were alone. "I'm not giving up. I truly believe the man I'm looking for is here tonight."

When the dance ended, Luc handed Bliss over to Lord Cranberry, a portly gentleman of advanced years who'd been waiting on the sidelines for his dance with Bliss.

Luc ran into Braxton as he pondered his next move. "Any luck?" Ram asked.

"I managed to eliminate three prime suspects, and all before the midnight buffet," Luc groused. "What the hell am I going to do now?"

"I wish I had answers," Ram said. "I believe Phoebe is signaling me. I'll talk to you later."

Luc wandered out to the veranda again, only this time he didn't linger. Instead, he descended the stairs to the garden and meandered down the path to the gazebo. If he was being watched, he could expect a visitor soon.

Luc hadn't been inside the gazebo ten minutes when he saw someone ambling down the path. He tensed, his nerve endings tingling in anticipation. In a few moments he might finally learn the identity of the man who had driven Sybil to suicide.

"I say, Westmore, is that you?"

Luc squinted into the darkness. It wasn't possible. Could it be? "Broadmore, is that you?"

"Were you expecting someone else? A

lady, perhaps? Surely not my wife. I believe Thomason is occupying her time right now."

"I am faithful to my wife, which is more than I can say for you."

"Bah! I'm as faithful to Lillian as she is to me."

"What are you doing out here?" Luc asked.

"Taking the air. Refreshing, isn't it? I've never seen such an exceptional night."

Luc glanced up at the stars. He had no reason to suspect Broadmore and thus was surprised when the man came up behind him and pressed something hard and cold into his back. A pistol? He started to turn.

"Don't turn around," Broadmore warned.

"So you're the one. I never suspected."

"Don't play coy with me. You knew it was me all along. What exactly did Sybil tell you?"

"That she was carrying her lover's child . . . her married lover. Did you know she asked me to marry her?"

Broadmore laughed. "Why didn't you? She would have made you an exceptional wife. She foolishly believed that once she was wed, we would go on as we were before she caught my bastard. But once I learned

neither saw a wraithlike figure slip into the gazebo.

Suddenly Luc felt a change in the atmosphere. He heard Broadmore suck in his breath, and then the gun pressing into his back shifted. He spun around, the blood freezing in his veins when he saw Bliss. The gun she held in her hand was pointed at Broadmore.

"Drop the gun, my lord. You're not killing anyone tonight. Are you all right, Luc?"

"Bliss! Bloody hell, what do you think you're doing?"

"Preventing you from getting killed. Step away, Lord Broadmore. I know how to use a gun and will shoot if you don't do as I say."

"Bitch!" Broadmore blasted. "Since when did you hide behind a woman's skirts, Westmore?"

Luc plucked the pistol from Broadmore's hand, and then just as quickly he relieved Bliss of her weapon. "You no longer need this, love. The situation has been defused. Go back to the house."

"I'm not going anywhere," Bliss huffed.

Bliss could tell Luc was seething despite the fact that she'd saved his life. Men were like that. They didn't want to give women credit for anything.

410

"You've married a firebrand, Westmore," Broadmore snarled. "I don't envy you."

"Nor I you," Luc replied.

"What are you going to do? If you charge me with attempted murder, you know it won't stand. There is no proof to connect me with the attacks upon your life."

"I saw and heard everything," Bliss challenged.

"You're a woman," Broadmore said disparagingly. "There's nothing either of you can do legally."

"Maybe not," Luc returned, "but I can ruin you. Once I feed information into the gossip mill, you'll be driven from London in shame."

Broadmore's bravado began to crumble. "I know you and Lillian were lovers in the past. She'll be ruined along with me."

"You should have thought about that before you ruined Sybil. The woman loved you, for God's sake. You, however, cared nothing for her. You saw her, wanted her, and took her innocence. Then you intended to abandon her."

"Surely you didn't think I would accept her bastard, did you? Once I learned she was increasing, I wanted nothing more to do with her."

"Scum!" Bliss hissed. "I'll do my part in

helping Luc ruin you."

"I have a son," Broadmore whined. "Would you condemn him for his father's sins?"

"I didn't know," Bliss whispered. "How old is he?"

"Fourteen. Percy arrived during the first year of my marriage to Lillian. Lillian and I truly do not like each other and have lived separate lives since his birth."

Bliss glanced at Luc, trying to communicate without speaking. Did he understand what she was trying to tell him?

"You should have thought about that before you seduced Sybil," Luc maintained. "Before your son is out of school, society will have moved on to other scandals."

"Luc," Bliss began, "perhaps we should —"

"You want me to forget about this?" Luc asked incredulously. "You think I should let him go? The man damn near put a period to my life."

"He has a son, Luc. The boy's life will be ruined along with his father's."

Luc stared at her a long time, so long Bliss nearly buckled beneath the burden of his perusal. After a weighty silence, he said, "Very well, but I'm not letting Broadmore off the hook that easily."

He turned to Broadmore. "My wife wants me to spare your reputation because of your son. If not for her, I would make damn sure you and your family suffered. But don't think you're going to escape unscathed. If I decide not to ruin you, there are conditions. First, if I hear that you've seduced another innocent, I will let everyone know you were responsible for Sybil's death. Second, I believe a very long sojourn in the country is called for. And third, one more attempt upon my life or that of my wife will negate everything I've just said. Have I made myself clear?"

"Perfectly," Broadmore spat. "You leave me little choice. I will pack tomorrow."

"One more thing," Luc said. "Take Lillian with you. She's a bad influence on my friend Thomason. A stint in the country will do her good."

Broadmore nodded stiffly and stumbled from the gazebo.

"Thank you, Luc," Bliss whispered. "I know he deserves far worse than he got, but there's a child involved and I didn't want him condemned for his father's sins."

Luc's expression did not bode well for Bliss. And she knew intuitively that it wasn't just because she had pleaded on Broadmore's behalf.

"What is it? What have I done?"

"Where did you get the pistol?" he asked through clenched teeth.

"Oh, that," she said blithely. "I bought it. One never knows when one might need to defend oneself."

"A woman should leave her protection to her husband," Luc shot back. "Whatever possessed you to follow me out here? You knew damn well I was setting a trap."

"You were nearly caught in your own trap," Bliss reminded him. "And you're welcome," she added sweetly, alluding to the fact that she had saved his life.

"You could have been killed!" Luc raged. "Broadmore meant business; he wasn't just play-acting."

"Neither was I," Bliss sniffed.

"I could have handled him by myself. I had things well in hand."

Her shapely brows shot up. "Did you? It didn't look that way to me."

"I was letting it play out. I had a pistol in my pocket and was about to distract Broadmore so I could relieve him of his. I don't ever want you to place yourself in that kind of danger again. I thought I made that clear when I got you out of that smuggling fiasco."

"Luc, I love you. I'll do whatever I think

necessary to save your life."

"Bliss . . . I . . . I —"

Whatever he was about to say was interrupted when a voice called from the darkness, "Westmore, are you in there? I can't seem to find Bliss. Is she with you?"

Braxton.

"Bliss is here. We're both fine."

Braxton burst into the gazebo, followed closely by Bathurst. "I hope we're not interrupting anything," Bathurst drawled. "We've been looking all over for you."

"Luc learned who was behind the attacks on his life," Bliss blurted out.

"Was it Mayhew?" Ram asked. "Never did like the man."

"This is going to surprise you as much as it did me. It was Broadmore."

"Never liked him, either."

"It doesn't surprise me, though he wasn't one I suspected," Gabriel mused. "What happened out here?"

"Broadmore pulled a gun on Luc and was going to kill him," Bliss explained. "If I hadn't followed Broadmore out here, Luc would be dead."

"Bliss, you exaggerate," Luc chided. "I had things well in hand." He sent her a strange look. "What made you follow Broadmore?"

"I saw you leave through the veranda doors and watched to see if anyone would follow. When I saw Broadmore slip away, I followed, though I couldn't leave immediately because I was dancing with Lord Sinclair."

"Tell us what happened," Ram urged.

Luc launched into a brief description of what followed after he was confronted by Broadmore. He ended the tale by giving Bliss a dark look. "I never suspected that my sweet little wife carried a pistol in her reticule."

"Brava," Gabriel said, grinning. "Sounds like something my Livvy would do. All joking aside, how are we going to ruin Broadmore?"

Luc sighed. "We're not. Bliss pleaded with me to place restraints on Broadmore's activities instead of ruining him. Once she heard he had a son, Bliss couldn't bear the thought of the son suffering along with the father. I hold the threat of ruin over Broadmore's head, and if he continues to debauch highborn innocents, I will make him very sorry.

"Another consideration was Sybil's elderly parents," Luc continued. "Learning that Sybil killed herself because she didn't want to shame them with her pregnancy would destroy them."

416

"You're more lenient than I would be," Gabriel said. "But as long as you can ruin him whenever you choose, I suppose he'll toe the line. We may have been the worst sort of rogues, but innocents were off-limits to us." He cleared his throat. "What I meant to say was that while we weren't angels, we wed the only virgins we seduced. That, and the fact that we were single, sets us apart from predators like Broadmore."

"Precisely," Ram agreed. "Shall we return to the ball? The guests of honor have been missing long enough."

Luc escorted Bliss back to the house. If their absence had been noticed, no one mentioned it. Phoebe and Olivia were briefed by their husbands, so they would understand why the Broadmores had left so abruptly.

Bliss was famished by the time Luc escorted her to the buffet table. Solving the mystery of Luc's attacker had lightened her mood considerably, and she was finally able to enjoy herself, though she couldn't say the same for Luc. There was still a quiet anger inside him just waiting to be unleashed, and she suspected a large part of it was aimed at her.

Bliss danced so much the rest of the evening that her feet felt numb, and she made acquaintances she hoped would turn into lasting relationships. She truly believed her acceptance into society was due as much to the dowager marchioness of Bathurst as it was to the Braxtons, who had sponsored her, and the Bathursts, who lent their support. The dowager had made it clear to all that she had put her stamp of approval on Bliss.

Luc hadn't asked her to dance again that evening. Nor had he moved from where he was holding up a column near the edge of the dance floor. She felt his eyes following her as she went from partner to partner, but when she tried to catch his attention, he deliberately looked away.

Luc was indeed angry. He didn't care how many people Bliss danced with, it was her disregard for her own safety that left him seething. He didn't want to rant at her before his friends so he hadn't belabored the point, but by no means did he intend to let it drop.

"You've got it bad, my friend," Bathurst said as he joined Luc.

"What in blazes are you talking about?"

"Think about it. You haven't taken your eyes off Bliss all night. Your heart is in your eyes, old man. You love her. I am well acquainted with the signs. I lived with them myself before recognizing the malady and finally acknowledging it."

"You're mad," Luc drawled. "Ours isn't a love match."

Bathurst's brows shot up. "Tell that to someone who will believe you. Does Bliss love you?"

A lengthy silence ensued before Luc spoke. "She said she did, but . . ."

Just then Bliss glanced over at Luc. There was no mistaking the message in the smile she gave him. Bathurst chuckled softly and slapped Luc on the back. "You poor bedeviled fool. You don't have a chance. Tell her how you feel before you explode. Well, I think I'll find Livvy and go home."

Luc thought going home sounded like a good idea. Bliss's thoughts must have run in the same direction, for she approached him before the next dance began and voiced her readiness to leave. They found the Braxtons, expressed their gratitude for launching Bliss into society and made their farewells.

They left as streaks of orange and purple dawn lit the sky and walked home in silence, Luc still seething and Bliss ignoring him.

It wasn't just annoyance with Bliss that kept Luc from speaking. His silence had as much to do with that telling conversation with Bathurst as it did with anger. Was he in love with Bliss? How could he be sure? Would admitting that he loved her irrevocably change his life?

They reached Luc's townhouse. Luc opened the door and Bliss swept inside. Without a word, she climbed the stairs to her bedroom. Luc followed in her wake, entering her room behind her and closing the door.

"It's late, Luc," Bliss said, yawning. "It was a wonderful party. I believe your friends accepted me."

Luc stalked toward her. "I don't care how late it is, Bliss. We need to discuss your interference tonight. Have you any idea what being an obedient wife means?"

She shrugged. "Not really."

His hands clenched into fists. "Have you no conception of danger? Are you afraid of nothing?"

"Very little. Should I be?"

"You should be afraid of me right now . . . very afraid. Damn it, Bliss! What if I had lost you? Broadmore could have turned and shot you in the blink of an eye."

Bliss gaped at him. "Would you care? You sound as if losing me would mean a great deal to you."

He grasped her shoulders, surprised to see that his hands were shaking. "Little fool. I love you." His words shocked him, but he couldn't stop now. "It would kill me to lose you."

Bliss gasped. "You love me? I thought . . . that is . . . you never said that before."

"It wasn't until you rushed headlong into danger that I realized how much you meant to me. I'm sorry, Bliss, I'm a selfish bastard. It never occurred to me that one woman could satisfy me for the rest of my life."

Slowly he began to undress her.

"Are you saying you intend to remain faithful forever, that I'll be the only woman in your life?" Bliss asked.

"You're asking a great deal of me, my love."

"If you can't promise me forever, then you don't really love me."

Luc grinned, his earlier mood considerably lightened. His adorable bride was demanding his soul, and he was all too eager to hand it to her on a silver salver. Life without Bliss seemed a boring prospect. In fact, he didn't know how he had conducted his life without her in it.

He had stripped her naked and brought her into his arms. "I'd promise you longer than forever if I could, but you'll have to accept forever. I do love you, Bliss. Now can we make love?"

"Oh, yes, please."

Luc flung off his clothes, swept Bliss off her feet and fell into bed with her in his arms. Weariness was forgotten as he aroused her with his mouth and tongue and hands. He brought her to the pinnacle, then denied her release and began all over again. When he finally thrust inside her hot center, she climaxed immediately. But Luc wasn't through with her. He deliberately held his passion in check while he slowly aroused her yet again. This time when she came, he was with her all the way.

Finally they slept.

Bliss had never been so happy. Everything was going wonderfully well. She loved Luc and Luc loved her. Nothing could hurt them now.

About a week after the ball, Partridge awakened them with news they neither expected nor wanted.

"Forgive me for awakening you, milord, milady," Partridge said through the door, "but there's a gentleman here to see you. I told him to come back later, but he said it was imperative that he see you. He said he and Lady Westmore were old friends."

"I'll be right down, Partridge," Bliss replied as she slipped on a robe.

"Who do you suppose it is?" Luc asked as he tugged on his trousers.

"I can't imagine." Bliss opened the door. Partridge wore a pained expression. "Did the gentleman give his name?" she asked.

"Aye, milady. He said his name was Fred Dandy, and that you and His Lordship would want to see him. He's quite . . . colorful, if I may be so bold as to say so, and very insistent."

"Show him into the breakfast room and offer him something to eat," Luc said. "We'll be down as soon as we're dressed."

Partridge withdrew; Luc closed the door behind him. "What do you suppose Fred Dandy wants?"

"We'll soon find out, won't we? It must be important, for him to show up here." Bliss sighed. "We seem to go from crisis to crisis. Do you think we'll ever be able to get on with our lives? I would like to have children, if you're agreeable."

"I never thought I'd hear myself say this, but I'd love to have children with you." He gave her a cheeky grin. "You could be carrying my child now. I've never taken precautions."

Bliss's hands flew to her stomach. "I

wouldn't mind. I just hope that whatever brought Fred Dandy here won't interfere with our lives."

"Nothing will interfere with our love, no matter how much our lives are disrupted," Luc asserted. He held out his hand. "Shall we find out what Fred Dandy and fate have thrown into our path?"

Bliss placed her small hand in Luc's larger one and together they descended the stairs.

Chapter Eighteen

Fred Dandy rose when Luc and Bliss entered the breakfast room. He was dressed in rough fisherman's clothing and seemed uncomfortable in his surroundings. Bliss saw that Partridge had furnished him with a hearty meal and that Dandy had polished off most of it.

"What brings you to London, Dandy?" Luc asked without preamble. "You're a long way from home."

"Ay, milord," Dandy said, sending a sidelong glance at Bliss. "Thank you for the breakfast, milord, and congratulations on your marriage."

His gaze found Bliss. His expression was intent, as if he was trying to convey a silent message. It didn't take Bliss long to discern that Fred Dandy wanted to speak to her in private, but she had no idea how to accommodate him.

"You're welcome on both accounts," Luc said. "How may I help you?"

"I'm looking for Millie," Dandy said, twisting his hat in his hand. "I came to

London to find her. I asked her to marry me some time ago, but she wanted to go to London, to see more of life. I figured she would have had enough of the big city by now and came to fetch her home."

"We haven't seen her, Fred," Bliss said. "We've been wondering ourselves what happened to her. His Lordship gave her enough gold guineas to keep her for a long time if she's frugal, so I don't think she's in trouble."

"I advised Millie to find my friend Bathurst when she arrived in London," Luc explained. "I told her he would help her, but Bathurst hadn't yet arrived in town. I have no idea where she might be."

"I ain't giving up," Dandy maintained.

"London is a large city. She could be anywhere."

"I'm just finding that out, milord. However, I'm determined. I know she done you wrong, but I'm willing to bet she's sorry."

"Indeed," Luc said. "It won't be easy to find Millie. Even if you do, you can't take her back to St. Ives. Are Captain Skillington and his men still in the area?"

Dandy's gaze found Bliss again, then skittered away. "They come to St. Ives more frequently than we'd like."

"You've put a stop to the smuggling,

haven't you?" Luc asked sharply.

Dandy flushed and looked away. "You see, milord, it's like this. Brady Bristol decided we couldn't afford to give up our lucrative business. He figured that if we were careful, we could still smuggle without getting caught."

Luc spat out a curse.

"What does my father say about that?" Bliss asked. "He promised to keep the villagers out of trouble."

"That's another reason I'm here. Jenny asked me to tell you the squire has taken ill again."

Bliss blanched. "How bad is it?"

"Bad. But the squire doesn't want you to come home. He says it's too dangerous."

"Oh, no! I'll leave immediately." She turned to Luc. "May I have the coach for my journey?"

"You're not going," Luc said firmly.

"You can't stop me."

"I can and I will. You heard Dandy. The villagers didn't heed my warning and are still involved in smuggling."

"But Papa —"

"I'll arrange for your father to be brought to London."

"It may be too late."

"It's the best we can do, love. It's too risky

for you to return to St. Ives." He turned to address Dandy. "If you do find Millie, you'll have to settle elsewhere. Maybe one day it will be safe to return to St. Ives, but not yet. Millie will be taken into custody and forced to testify against you and the others. She knows too much about your activities."

Dandy rubbed his chin. "I never thought of that. I can't make a living in London. I'm a fisherman, that's all I know. If Millie agrees, I'll find another home for us down the coast, someplace where I can ply my trade."

"You must love her a great deal," Bliss said.

"Aye," Dandy said. "I'm not leaving until I find her."

"Since you're so determined," Luc said, "I'll hire Bow Street Runners to find her. Come back in a few days and perhaps I'll have some information for you."

"I don't know what to say, milord," Dandy said gratefully. "I wasn't always as kind to you as I should have been, but you've proved a good friend to the men of St. Ives. Thank you."

"I wish Bristol shared your sentiments. He's putting the entire village at risk."

"Is Brady calling himself Shadow?" Bliss asked.

"Aye, he is."

She whirled on Luc, her excitement palpable. "If Brady is calling himself Shadow, then I am in no danger. I'm going home."

"We'll discuss this later," Luc said through clenched teeth.

Dandy must have taken that as a hint. "I'd best be on my way."

"Don't forget, check back in a few days and we'll see what the Runners have come up with."

"I'll see you out," Bliss said. "Luc, ask Partridge to serve breakfast in fifteen minutes."

Dandy followed Bliss to the front door. "I know you wanted a private word with me," Bliss said quietly. "What couldn't you tell me in my husband's presence?"

"Jenny said the squire is failing fast, and that you should come home immediately if you want to see him alive. I didn't know how your husband would react to Jenny's message."

"You saw how he reacted. He doesn't want me to leave."

"What are you going to do?"

"Go home, of course. Thank you for telling me, Fred, and good luck locating Millie."

After Dandy left, Bliss rested against the door a moment while she gathered her thoughts. She had to go home, and nothing Luc said or did would stop her.

Bliss hurried into the breakfast room. Luc was helping himself at the sideboard. She took her plate and joined him.

"Luc —"

"You're not going, Bliss. I'll make arrangements to bring your father to London. He'll get the best of care here."

"He could be too weak to make the trip. It's a long way to London."

"We'll just have to pray that he isn't. You know why you can't return. I love you, Bliss. I can't lose you."

"You won't lose me, Luc. I'm sure my return will receive scant notice. There's another Shadow now."

"I'd like to wring Bristol's neck," Luc groused. "I'm sure Skillington is aware of what's going on." A lengthy silence ensued. "I have a business deal in the works that needs my attention."

"You never mentioned it before. Is this something recent?"

"Not really. This deal was in progress before I left London. Braxton and Bathurst and I intend to make an offer for a defunct shipping line. We think we can make it profitable. Give me a few days to get things settled, and then I'll take you to St. Ives myself."

"How many days?"

"I'm not sure. These things take time. If we decide to buy, we'll have to deal with the bank and lawyers. The owner of the fleet lives in Portsmouth, so I'll be required to leave town for a few days."

"When will you leave?"

Luc gave her a curious glance. "Are you anxious to be rid of me?"

"You know better than that."

"We planned to leave day after tomorrow. It's a wonderful opportunity. We've been talking about the venture for some time. When I left London, Bathurst and Braxton decided to wait until I returned to inspect the ships and complete the deal."

"Do you promise to take me home when you return?"

"You have my word." He swallowed the last of his coffee and rose. "Well, I'm off. I'm to meet Braxton at White's." He brushed a kiss across Bliss's lips and left.

Bliss drummed her fingers on the table. How long would Luc be gone? No matter, she couldn't wait that long. Her papa could die before she arrived. When Luc left, she would go, too. She knew he'd be angry, but if he loved her he'd forgive her.

Bliss began preparing for her journey immediately. She packed a bag with a few essentials and slid it under the bed until she was ready for it. She didn't need much, for most of her clothing had been left at home when she was arrested and taken away. Her next decision, an important one, was to choose a mode of transportation. She could take public transportation; the mail coach arrived twice a week in St. Ives. Yes, she thought, that would do nicely.

Another consideration was money. Luc had given her pin money, of which she'd spent little. But it might not be enough. However, she knew where Luc kept funds for household expenses. Partridge often dipped into it to pay tradesmen. She doubted a few guineas would be missed.

Bliss felt as if she had betrayed Luc when he returned home for dinner that evening and greeted her sweetly. He looked tired. But after their vigorous bed play the night before, she was not surprised. She ordered dinner served in their room and followed Luc upstairs. She helped him bathe and suggested that he don his dressing robe since they were dining informally.

"Only if you put on your robe and join me."

Bliss complied, disrobing slowly for his benefit, while he poured them each a small brandy. They relaxed in chairs in front of the hearth while waiting for dinner to arrive.

"Did you meet with Braxton?" Bliss asked.

Luc sighed. "Do we have to talk business? I've had a hellish day."

"I was merely curious about your plans."

"Very well, if you're truly interested, I'll tell you. First, I hired Bow Street Runners to look for Millie. Then I met Braxton and we proceeded to Bathurst's mansion. We laid our plans for our joint shipping venture over lunch. There were numerous details, which I won't go into at this time, to consider before journeying to Plymouth."

"Must you go?"

"I don't want to but I must. Bathurst won't be accompanying us. He's been called away on estate business, so it's up to me and Braxton. Olivia has invited you to stay with her and the twins during my absence."

"I'll think about it."

"I shall miss you," Luc said. "Do you think we have time before dinner to —"

That question became moot when a discreet knock sounded on the door. "Our dinner," Bliss said, a wealth of disappointment in her words. She gave him an arch smile. "We'll definitely have time after dinner."

She opened the door; a succession of servants paraded in carrying trays. Mrs. Dunbar was the last to leave after making sure everything had been placed on the table to her satisfaction.

The food looked delicious, but their appetites seemed to run in a different direction. Their dinner grew cold as they cavorted naked on the bed.

"I don't want to leave you," Luc whispered against her ear as he thrust inside her. "Not when things are going so well for us."

Somehow Bliss gathered her scattered wits to reply, though it was difficult with Luc stroking inside her. "When do you leave?"

"Day after tomorrow."

That was the last word said on the subject, or any other subject, for a very long time. Their loving was slow and languid. No words were necessary to express their feelings, nor were any given. That had already been settled between them.

When they finally returned to their food, they found it cold and unpalatable. But instead of ringing for something else, they returned to the rumpled bed to resume their lovemaking.

Luc remained awake long after Bliss had fallen asleep in his arms. He had a bad feeling about leaving. It would be the first time he and Bliss had been apart since their hasty marriage, and Luc hated to leave Bliss alone. But the trip couldn't be put off. If he and his friends didn't act swiftly, the business could be snatched from them before the deal was closed.

It would be all right, he told himself. What could possibly go wrong? He stifled a chuckle. Any number of things, given Bliss's penchant for trouble.

On the up side, the Runners had been successful. They'd found Millie working in a respectable inn on London's east side. When Dandy arrived tomorrow, he would give him her address and leave the wooing to the fisherman.

Luc's side of the bed was empty when Bliss awakened the next morning. She slid out of bed and rang for Birdie. When she arrived, Bliss ordered a bath.

"Milord said you'd want a bath," Birdie said. "The water is already heated and the tub will arrive directly."

Bliss pulled on her robe and stared out the window while her bath was being prepared. There was so much to do today, she didn't know where to start. First on her list was purchasing a ticket on the first mail coach out of town the day after Luc was to depart. Once Luc returned and learned what she had done, she knew he would follow. She debated whether to leave him a note and decided against it. He'd know where she had gone and why she'd left.

After her bath, Bliss dressed and went down to breakfast. She found Luc in the breakfast room; Fred Dandy was with him. They had finished eating and were deep in conversation.

"You're just in time," Luc said when Bliss entered the room.

"Good morning, Fred," Bliss said as she helped herself from the sideboard.

"Good morning, milady," Fred replied. "I was just telling Lord Westmore how grateful I am for what he's done for me."

Bliss brought her filled plate to the table; Luc seated her. "What has he done?"

"I forgot to mention it yesterday." Luc grinned. "Something distracted me. The Runners found Millie. I just told Fred where he could find her."

"How wonderful!" Bliss exclaimed. "I suppose you're going to see her right away."

"Aye. But I'll be sure to heed His Lordship's warning. If Millie agrees to marry me, we'll make our home in another village, one where I can still earn a living as a fisherman.

Once we're settled, I'll return to St. Ives for my boat. As long as I can do what I know best, we'll get by."

"Come with me to my study. I'll give you a little something to start you off on the right foot."

"You've already done enough, milord."

"Perhaps, but it's to Bliss's advantage to keep Millie away from Skillington. I'm sure you're aware of that."

"Aye, I am, and it's good of you not to hold a grudge against her."

Luc stood, then walked to where Bliss sat. He bent and brushed his lips across her mouth. "As soon as I see Dandy out, I'll be on my way. There's a great deal to do before I leave tomorrow. I'll see you at dinner."

"Good-bye, Bliss . . . er . . . milady," Fred said.

"Give Millie my best and tell her I forgive her."

Bliss finished her breakfast in solitude. By the time she left the breakfast room, Luc and Fred Dandy had completed their business and departed.

Bliss left a few minutes later, informing Partridge that she was going for a walk in the park, and that a companion wasn't required. She sailed out the door before the butler could voice his disapproval.

It took but two hours for Bliss to complete her business. To her delight, the mail coach schedule fit perfectly with her plans. She purchased a ticket and returned home without arousing Partridge's suspicion.

That night she and Luc ate supper in the dining room and returned to their bedroom immediately afterward. Luc began undressing her the moment the door closed behind him.

Laughing at his haste, Bliss said, "We have all night, Luc."

"I know, but I've been thinking about this all day. It will be several days before we can make love again." He chuckled. "As often as we make love, I'm surprised you're not with child."

"It's too soon to tell," Bliss hedged. Intuition told her she was, indeed, with child, but she couldn't think about that now. Not when she was leaving without his knowledge or permission.

"Perhaps tonight will be the night I plant a babe inside you," he whispered as he carried her to bed, tore off his clothing and joined her.

They loved each other fiercely, without restraint or embarrassment. Bliss fondled, kissed and licked her way down Luc's body, and then took him into her mouth. Her tender torment didn't last as long as she would have liked.

"Enough," he growled, then lifted her away and flung her beneath him. He repaid her in kind, his mouth and tongue teasing the swollen petals of her sex, building her passion to a wild frenzy.

Then he drove himself inside her, thrusting and withdrawing, the exquisite friction bringing them both to climax. Afterward they slept, but awoke in the darkest part of night to love again.

The next morning while Luc was dressing, he asked Bliss if she had decided to stay with Olivia.

"I prefer to remain home," Bliss replied. "You'll only be gone a few days, and I'm perfectly safe here with your staff. It's not that I don't enjoy Livvy's company, I do. But it's rather silly to pack and unpack for such a short stay. She's but a few blocks away should I need her."

"As you wish. I didn't want you to be lonely during my absence and thought Olivia's offer a generous one. I'll send a note around explaining your decision. But you can always change your mind. I'll inform Partridge of the possibility."

All through breakfast Bliss avoided looking directly at Luc. She hated lying to him, but it couldn't be helped. If her father died before she reached him, she'd never forgive herself. And she prayed that Luc would forgive her for deceiving him.

Somehow Bliss got through the day. She felt as if everyone were aware of her plans, and did her utmost to avoid Partridge, who was more astute than the others. She spent time in the study because she felt closer to Luc there. When she left the room, his drawer was missing several gold guineas. Later, Bliss ate dinner on a tray in her room, for she couldn't bear eating in the dining room without Luc sitting across from her.

She went to bed early, well aware that the next few days would be arduous. Traveling by mail coach wasn't the most comfortable mode of transportation.

Bliss awakened early the next morning and summoned Birdie. She still had plenty of time, for the mail coach wasn't scheduled to leave until noon, and she'd been told it was usually late.

The first step of her journey was about to begin. Bliss drew in a steadying breath as she prepared to surmount the first obstacle that stood in her way.

"I've decided to stay with Lady Bathurst after all," Bliss told Birdie. "It's rather lonely here without Lord Westmore."

Birdie nodded knowingly. "His Lordship said you might. Shall I pack a bag for you?"

"I've already seen to it, Birdie. Tell Partridge I'll be down to breakfast in twenty minutes."

"Shall I help you dress and arrange your hair?"

"Thank you, no. I'm not going far, so I'll wear something simple. You can arrange my hair when you return."

Birdie curtsied and departed. After she left, Bliss pulled her bag from beneath the bed and checked the contents. Once she added her brush, she would have everything she needed. When Birdie returned, Bliss let her put the finishing touches to her hair.

Once she was all put together, Bliss descended the stairs. She was met at the bottom by Partridge, who was looking definitely put out.

"Birdie said you've decided to stay with Lady Bathurst, milady. Lord Westmore mentioned that you might decide to accept Lady Bathurst's hospitality."

"It's rather lonesome here without His Lordship," Bliss told the concerned butler. "For Lady Bathurst as well, I imagine. Lord Bathurst left London on estate business. We can entertain one another during our husbands' absence."

"Very good, milady," Partridge replied. "When will you leave?"

"As soon as I've finished breakfast. I'm already packed."

"I'll have Appleby bring the carriage around."

"That's not necessary. It's but a short walk and I could use the exercise. Since I won't be staying long, my bag is light."

"I wouldn't hear of it, milady, and neither would milord. Appleby will drive you to the Bathurst residence. Shall Birdie accompany you?"

"No. Lady Bathurst's staff is extensive, I'm sure she can provide whatever I need. Let Birdie enjoy a few days' rest."

"As you wish, milady."

Bliss nodded without enthusiasm. She should have known Partridge wouldn't allow her to go off alone. Her plan was a good one, however, and she wasn't going to abandon it just because a slight deviation was necessary.

Partridge stepped aside so Bliss could continue on to the breakfast room. She ate heartily, even stuffing a few rolls and an apple in her pocket to stave off hunger between stops. Less than an hour later, Bliss was waved off by Partridge and Birdie as

Appleby directed the horses the short distance to the Bathurst mansion.

Bliss's apprehension escalated as Appleby stopped at the front gate and let down the steps. What if Livvy happened to be looking out the window and recognized the Westmore carriage? What if one of the servants was watching?

"Shall I see you to the door, milady?" Appleby asked.

"That won't be necessary, Appleby. I can find my way to the door, and the bag isn't heavy."

Appleby, good employee that he was, looked doubtful. "Nevertheless —"

"Truly, Appleby, I'll be fine." Bliss was growing frantic. "You're dismissed." She hated to use that tone of voice, but she was desperate to be on her way.

Appleby didn't protest as he bowed, climbed into the driver's box and drove off. The moment the carriage was out of sight, Bliss trudged off with almost indecent haste. She didn't slow her pace until the Bathurst residence was far behind her. Then she hailed the first unoccupied hansom cab she saw and gave the driver her destination. She reached the mail coach station a good hour early, but waiting there was better than taking a chance on having her plans foiled by caring servants.

The journey to St. Ives wasn't an easy one, but Bliss hadn't expected it to be. During most of the trip she was buffeted about as the coach bumped along on rutted roads. She chafed impatiently at the frequent stops to take on and discharge passengers and deliver mail. The coaching inns on the route left a great deal to be desired, and Bliss was usually required to share a room with other female passengers. But she had considered all the pitfalls associated with her reckless flight and deemed them worthwhile.

During the seemingly endless trip across England, Bliss had plenty of time to consider the consequences of her rashness. If Luc loved her he'd forgive her, wouldn't he? She knew he'd come after her the moment he learned what she had done, and figured she had only a few days' head start. If Luc returned to London early and came after her on horseback, he might possibly catch up with the mail coach. That thought was not a pleasant one. She wasn't ready to face him.

Luc's business was taking longer than expected. The owner of the defunct shipping line was dithering about the offer Luc and

Ram had extended. He thought it not generous enough. Though Luc and Ram had examined the ships and deemed them seaworthy, they weren't interested in paying more than they were worth.

The two friends knew their wives would worry when they didn't return on time, so they dashed off notes and sent them off by messenger. If a deal wasn't reached by the end of the week, they would call the whole thing off and return home.

"Phoebe isn't going to be happy about this delay," Ram said once their letters had been dispatched.

"I don't suppose Bliss is going to like it either. She didn't want me to leave. She received word that her father was seriously ill and wanted to leave immediately to see to his recovery.

"She threatened to go alone, but I refused to allow it. I told her I'd go with her after our business was concluded, but she wasn't happy about the delay. I tried to impress upon her that St. Ives isn't safe for her anymore."

"She was cleared of all charges, wasn't she?"

"Aye, but if she were to go to St. Ives alone, she might be tempted to resume her illegal activities."

"Surely not," Ram said.

"You have but to recall Olivia's escapades as a highwayman if you doubt what Bliss is capable of."

"I see what you mean," Ram agreed. "Let's close this deal so we can go home to our wives."

Disheveled and weary from five days of hard travel, some of it in blinding rain, Bliss reached her destination in mid-afternoon, though one wouldn't know it for the dreary fog that all but eradicated the daylight. No one was on hand to greet her as she descended from the coach and retrieved her bag. But she hadn't expected anyone. The men were probably at the tavern bemoaning the weather, and the women were home preparing dinner for their families.

Gripping her bag, Bliss started up the incline that led to the squire's residence, her heart pounding with anxiety. What would she find when she arrived? Would she be too late? Or had her father made another miraculous recovery?

Bliss charged up to the front door and flung it open. The house was deathly quiet — too quiet. Had her worst fears been realized?

"Jenny, I'm home!"

Chapter Nineteen

Jenny came running from the kitchen, wiping her hands on her apron. Bliss dropped her bag and ran into Jenny's outstretched arms, hugging her fiercely.

"How is Papa?" Bliss asked. "He's not —"

"No, child, the squire is holding his own. After I asked Fred Dandy to deliver the note to you, I knew I shouldn't have made things sound so dire."

"How sick is Papa? Is the malady the same as before?"

"Aye, it appears to be the same. Only now we know what it is. A new doctor arrived in town. He took over Dr. Simmons's practice when Dr. Simmons declared his intention to retire. Dr. Landry had a London practice but gave it up because he preferred the country."

"Is Dr. Landry treating Papa?"

"Aye, and a good thing it is."

"What diagnosis did he give Papa?"

"It's his heart. Angina, I think the doctor called it. He's treating the squire with herbal concoctions and pain medication."

"What does it all mean?"

"It means that if the squire takes care not to exert himself and takes his medication faithfully, he'll be with us a few more years."

"I want to see him," Bliss said, unwilling to believe what she couldn't see with her own eyes.

"He's sleeping. I checked on him shortly before you arrived."

"What is angina?"

"The doctor said it's a weakening of the heart. There's some pain and spells of weakness that occur periodically. The squire is far from well, but I don't think he's dying."

Bliss nearly collapsed with relief. "Thank God for Dr. Landry. Dr. Simmons would have bled Papa and hoped for the best."

Bliss grew puzzled when she saw Jenny glancing toward the door. "Are you expecting someone?"

"Your husband. Where is he?"

"Luc couldn't make it, so I came alone. I feared Papa would die before I got here and so I left without him."

"I hope Lord Westmore sent you in his coach with plenty of outriders for protection."

Bliss cleared her throat. "I rode the mail coach, but I'm sure Luc will be following soon." No truer words were ever spoken.

Jenny looked astonished. "I can't believe Westmore would let you do such a rash thing."

"Luc doesn't know. He's away on a business trip. I didn't tell him I was leaving, but I'm sure he'll follow once he learns what I've done. He feared I'd get myself in trouble after Fred Dandy told us the villagers have resumed smuggling."

"We'll talk about that later," Jenny said. "You look like you could use a bath. I'll have Billy Pigeon carry water up for you. After you left, we hired him on permanently. And a godsend he's been. He takes good care of your father. Widow Pigeon helps out too."

"I'm glad you have help." Bliss picked up her bag and started toward the stairs. "I'm going to look in on Papa first. I promise not to wake him."

"His bedroom is still in the study. Dr. Landry said he shouldn't climb stairs even when he's well enough to move about. The study is large enough to accommodate him, and it's more practical."

"A good idea. Have Billy carry up the tub and water when it's ready. I won't be in Papa's room long."

Bliss opened the study door and peeked in

at her father. He was sleeping peacefully, his chest rising and falling steadily. She tiptoed to the bed and looked down at him. He was pale and had lost weight since she'd last seen him, but at least he was alive. And if Dr. Landry could be believed, he would recover.

Leaning over, Bliss placed a kiss on his forehead, and then she departed, climbing the stairs to her own room. It was just as she had left it. Her clothing still hung in the wardrobe and her personal items were lined up on the dressing table. Though it felt like home, there was a difference. Luc wouldn't be sharing the bed with her.

Bliss couldn't help thinking about Luc's anger once he learned she had left London against his wishes. Would her rash departure destroy the happiness they had found? Somehow she had to make him understand why she couldn't wait for him to accompany her.

The tub and bathwater arrived. Bliss banished her morose thoughts and concentrated on the bath she desperately needed. Her skin was gritty with road dirt and her hair a mass of tangles. After she washed her hair and scrubbed her body, she luxuriated in the tub until the water grew cold. Then she dressed in one of her old gowns and brushed out her hair until it dried, tying it back with a ribbon. Then she walked downstairs to see if her father was awake.

He was. Billy was arranging pillows behind him when she arrived. The squire's face lit up when he saw her. "Billy told me you'd come home. Come give your old Papa a hug."

Billy quietly left the room as Bliss flew to Owen's side and wrapped him in a bear hug. Then she sat on the edge of the bed and held his hand.

"I missed you, daughter," Owen said. "Are you happy in your marriage? I hope I didn't force you into an intolerable situation."

"Didn't you get my letters?"

"Aye, but I want to hear from your own lips that I didn't do you an injustice by demanding that Westmore wed you."

Bliss smiled as she recalled everything she and Luc had gone through to find happiness. "It wasn't easy at first. There was a lot going on in Luc's life that I wasn't aware of. But once he confided in me, things seemed to work out.

"I love Luc, Papa, and he loves me." She didn't want to tell him that she'd left without Luc's knowledge or approval lest it upset him.

"Where is the viscount?"

"He'll be here soon. He had some business to attend first. I came on ahead."

Owen frowned. "That doesn't sound like something Westmore would allow."

"Everything is fine, Papa," Bliss said before Owen could question her further. "I don't want to tire you, and I want to speak to Jenny, but don't worry, I'll be home for a while, so we'll have many opportunities to talk."

"Dr. Landry said I'm going to get better. Did you think I was going to die? Is that why you're here?"

"I was worried about you, but now that I see how well you're doing, I can relax and enjoy my visit." She kissed his forehead. "I'll return and have supper with you, if that's all right."

"I'd like that," Owen replied.

Bliss left Owen and joined Jenny in the kitchen. Mrs. Pigeon was there. She greeted Bliss warmly. "Can I help?" Bliss offered.

"You just sit there and chat with us while we work," Jenny said. "Thelma Pigeon and I have everything well in hand. Did you speak with your father?"

"I did. He appears weak, but his voice is strong. I hope Dr. Landry knows what he's talking about."

"He does. You can judge for yourself when he comes tomorrow to check on the squire."

Bliss slanted a glance at the widow before asking Jenny, "Can we talk freely?"

"Of course, dear. Thelma is aware of what's going on and doesn't like it any more than I do."

"We women are worried about our men," Thelma said. "Billy is all I've got. The excise men are still suspicious and keep tabs on us. And Brady Bristol is rash and unreliable. It's not like when you were in charge. You were more careful of our men."

"Yet the men follow him," Bliss observed.

"They like the extra blunt," Thelma explained. "Trying to eke out a living as a fisherman is a hard life. In the summertime the men can't get their catch to market before it spoils."

"Eventually they're going to get caught," Bliss predicted. "Westmore will be disappointed to learn that my experience taught them nothing. If not for Luc, I would have been tried and convicted of smuggling, and probably hanged."

"It's Brady's doing," Thelma said. "He talked the others into joining him. There's only been one delivery since you left."

"It only takes one to get a man caught. I

453

intend to speak to Brady in the morning. Someone has to talk some sense into him."

Bliss realized she sounded just like Luc when he'd first learned they were smuggling. He had warned her, and she had ignored him.

That evening, Bliss ate supper with her father. He didn't eat much, but enough to satisfy her. Then they talked until he started to nod off. Since she was tired herself after her extended trip, she went to bed right after she left him. And a lonely bed it was.

How long before Luc arrived? she wondered. Would he be so angry with her that he wouldn't come at all? On that unpleasant thought she fell asleep.

The next day Bliss decided to call on Brady. She wasn't looking forward to seeing him. She knew Brady to be stubborn and at times unreasonable. It was no secret that he'd always wanted to take her place as Shadow. He had gotten his wish, but his rash leadership could bring disaster to the villagers.

"Where are you going, dear?" Jenny asked as Bliss tied the strings of her bonnet beneath her chin.

"To see Brady. The weather is too unsettled today for him to take his boat out. It looks more like night outside than day with that fog rolling in from the sea."

"You'll probably find him at his house," Jenny said, "but I don't think you should go alone. His mother is visiting his sister in Penzance."

"I'm a married woman, Jenny. It will be perfectly all right. Besides, Brady and I have known each other since childhood. Pray that I'll be able to talk some sense into him."

"Oh, I will, Bliss, I will. I don't have a relative involved, but Thelma is concerned about Billy and so am I."

Bliss bade Jenny good-bye and walked out into the misty, damp day. Since St. Ives had many days like this, she was used to it, and London was often just as foggy and damp. The difference was, when she took a deep breath in London, the stench sometimes gagged her. But when she breathed in the clean fresh air of St. Ives, her lungs inflated with pure delight.

The village was compact, making it easy to get about. Bliss reached Brady's small cottage in no time. She rapped sharply on the door and waited. A few minutes later, Brady opened the door. His face lit up with pleasure when he saw her.

"I didn't know you were home," he said, grasping her hand and pulling her inside.

He closed the door and leaned against it, his gaze roaming freely over her face and figure with an intensity that made her uncomfortable.

"Did your high and mighty viscount tire of you already?"

"Why would you think that?"

"Just a hunch. Is Westmore with you?"

"Not presently, but he will be joining me shortly. Luc and I are very happy," Bliss said briskly. "I've come to talk some sense into you, Brady."

"Come into the parlor. There's a fire burning in the hearth to take the chill from the room. Would you like tea? That's about as efficient as I get in the kitchen."

"No, thank you, but I will sit down, if that's all right with you."

"By all means."

Bliss sat down on a settle and Brady took a chair across from her. "You look serious," he said.

"I am. You have to stop smuggling, Brady. Did you learn nothing from my experience?"

Brady bristled. "Of course I did. I learned to be more careful. I'm Shadow now, and you can't tell me what to do. I'm running things my way."

"Jenny told me Captain Skillington is still

suspicious, and with good reason."

Brady scowled. "We need the blunt. You have all the money you want; why do you begrudge your friends a little security?"

"I begrudge you nothing. But I'm too conscious of the consequences to sit back and let my friends get into trouble. You could all end up in jail . . . or worse."

"You can't talk me out of this, Bliss. This is my operation now. Everyone looks up to me as the leader. It always galled me to have to follow your orders." His eyes narrowed. "Besides, I've never forgiven you for falling in bed with a man you scarcely knew."

"Leave off, Brady. We've known each other long enough to dispense with the insults. I never agreed to marry you, and you know it. Sulk all you want; it won't change anything. I love Luc and he loves me. But I still care enough about you and my friends to want you all safe."

"You're wasting your breath, Bliss. Or should I say my lady?"

"Bliss will do. Why are you being so obstinate?"

"I could ask you the same thing. If I recall, you disregarded Westmore's warning despite being aware of the danger."

"I was a fool. When is your next delivery?"

"I hope you don't plan on joining us."

Bliss sent him a scathing look. "That part of my life is over. When, Brady? Tomorrow? Next week? Next month?"

He shrugged. "I don't suppose it will hurt to tell you. We expect another delivery any time now."

"Is that all you can tell me? How soon?"

Brady gave a huff of impatience. "You're no longer involved in our operation, Bliss. The less you know, the better."

"Brady, every one of the men involved is my friend. I learned my lesson, but obviously you've learned nothing. You're going to get everyone arrested, maybe even killed. Think of the wives and children who will be left behind to fend for themselves."

"That didn't seem to bother you. Why should it concern me?"

"Because I've come to realize the error of my ways. Please don't do this, Brady."

"Go home, Bliss. Your father has need of you. I've told you everything I'm going to."

Bliss was aware that her plea had fallen on deaf ears. Resolutely she stomped off, determined to save her friends no matter what the cost. What would Widow Pigeon do without Billy? She could name a dozen or more families that would suffer should their men be taken. Brady's sense of false security would be his downfall, just as it had been hers.

Bliss spent a pleasant week with her father. Her presence seemed to give him heart. Day by day he improved in small increments. She usually took her meals in his bedchamber, regaling him with amusing stories and telling him about Olivia's escapades as a highwayman and Phoebe's troubles with the government.

Dr. Landry's herbal medications seemed to be working. Owen was now able to leave his bed for short periods and sit in the sunshine on those days when it appeared through the clouds.

But even while seeing to her father's recovery, Bliss worried about her friends. Each night she stood at her window, watching for signs of unusual movement through the village.

Weary and covered with road dirt, Luc strode into his townhouse calling Bliss's name. Partridge appeared immediately.

"Milord, welcome home."

"It's good to be home, Partridge." Luc handed the butler his hat and cane. "Is my wife home?"

"No, milord."

"Where is she? Is she expected home soon?"

"Milady left the day after you went off to Plymouth."

Luc's mouth grew taut; his nerve endings tingled. The worst scenario he could imagine was that Bliss had disobeyed him and gone to St. Ives on her own. "Where did she go?"

"To Lady Bathurst, milord. She said she was lonely and decided to follow your suggestion to stay with Lady Bathurst in your absence. Shall I have Appleby fetch her home?"

Luc relaxed. "No need. I'll go myself after I bathe and change clothes. Send Plumb up — I need a shave after I've bathed. And tell Appleby to bring the carriage around in an hour."

One hour later, freshly shaved, bathed and immaculately dressed, Luc entered the carriage for the short ride to Bathurst's mansion. Minutes later, he strode up to the front door, anxious to see Bliss and hold her in his arms. He had missed her dreadfully and couldn't wait to be with her again. Tomorrow or the day after, he would take her to St. Ives, just as he had promised.

Luc frowned when he noted that the knocker had been removed from the door, an indication that the owners weren't in residence. His heart pounding erratically, Luc pounded on the door with the brass head of his cane. Minutes passed. He rapped again. Finally the door was opened by Bathurst's butler, Peterson, Olivia's former partner in crime.

"Lord Westmore," Peterson said. "No one is in residence. Lord and Lady Bathurst are expected home tomorrow. Would you care to leave your card?"

Luc's panic escalated. "Did Lady Bathurst accompany His Lordship? I knew he left to attend estate business, but I was told Lady Bathurst would remain in London with the children."

"Indeed," Paterson said. "But the dowager marchioness of Bathurst asked milady to visit while His Lordship was away. She takes such delight in the twins that milady decided to spend a few days with her."

"What about my wife?" Luc asked. "Did she accompany Lady Bathurst?"

Peterson's brow furrowed. "Lady Westmore, milord? I haven't seen her, though I assume she's expected, for a note arrived for her. It was sent by your butler. It's on the salver, waiting for her to claim it."

"May I see it?"

"Indeed." Peterson fetched the note from the salver and handed it to Luc. Luc tore it open and cursed when he saw it was the same note he had sent by messenger from Plymouth. Partridge must have sent it on here.

"You've not seen my wife?"

"I'm sorry, milord."

"Thank you, Peterson."

Luc returned to the carriage with uncommon speed. "Is anything amiss, milord?" Appleby asked.

"Everything is amiss," Luc said through clenched teeth. "Where did you take my wife after I left for Plymouth?"

"She asked to be taken to the Bathurst residence, and that's where I took her."

"Did you see her inside?"

"I offered, but she insisted on seeing herself to the door. When I protested, she quite emphatically told me to leave."

"I see," Luc said, and he did indeed see. His impulsive wife had traveled to St. Ives without escort or protector. "Take me home, Appleby. Then prepare a mount for me. I'll be leaving for St. Ives as soon as I've packed."

Luc entered the house in a rage. How dare Bliss attempt a dangerous journey like this without his knowledge! Didn't she trust him to take care of her and her father? He'd always known she was rash and irresponsible, but this went beyond anything he expected from her.

Partridge met him at the door, his smile fading when he saw Luc's scowl. "Was Lady Westmore not ready to return home, milord?"

"Lady Westmore wasn't with Lady Bathurst. She never arrived."

"But Appleby —"

"I've no time to explain. I'm leaving immediately. Send Plumb up to pack for me. I'll just have time to write a note to Lord Braxton, explaining my absence."

Less than an hour later, Luc was on his way.

Meanwhile, Bliss was monitoring her father's health according to Dr. Landry's instructions and at the same time keeping track of the villagers' movements. She had expected Luc to arrive days ago and wondered why he hadn't shown up yet.

Was he so angry with her that he no longer cared about her? She considered returning to London but hated to leave her father, even though Dr. Landry said he would recover, albeit slowly. But what if he had a relapse? Why couldn't Luc understand that Owen Hartley was her only living relative, and that the state of his health was terribly important to her?

Bliss had dinner with her father that night as usual and retired to her room. Waiting and worrying were taking a toll on her. She knew now that she was carrying Luc's child. Earlier today she had consulted with Dr. Landry, and he had confirmed her condition.

With so much to think about, sleep eluded Bliss. She walked to the window and stared out at the sleeping village. It was ten o'clock, the time when most villagers sought their beds. Bliss started to turn away when she saw a shadow pass beneath a tree. Then another, and another, until it seemed as if the entire village were on the move.

Instantly Bliss realized that the smugglers were headed toward the cove. Fear churned inside her, but there was nothing she could do to stop them.

Bliss turned away from the window. She knew from experience what each man was doing, what his individual duties were. What she didn't know was how Brady would react to trouble should it arrive unexpectedly. Or perhaps she did know. During their last encounter with the law, he had run off, leaving her alone and vulnerable. Fortunately, Luc had arrived in time to save her.

But getting shot hadn't been a pleasant experience.

Bliss heard the clock in the hall chime eleven. Minutes later she heard the clip-clop of horses' hooves against the cobbles. She turned back to the window. What she saw froze the blood in her veins.

Excise men!

There were about a dozen of them. They stopped in front of the house. She recognized Skillington as he dismounted and approached the front door. Then she heard a loud pounding on the wooden panel.

Bliss pulled on a dressing gown, opened her door and approached the staircase. Jenny stood at the bottom of the stairs, gesturing frantically at her.

"Stay where you are," Jenny hissed. "Let me take care of them. I'll delay them as long as I can. I don't want them to see you."

"I can't sit here and do nothing. While you delay them, I'll go down to the cove and warn the men."

"Billy let slip that tonight was the night, but I didn't tell you because I feared you would get involved. Your husband will have my head if harm comes to you."

"Let me worry about Luc."

Bliss had no qualms about helping her friends. Not if it meant saving the lives of people she had known all her life. Without a thought for her own safety, Bliss plucked a dark dress from her wardrobe and pulled it on. Voices drifted to her from the front door as she hurried down the rear staircase.

The night was perfect for smuggling. The thin sliver of moon was partially obscured by clouds, and a dense fog rolled in from the sea. If Bliss hadn't known the way, she would never have found it.

Luc knew it was late but he hadn't wanted to stop for the night when he was so close to St. Ives, so he had pressed on. It was an ungodly hour to arrive at someone's door, but that couldn't be helped. He had to know that Bliss was safe, and once he learned she had arrived unharmed, he would beat her black and blue. Either that or love her until she cried for mercy. Right now his sentiments ran toward the former.

Luc had nearly reached the squire's house when he noticed horses stomping and snorting at the front gate. An errant ray of moonlight reflected off brass buttons. Luc put two and two together and came up with the right answer.

Excise men!

After everything that had happened to her, Luc was stunned that Bliss had become involved again with smuggling. Was she still Shadow? He would wring her lovely neck if he learned she had resumed her life of crime.

Luc remained within the shadow of a lofty tree as he watched the revenuers ride off. Once they were out of sight, he approached the house and rapped sharply on the door.

"I told you all I know!" Jenny cried, flinging open the door. "What more do you want . . . Oh, Lord Westmore! I wasn't expecting you."

He swept past her. "Obviously. Where's my wife? What were the revenuers doing here?"

"Captain Skillington wanted to speak to the squire. He'd heard that a delivery of contraband was scheduled to arrive in the area and assumed the squire would know about it. I told him the squire was too ill to answer questions." She huffed in displeasure. "The foolish man wouldn't believe me until he saw the squire for himself."

"Where's Bliss?"

"I stalled them as long as I could."

"Where's . . . my . . . wife?" Luc's mouth was so rigid, it barely moved when he spoke.

"I sent the revenuers to the wrong cove to gain Bliss time."

"Jenny . . ." It was a warning, and Jenny knew it.

"She went off to warn the others."

"Bloody hell! Don't tell me she's taken up smuggling again."

"No such thing!" Jenny said, affronted. "Brady Bristol is Shadow now. Bliss tried to talk sense into him, but he wouldn't listen. She fretted endlessly about her friends but was wise enough to know there was nothing she could do about it."

"Why isn't she here? Why did she rush into danger when she knew what she was getting herself into?"

"Her friends . . . she wanted them safe."

"Where did she go?"

"To the cove."

"Which cove?"

"The one where you first saw her."

Luc sprinted out the door as if the devil's hounds were after him. His mind worked furiously. He knew it would take some time for the revenuers to reach the wrong cove, and that should allow him enough time to reach Bliss and warn her friends. Damn, he felt like he was reliving the past all over again. How many times must he rescue Bliss before she realized she could die down there on the beach?

Bliss ran as fast as she could, ran until her sides ached and her legs turned to jelly. She saw the ship, an undistinguishable shape in the darkness. A riding light showed from the masthead, but otherwise it was in darkness. Then she saw someone signaling from the beach. When she located the path, she slid nearly all the way down, calling Brady's name and then identifying herself.

Brady came running toward her. Grasping her shoulders, he shook her. "What in blazes are you doing here? I thought you wanted no part of this."

"I don't." She gasped for breath. "Revenuers. They rode into town around midnight. Jenny directed them to the wrong cove. You've got to leave immediately. Call the men back."

"I can't. The last wagon is being loaded now. We're almost finished."

"Now, Brady, now! Forget the wagon. Send the men on their way. The revenuers are mounted. They could have already learned their mistake and be on their way here."

"This is my operation, Bliss. I make the decisions. Get out of the way."

He shoved her aside. Bliss stumbled to her knees, then quickly scrambled to her feet. "Didn't you hear me? The revenuers are coming."

"We'll be out of here before they arrive."

He shoved her again. This time she fell on her rump.

"Damn you to hell, Brady Bristol. Touch my wife again and I'll hang you by your balls."

Bliss looked up at Luc and rocked back on her elbows. Fury blazed from his eyes; his body was stiff with it.

Never had she known such fear.

Chapter Twenty

Luc scarcely glanced at Brady as he grasped Bliss's hand and pulled her toward the path and safety. How could she do this to him? She might no longer be Shadow but she was still caught up in smuggling. Her need to warn her friends was no excuse for what she had done. What in bloody hell was he going to do with her?

What would he do without her?

That unpleasant thought firmed his determination to save her from her own foolishness.

Suddenly the night exploded around them. "They're here," Bliss gasped. "I thought there would be more time."

"Where can we hide?" Luc asked.

"Nowhere . . . except perhaps . . ."

"Where, Bliss? Time is running out."

And indeed it was. The revenuers were shooting at the dark figures on the beach from the top of the cliff. It wouldn't be long before they swarmed down the path to the beach.

"There's a finger of land that juts out into the water farther down the beach — a promontory of rocks and large boulders. We can hide among the rocks until it's safe to return home."

"Lead the way," Luc growled as the revenuers began storming the beach.

Bliss raised her skirts and sprinted along the sand.

Since Luc's legs were longer, he grasped Bliss's hand and dragged her behind him.

Some minutes later, Luc spotted the promontory. The boulders and rocks rose like dark sentinels against the black sky. He could hear Bliss panting, feel the drag of her feet, and feared she wouldn't be able to keep up the pace. Bringing them both to a halt, he swept her into his arms and carried her the remaining distance.

"Luc, put me down. I'm too heavy for you." Luc disdained an answer, preferring to preserve his strength for what lay ahead. He halted when he reached the promontory, raising his gaze to study the rocky protrusion.

"Is there a beach beyond the promontory?"

"No, the cliff reaches straight down to the water."

"Then we'll have to hide among the boulders," Luc decided. "I'll climb up first. Don't follow until I give the signal. Be careful — the rocks are slippery. I don't want you to fall."

"Wait," Bliss said. "Someone is coming." Luc paused and glanced behind him.

"Revenuers," she whispered.

Luc shoved Bliss behind him, ready to defend her with his life, but it wasn't necessary. A voice they recognized called out to them in a low tone.

"Bliss! Westmore! Is that you?"

"Brady," Bliss whispered. "He must have had the same idea we did."

"Billy is with me," Brady called out. "What are your plans?"

"We need to hide before the revenuers find us," Luc said when Brady and Billy came panting up beside them.

"Have you climbed those boulders before?" Brady asked.

"No, have you?" Bliss said.

"I have," Billy cut in, "several times. There are plenty of hiding places. I'll lead the way. Bliss can follow, and then Westmore. Brady, you bring up the rear. Be careful — it's black as pitch out here."

Billy scampered over the damp, lichen-covered rocks. Bliss followed in his footsteps, hampered only a little by her skirt.

She had climbed but a short distance when she glanced down, expecting to find Luc behind her. To her dismay, he was still standing on the wet sand. She started to call out to him, then gulped back her words when she saw a man running along the beach toward them. Fear pounded through her when she saw Luc and Brady pressed against a boulder, waiting to confront the man. Was he friend or foe? Bliss clung to the boulder, wishing she could melt into it. She could see their pursuer more clearly now and knew he was an excise man.

The revenuer skidded to a halt at the promontory, staring up at it. Unfortunately for him, he hesitated a moment too long. Brady stepped out from the shadows and clubbed him with a rock. He fell heavily and remained still. When Brady would have hit him again, Luc stopped him.

"You don't want to be charged with murder as well as treason, do you?"

Brady dropped the rock, and both men began climbing. "I'm right behind you, Bliss," Luc said. "Keep going. Billy is at the top waiting to help you."

The climb was slow but not particularly arduous. Twice Bliss felt loose rocks shift beneath her feet, but Luc's hand was always there to steady her. Finally she reached the top. Billy grasped her arms and pulled her up beside him. Luc followed and then Brady.

"What now?" Brady asked. "When that revenuer wakes up with an aching head, he's going to fetch his mates to look for us."

"We'll have to scale the cliff before he awakens," Luc said. "It's too dangerous to wait. Then you and Billy are on your own. Bliss is my responsibility; I'll keep her safe."

"I know the way," Billy said. "There's no path, so it might be difficult for Bliss."

"I've been down here before," Bliss said. "I sat on the promontory and fished with my father when I was a girl. Go ahead, Billy, I'm right behind you."

The climb was more difficult than Bliss had anticipated, especially in a skirt. When loose earth shifted beneath her feet and she started to slide, Luc steadied her from behind until she was ready to continue.

"I won't let you fall," he said.

Just when Bliss thought she couldn't climb another step, Billy's arms reached for her and hauled her up over the lip of the cliff. She sat on the ground, her chest heaving as Luc and Brady scrambled up after her.

"Are you all right?" Luc asked Bliss.

There was still enough anger in his voice to make her tremble.

"I'm fine."

"Good." He hauled her to her feet. "Let's get out of here."

"It's quiet on the beach," Billy said.

"The excise men are probably confiscating the brandy that you and the others abandoned. That should keep them busy for a while. It's time to split up. Good luck finding your way home."

"Shouldn't we leave, too?" Bliss asked.

"My horse is tethered out of sight. We'll wait until the moon slides behind a cloud, then make a break for the woods."

His voice was devoid of emotion, cold, curt, as if she were a stranger instead of his wife.

"Now," Luc hissed. Grasping her hand, he pulled her along behind him, taking a zigzag path across the open area to the woods.

He led her unerringly to his horse. Baron whickered softly in greeting. Without a word, he hoisted her into the saddle and climbed up behind her. Avoiding the path, they followed a circuitous route to the village.

To add insult to injury, the skies opened and it began to rain, a cold, saturating downpour. They were both drenched by the time they reached the village. Bliss huddled against Luc to soak up what little warmth she could from his body.

The village appeared quiet and peaceful as Luc directed his mount to the livery.

"I hope everyone gets home safely," Bliss said as Luc lifted her from the saddle.

Luc did not answer as he led his mount to a rear stall, rubbed him down and gave him a measure of oats. Then he crept to the door and checked to see if it was safe for them to leave.

"Let's go," he said. Gripping Bliss's elbow, he led her through the rain to her house. "Is the back door locked?"

"Probably, but the key is above the lintel."

They sloshed around to the rear entrance. Luc found the key and let them in, locking the door behind him.

Bliss gave a gasp of surprise when Jenny appeared from her room, her frightened features illuminated by the light from the candle she was holding. The light blinded Bliss and she blinked.

"Thank the good Lord you're both safe," Jenny said shakily. "You scared ten years off my life."

"It was close, but we escaped without

harm," Luc said. "I can't vouch for the others, however."

"You look like drowned rats. Go to bed," Jenny ordered. "You'll find fresh water in your room. I know you rode through the day and most of the night to get here, milord, so you must be dead on your feet. Sleep as long as you want, no one will bother you."

Bliss dawdled. Luc had scarcely spoken to her. He had been as cool and remote as a stranger, and she didn't relish being alone with him. She didn't know this Luc, didn't want to. She'd seen him angry before, but never had he been this distant or unapproachable.

"Thank you, Jenny. We'll talk tomorrow. Come along, Bliss."

Bliss stumbled up the stairs, conscious of Luc's unrelenting grip on her upper arm. She approached her room on wooden legs and paused before the door. Luc opened it, pushed her inside and shut the door behind him. Panic seized her when she heard the key turn in the lock.

"Get into bed," he ordered harshly.

"Luc —"

"You heard me. Get out of those wet clothes before you catch your death."

"Do you care?" Bliss muttered beneath her breath. Luc either didn't hear her or pretended not to as he bent to build up the fire.

Bliss began stripping, not to please Luc but because she was shivering in her wet clothing. Naked, she walked to the washstand, poured warm water into the basin and sponged her hands, face and body. Luc didn't turn around, though he must have known what she was doing. He was still facing the hearth when she retrieved her nightgown from a drawer and drew it over her head and down her body. Then, shaking from the cold — or was it fear? — she slid beneath the covers.

"Luc —"

"Don't say anything, Bliss. I can't handle it now." His hands were clenched at his sides, his back rigid.

He left his spot beside the hearth and walked stiff-legged to the washstand. He poured the water Bliss had used out the window and filled the bowl with fresh water. Then he peeled off his clothes and began to wash.

"Luc," she tried again.

His lips made a flat line across his face; his words were clipped. "Not now."

"We need to talk."

A bitter laugh was his only reply.

Sighing, Bliss fell silent as she watched

him through narrowed eyes. Firelight turned his taut muscles and corded tendons a deep golden hue. He was beautiful in a masculine way, and magnificently endowed.

Finally he tossed aside the drying cloth and approached the bed. Bliss swallowed hard. The chill in his manner and the glint of disdain in his eyes didn't bode well for her. The atmosphere was brittle with tension as he stared down at her. She met his gaze without flinching. She had never cowered in the face of danger and didn't intend to start now.

When Luc raised his arm, Bliss rose to her knees, ready to defend herself. "Don't you dare hit me, Lucas Westmore!"

Her words had the desired effect. Luc seemed to collapse inward. His face turned ashen and he began to tremble. "You thought I would strike you? My God, Bliss, how could you think me capable of such a cowardly act? I've never struck a woman in my life."

He dropped to the edge of the bed and buried his face in his hands. Bliss scooted over to make room for him. A desperate sound that could have been a sob worked its way up from his throat. Gingerly she touched his damp head.

"Luc, what is it? Talk to me."

When he finally turned to her, his cheeks were wet, his eyes glistening with moisture.

"Damn you! How could you do this to me? Don't you know I couldn't live without you?"

Luc couldn't stop shaking. At first, when Jenny had told him where to find Bliss, cold rage had overwhelmed every emotion but fear. He couldn't recall being so angry in his entire life. Adrenaline fed by grinding terror had driven his actions from the moment he learned that Bliss had gone off to St. Ives alone.

When she touched his shoulder, he shook her hand away. He couldn't bear to be touched right now. He was too raw. A kind of madness had come over him, and he had to get himself under control before he could face her. Little by little, anger and terror drained from him. He raised his head, his gaze colliding with Bliss's.

"I'm sorry," she whispered. "Forgive me."

Her apology surprised him.

"Tell me you had no part in tonight's fiasco. Tell me you're not Shadow."

"I'm not Shadow. I gave up that life when I married you. Brady is Shadow."

"So the reason you went to the cove was . . ."

". . . to warn my friends. I thought Jenny explained."

"Jenny would say anything to save your neck."

"Please believe me. If the excise men had not arrived when they did, I would have remained in bed during the delivery. You have to understand that I couldn't let my friends be arrested and hauled off to jail. I felt obligated to warn them."

Luc's face crumpled as he pulled her into his arms and whispered, "I love you." Then his mouth crushed down on hers. He kissed her with desperate need, his fingers gripping her shoulders, as if he feared she would disappear.

When Bliss realized Luc still loved her despite his anger, she felt as if a great weight had been lifted from her. She flung her arms around his neck and kissed him back, with all the love in her heart.

"Love me, Luc." It had been so long, and she craved the comfort of his body. She needed to be close to him again.

"Do you have any idea how eager I was to leave Plymouth and return to London and my wife?" he asked. "I planned to have a quiet dinner in our room and make endless love to you."

"I want that now, Luc. Let tonight be

your homecoming. I'm safe, you're safe, and our love is as strong as ever."

His eyes dark with desire, he drew her nightgown over her head and flung it away. Then he pressed her down into the soft mattress, kissing her again and again, their breath mingling, tongues meeting in a bold, sexual duel.

He cupped her breasts, erotically kneading them. He kissed her, touched her, showing her how much he cared, that all he wanted in this world was her lying beneath him. Her taste, her scent, her touch filled his senses, stoked his passion.

"I want you inside me, Luc."

Luc slid between her thighs, his sex thick, heavy with need, but he didn't enter her. With a passion hot enough to singe her, he licked and kissed his way down her body, suckling her nipples, nuzzling the tender underside of her breasts. Yet despite the blood pounding through his body, despite a hunger so desperate that he feared for his sanity, he nuzzled through the bright curls on her mound and closed his mouth over her sensitive feminine peak, flicking it with the rough pad of his tongue.

Bliss shuddered beneath him, lifting her hips and bringing her femininity deeper into his mouth. He worked her mercilessly, ruthlessly, until she screamed and shattered.

The pulsing urgency to sheath his rampant erection inside her scalding heat was so great that restraint was no longer possible. Sliding upward; he drove himself deep. He was iron-hard inside her; she thrust upward; he slid deeper. He worshiped the silk of her neck with his lips, tasting the dampness of her skin as he waited for her passion to ignite. She gasped; he moaned. Her inner muscles clenched, and he nearly lost it then. But he wanted to bring her to climax again before he found his own pleasure.

Bliss pressed upward, surrounding his waist with her legs, meeting his thrusts, her passion escalating. He pressed harder, deeper, faster. Abruptly she stiffened and gave a sudden gasp, arching hard against him as waves of pleasure gripped her. Her climax must have triggered his, for he lost himself moments later, falling mindlessly over the edge.

Slowly Luc's breath returned to normal. For the first time in his adult life, he no longer cared about maintaining his reputation as a rogue. Bliss's love had wiped his mind clean. His life of debauchery had ended the day he met her. He couldn't recall a more perfect moment than this and feared to move lest he break the spell.

Aware that he was too heavy for her, he shifted to his side. Bliss turned with him and buried her face in his neck, her head tucked beneath his chin. He held her until her trembling subsided. Complete and satiated, he welcomed the warmth of her breath and the sweet scent of sex that permeated the air around them.

Bliss sighed and gazed up at him. She could see his face clearly in the room brightened by the first light of dawn.

"Go to sleep, love. We're both exhausted."

Bliss shook her head. "I want to talk."

"I thought we'd already said it all."

"Perhaps you did, but I didn't."

Luc's brow furrowed as he pulled himself up, resting his head against the headboard. Bliss rose up on her elbows; he tugged her into his arms. "Very well, what do you wish to talk about?"

"Your anger. Aside from frightening me, I thought you were going to hit me."

"I would never strike you, my love. I've never raised a hand to a woman in anger and don't intend to start now."

"But you did raise your hand," Bliss pressed.

Luc looked bewildered. "I did? I don't recall. I've never been in a state of utter

485

terror before, and that's precisely what I felt when I saw you on the beach last night. Please believe me when I say I'd never do anything to hurt you.

"But," he added sternly, "I expect you to restrain your wild ways and behave properly during the remaining years of our marriage."

"Will you behave, Luc? Have I tamed your roguish ways?"

"You have most definitely tamed the wild beast in me," Luc laughed. "How could I want another woman when I have the best?"

"Ah, Luc, you are far too charming for your own good, but I believe you." She grinned at him. "I have something to tell you."

"What?"

"I no longer want those six months of fidelity you promised me."

Luc's brows shot upward. "Why not? Have you tired of me already?"

"Luc, how could you ask that? Six months simply won't do. I want forever."

"Forever is a long time for a remorseless rogue to remain faithful to one woman. How about a more reasonable one hundred years?"

Bliss stroked her chin. "Hmmm. Very well, I agree."

"Now can I go to sleep? I haven't had more than two hours of sleep at one time in a week."

"One more thing," Bliss said.

Luc groaned. "I've promised you my heart, my soul and one hundred years of my life. What more do you want?"

"Nothing. I'm with child."

His eyelids began to droop. "Ummm, that's nice, love."

"Are you pleased?"

Silence.

"Luc, please tell me you're happy."

"Of course I'm happy," he said on a long, exhausted sigh. "Good . . . night." He turned over and fell instantly asleep.

Disappointed by Luc's lukewarm response to her happy tidings, Bliss felt like hitting him. Instead, she pounded her pillow and followed him into sweet oblivion.

Luc awakened with an uncomfortable emptiness in his stomach. He cranked open one eye and then the other, surprised to see that daylight was waning. Had he and Bliss slept through the entire day?

Suddenly he jerked upright, his expression a mixture of shock and delight. "My God, I'm going to be a father!"

He glanced down at Bliss and found her staring at him, her green eyes glittering with mirth. "Welcome to the world of reality. It took you long enough."

"I suppose I heard what you said but was too exhausted to react. I'd been running on adrenaline since I left London, existing on little food and even less sleep. I don't know where I found the energy to make love to you last night."

"And you did it so well," Bliss teased.

"Am I really going to be a father?"

"Dr. Landry confirmed my own suspicions. Are you as happy about it as I am?"

"Strangely, I am," Luc mused. "I never aspired to fatherhood, but then I never met a woman I cared enough about to have children with until I met you. Having children is suddenly a wonderful idea. I'm glad you thought of it."

"It was bound to happen whether or not either of us wanted it, given the frequency of our lovemaking."

"Bliss, I —" His words ended abruptly and his face turned a peculiar shade of green. "Dear God," he whispered, trembling. "You were carrying my child when you went to the cove last night! Are you mad? Do you care nothing for the child you carry?"

He leaped from bed and began pulling on his trousers.

"Where are you going?"

"To kill Brady Bristol."

Bliss climbed out of bed and placed herself in front of him. "Luc, please calm down. What will that accomplish?"

"It will make me feel a hell of a lot better. I can't believe you would behave in such a reckless manner when you knew you were carrying my child." He pulled his shirt over his head.

"I wasn't expecting trouble, Luc. I merely intended to warn my friends and return home. I'm sorry." She touched her stomach. "Our child means everything to me."

Suddenly her face turned as green as her eyes, as green as Luc's had been earlier. One hand flew up to her mouth while the other clutched her stomach. "I'm going to —"

Luc reacted spontaneously and swiftly. He fetched the chamber pot, seated Bliss on the edge of the bed and held it while she lost the meager contents of her stomach. When she had no more to give, she shoved the chamber pot aside and collapsed on the bed.

"Are you all right, sweetheart?" he asked worriedly.

"That's the first time that happened," Bliss said, shuddering. "Might I have some water?"

Luc poured water into a glass and handed it to her. She rinsed out her mouth and wiped it on the towel Luc had provided. Then he sat down beside her and held her in his arms until she stopped trembling.

"I believe I could eat something now," Bliss said, perking up considerably. "I'm ravenous."

Astounded, Luc shook his head. "Is this what I'll have to put up with for the duration of your pregnancy?"

"I understand the sickness will only last a few weeks, but I'll probably drive you crazy in any number of ways until the babe is born. Expectant mothers can be demanding, capricious and totally unreasonable." She gazed into his eyes. "Can you tolerate that, Luc?"

"Aye, I can if you can tolerate my protective nature where you're concerned." He sent her a stern look. "There will be no more adventures for the duration of our marriage. If you enjoy the countryside, we can spend time at my estate in Kent.

"With my heir on the way, and more children likely in the future, the townhouse will no longer do for us. It was fine for bachelor digs, but now that I have a family, I'll need to purchase a more suitable residence, one large enough for your father and Jenny, should they decide to join us."

"Are you still angry with me?"

"Very angry, but I no longer feel like killing anyone. We aren't the same people we were yesterday."

"Of course we are. Nothing has changed."

"Everything has changed. You are no longer a smuggler but an expectant mother, and I have changed from rogue to doting husband and father-to-be. My sister will be stunned to see me settled down when she returns from abroad."

"Won't you become bored with your life?" Bliss teased.

Laughing, he pulled her into his arms and kissed her soundly. "My life will never be boring with you in it." He kissed her again. "Shall we tell your father and Jenny our good news?"

They dressed quickly and left the sanctuary of their bedroom. Delicious smells greeted them as they descended the stairs. Luc's stomach growled. "I hope we're not too late for dinner."

"You're just in time," Jenny said from the bottom of the stairs. "Billy told me he heard

491

you stirring. I knew you'd be hungry when you awakened, so I spent the day preparing your favorite dishes."

"I'm glad Billy returned home safely," Bliss said with marked relief. "What about the others?"

"All returned without mishap. Billy said everyone he's spoken to wants nothing more to do with smuggling. I believe their wives and families had something to do with the men's decision."

"I'm glad," Luc said. "I've been giving serious thought to providing the villagers with gainful employment. My friends and I just purchased several ships that will commence trading with the Americas. Any man who wishes can seek a berth on our ships."

Bliss squeezed his hand. "That's generous of you, Luc. I'm sure the villagers will appreciate your offer."

"Dinner is on the table," Jenny announced. "The squire feels well enough to join you. He's waiting in the dining room."

Bliss clapped her hands. "Wonderful! Will you join us, Jenny? You've been like a mother to me, and we'd like you to be present when we tell Papa our good news."

Jenny flushed with pleasure. "I'll join you as soon as the food is on the table."

"Papa!" Bliss exclaimed as she and Luc

entered the dining room. "I'm so happy to see you up and about. You must be feeling better."

"As well as can be expected." Owen shrugged. "Good to see you, Westmore. About time you showed up. It seems our Bliss got herself into a bit of trouble."

"You know?" Bliss gasped.

"Aye, daughter, and I'm not happy about it."

"I can assure you, sir, it won't happen again," Luc said firmly.

Jenny entered the room and slid into an empty chair across from Bliss. "I'm here. What is this good news you wanted to tell us?"

Owen perked up immediately. "Good news? Don't keep us in suspense, daughter."

"Perhaps we should eat first and save the news for later," Luc suggested. His stomach was touching his backbone.

"Oh, no, you don't," Owen blustered. "News first and then food."

Luc looked at Bliss and nodded. She cleared her throat and said, "I'm expecting a child in seven months. Dr. Landry has confirmed it."

Owen's face lit up. "Wonderful! Congratulations. Now I have something to live for.

And," he said, sending a sly look toward Luc, "Westmore has found a perfect way to keep you out of trouble."

"I have, haven't I?" Luc said, bursting with pride. "How clever of me."

Bliss kicked him beneath the table. "That's not all, Papa. Luc is going to buy a larger home, one that can accommodate you and Jenny as well as our growing family."

"I have no desire to live in London, Bliss, but I will visit from time to time, if Dr. Landry allows it. I'm still the squire here, and my people depend on me. I let them down during the worst of my illness, but Billy told me the villagers are no longer interested in smuggling, and that's gratifying news."

He picked up his fork and began to eat.

"I'm sorry you won't be joining us," Bliss said with obvious disappointment. She looked at Jenny. "I wish you could be with me during my confinement, Jenny. I'd feel better with someone I know in attendance."

Owen set down his fork. "Jenny can return to London with you if she wishes. In fact, I insist upon it. I'm sure Widow Pigeon will be happy to take her place as housekeeper. She can use the blunt now that Billy has given up smuggling."

Bliss clapped her hands. "Splendid! Will you, Jenny? Please? I really do need you."

Jenny appeared torn. She remained silent for a long time, until Luc said, "Please say yes, Jenny. I want my wife to be happy, and obviously, having you with her will please her."

"If Bliss wants me, of course I'll go. I know Thelma and Billy will take good care of your father during my absence."

Dinner progressed with more happy talk. Afterward, Owen retired to his room, Jenny disappeared into the kitchen, and Luc and Bliss wandered up to their bedroom.

"Do you feel better?" Luc asked.

"Yes, much better. Food did wonders for me."

"Me too, I was famished." He opened his arms and she walked into them. "Are you tired?"

"Not in the least. I slept all day. What did you have in mind?"

"I want to make love to you. Tell me you want me."

Her eyes glittered mischievously. "Only if you promise me something first."

"Anything."

"Don't change too much. I enjoy having

an experienced rogue in my bed."

His eyes crinkling with mirth, he bore her to the bed and proved that in some ways rogues never change.

Epilogue

One Year Later

Lady Mary Ann, Luc's sister, the Countess of Belcher, cradled her tiny nephew in her arms, crooning softly to him while his proud father looked on. The Honorable James Westmore cooed back, as if aware of his aunt's affection.

"He's precious, Luc," Mary Ann said. "You do know how lucky you are to have found Bliss, don't you? I must admit I despaired of ever seeing you wed, and I'm still not sure you deserve Bliss. I'll never know how she managed to change an unrepentant rogue into a loving husband and father."

"I'm not quite sure how she did it either," Luc laughed, "but I'm glad she did."

Still radiant after nearly a year of marriage, Bliss breezed into the nursery. "Plans for the christening are well under way," she said. "Our guests should begin arriving tomorrow. I'm so glad you came early, Mary Ann. At least one member of Luc's family will be on hand to celebrate with us."

Little Jamie began to fuss and Mary Ann handed him to Bliss, saying, "All that's missing is Father."

Luc snorted. "I was disinherited, remember. Why would he come to his grandson's christening?"

"People change," Bliss said on a hopeful note.

When the babe started rooting around at Bliss's breast, she excused herself and took Jamie off to nurse.

"The squire is downstairs in the parlor, Mary Ann. Shall we join him?" Luc said.

Mary Ann threaded her arm in Luc's and they descended the stairs together. "Your new home is impressive," Mary Ann said enthusiastically. "I'm sure Father would be proud of your accomplishments."

Luc gave a hoot of derision. "Father quite gave up on me. It's rather late for him to change his mind. Besides, he has a whole new family and doesn't need me."

They had just reached the bottom landing when the sound of carriage wheels announced an early arrival.

"I wonder who that could be," Luc said. "The guests aren't supposed to arrive until tomorrow."

Partridge came from the nether reaches of

the mansion to answer the door. Luc nearly lost the ability to breathe when he recognized the tall, imposing gentleman who swept past the butler with great presence.

"Father!" Luc and Mary Ann said in unison.

"Indeed," the Earl of Aldrich said as Mary Ann gave him a quick hug. "It's wonderful to see you again, daughter." He turned his gaze on Luc. "You've done well for yourself, Westmore. I could hardly credit it when I heard you had married. I can't wait to meet the paragon who brought about this miracle."

"Welcome, Father," Luc greeted. "I'm pleased you saw fit to attend my son's christening. As for Bliss, you'll meet her momentarily." Luc looked past him toward the carriage. "Did you bring your family?"

"Not this time. I came alone."

"Partridge will see to your bags. Come into the parlor and meet Bliss's father."

"Ah, yes, Squire Hartley. I'm most anxious to meet him. If not for his letter, I wouldn't be here now."

Luc's mouth dropped open. "Squire Hartley wrote to you?"

"Indeed. He told me what a fine, upstanding man you were, and how happy you've made his daughter. Thought I'd come down to London and see this marvel for myself."

Owen Hartley and Lord Aldrich were introduced, and it quickly became apparent that a friendship was being forged between the two men. When Bliss entered the parlor, she had no idea to whom she was being introduced until Luc said, "The earl is my father, and Mary Ann's, of course."

The earl lifted Bliss from her deep curtsy and kissed both her cheeks. "My dear, so you're the woman who brought my wayward son to heel. What a beauty you are. I'm still not sure you deserve her, Westmore."

"I'm the lucky one," Bliss said. "I couldn't ask for a better husband and father to our son." She reached out to Luc; he enfolded her hand in his and kissed her knuckles. "We love each other, my lord."

"I can see that," the earl said. "I was surprised, however, when the squire wrote that you'd named your son after me."

"Your name is James?" Bliss asked, surprised. She sent Luc a quelling look. "I didn't know. Your son never told me. I assumed he just liked the name, and it suited me as well."

"Sit down, my dear," the earl said. "I have some news to impart that I hope will please you."

Bliss sat beside Luc on the sofa. His expression gave away none of the turmoil he must be feeling, and Bliss squeezed his hand.

The earl cleared his throat and said, "I've reinstated Luc as my heir, and I'm extremely happy to find that my actions were justified. Luc will inherit my title and everything I own upon my death."

"Thank you, but that's not necessary, Father," Luc said. "I'm quite happy to remain a viscount. My half-brother is welcome to the title."

"Don't be difficult, son. The title is rightfully yours. Now that everything is settled, I'd like to see my grandson."

"I'll show you to the nursery," Mary Ann offered.

"I'll join you," Owen said. All three exited the parlor.

"What are you thinking?" Bliss asked when she noticed the pensive look on Luc's face.

"That I am blessed and don't deserve it. You know I don't care about the title; I'm just pleased to have Father back in my life." He paused, his expression thoughtful. "At one time I laughed at Bathurst and Braxton for choosing marriage over a life of debauchery and hedonistic pleasure. Then I

501

met you, a feisty outlaw who thumbed her nose at the king's laws. And a lovely nose it is." He planted a kiss on her upturned nose. "Now you're mine, my love, forever and ever."

She turned in his arms. "You're never going to regret choosing me over your former life," she promised. "I'll make sure of that."

"I haven't been sorry since the day we met." He gave her a quick kiss. "Shall we join our family in the nursery?"

"I can't think of anywhere I'd rather be. I love you, Rogue Westmore."

"No more than I love you, my sweet." He laughed. "Who would have thought the last rogue would be tamed by love?"

"Who would have thought a smuggler and a dissolute rogue had anything in common? It seems, my love, that we are evenly matched." She lifted her face to his. "How about a proper kiss before we join the others in the nursery?"

One kiss led to another. It was much later when, hand in hand, they ascended the stairs.

About the Author

Connie Mason is the bestselling author of more than thirty historical romances and novellas. Her tales of passion and adventure are set in exotic as well as American locales. Connie was named Storyteller of the Year in 1990 by *Romantic Times*, and was awarded a Career Achievement award in the Western category by *Romantic Times* in 1994. Connie makes her home in Tarpon Springs, Florida, with her husband, Jerry.

In addition to writing and traveling, Connie enjoys telling anyone who will listen about her three children and nine grandchildren, and sharing memories of her years living abroad in Europe and Asia as the wife of a career serviceman. In her spare time, Connie enjoys reading, dancing, playing bridge, and freshwater fishing with her husband.

The employees of Thorndike Press hope you have enjoyed this Large Print book. All our Thorndike and Wheeler Large Print titles are designed for easy reading, and all our books are made to last. Other Thorndike Press Large Print books are available at your library, through selected bookstores, or directly from us.

For information about titles, please call:

(800) 223-1244

or visit our Web site at:

www.gale.com/thorndike
www.gale.com/wheeler

To share your comments, please write:

Publisher
Thorndike Press
295 Kennedy Memorial Drive
Waterville, ME   04901